BISHOP'S REACH

Also by Kathryn R. Wall

In for a Penny

And Not a Penny More

Perdition House

Judas Island

Resurrection Road

BISHOP'S REACH

KATHRYN R. WALL

ST. MARTIN'S MINOTAUR ✖ NEW YORK

www.minotaurbooks.com

Library of Congress Cataloging-in-Publication Data

Wall, Kathryn R.
    Bishop's Reach / Kathryn R. Wall.—1st ed.
        p. cm. (A Bay Tanner mystery)
    ISBN 0-312-33795-7
    EAN 978-0-312-33795-7
    1. Tanner, Bay (Fictitious character)—Fiction. 2. Women private investigators—South Carolina—Hilton Head Island—Fiction. 3. Hilton Head Island (S.C.)—Fiction. I. Title.

PS3623.A4424B57 2006
813'.6—dc22

                                                            2006040514

First Edition: May 2006

10 9 8 7 6 5 4 3 2 1

To Norman,
who makes it all worthwhile

And to my niece Jennifer,
who daily demonstrates the true meaning of courage

ACKNOWLEDGMENTS

Those of you who haven't had the pleasure of visiting Hilton Head will search the map in vain for any mention of Bishop's Reach. Locals will, I hope, recognize it immediately as Broad Creek. Thus are the marketing gods appeased.

I've also taken liberties with Palmetto Bay Marina and some of its environs and procedures. I hope those who were kind enough to talk with me about boat servicing and repair will understand and forgive. To paraphrase one of my favorite authors, I reserve the novelist's right to make things up.

Thanks as always to the usual suspects: Jo and Vicky, who keep me focused on the task; Linda, Ben, Jen, and Emily for their support throughout the process; and Amy for her unfailing professionalism.

CHAPTER ONE

"GOT HIM!"

Erik Whiteside, his lean, boyish face flushed with triumph, filled the doorway of my tiny office. Behind him, midafternoon light drifted through the narrow windows in the reception area and bathed his white-blond hair in a soft halo.

I set aside the financial reports I'd been studying and tossed my reading glasses on the desk. "Got whom?"

My partner crossed the gray Berber carpet in two strides and dropped his six-foot-plus frame into the single client chair pulled up to my faux mahogany desk. "You're the only person I know who uses 'whom' in conversation," he said with his trademark grin.

"So I'm a grammar geek," I said, smiling back. "Get over it, and answer the question."

"Impatient as usual. This one's so good I'm tempted to make you work for it."

"Perhaps you might like to recall whose name you see on the bottom of your paycheck, such as it is."

"I believe that would be you, Lydia Baynard Simpson Tanner, for which I and my landlord are eternally grateful," he said.

Though I called him my partner, Erik hadn't managed to accumulate enough cash to buy an actual interest in Simpson & Tanner, Inquiry

2 ◇ K A T H R Y N   R .   W A L L

Agents, but he assured me he was close. My father, retired judge Talbot Simpson, and I had provided the initial investment enabling us to rent the small suite in a recently completed office complex midisland. My late mother's trust fund and the recovering stock market provided operating capital, supplemented occasionally by an actual paying customer. Erik earned his keep by providing a level of computer expertise unequaled outside a government agency.

I leaned back in the swivel chair and pinched the bridge of my nose. *Time to get my glasses changed,* I thought, another depressing reminder of my looming milestone birthday. "Are you going to answer me, or do I have to beat it out of you?"

He laughed. " 'They also serve who only stand and wait.' "

"Milton," I responded, "from 'On His Blindness.' When are you going to learn you don't have a prayer in this game? I practically had to memorize *Bartlett's* just to keep up with my father. Now knock it off and spill."

His brown eyes sobered. "I found Win Hammond. After nearly two years, I finally tracked him down."

"My God," I said, jerking upright in my chair. "How? Where? Is he still alive?"

"Pure dumb luck is how," he said, leaning forward to rest his elbows on the desk, "and yes, he's still very much alive." Erik consulted his watch. "And if everything works out, he should be landing in Savannah in about four hours."

My hand reached of its own volition for a nonexistent pack of cigarettes, although it had been nearly a year since I'd kicked the habit for the second time. I sighed in frustration and picked up a pen to keep my fingers occupied.

"So give."

"Well, you remember the postcard Miss Hammond got from her brother, right about the time . . ." His voice trailed off, and his eyes found mine. The events of that summer two years before—and the rippling aftershocks they'd created—had culminated in a number of deaths, some of which had struck very close to home.

"Of course I remember," I said. "He sent her the card after she got attacked. Postmarked from St. Thomas in the Virgin Islands."

Adelaide Boyce Hammond, frightened by her brush with death, had asked me to find her black sheep brother. Edwin Hollister Hammond III had abandoned family and country nearly twenty years before and had not been heard from until the mysterious communication which had provided neither return address nor any other useful contact information. Erik and I had been searching for him—off and on—ever since.

"Why is he coming here? And how . . . ?"

"A long time ago I put out a call on several of the message boards originating in the Caribbean, asking if anyone'd heard of him. I got a couple of responses early on, but they turned out to be false alarms."

My mind kept wandering to the scene where I actually told Miss Addie her beloved younger brother was coming home, to the joy on her weathered, octogenarian's face when I announced . . .

"Earth to Bay, come in please. Are you actually interested in hearing this, or should I just cut to the chase?"

"Sorry," I mumbled. "Of course I want to hear it. Caribbean message boards. False alarms."

The phone jangled in the outer office, and Erik half rose. "Let the service get it," I said, and he subsided back into his chair. "Go ahead."

"I got back on the trail yesterday when I heard from a woman in the British Virgin Islands, asking if I was still looking for information about Hammond. We exchanged several e-mails before I finally convinced her to do the right thing." He laughed. "I can be very persuasive when I put my mind to it."

I returned his smile. In his late twenties, with a long, rangy body and more than his share of blond good looks, Erik Whiteside oozed Southern charm. I couldn't imagine too many people of the female persuasion resisting him, even long distance. Still, it seemed strange the woman hadn't asked for some sort of reward.

"So what has Win been up to all these years? Where's he been living?" I tossed the pen back onto the desk and leaned forward.

Miss Addie's wish to see her brother once more before she died had seemed an impossible request, my failure to grant it a nagging guilt that had been quietly eating at me for months.

"Apparently he's been running a charter service out of Virgin Gorda. Sailing and fishing cruises for wealthy tourists. He's been going by the name of James Holland."

"No wonder you couldn't track him down. Why's he coming back to the States?" I glanced at the clock above my framed PI license on the side wall. "And how do you know he's on his way to Savannah?"

Again the phone rang on the desk of our phantom receptionist.

"Sure you don't want me to get it?" Erik asked.

"They'll call back if it's important. That's why we pay a fortune for the answering service. Go ahead."

The long and short of it was that Erik's informant, a sometime girl-friend of Hammond/Holland, had dropped by to find him stripping his place and throwing clothes into an old suitcase. When she'd asked Win where he was going, he'd become abusive, calling her names and literally throwing her out into the street. She claimed to have known for a long time about his real name and background. Apparently Win was like lots of people who sought refuge in the scattered islands of the Caribbean: He had a past he'd just as soon forget. They'd even laughed together about Erik's Internet inquiries the previous year. And, since there was nothing in it for her, she'd let it ride. But she'd written Erik's contact information on a slip of paper and tucked it into her wallet. Just in case.

"And she volunteered all this because . . . ?" I watched the red flush creep up my partner's neck. "You offered her money, didn't you? I thought we agreed—"

"I wired her five hundred dollars, okay? There was no way she was going to tell me anything without it."

He raised his head, and we stared at each other for a long moment.

"Your own savings, I take it?"

He nodded.

I sighed and leaned back in my chair. "Okay. I'll reimburse you out of the company account. But just this once. Next time, we need to discuss things before you go running off half-cocked."

"Thanks. You're right, but it seemed too good a lead to pass up."

And it had been. A quick check of the airline databases, only secure against amateur hackers not even remotely in Erik's league, had revealed Win Hammond's flight and its approximate arrival time.

"So did this mystery woman have any idea what's sending the long-lost black sheep of the Hammond family running for home?"

Erik shook his head. "She claimed not to know."

"I don't like the sound of this sudden decision to come back to the States after all these years. Five'll get you ten it's got something to do with money. Miss Addie isn't rich, but she's certainly comfortably well-off. This guy sounds like he could be nothing but trouble for her."

"Didn't you say they had other sisters? Maybe he plans on hitting them up for room and board or a fresh stake or whatever it is he's got in mind."

I shook my head. "Not likely. One of them's in a nursing home, and I remember the other one seemed to have gone through whatever inheritance she'd received. No, I think Miss Addie's the target. His flying into Savannah pretty much clinches it."

I ran a hand through the tangled mop of my hair. It had grown out to nearly the length it had been before they'd hacked it all off in the emergency room that awful summer I first got involved in Adelaide Boyce Hammond's problems.

"How am I going to tell her the brother she's idolized all these years may be dropping back into her life just for a handout?"

"You don't," Erik said, and my head snapped up. "Don't get all riled up, Bay. I'm just saying it's really none of our business. We tell her he's coming, give her a little warning so the poor old thing doesn't have a stroke when she opens the front door, and let it go at that. What happens afterward is between the two of them."

I knew he was right, but the idea of anyone's taking advantage of Miss Addie set my teeth on edge. She and my late mother had been the cream rising to the top of local society, both of them products of family trees stretching back to the founding of the country. Having withstood the humiliation of the War of Northern Aggression, both families, along with so many others in our little corner of the South Carolina coast, had retained the casual arrogance that went with old money and older lineage. Despite it all, Adelaide Boyce Hammond remained one of the kindest women I'd ever encountered. Her sleazy brother would have me to deal with if he thought he could just show up after all this time and run any sort of scam on the old lady.

"So what's the plan?" Erik's voice cut across my reminiscences.

"I need to go talk to her in person. I don't think this is something I should do over the telephone."

"I agree. What do you want to do about the brother? Want me to meet him at the airport?"

I thought about it for a moment. "No, I can't see any point to that. I do think it wouldn't hurt, though, for you to tail him and keep me posted. If he doesn't head straight for Hilton Head, I'll need to know where he's going. Maybe I should hold off alerting Miss Addie until we actually see the whites of his eyes."

"Good thought. That way we won't get her hopes up if he doesn't actually intend to contact her."

"I can't believe it isn't the whole point of this sudden trip home. That's what your e-mail lady implied, right?"

Erik shrugged. "Yeah, but remember she's an *ex*-girlfriend, so her information may not be entirely reliable. A woman scorned and all that."

If he intended to get a rise out of me or engender another quotation contest, I had to disappoint him.

"Why don't you grab some dinner and head on out to the airport? I've got paperwork to finish up on the Matheson file. I'll probably be here another hour or so. After that you can reach me at the Judge's or on my cell. I should be home by eight."

"Command performance?"

I answered his rhetorical question with a smile. When my father asked me to stop by at Presqu'isle, the old family mansion on St. Helena

Island, I generally didn't have the option of saying no. Besides the fact I'd spent most of my life dancing to his tune, his health had deteriorated over the past few months, especially after his harrowing ordeal the previous year. He'd been looking more frail than usual lately, and I'd made it my business to keep a close eye on him. Not that Lavinia Smalls, his companion-housekeeper and the woman who had practically raised me, didn't guard him like a fierce old bird with her hatchlings, but still . . .

"Take some money from petty cash for expenses," I said, "and bring me back your receipts."

"Aye, aye, Captain," he said, saluting as he rose. At the door, he paused and looked back. "By the way, what's the verdict on Matheson? Is he messing with his partner?"

"About money? Probably. I don't have that nailed down yet. Literally? Again, it's hard to say. What do you think? You've been following him off and on for the past week or so. Any indication he swings both ways?"

Erik shook his head. "They spend a lot of time together, but it's mostly in public places—restaurants, bars, the golf course. I've never seen any indication they're more than business associates, much as Mrs. M. would like to believe he's in the closet."

I shook my head. "I swore when we got into this inquiry agency stuff I wouldn't mess with anything remotely resembling a divorce, and now look at us." I couldn't keep the disgust from my voice. "I thought it was a straight case of cooking the books, something I could verify with half my brain tied behind my back. I did a ton of those when I had the CPA practice in Charleston. Then all of a sudden we're following potentially philandering husbands all over the damn island. I'm almost inclined to give Grace Matheson her retainer back and tell her to find someone else."

"That'd be a shame considering all the time we've both put in on it," Erik said in the maddeningly reasonable tone he sometimes adopted when he felt I was about to go off the deep end. "What does Ben have to say about it?"

I could feel my ears turning red as Erik studied me from the doorway. Most of the time I tolerated his teasing and ragging, almost as if he were an annoying younger brother. Since I'd grown up without any siblings to practice on, I sometimes didn't know quite how to deal with it. His mention of Ben Wyler, our silent partner and former New York City homicide detective, had been meant to aggravate me, and it worked. We'd needed someone with police experience to allow us to obtain our investigator's license from the state, but that had been the sum total of Wyler's involvement, and I intended to keep it that way. I still hadn't sorted out my feelings about the man who had tried to have me arrested for murder.

"Get your butt in gear, Whiteside," I said, "or the plane'll be on the ground before you get off the island. You're going to hit the late-afternoon traffic."

With tens of thousands of tourists streaming across the bridges for the start of the summer beach season, our rush hour had become more than its usual nightmare.

"You, too," he said, ignoring the jibe and glancing at his watch. "If you're headed for Presqu'isle, you'd better get moving yourself."

He had a point. I heard him unlock the drawer in the receptionist's desk and lift out the petty cash box. I stuffed the Matheson papers into my briefcase just as the outside door opened. I looked up to see a statuesque blonde in a raspberry silk shift that did nothing to disguise the contours of her body. She paused just across the threshold. I couldn't see Erik's face from where I sat, but I could almost guarantee his jaw had dropped at least a couple of inches.

"May I help you?" I heard him say, his words followed by the soft closing of the door.

"I don't know," the woman answered, her voice low and hesitant. "Is this the detective agency?"

I shifted around in my chair trying to get a better view of the outer office without being too obvious. I could just make out the line of Erik's shoulder as he stood facing the newcomer.

"Inquiry agency," he said, and I smiled. We were very firm about dispelling the notion we were your average sleazy husband-chasers, although Grace Matheson was making it very difficult to maintain that illusion. "I'm Erik Whiteside."

I watched the handshake, the woman's fingers seeming to hesitate a little as they met Erik's, a tremulous smile lifting the corners of her wide mouth. She nodded, but didn't reply.

"Something we can help you with?" Erik asked. "Why don't you have a seat over here?"

He guided her toward the single easy chair across the room from the small desk, and for a moment they both stood framed in the doorway to my office. She looked to be in her early twenties, not beautiful in any classic sense, but striking, her long tanned legs thin and shapely beneath the short hem of the shift, her pale hair falling in soft waves to her shoulders.

I moved from behind the desk. I wanted Erik on his way to Savannah, and I figured this would turn out to be just another cheating-man scenario, when the woman said, very succinctly, "I want to report a rape."

CHAPTER
TWO

I MADE IT OUT TO THE RECEPTION AREA IN TIME TO catch Erik's stunned expression and forestall his stammering reply.

"I'm Bay Tanner, Ms. . . . ?" I said, extending my hand.

The pale blue eyes lifted to mine. "Swensen. Britt Swensen."

The quick, darting look away and about a quarter-inch of dark roots peeking through the blond mane told me it probably wasn't her real name, but I let it go.

"Why don't we step into my office? I'll be right with you." I waited until she'd seated herself in the client chair before turning to Erik. "You'd better get on the road," I said.

"Sure you don't want me to stick around? This doesn't sound like our run-of-the-mill case."

I glanced over my shoulder and lowered my voice. "It sounds like I'll be hustling her off to the sheriff's office in a few minutes, but I want to get her calmed down first. She looks about ready to shatter."

Erik scooped the two twenties from petty cash off the desk and shoved them in the pocket of his khakis. "Okay. Give me a shout on the cell if you need me for anything. I'll check back in when I see where Win Hammond is headed."

"Good. Take it easy out there."

"You bet," he said and slipped out the door.

I noticed the message light blinking on the reception area phone and wondered if Ms. Swensen had been trying to call us before she appeared on our doorstep. I straightened the wrinkled skirt of my sleeveless cotton dress and wished I'd put on something a little more professional. I moved back into my office, seated myself in the high-backed chair, and opened the top right-hand drawer.

"Before we begin, Ms. Swensen, I'm going to ask your permission to tape our conversation. It saves me having to take notes, and it protects both of us down the road if any sort of questions arise. Do you have a problem with that?"

She shook her head, and I switched on the recording equipment.

"I'm sorry, but you'll have to say it out loud. For the machine."

"Oh, yes. Of course. I mean, of course, it's okay to use tape." She paused for a moment, then added, "But what if . . . ? I mean, what if you won't take my case or something? What happens to the tape?"

Good, a clever one, I thought. Working with intelligent clients made my job a lot easier. "If we decide not to do business together, I'll give you the tape, and you can do whatever you like with it. Fair enough?"

Britt Swensen nodded.

"Okay, for the record, will you give me your full name, local address, and phone number?"

She hesitated, and I figured we'd hit the moment of truth pretty early. If she wanted to maintain the fiction of her Scandinavian alias, I'd have to go with it. On closer inspection, I'd decided she was older than I'd first estimated, maybe around thirty, and the years didn't sit well on her face. Or maybe the trauma of whatever had happened to her had etched those worry lines between her eyes and drained the natural color from her cheeks.

"Ms. Swensen?"

The woman sighed. "That's not my real name. I only use it for . . . it's sort of my stage name."

"I see. You're an actress?"

"Sort of. Look, can I just tell you what happened?"

"Sure. But how about giving me your real name first."

"Karen Zwilling." She spelled it and added her address, an upscale condominium complex on the southern tip of the island.

"Fine. Now tell me how I can help, although if you were in fact raped, I have to advise you to go straight to the sheriff. I know some people there, and I'd be glad to go with you. I can get you to the right person."

Her head had begun shaking violently the moment the word "sheriff" came out of my mouth. "No. No cops. They'll just . . . they won't understand."

"Okay, we'll table that for now. Go ahead."

I leaned back in my chair, fairly certain I knew the outline of the story I was about to hear. Though I'd been a licensed private investigator for only a little more than eight months, I'd been around for way too close to forty years. After the murder of my state's attorney husband, I'd found myself embroiled in more than my share of the seamier side of our little slice of paradise. Just as the grace and beauty of our antebellum culture had masked the cancer of slavery, so our modern image of Southern gentility and world-class resort living hid the same human frailties and misery to be found anywhere else in postmillennial America. We just concealed our problems with a little more élan.

As I'd suspected, Karen Zwilling worked for one of the dozens of escort services you could find simply by consulting the Yellow Pages. The Judge and I had gotten into a discussion about it one day, and my appalling ignorance about this facet of island life had sent me flipping through the local phone directory, astonished at the number and variety of services offered. Clever minds had been at work in coming up with some of the euphemisms: escorts, dancers, cheerleaders, beach babes, lingerie models, vixens. My favorite, though, was caddies. I could just hear some Midwestern businessman trying to explain to the little woman about golf course attendants who looked and dressed like *Playboy* centerfold wannabes.

My potential client, however, insisted she wasn't a prostitute, and I nodded as if I believed her.

"I'm not saying some of the girls don't . . . you know, become *inti-*

mate with their dates, but it's strictly up to them. I mean, they do it because they want to, not because it's what they're getting paid to do. Our instructions are very clear. We provide companionship and someone for them to talk to over dinner. That's all."

"But you are saying you went out on a date with a man who paid for your . . . companionship, and he raped you?"

"He . . . he seemed okay," Karen Zwilling said, her eyes downcast. She twisted a nicely cut emerald around and around on the third finger of her right hand.

"Let's get specific," I said brusquely. "I still believe I'm going to recommend you take this to the authorities, but let me hear your story before I decide."

Her head snapped up at my words, and for the first time I saw anger smoldering in her soft blue eyes. "Story? Do you think I made this up?"

"I have no idea. Why don't you just tell me," I said calmly, leaning back in my chair and folding my hands in my lap. "We'll reserve judgments for later."

Karen Zwilling squared her shoulders. "I arranged to meet him last Friday night, at the bar in the Crowne Plaza, where he was staying. He took me to dinner, then—"

I held up my hand to halt her in midsentence. "Wait a minute. Had you met him before? How did you recognize him?"

Her smile, though tentative, altered her face completely. She looked, at that moment, barely out of her teens. "The usual. I had a white rosebud pinned to my dress."

I waited without comment for her to continue.

"Anyway, after dinner we went to this jazz place and had some drinks, then he asked if I wanted to see his boat. He said he'd just had it brought up from his place in the islands, that he was having some sort of repairs done on it. He said we could have a nightcap on board." Her smile this time seemed less little-girl-lost and more like that of a woman who'd been around the barn a few times. "I knew what he wanted, of course, so I told him that wasn't part of the package."

"And what did he say?"

"He seemed to take it okay, said he just wanted to show off his 'baby.' " The young woman shook her head. "The damn thing was the size of a house! I know it was stupid of me to go there with him, but I couldn't resist. I mean, I've never seen anything like that except on TV."

I smiled at the wonder in her voice. "Where was the boat docked?"

"Somewhere on the south end, I think. I've only been here a couple of months, and I'm not real familiar with the island, except for the main drag." She blushed. "Besides, like I said, we'd had a few drinks."

"How about the name of the boat? Did he tell you, or did you see it painted on the outside somewhere?"

Karen Zwilling shrugged. "He told me, but I don't remember. Something to do with music, I think, but . . ." Again she colored up. "Sorry."

"Never mind. We'll work on that later. So you went on board with him. Then what happened?"

The brief pleasure of the memory drained from her face. "We went inside to look at the cabins, and he threw me down on a bed and raped me."

The matter-of-fact statement had more power than if she'd screamed and shouted and beat her breast. It made me wonder if it had happened to her before.

"You actually said no? You resisted?"

The look she turned on me then would have melted steel. "The bastard was big—around six feet, a couple of hundred pounds." She sighed. "Look, after I realized I couldn't stop him, I just . . . let it happen. I didn't help, but I didn't fight him either. I figured it was better just to get it over with."

I suppressed a shudder at her calm acceptance. "What happened . . . after?"

"He apologized. Said he'd gotten carried away by the booze and the moonlight." Karen snorted. "And my incredible beauty. He offered me money."

I waited for her to tell me she'd flung it in his face. Sometimes my own naïveté surprises even me.

She looked up and correctly read my expression. "Hey, it was five hundred bucks. He just peeled it off a roll from his pocket. He begged me to keep it, to make up for, you know, whatever. He seemed really sorry."

"So you took the money."

"Damn right I took it! The son of a bitch raped me! I could've had his ass thrown in jail, and he knew it."

I phrased my next words carefully. "Karen, you had sex— unwillingly, you claim—" I held up my hand to forestall the outburst I could see coming. "And you accepted money for it. That's a pretty straightforward definition of prostitution."

Karen Zwilling popped up out of the chair as if she were a marionette and someone had jerked all her strings at once.

"Wait!" I said, holding out a placating hand. "Just wait a second. Hear me out."

She hesitated before resettling herself in the padded chair. "This is pointless if you don't believe me."

"I didn't say I don't believe you. I'm trying to tell you what it will look like to the police."

"Which is exactly why I didn't go to them. Don't you think I know how it looks?" She sighed, and a lot of the fight went out of her. "I'd just about decided to let the whole damn thing go, get myself checked out in case he had something, you know? But then I talked to my friend Layla."

It didn't take a detective to figure the next part out. "And the same thing had happened to her?"

"Yes. Almost exactly."

"Same guy? Same hotel?"

"No. She met him at the Hilton on Saturday. But it was the same routine, and the description fits. He used a different name, sort of a variation on the one he gave me, but he took her to the same yacht. Except she only got a couple of hundred." Her voice sounded almost smug.

I shook my head. This whole thing was fast becoming very weird. "And she didn't report him either?"

"No. That's why I'm here." She swallowed hard, and for the first time she met my eyes directly. "Look, it's not some kind of sorority, you know? We don't all get together and have pajama parties and paint each other's toenails. But I've been thinking he might be doing this to a lot of the girls, and no one's doing anything about it because everyone figures like I do, that nobody'll give a damn if a few 'escorts' get what's coming to them."

"What is it you want me to do?"

Karen lifted her straw bag from the floor, searched its contents for a moment, and pulled out a checkbook. "I want you to find the bastard and shut down his little operation before someone really gets hurt." She rummaged again and produced a gold pen. "How much do you charge?"

I reached into the left-hand drawer and pulled out our standard contract and a rate sheet. "Read this over, and I'll be right back."

I slid the paperwork in front of her and stepped through the door, easing it closed behind me. I had about three minutes to decide if I wanted to embroil us in something as potentially dangerous as tracking down a rapist. I knew what I should do was to pick up the phone and call the sheriff's office. I could dump the whole thing in the lap of my brother-in-law, Sergeant Red Tanner, and urge him to get the information to the right detectives. Surely with two victims telling identical stories they'd have to take it seriously. On the other hand, a nagging voice in the back of my head kept repeating, why would they? I still had a problem believing a woman who worked in Karen's profession didn't knowingly lay herself open to all kinds of kooks and weirdos. Occupational hazard. Why would the cops think any differently?

I lifted the receiver and held it against my chest for a moment before drawing a long breath and punching in the familiar numbers.

CHAPTER
THREE

*L*AVINIA SMALLS ACCEPTED MY APOLOGIES AND PROM-
ised to convey them to my father. I knew he'd rant and carry on
for a while, more because his wishes had been thwarted than for any
genuine regret at not seeing me across his dinner table.

I walked back into the office to find Karen Zwilling scrawling her
signature on the bottom of the contract. On top of it lay a check for five
hundred dollars made out to Simpson & Tanner. Neither of us com-
mented on the synchronicity of the amount.

"Will that be enough?" she asked as I slid back into my chair. "To
get started?"

"Certainly. You understand the hourly rate doesn't include expenses?"

"I read the paperwork. Layla and I are going to check around and
see if anyone else wants to contribute. If not, we can handle the expense,
for a few days anyway. How long do you think it'll take?"

I shrugged. "No idea, really. It all depends on how much information you can give me about this guy. The more I know, the less time I'll
have to spend tracking him down." I paused, making sure I had her full
attention. "There's one thing we haven't talked about. What does a sat-
isfactory resolution of this look like in your eyes?"

"I don't understand."

"Say we locate this guy for you, which shouldn't be too hard if he's still on Hilton Head. Then what?"

Her gaze held mine, but still she didn't speak.

"What happens next? Do you want us to gather enough evidence to make a case to the sheriff? Do you want him arrested? Run out of town on a rail? What?"

Her laugh made me understand how a man could find her irresistible. It changed her whole face and body language. "I don't suppose you'd consider just having someone beat the crap out of him, would you?"

I smiled back. "Not on our menu of services, I'm afraid. Seriously, Karen, what do you hope to accomplish?"

"I don't know yet. Just find the bastard, and we'll worry about it then."

I didn't exactly like the idea of an open-ended investigation, but the client, like the customer, is almost always right. I removed a yellow legal pad and a fresh pen from the center desk drawer. Even with the tape recorder running, I felt better taking notes.

"Okay," I said, "tell me everything you remember."

By the time I ushered Karen Zwilling out of the office, I had enough information to make locating Randolph Remington Wade a lot easier. I wondered briefly why the women hadn't just cornered the man themselves since they seemed to know so much about him. I shrugged and locked the outside door behind me. Maybe they thought being confronted by someone quasi-official would carry more weight. I tossed my briefcase onto the passenger seat and climbed into the T-Bird.

Spring had decided to skip the Lowcountry, and we'd gone from the lovely sixties of March directly into the nineties of late summer, even though we were barely into June. I left the convertible top in place and cranked up the air conditioning. I gave a brief thought to stopping by somewhere to pick up a sandwich, then decided I'd scrounge something up at home. Since I'd finally learned how to cook, Dolores Santiago, my part-time housekeeper, had reduced her schedule to only two days a week, and this wasn't one of them. I would have no lovingly prepared meal waiting for me to heat up in the microwave.

I pulled onto Route 278 and joined the evening rush hour, relatively moderate in the eastbound lanes. The real crunch came when the thousands of workers who couldn't afford to live on Hilton Head battled their way home to the small communities on the mainland where housing could still be found for under six figures. Our unemployment rate, especially during tourist season, was practically nonexistent, but it made for horrendous bottlenecks every afternoon between three and six.

It took only a few minutes before I turned off at the entrance to Port Royal Plantation, received a smart salute from the uniformed woman at the security gate, and wound my way past one of our three golf courses to my beachfront home. My late husband Rob and I had always called it our "cottage," but its three bedrooms and two baths sprawled across a generous lot just behind the rows of sand dunes that protected us from the gentle Atlantic rollers.

Inside I tossed my briefcase onto the white sofa in the great room and climbed the three steps up into the kitchen. Built over the garage, it had been completely remodeled after an explosion had destroyed that entire end of the house. I pulled open the refrigerator door, glancing over my shoulder as the phone rang shrilly in the emptiness. I moved over to the built-in desk and checked the caller ID before picking up.

"Hey, Red!"

"Hey, yourself," my brother-in-law said. "I'm amazed to find you home. I intended to leave you a message."

"Actually I was supposed to be having dinner with the Judge, but I got stuck at the office and couldn't make it."

I felt the temperature drop a few degrees as the frosty silence from the other end of the phone stretched out. While my dead husband's brother understood my desire to make use of the skills I'd acquired over the past couple of years, *Sergeant* Tanner didn't entirely approve.

"Anything I should know about?" he finally asked.

Technically speaking, allegations of rape were precisely the kinds of things he should know about. But Karen Zwilling's signature on a

Simpson & Tanner contract—and her five-hundred-dollar check—guaranteed her confidentiality.

"Nothing I can't handle," I said with more confidence than I had any right to feel. "So what's up? What's the message you were going to leave me?"

I could almost see him shaking his head in that condescending way he had, as if I were a kid caught playing with matches.

"I'm off at four on Friday, and I thought we'd run over to Savannah and catch a Sand Gnats game. I'll pick you up around five thirty."

My enthusiasm for baseball had been instilled in me at an early age by my father, a lover of the purity and symmetry of the game. The minor league team, a farm club of the brand-new Washington Nationals, came as close as we were going to get to professional sports this side of Atlanta.

"Sounds like fun," I said, "but I don't think I can make any definite plans. I've got this new case, and Erik—"

"C'mon, Bay, lighten up. I know you like playing detective, but get serious. What could be more important than baseball?"

Playing detective. If he'd been in the room, I would have thrown something at him. We'd been over this ground so many times, in so many different ways, and still Red seemed unable—or unwilling—to get it.

Ever since his brother's murder, coming right on top of his divorce, we'd been spending a lot of time together, taking in dinners and movies and just generally hanging out. I never thought of them as dates, although it seemed Red had other ideas. I could handle that. What I couldn't tolerate was his patronizing attitude toward my new profession.

Besides, having my father meddling full-time in my personal business was just about all I could handle. I didn't need two men trying to tell me how to run my life.

"Bay? You still there?"

"I'm here. Look, I can't make plans for Friday, okay?"

"But I already have the tickets." He sounded like a petulant little boy.

"Hang on," I said, the beep in my ear signaling an incoming call. "I think this might be Erik, and I've been waiting to hear from him. Can I have a rain check on the ballgame?"

He made sure I heard his deep sigh. "Sure. No problem."

"Great. Gotta run. Talk to you soon."

I switched to the incoming call, promising myself I'd make it up to Red later.

"Hello?"

"Bay, it's Erik."

"What's happening? Did you locate our long-lost boy?"

"Yeah, eventually. Did it ever occur to you that neither one of us has a clue what the old guy looks like?"

I would have laughed if it hadn't been so pathetic. Every time I got up on my high horse about playing Bay Tanner, Girl Detective, some stupidity like this popped up to remind me I often didn't have a clue what the hell I was doing.

"A minor detail which I'm sure you found a way to overcome," I said.

"Yeah. I marked out three possibles when they came off the plane, then beat it down to the luggage carousels and tried to blend in with the passengers. I checked most of the name tags on the bags as they came off. I think I gave a pretty convincing impression of a guy hunting for a lost suitcase."

"So you fingered Hammond's bags and waited to see who claimed them. Very inventive."

"Thank you, ma'am. Anyway, he got on the shuttle for Hilton Head. We just pulled out of the airport lot, so you've got about an hour to high-tail it over to Miss Hammond's and prepare her."

I looked longingly back toward the refrigerator and patted my growling stomach. So much for dinner. "Is he on the bus that drops people off directly at their individual destinations?" I asked.

"Yup. Which could give you a little more time, unless they take the Cross Island and do the south end of the island first. No way to tell."

"Good point. I'd better get over there."

The Cedars, the high-end retirement community where Adelaide Boyce Hammond owned a condominium, was an oak-laden, gated enclave with tight security, sprawled next to the marsh and the wide expanse of Bishop's Reach. I wondered how her brother planned on breaching the walls.

"He may be staying somewhere else overnight," Erik said when I'd voiced my concerns. "All I can do is stick close to the shuttle and let you know where he gets off."

"Did he make any phone calls from the airport?"

"Nope, but he could have a cell."

"Okay, I guess I'd better get myself over there. I'll call and tell her I want to drop by for a visit."

A part of me couldn't help itching to get the new investigation under way. I'd hoped to be able to hit a couple of the hotels later in the evening to see if I could scare up this Wade character, but I knew precisely where my real responsibility lay.

"Let me know the second you're sure where her brother's headed."

"Will do. Give Miss Hammond my best."

I flipped through my address book, then let the phone ring eleven times before hanging up. She might be down in the dining room or out with friends. Either way I had a short reprieve. I whipped open the freezer door, popped a package of scallops into the microwave, and hit Defrost. A little garlic and olive oil, some al dente pasta, and I'd be in business.

Half an hour later I tried her again, then replaced the phone and carried my steaming bowl to the glass-topped table in the alcove of the kitchen. The *Island Packet* still lay folded where I'd left it that morning. I'd taken a short run and cut things too close. Breakfast had been half an English muffin mounded with extra-crunchy peanut butter wolfed down on my way out the door. Since we staffed the offices of Simpson & Tanner only three days a week, I felt an obligation to be there on time, even though no one would be chiding me for punching in late. I ran the show, such as it was.

I twirled linguini onto my fork and studied the front page. Most of the national news concerned the chaos in the Middle East, and I scanned quickly by it. The local items were dominated by the imminent arrival of several heads of state for the G8 economic summit being held on Sea Island, south of Savannah, in just a few days. I forced myself not to let my mind drift to the painful associations that event conjured up. In spite of my best efforts, I couldn't help wondering if my former lover, Interpol agent Alain Darnay, lurked in the shadows somewhere nearby. Before he'd abruptly abandoned me in the middle of one of the worst crises of my life, he'd been heavily involved in planning security for the conference.

"Bastard," I muttered around a mouthful of pasta and congratulated myself on having advanced to the stage where I could say it without the accompanying exclamation point.

My cell phone rang just as I finished stacking things in the dishwasher.

"Bay, this is going to take longer than I thought," Erik said, an unusual level of frustration seeping into his voice. "We've stopped at two motels already, one in Hardeeville and another by Sun City. The bus is loaded, so I have no idea when we'll get to Hilton Head."

"Not a problem," I said as I moved into my bedroom and began a one-handed effort at peeling off my work clothes. "I haven't been able to get Miss Addie on the phone."

"Are you concerned?" he asked.

"No. She often eats in the dining room in the community center there. Or she could be out with some of her old cronies."

"Well, I don't think I'm going to have an answer for you anytime soon."

I paused to consider my options. "Tell you what. I'm going to go out and do a little snooping around on this rape case. I can get hold of her as soon as—"

Erik cut me off. "Rape case? That woman was on the level?"

I'd forgotten my partner had no idea about Karen, alias Britt, and her allegations. I worked my way out of my crumpled cotton dress and stuffed it in the clothes hamper while I filled him in.

"So I think I'll go take a little prowl around some of the big resort hotel bars and see if anyone answering Romeo's description is hanging out."

"I don't like it," Erik said. "You should wait for me. I can just run the hotel registrations on the computer."

I bit my lip. *Make that* three *men trying to run my life.*

"What fun would that be? Besides, I'm just going to reconnoiter." I liked the way the word rolled off my tongue, the quasi-military sound of it giving me a little adrenaline buzz.

"Okay, you're the boss. Just be careful."

"Not a problem. Listen, give me the word the minute you know where Win Hammond ends up."

"Ten-four."

Reconnoiter. I pulled open the door to my walk-in closet and scanned its contents. I selected a slinky black jumpsuit whose jersey material clung to me in all the right places but still managed to conceal the ugly scars that crisscrossed my left shoulder. They were old wounds, lasting reminders of the horror of my husband Rob's death, of his plane exploding on takeoff and the rain of hot metal which had left me scarred forever in more ways than one. I touched the puckered skin where I'd taken a bullet in that same shoulder over a year before and wondered if it was courage or stupidity that drove me toward placing myself in harm's way.

Neddie Halloran, my psychologist friend in Savannah, said it had more to do with my need to be accepted, to be admired, a result of my less than idyllic childhood and my mother's constant criticism. But that was ridiculous. At first it had been about revenge for Rob's murder and protecting my family from the monsters who had caused it. Eventually I learned to love the solving of the puzzle, the rush of winning in a game where failure held more than the usual consequences. And, like turning out a perfectly balanced set of accounting records or parlaying a gut feeling into a stock market killing, I was pretty good at it. Most of the time.

I piled my hair on top of my head in a casual jumble of reddish brown curls. I touched up my mascara, grimacing at the tiny lines radiating out from the corners of my eyes. The completion of my ensemble involved tucking the tiny Seecamp pistol, along with my cell phone and some cash, into a sleek, black handbag.

I tried Miss Addie once more as I slipped into the Thunderbird, a tiny kernel of concern worming its way into the back of my mind as the phone rang unanswered in the old woman's apartment.

CHAPTER FOUR

THE CROWNE PLAZA HOTEL SITS DIRECTLY ON THE OCEAN next door to the world-famous Van Der Meer Racquet Club inside Shipyard Plantation. Its elegant lobby soars to a three-story atrium beneath which small groupings of overstuffed chairs and sleek leather love seats invite hushed, intimate conversations.

I veered right toward the cherry-paneled reception desk where three young women in crisp white shirts and navy blue blazers huddled together in earnest conversation, the check-in rush apparently over for the day. I cleared my throat, and a thin blonde with her hair brushed back in a slick man cut separated herself from the group.

"May I help you?"

"Yes. I wonder if you could ring someone for me. I don't know the room number, and I understand you don't give those out."

"No, ma'am, we don't. What's the guest's name?"

I palmed the piece of paper I slid from the pocket of my jumpsuit and glanced down at it. "Randolph Wade."

"One moment, please." Her fingers flew over the keyboard and a slight frown puckered her tan face. "We don't have anyone by that name registered with us."

"Maybe it's under Remington Wade. Or it could be Wade Randolph." She cocked an eyebrow at me, and I hurried on. "They're cousins. They're sharing the room."

"Of course they are." Again she tapped keys, and again she shook her head. "No, I'm sorry. Are you certain you have the right hotel?"

"Maybe they haven't checked in yet," I said, her suspicious gaze making me squirm a little. "I'll just wait in the bar and see if they show up."

"Why don't you do that. Our lounge is down the hall to your right." She aimed a well-manicured finger toward the tall windows. "Would you like me to have you paged if . . . when they arrive?"

"No, thanks. I'll check back."

That went well, I said to myself. I thought it had been a pretty damned good cover story, but it obviously needed work.

So neither of the names this bozo had given the women from the escort service had been legit. Maybe he'd used some other combination. Or maybe he'd lied about being registered. You didn't have to be a guest to gain access to the public rooms. Anyone could walk in just as I had done and make use of the several restaurants and bars serving the sprawling hotel.

I crossed the lobby and turned down the hallway toward Signals Lounge, my high-heeled sandals clicking loudly on the parquet floor. The doors stood open, and soft background music drifted out. Inside, about half the seats were occupied, not bad for a Wednesday night on the cusp of tourist season. I found a small table near the empty bandstand and settled myself in. A young woman, pretty in a clean Midwestern way, materialized almost immediately.

"Hi! Can I get you something?"

"Perrier and lime," I said, and she bounced away.

I crossed my legs and leaned back in the chair. If I hadn't quit smoking, I would have used the ritual of lighting up to cover my quick perusal of the lounge's male customers. As it was, I had to do it a few quick glances at a time, trying not to make eye contact with anyone. Couples made up most of the clientele, and I skimmed over them. Not that husbands didn't constitute a bulk of the escort services' business, but it would be tough to ditch the wife for an entire evening. One table held four older men, probably vacationing golfers. A few unaccompanied guys, mostly younger, occupied about a third of the high-backed stools, all of them intent on their beers and the baseball players cavorting mutely on a screen behind the bar.

Karen Zwilling had described her attacker as a large man, perhaps six feet tall, two-hundred-plus pounds, with black hair graying at the temples. A flashy dresser, favoring what she referred to as "sherbet chic," which I took to mean pale, pastel shirts and soft, ivory-colored linen trousers. Without prompting, I could envision the tasseled loafers worn without socks. The rest of her description, verified she said by her friend Layla, included a sharp face, a demeanor they described as suave, and a stunning gold Cartier wristwatch.

The perky waitress delivered my overpriced French water and scooted away.

I shifted around in my seat and picked up the glass, giving me the opportunity to scan the other side of the room. Nothing. Maybe it was too early. I took a couple of sips and let my gaze wander through the open doors and the floor-to-ceiling window across the hall to the verdant courtyard surrounding the pool. Though out of sight from my vantage point, I knew the ocean rolled on in its endless rhythm just the other side of the screening palms.

"Excuse me."

The voice at my shoulder made me jump a good two inches.

"Sorry, ma'am. Didn't mean to startle you."

I stared into the face of a middle-aged man, one hand on the marble-topped table and the other latched firmly onto the back of my chair. A big clump of blond hair sat smack in the middle of his scalp, a vain attempt to detract from his receding hairline. The cloying sweetness of his cologne attacked my nose and settled in the back of my throat.

"I don't mean to interrupt," he said in a slow drawl which might have been local but sounded more like Texas, "but I was wonderin' if I could buy you a drink."

I leaned as far away from his eager face as I could without falling out of my chair.

"No. Thank you." I turned back toward the window and concentrated on the parade of late-evening swimmers wandering back to their rooms from the pool.

"It's just you look so lonesome, darlin', sittin' here all by yourself. Thought you might like a little company."

I swiveled my head back around and fixed him with the withering stare that came standard with my mother's Tattnall-Baynard genes. "I said no thank you."

"Aw, come on, sweetheart, no need to be that way." He gestured toward the table of golfers I'd noticed earlier on the far side of the room. "My buddies and me are just lookin' for a little companionship. We don't mean no harm."

I glanced in the direction he'd pointed. Three other paunchy, fifty-ish men stared back, anticipatory smiles pasted on their sun-weathered faces. One of them lifted a martini glass and said something to the others, and they burst into drunken laughter. I jerked the chair out from under my admirer's hand and stood. He straightened as well, a little abashed that in my high-heeled sandals I topped him by a good five inches. I retrieved my bag from the table and waved it under his nose.

"Know what I have in here?" I asked in a soft, seductive whisper.

He grinned, and I could see all sorts of enticing possibilities running through his dirty little mind. I made a show of undoing the clasp and slowly easing the bag open, almost like a stripper peeling a fishnet stocking off a shapely leg. He swallowed hard and glanced back toward his audience. I put my hand in the clutch and moved it closer so he could peer inside. I heard his gasp as his fuzzy brain registered my fingers fondling the Seecamp.

"Are we understanding 'no thank you' a little better now?" I asked.

I didn't think he'd probably moved that fast in twenty years. He was back with his buddies, whispering and gesturing, by the time I had slipped a ten onto the table and moved toward the door.

I walked briskly through the lobby and handed my ticket to the youngster at the valet stand. I could hear Neddie tsk-tsking about this love affair I seemed to be having with life in the fast lane, but I hadn't felt this alive since Rob's murder. It sure beat the hell out of endless columns of debits and credits. Any old day.

I changed tactics at my next stop. I parked in the side lot next to the Hilton Resort in Palmetto Dunes, used my cell phone to get the hotel number from information, and dialed the front desk. This time I posed as a harried secretary who had screwed up her boss's appointment book. I asked the helpful young man to check all the possible permutations of the name Randolph Remington Wade, but again I struck out. Maybe I'd have to revise my earlier assessment that tracking this guy down wouldn't take much time or effort.

The cocktail lounge inside the Hilton is much less intimate than its counterpart at the Crowne, with banks of windows giving out onto the lushly landscaped grounds. The Regatta caters to a younger clientele with a DJ during the week and a live band on Friday and Saturday nights. Again the room was nowhere near full, and several couples writhed on the dance floor to what sounded to me like cat screeching set to a pounding beat.

God, another sure sign of encroaching old age, I thought. *I'm criticizing the kids' music.* Next thing you knew, I'd be humming Barry Manilow songs in the shower.

Deciding that a moving target would be harder to hit on, I stepped up to the bar, paid for my Perrier, and surveyed the room. None of the men came even close to Karen's description. I wove my way through the tables and out to the boardwalk connecting several of the resort's facilities. I found a bench that gave me a good view of the entrance to the bar and sat down gratefully. It had been a long time since I'd spent that many hours in high heels, and my back had begun to ache just a bit.

I watched the sky above the ocean deepen from soft orange to violet to a rich, deep purple as the sun set over the mainland. The day's humidity still saturated the air. I pushed away a few damp tendrils of hair

that had escaped my topknot and lay in soggy strands against the back
of my neck. I rubbed the sweating iciness of the glass across my forehead and wondered what my next move should be. I sure as hell
couldn't wander into every bar on Hilton Head Island in the hope of
running across Karen and Layla's attacker. The fact he had given different names to the women—and that both of them were probably
phony—upped the stakes considerably. Apparently he hadn't used either of them to register at the two resorts, and there was no guarantee
he had even been a guest at all. In this era of heightened suspicion and
security, no one in any legitimate hotel would ever let me have a look at
their registration records this side of a subpoena. I'd probably have to
end up letting Erik work some of his hacker's magic on their computer
systems. My only other alternative would be to sit at the desk for the
next week or so and call every one of the hundred or more places this
guy might be staying. And if he'd rented a private condo, it might
prove impossible.

I sighed and set the slippery glass beside me on the bench. My best
bet seemed to be the boat. I didn't think he could gain access to a yacht
he didn't own, but I really had no idea what kind of security the mari-
nas maintained, especially at night. Something else to put on my check-
list. Neither of the women recalled the name of the seagoing love nest,
but vessels of that size shouldn't be too hard to spot.

Maybe there was some way I could make him come to me . . .

The familiar strains of Beethoven's Ninth drifted out of my clutch
bag, and I retrieved my cell phone. In the dim glow from the widely
spaced light fixtures, I couldn't make out the identity of the caller.

"Bay Tanner."

"Bay, it's me." Erik sounded excited and slightly out of breath.

"What's the matter?"

"Nothing. I mean, this is really weird, but it's not a problem. At
least I don't think so, but maybe you'll—"

"Erik, what are you talking about?" I could feel my muscles tensing
in anticipation of bad news.

"Win Hammond just got off the bus."

"Oh, no! He's at Miss Addie's already?" I left my glass sitting on the bench and strode as rapidly down the boardwalk as the heels of my sandals would allow.

"No, wait! Slow down. He's not at The Cedars."

My heart dropped back into its normal rhythm, and my speed slowed to a measured walk. "Then where is he? You sound as if it's trouble."

I could hear concern edging his voice. "Port Royal. The shuttle stopped at the Westin, and he got out with a few other people."

"So he's taking a room for the night. I see this as a good thing. It gives me time to get over to Miss Addie's and prepare her for tomorrow."

"No, you should come home."

I'd reached the Thunderbird, tucked into the side lot now deeply shadowed by overhanging oaks and swaying pines. I jumped, startled by the bright chirp in the humid darkness as someone a few cars over punched a remote to lock his doors.

"Why?" I asked, tossing in my bag and sliding after it into the seat.

"Because Win Hammond talked a while with the concierge, checked his bag there, and headed off down the beach."

"I don't understand."

"Let me finish. I had to scramble to park and catch up with him, but he looks pretty worn out, and he didn't really know where he was going, so I was able to keep him in my sights. He walked about a half mile, then suddenly veered off on a path away from the water."

My hand paused over the key in the ignition as I waited for the finale.

"He used a penlight to check something on a piece of paper he took out of his pocket, then disappeared behind the dunes. Next thing I know, he's collapsing into a chair on the back deck of your house."

I took my time, obeying all the speed limits and traffic signals, and pulled into my driveway about twenty minutes later. I'd needed the space to try to wrap my head around the idea of Adelaide Boyce Hammond's wayward brother using his first hour on the island to sneak onto my property. I pushed the garage door opener, eased the T-Bird inside, then trotted up the steps and into the house.

Voices drifted to me from the deck, although I couldn't make out who sat in the shadowy darkness of the screened-in area. I marched across the white-carpeted great room, flung back the door, and stopped dead at the three faces squinting up at me from various pieces of wicker furniture.

Erik was the first to speak. "Hey, welcome home! Can I get you something to drink?"

My partner sprawled in one of the cushioned chairs, a bottle of beer dangling from his hand. A man I assumed to be the fugitive, Win Hammond, reclined on the chaise, his face lost in the shadows. An empty tumbler rested on the side table at his elbow. But what had halted me in the doorway was the lined face, creased in a wide smile, caught in the soft glow of the single lamp.

"Oh, Lydia, isn't it wonderful?" Adelaide Boyce Hammond sighed as I stepped onto the porch.

CHAPTER FIVE

I COLLAPSED INTO THE ONLY REMAINING CHAIR AND ALlowed Erik to fetch me a Diet Coke. I had neither the will nor the inclination to play hostess. When he'd set the icy glass down beside me, I leaned forward, my arms resting on my knees.

"Now just what the hell is going on here?"

Both Erik and Miss Addie spoke at once, and I raised my hand for silence.

"One at a time. Erik, maybe we ought to start with you." I felt like the captain of a military unit conducting a debriefing.

"I think it'd be best if we let Miss Hammond go first," he said, avoiding my eyes.

I knew he had an inkling of how upset I was. I didn't mind hosting the welcome-home party for Edwin Hammond. I just would have appreciated being the one doing the inviting.

I glanced across at my late mother's best friend. The last time we'd had lunch together, I'd thought Miss Addie had aged considerably in the few intervening months since we'd spent any significant time together. Always sprightly, with a soft, cultured drawl that hid a quick, clever mind, the old lady had seemed lost that day, her thoughts drifting away from the conversation. I'd had to nudge her back to the subject several times, and I remembered thinking perhaps her eighty-plus years had finally taken a toll on her memory and concentration.

That evening, the lines in her face eased by the warm glow of the lamplight, she might have been a young woman. But her eagerness and excitement seemed tinged with something I couldn't quite put my finger on, something which made me wonder if her brother's sudden appearance wasn't as welcome as I'd always assumed it would be.

"Lydia, dear, I really should apologize for all of us barging in like this. It's all my fault, really it is. Please don't be angry with your young man." Her smile drifted toward Erik and came to rest on her brother. "Or with Win. It was my idea entirely."

I swallowed hard when I saw tears pooling in her faded eyes and reached quickly across to lay a hand on hers, liver-spotted and trembling slightly where it rested in her lap. "No need to apologize, Miss Addie. You know you're always welcome. I'm only trying to understand what's going on. I was just about to head over to your place and warn you about Win's arrival. I had no idea you already knew he was coming."

She extricated her hand so she could bring a glass of ice water to her thin lips. She replaced it carefully onto its coaster before continuing. "I know, dear. I wanted to tell you, really I did, but Win . . . that is, we . . ."

She hesitated, glancing at her brother as if waiting for him to come to her aid, but he remained mute, his arms folded on his chest, his long legs crossed at the ankles. I still hadn't gotten a good look at his face, and he didn't seem inclined to move out into the light. At our introduction, he'd merely nodded in my direction, failing to offer a hand. With little to go on but Miss Addie's stories, I'd already formed a mild dislike for this spoiled, arrogant man who'd abandoned his sisters in a fit of pique when he'd been disinherited. I had a few hazy memories of my own as well, and they didn't help his case any. His actions so far had done nothing to soften my opinion.

"Let me," Erik said, smiling across at the old woman. "I think I know most of it by now."

I leaned back in my chair.

The recitation took just a few minutes. The story made a certain amount of sense, although there were gaps and inconsistencies I'd want to examine later. I wished I'd had an opportunity to flip on the small tape recorder I carried in my tote bag, but it lay on the bed where I'd dropped it before embarking on my tour of Hilton Head's nightlife.

The *Reader's Digest* condensed version was that Win Hammond supposedly owed money to some very unsavory people, and he had appealed to his sister to bail him out. To her credit, Miss Addie hadn't rushed down to the nearest Western Union and wired him the cash. Instead she'd sent him a plane ticket.

"Miss Addie, why didn't you tell me?"

The question hung in the air between us for a few seconds before she answered.

"I know I should have, Lydia, really I do. But you'd already done so much for me. If it hadn't been for you, I might have been out in the street myself."

I squirmed, uncomfortable with her praise. True, my resolution of the Grayton's Race development debacle had saved Miss Addie from losing almost all her capital, and I had paid a heavy price for my involvement. But that was old news. Ancient history.

Erik resumed the story. Win's creditors, it seemed, hadn't been the kind to accept partial payments or to file papers in small-claims court.

"It seemed best for him to get out of there," my partner continued. "The two of them were afraid the bad guys might have figured out the connection, so they decided it might be a good idea for Mr. Hammond to keep a low profile once he got back in the country." He smiled at Miss Addie. "She thought this would be a safe place to meet."

"Lydia, dear, please don't be angry." Miss Addie had begun to twist the folds of her lavender dress. "I . . . I was afraid if I told you about Win's troubles you'd have to report him to the police. Because of your being a private investigator and all. I was just going to pick him up and take him somewhere safe." Her voice cracked on the last word. "But Erik found us in the driveway, and he sent the cab away and told us to wait for you inside."

I crossed the room and knelt next to her chair. I gathered her trembling shoulders into my arms and hugged her gently. "It's okay, Miss Addie. Really. I'm not angry. I'm just very confused. Why didn't you just check him into a hotel?"

Erik smiled. "Mr. Hammond was afraid he might be followed from the airport." He and I exchanged a look.

I whipped my head toward the mystery man sitting silently in the shadows. "What kind of people have you gotten yourself mixed up with?"

I was getting pretty damned tired of everyone explaining his actions and making excuses for this man who stretched like an aging sunbather on my chaise longue.

When he failed to respond, I rose and moved closer to where he lay. "Hey! Since you seem to be the cause of all this trouble, don't you think you owe us the courtesy of at least contributing a few words to the discussion?"

I peered down into a still handsome face ravaged by time and constant exposure to sun and wind and salt spray. His skin had the tone and texture of a weathered baseball glove. His eyes, a startling deep blue, regarded me with total unconcern and what might have been a hint of contempt. His full, cracked lips barely moved when he spoke.

"I thought your boy and Sissy were doin' a fine job of it," he drawled, his years away from South Carolina apparently having done little to erase his accent.

Across the room I could feel Erik bristle.

"My *boy?*" I leaned in until our faces were only a few inches apart. "You have a nerve, pal."

The acrid aroma of his breath carried me back to steamy summer afternoons on the verandah of Presqu'isle, my hoydenish self trapped in ruffles and scratchy crinolines, and an impossibly good-looking man who smelled of rum and pinched my cheek. I recoiled without being aware of it, but I could tell he'd noticed.

I straightened up and took a step back. "Now sit up and help us figure out what the hell we're gonna do with you."

The slow smile transformed him, and I had no trouble understanding his legendary success with women. His languid gaze slid from my face down to the black jersey clinging to my breasts, and I gave a fleeting thought to slapping his face. I stepped aside as he swung his legs over the edge of the chaise and ran a hand through his tousled salt-and-pepper hair, luxuriantly thick and lying in loose waves down to the collar of his pale blue shirt.

"We'll get out of your way," he said, rising so suddenly I stumbled to keep from getting run over. He extended a hand in Miss Addie's direction. "Come along, Sissy. Let's leave your friends in peace."

Adelaide Boyce Hammond hesitated, her gaze sliding from her brother's outstretched arm to my stony face and back again. "I don't know, Win. I mean, shouldn't we . . . ?"

"Sit down, Mr. Hammond," I said, returning to my chair. "Let's think this through before you go running off half-cocked."

He smiled as if he'd known all along I wouldn't throw him out, then draped himself back across the chaise. "I'm completely at your service, Miss Lydia."

I knew from the mocking tone of his voice and the way his deep-set eyes sparkled with the mischievousness of a small boy that he remembered those days on the verandah as well as I did. I wondered if his blatant sexuality had been apparent even then to the child I had been—if I had shrunk from it without really understanding exactly what had made me uncomfortable. I wanted to tell him to crank it down a few notches, that I wasn't buying, but I didn't want to upset Miss Addie.

I ignored Win's obvious come-on and spoke to his sister. "What exactly did you have in mind when you came up with this . . . plan?"

Miss Addie smiled, first at her brother, then at me. "It sounded so exciting! Win would take the shuttle and pretend to check in to the Westin, then walk down the beach to your house. I was supposed to get in a cab, meet him here, and take him back to my place." Her voice dropped to a conspiratorial whisper. "We were going to sneak up the stairs instead of using the elevator. No one would have known a thing! Next day I'd go back and claim his things from the hotel and bring them to The Cedars."

The poor old woman had obviously been indulging in an overabundance of enthusiasm for the mysteries I often loaned her, even though the whole thing sounded more like something out of a Three Stooges skit than an Agatha Christie plot.

"I see," I said, nodding. "Very clever. Then what?"

Miss Addie looked suddenly lost. "I don't understand."

I sighed and ordered myself to stay calm. "After all this skulking and sneaking around, what did you plan on doing next? I mean, you can't exactly stay holed up in your condo for a couple of years until the heat dies down."

She seemed to sag in her seat. "Oh, dear. I'm afraid I hadn't gotten quite that far."

Win Hammond's indulgent smile and soft pat on his sister's shoulder did a lot to rehabilitate him in my eyes. "We'll worry about that later, won't we, Sissy? Come on now, I think it's high time we let these folks get some sleep." He stretched and levered himself out of the chair. "I'm pretty tuckered out myself."

"Lydia, will you call a cab for us?" Miss Addie, too, looked done in.

"Don't be silly," I said, almost at the same moment Erik piped up, "I'll drive you."

"We'll all go," I said, "and we'll stop at the Westin on the way and pick up your bag. Just let me get my purse."

"That's right kind of you, Miss Lydia," Win drawled, his eyes saying things no man his age had any right to be thinking about a woman young enough to be his daughter.

They followed me out into the great room, Erik carrying the dirty glasses toward the kitchen while I hurried down the hallway to make a quick stop in the bathroom. I thought about using the phone in there to contact Red and see if there was any way to verify this cloak-and-dagger stuff about irate creditors of dubious character tracking the aging beach bum from Virgin Gorda to Hilton Head. I tucked the escaping tendrils of hair back onto the top of my head and decided it could wait until morning. I'd put Erik to work on the computer. I had a hunch it might all be a scam to separate Miss Addie from her inheritance, and that these shadowy figures were probably nothing more than an embellishment to make Win's story more convincing. Once again I vowed to fight the old reprobate tooth and nail if I became convinced his only aim in coming home had been to cheat his sister. I also wanted to check in with the Judge to see if he could remember the details of—

A loud *thunk* followed by a sharp squeal of alarm cut my thoughts off in midsentence. I dropped my hairbrush and bolted down the hallway to find Edwin Hollister Hammond III face down on my great room carpet.

CHAPTER SIX

"So HOW MUCH DID HE HAVE TO DRINK?"

I kept my voice low, although I didn't think the blast of an air horn could have been heard above Win Hammond's monumental snores. I'd made Miss Addie comfortable in the guest room. She'd refused to accept one of my chaste cotton nightgowns, insisting instead that she'd "just take a little rest" fully clothed on top of the duvet. I'd helped her slip off her low-heeled pumps and draped a light throw over her against the chill of the air conditioning.

I glanced over my shoulder toward the great room where the old man lay stretched out on his back on my white sofa, one arm dangling over the side, his fingers brushing the carpet. It had taken every ounce of strength Erik and I had to wrestle him off the floor. I'd wanted to call the paramedics, even after we'd determined he seemed to be breathing steadily, his heart pumping along slowly and rhythmically, and his mumbling incoherence proving he hadn't lost consciousness. Miss Addie, no doubt fearful of revealing his whereabouts, had overruled me. Erik, too, seemed convinced the man was simply drunk.

"He had a couple of stiff Scotches," Erik said, blowing across the surface of his second cup of coffee and avoiding my eyes. "You had an open bottle in the cupboard."

"It's been up there for years." I set my mug of tea down on the kitchen table. "But we have no idea how many he had on the plane. Or before he got on." I shook my head. "God, I thought he'd dropped dead in my living room. I almost had a heart attack myself."

Erik grinned. "Yeah, with your history the last thing you need is another body turning up in your vicinity." He flinched at the glare I shot him but refused to back off. "If Ben Wyler were still working for the sheriff's office, he would have had a field day with that."

"Thank God for small favors." I sighed deeply and worked my neck from side to side, hoping to break loose the tension settling into my muscles. "So what the hell am I supposed to do with them? Are you buying this stuff about loan sharks being hot on his trail?"

"I'm having a tough time with it," Erik said. "I'm more inclined to think it's something he's cooked up to enlist his sister's sympathy, maybe make it easier to scam her out of some of her money." Again the wide grin split his boyish face. "You have to give the old girl credit, though, don't you? I mean this sort of James Bond scenario she cooked up . . ."

"I know. I remember one time she told me this story about how she and Win used to play together in the attic. Apparently it fell to her to look after the baby of the family, her being the old-maid sister and all. Anyway, they'd dress up in old clothes they found in trunks and perform Shakespeare. She says he was a pretty good actor. Maybe he's just picking up where they left off all those decades ago." I shook my head. "Whatever games he's playing now, I need to figure out a way to convince them both it's safe to go home." I glanced up at the clock over the sink. "It's after one, and I need to get some sleep."

As if on cue, Win Hammond stirred, snorted, and came suddenly awake. I watched his head rise above the back of the sofa as he pushed himself upright. He ran a trembling hand through his thick, graying hair and shook himself, like a dog with a wet, soggy coat. He turned bleary eyes toward the kitchen and found us watching him.

"Good morning," I said, the sarcasm slipping past my best intentions to be civil.

"Good morning to you, Miss Lydia," he replied in the mocking tone I was fast becoming used to. "I believe I would sell my soul for a cup of that coffee I smell percolatin' out there."

"Help yourself."

"Bay," Erik began, but I cut him off.

"I want to see if he can walk without falling down," I whispered as Win Hammond levered himself carefully to his feet.

On wobbly legs he managed to maneuver across the wide expanse of carpet and up the steps into the kitchen. I brought him his coffee and set it in front of him. "Milk? Sugar?"

His wan smile as he shook his head still held traces of the lady-killer he must have been in his youth. "Thank you, no." He clasped the cup in both hands and sipped, a soft *aah* escaping as he set it back on the table.

"Heaven," he breathed, and the small jolt of caffeine seemed to restore him. "My apologies, my dear, for the unforgivable faux pas of passing out on your living room rug. I'm afraid I've been too long out of genteel company."

Much as I wanted to despise the man, I found myself being sucked in by his charming, old-school manners. "Better here than at the airport. Or on the bus." I paused to make sure I had his full attention. "Does this happen often?"

"No. Actually, I'm usually able to hold my liquor quite well, although I'd be less than candid if I said this was the first time it's happened. You're concerned, of course, for Sissy."

I nodded.

"Don't be, my dear Miss Lydia. I believe my distress may have been compounded by the . . . *er,* haste with which I made my travel arrangements and the naturally overwhelming emotion at being reunited with my dear sister after all these years."

The needle on my bullshit meter quivered toward overload, but I couldn't suppress a smile. I'd done a little mental arithmetic and figured he had to be in his early sixties, but his life on the sea had hardened his body. There didn't seem to be an ounce of fat on him. Cleaned up and sober, Win Hammond would be a serious heartbreaker. The little old ladies of the Lowcountry would need to be on their guard.

I didn't want to get into a heated discussion at nearly two in the morning, but I wanted to make certain he understood my position. "I won't tolerate her being hurt. Emotionally, financially, in any way whatsoever. Are we clear?"

The man's bleary eyes regarded me across the rim of his coffee cup. "Perfectly, Miss Lydia."

I leaned back in my chair, satisfied for the time being that the lines in the sand had been drawn and acknowledged. "And please quit calling me by that ridiculous name," I said. "I've been going by Bay since I was in grade school."

"As you wish." He finished the coffee in one long swallow. "Is Sissy asleep?" he asked, his eyes straying toward the hallway that led to the bedrooms.

"Just resting," I said.

He smiled at Erik. "Is your kind offer to carry us home still open, young man?"

"Certainly, sir. If you're ready to go."

I would have kicked him under the table if I could have reached him. *I* was ready for this whole crazy circus to move on to the next town, whether they were or not.

"I'll wake Miss Addie," I said and moved toward the hallway.

At three thirty I stumbled back into the house, my body sagging with fatigue, but my mind zipping along at full throttle.

We'd picked up Win's bag at the Westin and finally escorted the two Hammonds into Miss Addie's condo with a minimum of additional fuss. I'd even convinced her to let us take the elevator instead of skulking up the stairs since the likelihood of anyone in the complex being out and about at that hour of the morning seemed relatively slim. I'd also had to talk her out of making her brother hunch down in the back seat of Erik's Expedition while we cleared security at the front gate of The Cedars.

I went through the motions of preparing for bed, although I had a pretty good idea I wouldn't be doing much sleeping. I thought about taking a pill, but it seemed sort of pointless when there wasn't much left of the night. And I couldn't spend all day in bed. In spite of my brother-in-law's skepticism, I had actual clients who were paying for my time. Besides, Dolores came to clean and mother me on Thursdays, and I'd be ashamed to have her find me languishing in my bed, no matter how late I'd tumbled into it.

I pulled on an oversized T-shirt and scrunched down against a bank of pillows propped up against the headboard, the files I'd brought home with me open on my knees. Grace Matheson had been positive her husband had been systematically looting the company he and his best friend, Cliff Morningside, had started over a decade before. CM^2 Supply catered to the hospitality industry, providing everything from linens to tableware to pots and pans for the kitchens of the island's scores of restaurants, from small delis to the high-end dining rooms of the big resort hotels. Grace had been able to remove financial records from her husband's desk at home and make copies for me. I'd been over the numbers several times and had to agree something didn't look right, but I hadn't been able to put my finger on exactly what had set my antennae quivering. If there was in fact financial chicanery going on, I knew I would eventually tumble to his scheme, but my frustration level with good ol' Chuck had been rising into the danger zone for the past few days.

I stretched and shifted position, letting the papers slide onto the bed. The real problem with the case was Grace Matheson. I hadn't understood why she'd be hiring someone to expose her husband as an embezzler—that is, until she announced she intended to divorce "the lying scumbag" and wanted to prove he had squirreled away assets to keep them out of her property settlement. She'd tossed in the idea Chuck and Cliff were more than business partners almost as an afterthought, offering me a huge bonus if I could nail her husband in a compromising position with his old college pal. I'd come close to throwing her out of my office at that point. At nearly five o'clock in the morning, a part of me desperately wished I had.

Erik had reminded me, though, that her money was green and that securing grounds for her divorce action didn't constitute the real heart of the case. Still, it made me feel grubby somehow, and I vowed to concentrate on the financial end of my mission and stay the hell out of Chuck Matheson's love life.

I didn't remember falling asleep, but Dolores Santiago's soft humming penetrated my consciousness at about the same time the narrow shaft of light from a slit in the drapes fell across the bed. I groaned and flung an arm over my face.

"Ah, *Señora. Buenos días.*"

I pried open one sleep-encrusted eye and squinted at her. "Good morning. What time is it?"

"*A las diez, Señora.*"

Ten o'clock. *Damn!*

My brain refused to make connections with my mouth. I rolled over, away from the light, and heard the crinkle of paper. I eased my leaden body up off the Matheson file and headed for the bathroom.

"I make the tea," I heard Dolores call as I cranked the shower up to just short of scalding.

I became reasonably coherent somewhere between the French toast and my second cup of Earl Grey. Over the years I'd given up trying to convince Dolores of my preference for light or nonexistent breakfasts. I simply smiled, ate, and added a couple of miles to my erratic running regimen.

"You have the little party last night?" Dolores stood at the sink rinsing out glasses before loading them into the dishwasher, another habit I couldn't seem to break her of.

"Sort of, although it wasn't something I planned," I said, hitching the belt on my old chenille bathrobe a little tighter. I hadn't been up to deciding what to wear.

My head jerked up at the sound of the phone, and I made a note to remind myself not to do that again. My eyes felt as if someone had dumped a pound of sand into them.

"I get, *Señora.* You eat."

I mopped up the last of the syrup as Dolores carried the handset toward the table. "Take a message," I whispered, waving her away with my free hand.

"It is *el Juez,*" she said.

No way the very Catholic Dolores would let me get away with avoiding my father. She believed strongly in keeping all the commandments. I sighed and took the phone.

"Good morning, Daddy."

"I trust whatever you had to do last night proved productive."

I was in trouble. "Not exactly," I said, "but it was necessary."

"A new case? Were you planning on informing me anytime soon?"

The sarcasm struck home. Because he'd been confined to a wheelchair for years and pretty much housebound following a series of small strokes, I sometimes forgot he had a stake in the agency which bore his name as well as mine.

"Of course I was. The whole thing just materialized late yesterday afternoon. And then last night—"

I'd almost blurted out the Miss Addie scenario before my fuddled brain had a chance to weigh the pros and cons of it. My father had been a highly successful attorney before being elected to the bench. Despite his infirmity and his advancing years, his mind remained as sharp as when he had skewered opposing witnesses and their lawyers with equal zeal. The cross-examination he'd subject me to if I got into the tangled tale of Win Hammond could last until dinnertime.

"You were saying? About last night?" he boomed, his strong voice belying his withered legs and useless left arm.

"I did a little research," I said. "On the new case." Inspiration struck. "In fact, I'm just heading off for an appointment right now. Gotta run, or I'll be late."

I glanced up to see Dolores eyeing me gravely. Lying to my father probably counted as two strikes against my immortal soul.

"We'll expect you for dinner tonight. Six o'clock. You can report to me then. And Bay? Don't disappoint Vinnie again."

"No, sir. I'll see you then."

I punched the disconnect button and set the phone on the table. Dolores reached around me to remove my empty plate and dirty silverware. Her round, olive face had set into squint lines of disapproval.

"Hey, lighten up, okay? I just didn't want to get into it right now. Don't tell me you've never told a fib in your life."

She carried the dishes to the sink. "This fib, it is like *la mentira*? The lie?"

"Close enough," I said.

I picked up my mug and pushed back my chair, moving slowly down the steps and out from under Dolores's disapproving glare. I retrieved the Matheson file from my bed and carried it across the hall into the third bedroom, which Rob and I had converted years before into a home office. As I reached for the phone to set Erik tracking down hotel registrations, it rang under my hand.

I jumped and heard Dolores call, *"Señora?"*

"I've got it!" I yelled back. "Bay Tanner," I said more softly into the phone.

"Mrs. Tanner? It's Karen. Karen Zwilling."

"Good morning," I replied, immediately on alert from the panicky rush of her words and the tremor I could hear in her low voice. "What's the matter?"

"I'm sorry to call you at home, but I tried the office and . . . Did you see the paper this morning?"

"No, I didn't." I hadn't wanted to overtax my sluggish brain with either the uniformly negative national news or with the mundane doings of our local movers and shakers. Even my horoscope seemed beyond me that morning. "Why?" I asked when she didn't continue.

"They found a body last night. On the beach."

There could be only one reason for her call. "And you think it's your rapist?"

She hesitated again. "I don't know. Maybe. It could be."

"What makes you think so?"

"The description fit—height, weight, that stuff. The paper said he didn't have any identification on him, and the sheriff is asking anyone who might have information . . . I can't go to the cops! I won't! They'll think—"

"Whoa, Karen! Slow down. First of all, it might not even be the same guy. Let me make some calls—"

"It's the watch. The Cartier. It has to be him. They're going to think we killed him!"

It took me a full ten minutes to get her calmed down. It could have been an accident, a simple drowning or a heart attack, I said, but she didn't seem to want to believe it. I told her to stay put, keep her mouth shut, and wait for me to get back to her. I grabbed the *Island Packet* from the kitchen table, scanned the brief article twice, and tossed the paper onto the desk.

I picked up the phone and dialed Ben Wyler.

CHAPTER SEVEN

J ALSO PUT IN A CALL TO RED BEFORE MOVING ACROSS the hall to get dressed. The dispatcher said he had responded to a burglary call and would give him my message when he checked in. I hated to use his cell number when I knew he was in the middle of a situation.

Ben Wyler had insisted on meeting me for lunch. I hadn't wanted to admit I'd just finished breakfast, so I held him off until one o'clock. He'd recently moved into a small house in Sea Pines, and we decided on Jump & Phil's near the main gate to Charles Fraser's visionary development, the very first on the island. I often wondered what Hilton Head might have looked like if Fraser hadn't been so obsessive about preserving the environment and natural habitat as an integral part of his plans and hadn't been so insistent that subsequent projects follow his lead.

We'd be ass-deep in honky-tonks and fifteen-story hotels blocking out the view of the ocean, I thought as I negotiated the famed circle on the south end of the island, barely missing a sleek Mercedes from New York that decided to change lanes at the last possible moment. I waited for a long stream of traffic exiting Sea Pines to clear before turning left into the small plaza set back in the trees. I finally found a parking space halfway to Pope Avenue and wove my way on tabby sidewalks to the outdoor seating area of the local pub and restaurant.

I almost didn't recognize Ben Wyler. He sat just inside the door, a red baseball cap pulled low on his forehead and wire-rimmed half-glasses perched on the end of his nose as he studied the menu. His gray T-shirt looked damp around the neck as if he'd been doing something strenuous, and the navy blue shorts stopped midthigh on a pair of very nice legs. I couldn't remember if I'd ever seen him in anything other than an expensive suit and designer tie. He glanced up as I pulled out the chair across from him.

"Bay. Good to see you."

"You, too," I said, neither of us making a move toward any sort of physical contact, not even a handshake.

Our relationship, such as it was, had been forged during a period of my life when all the horror of my husband's murder and its ugly aftermath had seemed to coalesce into a nightmare of suspicion and terror. Ben Wyler, former New York City homicide detective and temporary death investigator for the Beaufort County Sheriff's Office, had been smack in the middle of it—literally. He'd taken a bullet I remained convinced had been meant for me.

"How's the leg?" I asked, dropping into the chair opposite his.

His hand worked on his left thigh, unconsciously massaging a wound which had long been healed. "Not bad," he said, "although I'm getting pretty damn good at predicting rain."

I smiled. "I know what you mean. I have the same trouble with my shoulder."

"Don't know what the hell we're gonna do when we get old," he replied and glanced back down at the menu. "You come here a lot?"

"Red and I tend to hang out here."

I could feel the mood shift even though I couldn't see his eyes. "Ah, yes, the ever-present Sergeant Tanner."

The two men had taken an instant dislike to each other, and Wyler's resignation following his shooting hadn't done anything to ameliorate the situation. The detective hadn't exactly been at the top of my hit parade, despite his heroics, which is why I had been totally shocked when, out of the blue, he'd volunteered to front Simpson &

Tanner for our PI license. He swore he expected nothing in return, no slice of the profits—if there ever were any—or any active participation in the agency whatsoever. All he asked was to be cut in on any unusual or interesting cases that might come our way.

I felt certain Karen Zwilling's situation qualified on both counts.

I ordered a Caesar salad, and Wyler opted for a steak sandwich. With drinks in front of us, he leaned back in his chair and regarded me over the top of his glasses.

"So. Tell me what you know about this dead guy," he said.

"I don't know any more than what I read in the paper. It obviously happened too late for them to get anything but a couple of paragraphs in there. Probably be more tomorrow."

On the phone I'd outlined Karen's story for him, leaving out names. He'd gone silent on me then, finally saying we should meet for lunch and talk it over.

"I made a couple of calls after we talked," he said and leaned in closer. "This isn't for publication, understand? You watch all those TV cop shows. You know they like to hold back one or two pertinent facts to help weed out the kooks."

"Sure. So what did you find out?"

He glanced over both shoulders as if everyone in the neighborhood bar might be straining to overhear his words. "Somebody beat the crap out of the guy. Broke just about every bone in his face. They found a couple of slivers of wood in some of the wounds, so part of the damage might have come from a branch or a piece of lumber."

I wished he'd waited until after lunch to get down to the forensic details. "So there's no chance it was an accident."

"None at all. They figure the body must have washed up sometime between nine and midnight last night, though it's going to be tough to pinpoint time of death. Looks like the stiff spent at least some time in the water."

I almost said, *I have an alibi,* then decided against it. I didn't find the idea particularly funny, and I was pretty certain Wyler wouldn't, either. Instead I asked, "No sign of a weapon?"

"If he did use something besides his fists, he probably chucked it in the water with the body. Could be halfway to Africa by now."

The waitress appeared and parceled out the food. Ben Wyler doused his steak in Worcestershire sauce and dug in.

"So the cause of death is one of the things they're going to hold back from the press. Anything else?"

The former detective swallowed before replying. "The reason they couldn't ID him is that anything about who the hell he was had been stripped from the body. Took his driver's license, credit cards, all that stuff."

"So why couldn't it just be a simple robbery gone bad?" I asked.

"Not a chance. No self-respecting mugger would have left such a swanky watch. That baby has to be worth at least a few grand." He paused to sip from his Bloody Mary. "And they went to a lot of trouble to mess up his face."

"What do you mean?"

"Way I hear it, there was a wound in the back of his head, too. I'm guessing somebody hit him from behind, knocked him out or at least stunned him, then came around front and finished off the job." He shrugged and studied me over the rim of his glass. "Sort of makes you wonder why, doesn't it?"

I pushed my half-eaten salad away and leaned back in my chair. "So what do you think I ought to do? Can I give the information to Red without revealing our client's name? Right now she and her friend apparently know a whole lot more about this guy than anyone else."

Ben Wyler pointed his upraised fork in my direction. "You gonna finish that?" he asked, pulling the bowl toward him when I shook my head. He stabbed a few romaine leaves and paused. "I think you should sit tight for a day or so, see if anyone else comes forward. Maybe someone will file a missing-persons report. Or could be someone'll recognize the watch. Lots of possibilities." He stuffed salad into his mouth, and I waited for him to chew and swallow. "Plenty of time for you to spill your guts if nothing else turns up."

I had a feeling Red would have given me different advice, but Ben

Wyler was a civilian again, and the constraints of being an active-duty cop had been left behind with his badge. Besides, like it or not, he had a vested interest in Simpson & Tanner, Inquiry Agents. I didn't think he'd advise me to do anything that might put the agency in jeopardy.

I hoped.

Thunderheads had piled up out over the ocean by the time I finished all my phone calls, but I decided to try and get in my run anyway. Dolores had left about three, admonishing me not to forget about the casserole she'd left in the refrigerator as she made her way down the hallway. I smiled at the steadiness of her gait, the dragging limp she'd had to live with for long, agonizing months finally cured by her own strength of will and endless hours of physical therapy.

I came pounding up from the beach just moments before the first dime-sized drops of rain plopped onto the layer of pine dust coating the deck, grabbed a quick shower, and was on the road to St. Helena as the storm moved inland. For some reason the gods had smiled—maybe the rain had chased all the tourists indoors—and the traffic off island zipped right along. Even the usual bottleneck at the Moss Creek light flowed smoothly.

I put the driving on autopilot and let my mind drift to the conversations I'd had after I'd left Wyler in the parking lot of Jump & Phil's. I still didn't understand the necessity of our meeting in person. Everything we talked about could have been handled just as well over the telephone. He'd let me pick up the tab, though, so maybe he'd simply taken advantage of the chance for a free lunch.

Karen Zwilling had calmed down considerably, and I could hear the relief in her voice when I relayed Ben Wyler's advice, disguised as my own. I told her to make certain her friend Layla kept her mouth shut as well. I promised her I wouldn't do anything about talking to the cops until the two of us had a chance to discuss things first.

Red had been about to go off duty when I finally caught up with him. He wouldn't give me one bit of information about the murder on the beach the night before, basically telling me to butt out and mind my own business. I figured he was still testy from our little dustup, so I thanked him sweetly and did my cursing after I'd hung up the phone.

I hadn't been able to reach Erik. His part-time day job in the computer department of the big office-supply chain on the south end of the island kept him busy until well after six, so I left a message on his voice mail.

I snapped myself back to reality in time to realize the traffic had reached the stoplight in downtown Beaufort at the foot of the bridge to Lady's Island. Thankfully the span had not been forced to open to allow a boat to pass underneath. We crawled across toward the causeway out to St. Helena, and fifteen minutes later I wheeled into the semicircular driveway in front of my family home.

Presqu'isle dozed in the late-afternoon sun, its split staircase and wide verandah dappled in shade from the towering live oaks that surrounded the property and lined the rutted lane leading up from the highway. Though my childhood had been anything but idyllic inside its stately halls, the house had grown on me in recent years. I no longer felt as if I'd like to tear it down and turn the whole thing into a parking lot after the Judge passed away.

I climbed the steps and let myself inside, annoyed as always by the cool, dry air of the climate-controlled environment my mother had thought imperative to keep her treasured paintings and family antiques in perfect condition. This lack of any hint of freshness—the cool breezes off St. Helena Sound just beyond the rolling back lawn or the sweet perfume of confederate jasmine twining around the tabby foundation—added to the sterility, the lack of life I'd always sensed in the old place. It had been like growing up in a museum.

"It's me," I called just as the grandfather clock in the hallway began its solemn tolling. Six o'clock. Right on time. I smiled and strode across the heart pine floor in the direction of the kitchen. "Lavinia? Daddy?"

"You're late," my father grumbled from his wheelchair pulled up to the scarred wooden table in the wide, sunny kitchen.

"I am not. Listen." As I dropped into my seat, the last of the six stentorian notes died away. "See? Exactly, precisely on time. Prompt to a fault, that's me."

"Let's eat," he said, and Lavinia Smalls turned from the stove to set the last of the serving dishes on the table.

"Hello, Bay," she said, her smile splitting a handsome face the color of polished oak. "I'm glad you could make it tonight."

If there was a rebuke there, I let it go. "Me, too. Sorry about yesterday. I got hung up at the office."

"I want details," my father barked, "but not until after dinner. Vinnie, will you ask the blessing?"

I stared open-mouthed at my father, his head bowed, his good hand pulling his useless one into his lap in as prayerful an attitude as his infirmity permitted. Lavinia reached across to pat my arm, a twinkle in her deep-set eyes.

"Certainly, Tally, I'd be happy to."

I lowered my head, unable to fathom what had driven my agnostic father to get religion all of a sudden. Intimations of mortality, perhaps? The idea made me shudder in the cool dryness of the old mansion.

Lavinia kept her imprecations blessedly brief, and I raised my eyes again to study my father. He looked good, his color healthy, his wise gray eyes bright beneath the cap of snow white hair which never seemed to lose its thickness.

Lavinia had prepared crab cakes, and we tucked into the meal with little conversation above requests to pass the sweet potatoes or the salt and pepper. I finally sat back, completely stuffed, and watched my father struggle to corral the last of the slippery kernels of corn he'd been chasing across his plate.

"Want me to get that?" I asked, a spoon poised in my hand.

He glowered up at me from beneath shaggy white eyebrows. "Did I ask for your help?"

"No, sir," I said meekly.

"That was quite uncalled for, Tally." Lavinia's tone reminded me of days gone by when her sharp retorts about minding one's manners had been directed almost exclusively at me.

I didn't expect the Judge to apologize, and he didn't disappoint me. Lavinia and I exchanged an exasperated look over his head as she rose to fetch the coffeepot.

"Would you like some tea?" she asked, and I shook my head.

She removed the plates and poured for my father. He added cream from the pitcher and used the controls on the handle of his motorized wheelchair to ease himself back from the table. Lavinia waved away my offer to help and busied herself at the sink.

"So what's the new case?" my father asked in a voice which had lost most of its querulous undertones.

I glanced briefly at Lavinia's back. Technically, she didn't have a right to hear any of the details of Simpson & Tanner's cases, our confidentiality clause extending only to the actual members and employees of the firm. But she'd been sharing the secrets of Presqu'isle since before I'd been born, and I knew whatever she heard would be kept to herself. Besides, she had as little curiosity about her fellow man as any woman I'd ever known.

I pushed my own chair back, clasped my hands behind my head, and gave my father a concise rundown on the accusations of Karen Zwilling, my striking out at both hotels the night before, and the discovery of a body which might be that of the alleged rapist. I reported my conversations with both Red and Wyler.

The Judge's response consisted of a distracted, "Hmmm," and the rhythmic drumming of his fingers against the plastic of the wheelchair's armrest. I recognized both as signs his mind had been fully engaged by the problem, and I should be quiet and let him think.

I rose and pulled a towel from the hook next to the sink and set in drying the plates and glasses Lavinia had stacked in the drainer. She almost never used the dishwasher except on holidays or after the rare party held at Presqu'isle. She smiled as we worked, the silence of the room broken only by the occasional clink of silver against china.

"The man was obviously using a false name." The Judge's courtroom baritone cracked across the room, making both of us jump.

"Of course, but the question is, why?"

"Any number of reasons," my father replied. "A suspicious wife, for instance. Or a pack of creditors on his heels. Doesn't necessarily have to be something illegal."

"I didn't say it did. But if the body is in fact Karen's rapist, I certainly doubt this is the first time he's done it. She described a man in his late forties. Seems a little odd someone would wait that long to begin a life of crime, especially rape."

"True. Still . . ." The Judge paused and slurped down the last of his coffee. "Let's go ponder on it. I could use a cigar."

His eyes bored into the back of Lavinia's head, daring her to object. The only indication she gave of having heard him at all was a barely perceptible tightening of her shoulders.

"Will you join us?" I asked, uncomfortable with what I saw as my father's attempt to bait the woman who had loved and cared for him for more years than I'd been alive. He'd always been irascible, but lately his remarks had begun to cut very deep. I could handle the cranky old curmudgeon. I wasn't so sure about Lavinia.

"Thanks, but no," she said without turning around. "I have things to tend to."

"Anything I can help with?"

She shook her head and began pulling items out of the cupboards.

"Okay," I said, certain we were in for a smashing dessert. When Lavinia got upset, she baked.

I followed the soft *hiss* of the wheelchair's tires as they rolled across the worn wooden planks and into the Judge's study. Right after his first stroke, Rob and I had had it remodeled into a bedroom/sitting area with an invalid-accessible bath. My father slid expertly into his spot next to the low cherry table and waved a hand in the direction of his old bureau.

"Get me a cigar. Top—"

"I know where you stash your Havanas." I jerked open the dresser drawer and rifled through his folded pajamas and handkerchiefs, then tossed the panatela at him. He caught it deftly in his right hand. "You know," I added, dropping into one of the Queen Anne chairs pulled up next to the empty fireplace, "your temper is getting out of control."

He clipped the end of the cigar by anchoring it between his dead hand and his immobile left leg, a system he'd been perfecting ever since Lavinia had refused to participate in the ritual. If my father chose to ignore his doctor's advice and keep on smoking, she certainly didn't intend to give him aid and comfort. He pulled the crystal lighter from the table and snapped it angrily to flame. Within a few puffs, the room had filled with the not unpleasant odor of fine tobacco. I inhaled, surreptitiously drawing in the secondhand smoke.

"Out of control, huh?" my father said. "I find your accusation entirely without merit."

"Well, you can snap at me all you want, but I'd give serious thought to laying off Lavinia. In case you haven't noticed, the woman keeps you alive."

He didn't respond, and I rose to cross to the window seat set into the bay at the back of the house. I tucked one leg up under me and let my eyes roam out across the lawn to the narrow strip of marsh bordering the placid waters of the Sound. Evening had begun to settle over the mainland, a smattering of lights winking on along the shoreline.

"I don't mean to be unkind."

I turned, surprised by the soft sadness in his voice. "I know you don't," I said, "but it still hurts."

The silence stretched out, the deep bass ticking of the grandfather clock marking off the minutes. My father cleared his throat but didn't speak. I let my gaze drift again toward the water.

"I'm going to pursue this rapist thing until we know for certain whether or not he's the body they found on the beach," I said.

"Good. I'll make some calls tomorrow and see if I can shake some useful information out of any of my contacts. I'll keep you apprised."

"Good," I echoed, hearing the dismissal in his tone. "I guess I should be getting home."

I rose and hesitated next to his chair. Usually I dropped a brief kiss on the top of his head as I left, but I settled for a casual pat on the shoulder as I moved into the hallway to call good night to Lavinia. I let myself out and paused on the verandah to inhale the sweetness of the salt-tinged air and listen to the muted chorus of cicadas and tree frogs rippling across the humid Lowcountry night.

"Love's a bitch," I said to no one in particular and trotted down the steps.

As I slid into the damp leather seat of the Thunderbird, the cell phone sounded its notes. With a sigh, I lifted it from my purse.

"Bay Tanner."

Miss Addie's voice trembled, but the words rang loudly in my ear: "He's gone!"

CHAPTER EIGHT

ℐ MADE GOOD TIME THROUGH THE SPARSE LATE-NIGHT
traffic and pulled up to the gate at The Cedars a little before
ten o'clock. Miss Addie had followed my instructions and called in a
pass for me. I thanked the uniformed sentry and eased along the tree-
lined drive toward the back of the property. Marsh Edge, the three-story
building which housed her condominium, blended seamlessly into the
live oaks and sycamores highlighted by the scattered security lights.

Miss Addie had been watching for me. The door opened just as I
angled my finger toward the bell.

"Oh, Lydia, thank goodness you're here!" she said in a rush, waving
me in with a trembling hand as she stepped back into the foyer.

I moved past her and into the large living area crammed with
enough Hammond antiques and paintings to stock a good-sized gallery.
Though it had been months since I'd been inside the condo, it seemed
as if not one piece of Dresden or Lalique had been moved since my last
visit. The stunning silver service had been laid out on the Hepplewhite
table in front of the magnificent Empire sofa.

"Sit down, my dear. Let me pour you some tea."

"Thanks. Miss Addie, I don't understand . . ."

"In a moment." Her faded eyes avoided mine as she seated herself
on the pale gold velvet and patted the cushion beside her. "I've always

believed in the restorative power of tea. The British are so wise about these things."

I dropped my bag on the creamy carpet and joined her on the sofa. "But if you really think something might have—"

"Lemon and one sugar, have I got that right, dear?"

I drew a deliberately calming breath and released it slowly. If Miss Addie's mind had picked this particular time to take another trip back to Neverland, it could turn out to be a very long night.

"Yes, that would be lovely," I said.

Adelaide Boyce Hammond handed me the delicate Spode, a tiny silver teaspoon resting on the saucer. I waited while she served herself. She smiled at me over the rim of her own cup as we both sipped.

"There," she said with a contented sigh, "isn't this nice?" She returned her saucer to the table. "Are you feeling better now, my dear?"

I didn't know how to answer. Someone had written an entirely different play from the one I'd expected to perform in, and they'd forgotten to give me a script. I ad-libbed as best I could.

"Yes, thank you, much better." I looked pointedly at the closed door of the guest room. "And how's your brother settling in?" I kept my tone light, as if my question was nothing more than polite inquiry.

Her face fell, and I watched awareness of the situation creep back into her soft eyes. "I wandered there for a moment, didn't I?" Her voice quivered with imminent tears.

"No," I said in a rush, "no, of course not. You're fine."

Her look told me she appreciated the lie. "Win didn't want to go down to the dining room for dinner," she said in a more matter-of-fact tone. "I ordered from one of those delivery services. A quite lovely meal, considering they had to bring it all the way from the Marriott Hotel. And still warm. Imagine. I do so love Conroy's, don't you?"

I feared she might be wandering off track again, so I spoke briskly. "Miss Addie, where is Win? How long has he been gone? Did he pack a bag? If you want my help, you have to give me some straight answers."

I watched her fight her own confusion. "Yes, of course you're right. I took a little walk, as I always do after a meal, so good for the constitution. Papa always . . . Well, I couldn't have been out for more than half an hour. When I came back, I knocked on his door to see if he wanted coffee or tea, and he didn't reply. I thought maybe he'd dropped off for a little nap, understandable after all . . ."

I loved this little old woman, but she was about to drive me stark raving mad. "So he wasn't in his room. Maybe he just went for a walk, too. How long ago was that?"

Miss Addie sniffed a little at my rudeness and squinted at her watch. "About eight o'clock. There isn't anyplace to go from here, you know. Not on foot. When he hadn't returned in an hour, I . . . well, I admit it. I looked in his room."

"And?" I chewed on my lower lip to stifle my frustration.

"Some of his things are gone. From the bathroom, don't you know. Toothbrush, his shaving things. His only good pair of shoes."

Either Miss Addie had been paying really close attention, or her brother had let her unpack for him. I had no trouble envisioning him lounging on the bed while his eighty-year-old sister stored away his possessions. I had a feeling Win Hammond had no problem allowing women of all ages to cater to his needs.

I glanced at my watch. "You know, it's only ten thirty now. Maybe he's just gone out to see some old friends. Someone could have picked him up. To have a drink or something." I was fairly certain Miss Addie didn't keep anything stronger than sherry in those cut crystal decanters lining the massive mahogany sideboard, and Win had already demonstrated his preference for Scotch.

"Then why didn't he leave a note?"

Because he's a self-absorbed bastard without the slightest interest in anyone's feelings but his own, I longed to say. Instead I shrugged. "Maybe he just forgot. He's been used to living alone for a long time. He's probably not accustomed to accounting for his whereabouts."

Miss Addie reached for the teapot and freshened our cups. She raised hers and sipped, then said, "I think those awful men have done something to him. I think we should notify the police."

I stared at her for a moment before she rose and crossed to the telephone hanging on the wall near the kitchen. "We'll call that nice young man, the one you're related to. Do you remember the number, dear?"

I shook my head as I wove my way through the furniture crammed into her small living space. "That's okay," I said, removing the handset from her and setting it back onto the base. "You just finish your tea. I'll take care of it."

The sweet smile I found so enchanting lit her face, and she reached to cup my cheek in her withered hand. "Such a good girl," she said, patting me gently. "I always told your mama you'd turn out fine if she just let you be."

I smiled as I edged through several generations' worth of Hammond family antiques to the spare bedroom.

Either Win Hammond traveled light, or he had accumulated a paltry number of possessions during his twenty years of self-imposed exile. I started in the adjoining bathroom, verifying the absence of the masculine counterpart of a makeup bag. The day-to-day toiletries were indeed gone. I pulled back the shower curtain. He'd left behind a nearly empty bottle of shampoo, a brand I'd never heard of, probably bought on Virgin Gorda or one of the surrounding islands. A damp towel lay crumpled across the rim of the tub.

In the bedroom, the closet contained three wildly flowered sport shirts, one pair of rumpled khakis—no doubt the ones he'd worn on the plane—and two pairs of sandals, one cheap flip-flops, the other fine leather huaraches. A guayabera in what felt like an expensive linen fabric completed his meager wardrobe. I also took note of two empty hangers in the middle of the other five.

The dresser offered a little more hope that Miss Addie's brother hadn't just changed his mind about staying with her and taken off again for parts unknown. T-shirts and a variety of shorts filled the first two drawers. Captaining a fishing boat on a tropical island obviously didn't require anything more formal. He had a full complement of underwear, although I didn't find a single pair of socks. Neither did I come across the real essentials, like his wallet and passport, although a handful of strange-looking coins filled a dainty china bowl on the top of the antique oak dresser. I picked one up at random and found the profile of Queen Elizabeth in her younger days gazing back at me.

I checked the nightstands and found nothing, not a single scrap of paper or any clue whatsoever as to where Win Hammond might have disappeared to. Or why. Except for the missing toiletries and shaving gear, he might have been, as I'd first suggested to Miss Addie, out for an evening with friends. Although . . .

I stepped back into the living room where she sat cradling the delicate teacup in her hands and gazing at a portrait of a man in a heavy gilt frame, one of the many oil paintings crowding her walls. I moved silently across the carpet. It could have been Win, but the dress told of an earlier, more formal time, as did the stilted pose. I guessed their father, Edwin Hollister Hammond II. I remembered once asking the Judge why no one in our circle ever named their sons "Junior."

"Miss Addie?" I said softly, afraid of startling her.

Reluctantly she pulled her eyes away from the painting. "Yes, dear?"

"Where is Win's suitcase?" Erik had told me how out-of-place the battered old Gladstone bag, a holdover from another era, had looked among the brightly colored nylon on the baggage carousel at the airport.

"Suitcase? Why, in the storage closet, I believe. Just down the hall. Every apartment has one, you know."

"May I take a look?"

"Of course. Now where did I put the key?" She crossed the room and began pulling bits of paper and used rubber bands from one of the drawers in the sideboard. "Yes, here it is. But I don't understand . . ." She sighed and lowered herself slowly back onto the sofa. "Whatever you think best, dear."

I saw her faded eyes drift again to the portrait as I lifted the key from her twisted fingers and slipped out the door.

———

I found Miss Addie's storage room with no problem, but not her brother's suitcase. A few boxes lined the six-by-six-foot space, but most of the Hammond treasures were crammed into her condominium.

I pulled the door closed and slipped the key into the lock. *So he left his clothes and took the suitcase.* That made absolutely no sense at all. The whir of the elevator made me pause. I have no idea what set the alarm bells clanging in my head, but I suddenly found myself slipping back inside the storage closet leaving the door slightly ajar. Through the thin crack I watched a man step out onto the plush carpet and look both ways as if he were preparing to cross a busy street. Medium height, well built, in a black polo shirt and gray slacks. Dark hair. In the dim glow from the recessed overhead lights, I couldn't make out much of his face, except to notice he had a great tan.

The man turned right, paused in front of Miss Addie's apartment, and rang the bell. I pushed the door open a little wider and cursed myself for having left my pistol locked in the floor safe at home. I'd scared myself a little after my exhibition with the drunken golfer the night before, and I'd decided not to carry the gun unless I felt I might be about to put myself in a potentially dangerous situation. I hadn't figured dinner at my father's would qualify.

The man pushed the bell again, and I wondered if Miss Addie thought it was me. I'd actually left her door on the latch so I wouldn't have to bother her when I came back, and she probably couldn't figure out why I didn't let myself in. Then the panel swung open, and I could just make out her thin, reedy voice.

"Lydia, dear, I thought . . . Oh! Who are you?"

The man took a step back, and a little of my fear subsided. "I'm sorry to disturb you, ma'am," he said, "especially at this late hour. But I'm wondering if I might speak to James for a moment."

I could picture the confusion on her face. "James? I'm sorry, there's no one here by that name. Perhaps you have the wrong apartment?"

"No, I don't think I do." His tone had hardened. "James Holland. He just arrived from the Caribbean."

I doubted Miss Addie had any idea her brother had been using a phony name during his sojourn in the tropics. I drew myself up to my full five feet, ten inches and stepped into the hallway, slamming the storage closet door behind me. His head whipped around in my direction as I marched toward him.

"Can I help you with something?" I asked, stopping a few feet away and forcing him to turn away from Miss Addie. "Go back inside and close the door," I said to her in a tone I hoped conveyed the message she should just do it and not ask any questions. To my complete surprise, she did exactly that. I heard the deadbolt snap into place.

"And you are?" Up close his voice had a slight lilt to it, and I realized his dark complexion probably came from some sort of mixed Jamaican heritage.

"Bay Tanner. I'm Miss Hammond's niece," I lied. If you counted my fictitious cousins, the Randolph Remington Wades, I'd been acquiring all kinds of bogus relatives over the past couple of days. "I'm afraid the person you're looking for doesn't live here, Mister . . . ?"

"I was told he did." His tone seemed more arrogant than threatening, but I still wished I had the little pistol tucked into the pocket of my shorts.

"Then I'm afraid someone gave you bad information," I said. "Now if you'll excuse me, I have to get my aunt settled for the night." I gripped the doorknob, fully aware I couldn't get in unless Miss Addie released the deadbolt, but hoping my performance had passed muster.

His liquid brown eyes held mine for what seemed like an hour, then he smiled, revealing sparkling white teeth. "I'm sorry to have troubled you. And your aunt. Have a pleasant evening."

I waited until the indicator lights on the panel above the elevator assured me he'd gone all the way down to the first floor, then whirled and pounded on the door. "Miss Addie! He's gone. Let me in."

I listened for the slide of the bolt and slipped inside. I reset all the locks and leaned back against the panel, my heart racing. Adelaide Boyce Hammond stared at me from a few feet away, one bony hand clutching the collar of her pale blue dress. Her face had gone pasty white.

I was beside her in two steps. "Miss Addie, are you okay?" I gripped her shoulders and felt her quivering like a frightened rabbit. "Come and sit down. I'll make some fresh tea."

I guided her to the sofa and eased her onto the cushions. I stepped back and suddenly realized she had been shaking not with fear but with laughter.

"Oh, Lydia, my dear, wasn't that exciting? I swear I haven't had such a fright since Papa made me take Edwin through the fun house at a traveling carnival when he was just a boy. Do you think he was one of those men my brother owes money to? That he followed him all the way from Win's island?"

I stared at the old woman in a mixture of confusion and exasperation. "It's not a joke, Miss Addie," I said as sternly as I could. "This isn't a novel. Or a game. I want you to promise me—"

"Of course, dear, of course," She waved away my concern with a flick of her spotted hand. "But do you think I should get a gun? I used to be quite a good shot, but that was with a rifle. Papa taught me, you know."

She beamed at me, and I dropped my head into my hands. "Lord help us," I muttered through clenched teeth.

"Amen," Miss Addie chirped.

CHAPTER
NINE

BLEARY-EYED, I REMOVED THE KEY AND PUSHED OPEN the door to the office at almost precisely nine o'clock on Friday morning. I heard the slam of a car door and watched Erik Whiteside stride toward me across the parking lot.

"Morning," he called, and I grunted. "Bad night?" he asked, following me inside.

The message light on the telephone blinked furiously. I ignored it and carried my briefcase into my office. "Will you get those?" I asked, canting my head toward the phone.

"Sure." Erik slid into the chair behind the receptionist's desk and pulled a message pad out of the drawer.

I set the Styrofoam cup of tea I'd picked up at Starbucks on the desk and dumped out the Matheson files I'd taken home with me. I drew in a long, deliberate breath and exhaled slowly. Somehow being back in the professional environment of an office had rekindled my nicotine longings. Every time I stepped into Simpson & Tanner, Inquiry Agents, I ached for a cigarette. I booted up the computer and squirmed in my chair.

"Didn't you pick these up before you left on Wednesday?" Erik spoke from the doorway and waved a handful of message slips in my direction.

"Obviously not," I snapped, then held up a placating hand. "Sorry. To answer your previous question, yes, it was a very bad night. Win Hammond's taken off again."

Erik took the client chair, and I recounted the events at Miss Addie's apartment.

"Got any ideas?" he asked when I'd finished.

"I'm beginning to think maybe we have to revise our opinion about his story. The guy who came to the door knew his James Holland alias and that he'd just come back to the States from the Caribbean. He sounded Jamaican, with that sort of singsong quality to his speech. And it took him less than twenty-four hours to find out where Win was staying."

"Maybe the old guy has gotten himself mixed up with some sort of tropical version of the mob. Or maybe it was the cops."

The last was a scenario I hadn't considered. "You think the man last night might have been some foreign cop? Why didn't he identify himself?"

Erik shrugged. "Hard to say. I'm just tossing out ideas here. You'd know better than I would about that kind of stuff."

The face of Alain Darnay, my former lover who had been working undercover for Interpol the first time I'd met him, flashed across my mind. I kicked the image viciously back into its hole.

"Anyway, we need to find Win. I'm afraid for Miss Addie. Somehow the guy got past security, and she keeps drifting in and out of coherence to the point I think she'd probably invite him in for tea the next time he shows up." I sighed. "I almost scooped her up and carried her back to my house last night."

"I'm surprised you didn't."

"I would have had to do it literally. The old girl can get feisty when she sets her mind to it."

"Why do you think Win took the suitcase with him?"

"The only logical explanation is that there's something hidden in it."

"Like?"

I shrugged. "Could be anything. Money, drugs, documents—who knows?"

"With all the heightened airport security these days, I find it hard to believe you could smuggle anything into the country," my partner said. "Especially from that area of the world."

"Win probably still has a U.S. passport. If he was clever enough with the hiding place, I think he could do it. He's Anglo, well-spoken, older. Not exactly the profile of a terrorist or a drug courier."

"I hate to think you're right, but you probably are," Erik said. "So where do we start to look for him?"

"Can you find out if he's got credit cards? And if he's used them lately? It might tell us if he's still in the area."

"Not legally, but you don't want to know about those things, right?"

"I'm sorry, I didn't quite hear that last remark," I said, and he grinned.

"Gotcha." He rose, then hesitated in the doorway. "Oh, here're the messages." He placed the stack on my desk.

"Anything important?"

"The girl Karen who said she was raped. And Ben. I'll get busy on the computer." Erik preferred his own laptop, hooked up through a cable modem that guaranteed him the fastest access to the Internet. He generally worked from the receptionist's desk or from his own apartment.

"Hey, while you're at it," I said, scribbling on the notepad in front of me, "check out these names. See if any of them is registered at a local hotel."

"Can do," he said with a mock salute.

I sipped my cooling tea and studied the five pink message slips. Karen Zwilling had called twice before finally appearing at our office on Wednesday afternoon. Someone wanted me to lease a fabulous copy machine. And Ben Wyler had left two messages within fifteen minutes of each other late Thursday night. Both instructed me to call him ASAP. I picked up the phone and punched in his home number.

"Wyler."

His blunt, New York style irritated a lot of folks in this land of the languid drawl, but I found it refreshing. I'd spent most of my college and graduate school years at Northwestern near Chicago. Sometimes I longed for that flat, Midwestern twang and a penchant for plain speaking.

"It's Bay," I said. "I got your messages. What's up?"

"Got an identity on our mystery corpse," he said without preamble or small talk. "I don't know if it'll make the papers, but I wanted to give you a heads-up."

"Tell me." Every time I talked with Wyler I found myself adopting his clipped, verbal shorthand.

"Some kids found his wallet up by the dunes. Perp musta tossed it in the ocean, but it washed back up. They took it to the beach patrol, who called the deputies. Emptied out except for his driver's license. The wallet was soaked, but enough of the license survived to make out a few of the details."

"So who was it?" I could almost see his grin, enjoying his game of making me drag the important stuff out of him.

"Randolph Remington Wade of Atlanta, Georgia."

"Karen's rapist!"

"Yeah, looks that way."

"They're sure?"

Wyler grunted. "General description on the license pretty much fits the dead guy. Nobody else close reported missing."

"Will they fingerprint him? Check to see if he has a record?" I wanted to be as certain as I could be before I reassured Karen Zwilling her attacker wouldn't be bothering her or her friends again.

"Why would they? Unless you spill your client's rape accusation, there's no reason to."

"Did someone identify the body? Someone who knew him?" I asked.

"Negative. But they traced him to the Holiday Inn Express down off Pope Avenue. Desk people there remember him. Well, actually they remember his clothes and his watch more than his face, but there's not enough left of that to worry about."

I shuddered, remembering another man, his face destroyed by a shotgun blast. Thank God I'd never had to look at it myself.

"So what do you think I should do? About my client."

"I think we need to get our heads together and talk about it. You free tonight?"

The question took me by complete surprise. What was up with this guy? Was he looking for another free meal?

"Actually, I'm in the middle of another case right now. Something personal. I need to locate someone who's sort of disappeared."

He snorted. "How does somebody 'sort of disappear?' "

"It's a long story," I said.

"Good. We can work on that one, too. How about Eugene's? Say eight o'clock?" He hesitated. "I can pick you up."

This had begun to sound less and less like a business meeting. "I don't know," I said, stalling for time. I couldn't get a handle on what Wyler was up to. "I've got a few places to check out, and—"

"Then I'll meet you there. Around eight. And, hey," he added, his cynical grin evident in his voice, "this isn't a date or anything. Strictly business." Again he paused. "Wouldn't want you to go getting your hopes up or anything."

I stifled the curse word trembling on the tip of my tongue. "In your dreams, Wyler. I'll try, that's all I can promise."

"Fair enough. I'll see if I can wring any more info outta the sheriff's office before then. See ya."

I stared at the handset and listened to it click over to a dial tone as Ben Wyler hung up on me.

"Bay?" Erik stood framed in the doorway.

"Hmm?" I placed the phone back in its cradle.

"This Wade guy was staying at the Holiday Inn Express. He's still registered, but no one's seen him around in a couple of days."

"I know," I said, glancing up. "That was Wyler. They found the corpse's wallet on the beach. Cleaned out except for Wade's driver's license."

"Well, that's one case we can put in the win column. At least he won't be bothering the local talent anymore."

"I don't think it's over yet," I said, leaning back in my chair.

A couple of things had been nagging at me during Ben Wyler's recitation, and I spent the next few minutes itemizing them for Erik. First off, it seemed awfully convenient for his wallet to have turned up, just down the beach from his body. If someone had gone to the trouble of disfiguring him to prevent easy identification, why leave something like that lying around? All his credit cards had been lifted, the wallet supposedly chucked into the ocean. Why not take the license as well? For that matter, why not just take the whole damn thing?

And then there was the watch. According to both Karen Zwilling and Ben Wyler, it had been worth several thousand dollars. Why leave it behind? Karen had said he carried a roll of cash in his pocket, which the killer had obviously stolen, so why overlook something he could pawn? Maybe not around here, where a piece so distinctive would be easy to trace, but surely in Charleston or Savannah.

I didn't expect Erik to provide answers to my rhetorical questions, but he agreed the whole scenario had a lot of quirky twists to it.

"Ben said the guy was from Atlanta?" he asked, and I nodded. "Why don't I check him out? See if he's been in the papers or arrested for anything up there? It wouldn't take more than a couple of hours at most."

"Good idea. I guess we could bill it against Karen Zwilling's retainer, although I don't really feel as if we've done much to earn it. Hell, she called me about the article in the paper, or I might never have known about the guy's death at all."

"There's another part of this we haven't discussed," he said, and I waited for him to elaborate. "Our client's got a really good motive for whacking this Wade."

"I know. It's the first thing I thought of when Wyler confirmed his identity. Even if she didn't beat him up herself, she certainly could have hired someone to do it. I need to run this by the Judge and see where we stand. Legally, I mean."

"You're thinking we might have to reveal her name to the cops?"

"I don't want to, not unless she begins to look like a really viable suspect." I shook my head and leaned back in my chair. "Sure is a hell of a lot going on all of a sudden. Did you do any good with Win Hammond's credit cards?"

"Not so far, but I'll keep at it. Anything else we should be doing on that front?"

"I told Miss Addie to let me know immediately if she heard from him. I also warned her about answering the door, making sure she knows who's out there before she opens up, but I don't have a lot of faith in her memory these days. I think I'll give her a buzz. Maybe she can recall the names of some of his pals from the old days, anyone he might go to for help. I tried last night, but she wasn't really up for it."

"I'll get on Atlanta," he said and stepped back toward the reception desk.

As I punched in Miss Addie's number, my eyes fell on the Matheson files. Maybe we needed to hire some help. For some reason I didn't want to examine, the slightly off-center face of Ben Wyler popped into my head.

Adelaide Boyce Hammond managed to dredge up three names from her brother's past life in Beaufort, although she thought one of them might have died recently. I repeated my suggestion that she come and stay with me for a few days, but she insisted she'd be fine. Besides, she told me, she needed to be there when Win came home.

All three of the men had current listings in the Beaufort phone book. I jotted them down and leaned back in my chair, weighing whether or not to concoct some cover story or just go with the truth. I had plenty of ammunition in the form of my late mother's social connections to get my foot in the door. I just couldn't decide if it would be enough to induce one of Win's old cronies to give him up.

In for a penny, I thought, and dialed the first number on my list.

Ten minutes later I'd left two messages and offered my condolences to John Wendell Estes's daughter, in from Raleigh to help settle his affairs. He'd suffered a massive coronary on the ninth tee of the Oyster Reef golf course the middle of May.

I checked my watch. At a little after ten thirty, my father's day should be in full swing. Placing and receiving phone calls to guarantee his being kept up-to-date on all the significant happenings around the county occupied pretty much all his waking moments. I lucked out, and he answered on the second ring.

"Hey, Daddy. How are you this morning?"

"Fine. Why shouldn't I be?"

I sighed. "No reason. It's just a greeting, not a request for a medical update."

He chuckled. "I am turning into a cantankerous old coot, aren't I?"

"I couldn't have put it better myself. Listen, I need to ask you a couple of things about Edwin Hammond." I braced myself for the explosion of questions and for a thorough tongue-lashing for not having spilled the entire story the night before, but the Judge surprised me.

"Heard he's back in town. Well, over to his sister's on Hilton Head anyway. You tell Addie to keep an eye on him. And her checkbook locked up." I pictured his leonine head shaking from side to side. "Don't imagine the boy's changed all that much in twenty years."

"Where'd you hear about it?" I asked.

"I'm not sure. Charlie Seldon might have mentioned it this morning." The retired county solicitor was one of my father's oldest friends and one of the most reliable links in his information network.

"Do you know the story? About why he took off in the first place and then never came back? Miss Addie told me his father disinherited him for some transgression or other, and he packed up and left without another word right after the reading of the will."

My father snorted. "That's the story they put out. But, if I recall, he'd gotten himself mixed up with some shady characters, and Edwin—the father—had had to bail him out of a number of scrapes over the years. What the will actually said—and my sources on this are extremely reliable—was that Win had already used up his inheritance in blackmail and hush money his daddy'd had to pay out over the years, so he could just go whistle up a stump for any more." He paused to chuckle. "Or words to that effect."

"Blackmail? That sounds pretty heavy."

"Not really. Most of the boy's sins had to do with women. A lot of 'em married. And a lot of their husbands not averse to lookin' the other way if the price was right. He was a damned attractive man, even into his forties. Probably what drove poor Mayelle to an early grave."

As I recalled, Mayelle Hammond, the family matriarch, had lived well into her seventies. Maybe from my father's perspective that seemed way too young to die.

"Well, he's disappeared from Miss Addie's condo. She came back from a walk last night, and he was gone."

I related the details of the missing suitcase and toiletries as well as the mysterious visitor. I waited while my father absorbed the information.

"Did you do an inventory?" he asked.

"Of what?"

"Addie's things. Jewelry, silver, all that hideous bric-a-brac her mother collected." He paused for effect. "Anything small enough to fit in a suitcase."

The idea had never once crossed my mind, and for the second time in as many days I wondered where I had gotten the nerve to charge people for my investigative services.

"No, I didn't. I was too busy trying to talk her out of getting a gun so she could defend her brother against his howling pack of creditors." I hesitated and shook my head. "You really think he's sunk so low he'd steal from his own sister?"

"The boy always could rationalize his actions. I can see him thinkin' the stuff rightly belonged to him anyway. Just getting his own back."

The Judge had a point. I added a return trip to Miss Addie's condo to my growing list of things to do. I could hardly suggest to her that her brother might have stayed only long enough to rip her off. I'd have to do my own reconnoitering—that word seemed to be slipping more frequently into my vocabulary—and see if I could spot anything missing. It brought back painful memories of the last time Miss Addie's belongings had been the target of would-be thieves.

My father promised to alert his network to be on the lookout for Miss Addie's brother and seemed pleased to be able to contribute to an actual ongoing case, even though no one was paying us for it. Still, friendship had its claims, and they couldn't be ignored. If Win Hammond had showed his face in Beaufort or its environs, someone would know about it.

You have to love small towns, I thought as I flipped open the Matheson file and prepared to immerse myself in the beauty and logic of rows and columns of numbers. If only people could be so predictable.

Erik's whoop from the outer office brought my head up.

"What?" I called over the hum of the laser printer gearing up for action.

"Hang on a sec."

I tapped the end of my pencil against the smooth top of the desk. A moment later my partner stood in the doorway dangling a sheet of paper between his thumb and index finger.

"You're gonna love this." He crossed the short distance and flipped the printout in front of me.

The reproduced photograph had obviously come from the society page of the *Atlanta Journal-Constitution*. The date on the running masthead indicated the story had appeared a few months before. Two couples in formal evening dress stood arm in arm, their wide smiles lighting up the page. Three of them looked to be older, maybe in their sixties. The fourth, a tall man in a tuxedo which molded itself to his well-muscled body, dominated the picture, although his face was turned slightly away from the camera. My eyes dropped to the caption:

Mr. and Mrs. William (Nancy) Lederer share a laugh with "Star"
Ryan Kennedy and her escort, Randolph Wade, at Saturday night's
gala ball to kick off this year's United Way campaign. Both women
were cochairs of the event held in the Grand Ballroom of the Ritz-
Carlton in Buckhead.

"So that's our boy," I said. "Good-looking guy, at least from what
you can see of him. I wonder what he's doing hanging out with all the
old folks."

"Check out the diamond necklace around his date's neck. And the
way she's gazing up at him. I'm guessing Ms. Kennedy has found herself
a boy-toy."

"A boy-toy?" I laughed out loud, and Erik's face reddened. "No,
you're probably right. It's just I haven't heard that expression in a long
time. You're saying Wade could have been a gigolo."

Erik shrugged. "Just a guess. Want me to keep digging on him?"

"Definitely. And while you're at it, see what you can find out about
this Kennedy woman. Her face looks familiar, although I can't put a
finger on why right now. Who the hell would call their daughter 'Star'
anyway?"

"Don't go there, Miss Bay," Erik said, grinning as he headed toward
his desk.

I tossed my pencil at his retreating back, pulled another one out of
the drawer, and bent my head to the Matheson papers. I'd already
slogged my way through three years of accounting records, coming up
with nothing more concrete than a gut feeling his scam had something
to do with inventory. I promised myself this would be the day I finally
figured out how old Chuck had been slowly draining assets out of his
company if I had to drive down to CM^2 Supply and count napkins and
tablecloths myself.

Sometimes it scares me how prophetic some of my screwier
thoughts turn out to be.

CHAPTER TEN

*T*HE CALL CAME IN CLOSE TO NOON, JUST ABOUT THE time Erik and I were trying to decide what to do about lunch. We usually took turns picking the restaurant or fast-food chain, but the rest of the routine rarely varied: Erik did the flying, and I did the buying. I'd just about talked him into Chinese when the phone interrupted.

I reached for the receiver, but Erik grabbed it from beneath my hand. He had a theory it sounded more professional if the owner of the business didn't answer her own calls.

"Simpson and Tanner," he said in his low, soft drawl and grinned up at me. "May I ask who's calling? . . . I'm sorry, she's not in the office at the moment. May I take a message?"

I shot him a quizzical look, and he shook his head, holding up an index finger.

"Yes . . . Okay, certainly. I'll see she gets the information as soon as she returns. Is there somewhere she can reach you?" He pulled a pad toward him. "Uh-huh. Right. I've got it," he continued as he scribbled. "Yes. The minute she comes in . . . I understand . . . Yes, I will . . . Definitely. Good-bye."

He slid the receiver back into its cradle and added a few more words to the top sheet of the message pad.

"It can't be a bill collector," I said, leaning over the desk to try and decipher his writing upside down. "I just paid everything last week."

He ripped off the paper and handed it to me with a flourish. "Grace Matheson."

I wrinkled my nose. "That woman makes my skin crawl. What does she want now?"

"She said if you want to catch her husband and Cliff Morningside you should get over to the store right away. She claims they're inside, just the two of them, with all the doors locked and a homemade 'Temporarily Closed' sign in the window."

"God, it's not enough she's paying us to hound the poor man. Now she's tailing him herself, too?"

"I have no idea. She just said she knows what they're doing in there, and you should grab a camera . . ." He paused to consult his notes. "And, quote 'Nail the bastard,' end quote." Erik shook his head in amazement. "And you wonder why I'm in no hurry to get married."

I smiled in spite of my aggravation. "Your day will come. Anyway, I'm not going to go sneaking around Chuck Matheson's business, peeping in windows with a 35mm camera slung around my neck like some sleazy divorce investigator." I ran a hand through my tangled hair. "I'm just going to give the woman her money back and wash my hands of the whole thing. I should have listened to my instincts and thrown her skinny butt out the first time she plopped it into my chair."

Erik laughed. "I can't say I blame you." Then his voice sobered. "But if liking the client is going to be the main criteria for accepting a case, we're going to be out of business in short order, don't you think?"

"You're right. But I still refuse to go chasing after errant husbands, no matter how much money we're getting paid. We have to have some standards."

"Why don't I take a swing by CM^2 Supply while I'm picking up lunch? If you call in the order to the Imperial Dragon, I can grab our stuff and check out the building on the way back."

I hesitated. "Okay. But no camera and no peeking in windows, got it?"

"Yes, ma'am, loud and clear." He set his sunglasses on his nose and pulled a ring of keys out of his pocket. "I'll have General Tso's chicken with fried rice."

"Got it. Be careful," I added, handing him a twenty from my wallet. He grinned and headed out the door.

I didn't begin to worry until one o'clock.

I'd immersed myself once again in the CM^2 accounting records, determined to salvage at least some of my professional pride and find a way to keep as much of Grace Matheson's retainer as I could justify. I'd zeroed in on a subaccount in the Non-Operating Expenses section of the prior year's profit-and-loss statement, something labeled Non-Recurring Spoilage. The number had increased significantly over the year before and again over the year before that. I sat back in the chair, my hand once again reaching automatically for a cigarette, and thought about the concept.

Spoilage. I associated the word with perishable things—meat or vegetables—something you'd find on the books of a grocery store. These guys dealt in tangible goods, like linens and china. They also handled glassware, so I supposed there could be some losses there. But then wouldn't it be called breakage? I scanned the chart of accounts and found nothing close. I clasped my hands behind my head and stared at the strip of wall over the doorway.

Okay. Say this was how Chuck Matheson had been ripping off his partner. How would he go about it? I conjured up a mental picture of their small warehouse on Hunter Road as I'd seen it on my initial foray to case it out. A few parking spaces out front, a fairly large showroom with samples of their goods displayed behind a counter with catalogs from their major suppliers available for browsing. I'd driven around the back past a loading dock. The rolling overhead door stood open, and a quick glance revealed boxes stacked neatly on rows of metal shelves.

Grace had told me there were two offices behind the showroom, Chuck and his partner, Cliff Morningside, sharing one space, the other used by their small sales staff. The two owners also divided the paper-work between them, including the preparation of financials and year-end taxes, saving money by retaining an accountant only for the occasional consultation. The men relied on a canned accounting program and each other's integrity. A big mistake, in my estimation, but then no one had asked me.

I'd let my mind play with a scenario in which inventory got siphoned off, the discrepancy being buried in this Non-Recurring Spoilage account, but actually being diverted—where? The only way that made sense would be if Chuck was selling the stuff off the books and pocketing the cash. I chewed on the end of the pencil and thought about it.

Okay, it could work. Entries crediting inventory and debiting this expense account would avoid any discrepancies when they did their annual physical counts; the cost of goods sold percentage would be in line with industry norms and their prior experience. If Cliff didn't pay close attention to this often overlooked section of their financial statements, he might not tumble to it at all.

Chuck would need an accomplice. Maybe more than one. I knew a lot of business got conducted under the table, from off-the-books employees to kickbacks. While I certainly believed most of the restaurants on Hilton Head were operated by honest people, I wasn't naïve enough to believe there weren't a few bad apples stinking up the barrel.

But how could I prove it?

My stomach rumbled, and I glanced at the clock. Ten after one. What the hell could be taking Erik so long? I punched in his cell phone number, prepared to chew him out if my shrimp and broccoli came back cold, but I never got the chance. The voice mail kicked in after five rings, and I felt the first quiver of alarm ripple its way into my chest.

CM^2 Supply's parking lot stood empty.

I drove all the way around the building. The overhead door had been rolled down, and no trucks sat waiting to unload. I pulled in out front and approached the door to find the hand-lettered sign Grace Matheson had told Erik about. Inside, the lights gleamed off the glass countertop and an array of stemware displayed along one wall. I cupped my hands around my eyes and squinted through the windows, but the place seemed completely deserted.

Back in the car, I tried Erik's number again and got no answer.

"Damn it!" I muttered and cranked the engine of the T-Bird to life.

The young Asian man at the Imperial Dragon carryout said our order had been picked up over an hour ago and seemed confused by my questions. Back out in the midafternoon heat, I paused on the sidewalk of Port Royal Plaza with tourists milling around me and tried to decide what to do. This was all so un-Erik-like. Why had he turned off his phone? And where the hell was he?

I swung through McDonald's at the other end of the shopping center and ate French fries out of the bag as I headed back to the office. I saw no sign of Erik's hulking Ford Expedition among the vehicles baking in the sun, but a woman paced in front of our office door. I grabbed my substitute lunch off the passenger seat and went to confront Grace Matheson.

"Where the hell have you been?" she demanded as I approached, key in hand.

I bit my tongue. "I had an appointment out of the office."

I saw her glance contemptuously at the McDonald's bag as I let her precede me into the reception area.

"Where's your partner then? This isn't a very professional way to run a business, you know."

I couldn't argue with that. I led the way into my office and moved around behind the desk. "Please have a seat. Actually, Mr. Whiteside was checking out the information you gave him this morning."

The short, compact woman had the deep tan and taut body of a tennis player. Her long, blond hair had been pulled up into a ponytail, and a visor kept the bangs out of her eyes. She might have been pretty if she ever smiled. Her fingers toyed nervously with the top button on her pale green polo shirt.

I wiped my fingers surreptitiously on a paper napkin from my lunch bag. "Is there something I can do for you?" I asked, giving her my full attention.

A lot of the imperiousness had seeped out of her face, and I couldn't quite interpret the look that replaced it. Sadness? Embarrassment? Fear?

"I'd like you to drop the whole thing," she said, her eyes not meeting mine.

"I beg your pardon?"

"I want you to stop investigating my husband."

"Mrs. Matheson, I don't understand. I have a good line on how he's siphoning off money from the company. I can show—"

"No! I want you to stop the whole thing, right now." She rifled through her large tote bag and came out with a checkbook in her hand. "How much do I owe you?"

I stared at the top of her head as she fumbled with a pen. "You're terminating our contract?" I said.

"Yes. And I'm perfectly within my rights. I read the fine print." She glared at me across the desk.

"Of course you are," I said, not sure whether I felt relieved or angry. "I'll have to total up the hours we've spent and the expenses we've incurred on your behalf. I'll be happy to send—"

"Just estimate. I want this over with. Will another thousand cover it?" She scratched the pen across the face of the check before I had a chance to reply.

I'd purposely inflated the retainer since I'd had no idea what I might encounter in her husband's business records. Doubling it would be more than fair.

"Yes," I said, "but it's probably too—"

"Here." She ripped the check off the pad, tearing the top left-hand corner in her haste, and thrust it at me.

I took it from her quavering hand. "If you'll give me just a moment, I'll get the photocopies of the financial records together for you."

"I don't want them back. Just shred them." She rose abruptly and stepped toward the door, then paused and looked back. "The confidentiality clause still holds, right? You're ethically bound not to reveal anything I've told you or anything you found out."

"You're correct."

"Just make sure you don't violate it, or I'll sue. I really will."

She nearly sprinted across the gray carpet. The door banged closed behind her.

I stared at the empty reception area until the telephone chimed. I let it ring four times before deciding to pick up.

"Simpson and Tanner."

"Bay." Erik's breathless voice brought me to full attention.

"What's wrong? Where are you?"

"I'm at the hospital."

I gasped, and he rushed to continue.

"No, it's not me. I'm fine. I'm in the parking lot by the emergency room."

"What's going on?"

"I've been trailing the supply guys for the last hour or so. Morningside took off in a company van just as I was pulling into their warehouse, and the other one jumped in his car and followed him."

"Chuck Matheson was following Cliff Morningside?"

"Right. Chuck was trying to be cool about it, not be spotted, so I figured I should see what they were up to. Considering the things old Gracie has been accusing him of."

"Understood. So you joined the convoy." If Erik had ended up anywhere else but at the emergency room, I might have found a little more humor in the mental picture his words conjured up. "Why are you at the hospital?"

"Hang on a minute. I tracked them to the Quality Inn. You know, the motel on the north end? The one by the restaurant that used to be Shoney's?"

"I know where it is. They actually went to a motel?" Maybe Grace had been right all along. "Then what?"

"Chuck followed Cliff, and I followed both of them. Cliff already had a key, so he parked in the back. Walked right up and into a room on the second floor. A couple of minutes later Matheson banged on the door, screaming at the top of his lungs for Cliff to let him in. The door flies open, and next thing I know the two of them are wrestling around on the balcony."

"You're kidding!"

"It gets worse. Before I can even make a move to try and break them up, Cliff goes right over the railing."

"My God! How bad is he?"

"Landed in some shrubs which helped to break his fall, but it looks like he has a broken arm. Maybe an ankle, too." Erik paused and exhaled loudly. "People came running out of their rooms. I think one of the cleaning ladies called for the rescue squad. Anyway, I hung back to see what happened next. Just as Chuck was about to hop in the ambulance to ride with his partner to the hospital, a sheriff's car wheeled in, yanked him out, and put him in the back of the cruiser."

"My God," I said again.

"I know. I tailed behind, and they all went to the hospital. The deputies are in there now with Chuck. I tried to get close enough to hear what was going on, but they cleared out everybody who wasn't waiting to see a doctor. But I think I got enough to figure it out." He paused.

"What? Tell me."

In the dramatic fashion I'd come to expect from my young partner, Erik said, "Cliff Morningside went to the motel room to kill himself, and Chuck was trying to stop him."

CHAPTER ELEVEN

I MANAGED TO CHOKE DOWN ABOUT HALF THE COLD Quarter Pounder, then carried the remainder of the sandwich along with the soggy fries out to the Dumpster. Erik pulled in just as I headed back to the office. I waited for him to climb down from the Expedition, two Styrofoam carryout boxes tucked under his arm.

"If we had a microwave, I could nuke these," he said.

"We don't even have room for a coffeepot."

He dropped the containers of congealed Chinese food on the reception desk, then trailed behind me into my office and sagged into the client chair.

"That's an adventure I don't care to repeat anytime in the near future." He cupped the back of his head in his hands and stretched out his khaki-clad legs.

"Did you get tangled up with the cops? Did they know you'd been tailing Matheson?"

He shook his head. "No, thank God. I waited a few minutes, and the deputies came out alone, so they must have decided not to hold Chuck for anything. At least not right then."

"I have more interesting news." I paused. "Grace Matheson fired us."

"*What?* Why'd she do that?"

I shrugged. "She didn't give me a reason, but I'm wondering if maybe she heard about what happened at the motel. Although I'm damned if I can figure out why that would have spooked her."

Erik thought about it for a moment. "I don't see how she could have known. Unless . . ."

"Unless she was tailing you tailing Chuck tailing Cliff. Whatever the reason, she gave me another grand, and we called it even."

"I can't say I'm disappointed, and you're probably thrilled to be out of the Peeping Tom business."

"I am, although I'd just figured out how her husband has been skimming money from the company." I took a minute and gave Erik the condensed version of my theory. "But it's officially not our problem anymore, and yes, I'd have to say I'm more relieved than disappointed. Now we can concentrate on the dead rapist and trying to locate Win Hammond. I think that's enough on our plate, don't you?"

"Definitely."

"Did you find out anything else about Wade? Ben Wyler wants to meet with me tonight so I can share whatever we've got with him." I pointed a finger sternly in his direction as I watched the knowing smile slide into place. "And no cracks. This is business. B-u-s-i-n-e-s-s, got it?"

"Yes, ma'am." He tried unsuccessfully to look contrite. "I did find a couple of other articles from the paper, but I didn't get a chance to print them. I'll do it now." He hesitated in the doorway. His face had lost its teasing look. "Do you have any clue why Cliff Morningside would want to kill himself? I've been trying to put together something that makes sense, and all I can come up with is that he and Matheson really were involved—you know, sexually—and someone found out. Like maybe old Gracie?"

"I have no idea," I said, "and it's counterproductive to worry about it. Just write up a set of case notes for what happened today, and I'll close the file."

"You're the boss. Still, it does seem pretty weird."

I couldn't argue with that. I picked up the phone and dialed Adelaide Hammond's number while I gathered together the Matheson papers scattered across my desk and shoved them back into the file folders.

"Miss Addie, hi. It's Bay," I said when she picked up.

"Hello, my dear. Have you found Win?" The plaintive undertone of her question made my heart hurt.

"No, ma'am, I sure haven't. I take it he hasn't been in touch with you?"

The long sigh provided her answer. "No, not a word. I don't understand. You don't think something's happened to him, do you?"

"No, of course not," I rushed to say, although the conviction in my voice was at least partly feigned. "I'm sure he's just gotten caught up reminiscing with some of his old friends and lost track of time."

Speaking of which, it occurred to me I hadn't gotten a response from the two men whose names Miss Addie had given me and with whom I'd left messages earlier in the day. I pulled out the notepad on which I'd scratched their numbers so I could have another run at them when I finished my call.

"It's unlike him to be so . . . so *inconsiderate*," she said with some asperity.

Sounds exactly like him, I thought, and wondered if Miss Addie's mind was wandering again. What I said was pretty much the same thing I'd told her the night before. "He's probably just not used to having someone else to think about. Try not to worry. Listen, Miss Addie, I wonder if I could stop over this evening for a couple of minutes."

"Why, of course, dear. You know you're always welcome."

I could hear the unasked question in her voice. The lie came too easily to my lips. "I want to take another look through Win's things. Maybe I missed something last night."

"Of course. I should be back from dinner about seven. Will that be all right?"

"Perfect." It would take about five minutes to get from The Cedars to Eugene's and my mysterious rendezvous with Wyler at eight o'clock. "I'll see you then."

I looked up to find Erik filling the doorway. "Here's the rest of the stuff on Randolph Wade. Two more swanky affairs in the company of 'Star' Kennedy." He placed the copies on my desk. "I wonder why they always put quotation marks around her first name."

"Maybe it's a nickname."

I skimmed through the articles, one with another photo accompanying it. Again the older woman gazed adoringly up at her escort. I tried unsuccessfully to mine my memory for why her face looked so familiar.

"And I can't find any information about Win Hammond's credit cards," he said. "I'm thinking if they were issued in the British Virgin Islands, my usual sources may not have them listed."

"Well, it was worth a try. The Judge has his network on the case, so if Win is hanging around Beaufort, we'll hear of it sooner or later. I'm going to stop in at Miss Addie's and check the place out again. My father suggested her brother may have helped himself to some of her more portable treasures before he hit the bricks."

"If he did, I'll wring his damn neck when we track him down," Erik said.

"I'll hold him for you," I replied. "You might as well knock off for the day," I added after a swift glance at the clock. "I need to get home and clean up."

I heard his soft chuckle and again waved my finger at him. "And don't you dare say anything about a date, or you'll be the one with fingers wrapped around your neck."

"My lips are sealed. I'm working at the store tomorrow, so call me there if anything interesting turns up."

We wished each other a good weekend, and a few minutes later I heard the front door close. I tried the numbers again for both Win's former friends and again ended up reaching only their answering machines. I tucked the note with the numbers into the pocket of my slacks, shoved all the Matheson folders into the Closed Files cabinet, and slipped the newspaper articles about Randolph Wade into my briefcase. I had my hand on the doorknob when the phone rang.

"Bay, it's me," my father said.

"What's up?"

"I think I may have a line on Edwin Hammond. At least his where-abouts around three o'clock this afternoon."

I set the briefcase and my bag on the desk and moved around to the receptionist's chair. "Where?"

"You remember the old Hammond place? On Federal Street over in The Point?"

The cluster of historic, antebellum homes sat on a peninsula bounded by a sharp bend in the Beaufort River. The former summer houses of wealthy planters from the outlying islands attracted thousands of visitors each year. Images of their columns and porticoes and long verandahs doubtless graced vacation photo albums from Massachusetts to California. The Hammond mansion had passed out of the family decades before and, like so many of its neighbors, had found its way into the hands of carpetbaggers.

"Wasn't theirs the one with the huge live oak with its branches crawling all over the front lawn?"

"Right. Anyway, Boyd Allison says he saw someone standing out front, just staring at the house. Older man, hair beginning to go gray, in dark slacks and a beige jacket. Says he caught his eye because it's about ninety-eight degrees out there, and nobody in his right mind would be wearin' a coat."

"Did Boyd recognize him?"

"He says it could have been Hammond, but he hasn't seen him in so many years, he couldn't swear to it. He made a couple of passes, Boyd that is, then had to stop and drop off some papers to his sister. When he came back, about twenty minutes later, the man was still there. Boyd says he stopped and asked if he was lost, if he could help him find wherever he was lookin' for, but the man said no thanks." The Judge paused. "Boyd glanced in his rearview mirror as he drove away, and the man still hadn't moved."

I checked my watch. A few minutes before five. "You don't think there's a chance he's still there, do you?"

"No. I phoned old Mrs. Russell—remember everyone called her

Aunt Deed? She lives just a couple of doors down from the Hammond place. She checked and didn't see anyone loitering around. That was about ten minutes ago."

"It must have been Win. Why else would someone be standing for hours staring at his old family place?"

"I concur."

"Well, at least we know he's probably still alive and kicking. Good work, Daddy."

He chuckled. "Somethin' to be said for being older than God and knowin' everybody in the whole damn county."

"Speaking of which, can you check out a couple of names for me? Miss Addie thinks they're people from the old days Win might go to."

"Sure."

I pulled the paper out of my pocket. "Bobby Delacroix and Ray Don Rydel. I've tried calling both of them but only got their machines."

"Names sound familiar, but I can't say I remember a whole lot about either one of them. Let me get the boys workin' on that, too. I'll let you know."

I smiled at the energy and enthusiasm in his voice. Maybe work was the cure for his bouts of bad temper. Even if he couldn't get out and around, he could still make a significant contribution to the efforts of Simpson & Tanner.

"I'm going out tonight, so call me on my cell if you have news. I'm stopping at Miss Addie's to see if anything's missing. Besides her brother."

"Good." The Judge paused. "Going out where?"

"Not that it's any of your business, but I'm having dinner with a friend."

"Anyone I know?"

"Good-bye, Daddy." I hung up on his booming laugh, a sound I'd heard way too little of recently.

The Friday afternoon line of vehicles backed up at the Port Royal Plantation security gate stretched almost to the highway. By the time I pulled into my driveway, I knew I'd have to scramble to get showered and changed if I wanted to inventory Miss Addie's condo on my way to meet Wyler.

I stepped into her front room a little after seven.

"Why, Lydia, don't you look lovely!" she said, swinging the door wide.

The cream-colored, short-sleeved dress had been one of those I'd had specially designed to hide the scars that scored my back and left shoulder. Halfway between "date" and "business," I thought it pretty well summed up the evening.

"Thanks."

I refrained from asking if she'd heard from Win. She'd have told me first thing if she had.

"Do you have time for a glass of tea? I've made some fresh."

"That would be nice," I said, and she bustled off to her small kitchen. I never ceased to marvel at the innate hospitality Southern women of her generation displayed. No matter how long one had been acquainted or even on intimate terms with them, a guest was always a guest.

I took the opportunity of her absence from the room to prowl among the crowded tables looking for telltale signs of theft: gaps in the massive clutter of her mother's vases, statues, and geegaws, patches of clear wood in a cluster always slightly dusty. No one, not even Miss Addie, could probably itemize everything that *should* be there. I found nothing that seemed out of place.

"Here you are, dear," she said, setting a small silver tray with two glasses down on the Hepplewhite.

"Thank you." I seated myself beside her on the gold sofa.

"I take it you're on your way to dinner," she said. "I so seldom see you these days in a dress."

"Yes, I'm meeting a friend." I paused, fumbling in my mind for some way to broach the unpleasant subject of my visit. "Is everything okay here? In the apartment, I mean? You haven't had any more trouble with anyone disturbing your things like . . . that summer?"

Her faded eyes regarded me across the tops of her wire-rimmed glasses. "Trouble? You mean, someone trying to rob me?"

"Well, yes. You have so many lovely things—"

"Win would not steal from me."

The iron in her voice surprised me. "I'm sorry. I didn't want to upset you, but I had to consider the possibility. You have to admit his behavior has been very strange."

Miss Addie's smile carried a hint of sadness. "Yes, dear, you're right of course. His just picking up and disappearing right after I'd found him again has been most distressing. But you don't know him. It's exactly the sort of thing he used to do that drove poor Papa to distraction. My brother has always been spoiled—he was the baby, and the only boy, you see—so we've always made . . . allowances." She sighed, and her shoulders slumped. "I thought perhaps he'd grow out of it."

I set my tea glass down and reached for her hand. "One of the Judge's friends is pretty sure he saw Win today in Beaufort. At least someone fitting his description was standing in front of your parents' old place on Federal Street."

"And he seemed to be all right?"

"Far as Boyd could tell."

"Then he'll be in touch when he's ready. Thank you, dear. I feel so much better."

Her easy acceptance surprised me, but she knew the man a lot better than I did.

I glanced at my watch. "I really have to be on my way," I said, rising. "Will you be okay? You haven't had any other visitors, have you?"

She shook her head. "No. I did get one phone call, but the person hung up as soon as I answered. Probably one of those horrid people trying to sell me something. I do wish they'd find more fulfilling employment."

I smiled as she trailed behind me to the foyer. "Well, don't open the door unless you know who it is." A thought struck me. "Even if it's someone claiming to be from the electric company or something like that. Just tell them you're unwell, and they need to come back later. Then call me. No matter what time. Promise me?"

Miss Addie patted my arm. "Lydia, don't fuss. I've lived alone more than half my life."

"I know." I bent to gather her frail body into a soft embrace. "I just worry about you. I couldn't stand it if anything happened to you."

I surprised both of us with the depth of my emotion. My mother had been dead for close to twenty years, and I couldn't remember ever feeling the sweet concern for her that I did for this woman with whom I had no claim of kinship.

"I know," she whispered against my shoulder, "I know." She disengaged herself and stepped back. "Now run along and enjoy yourself. Don't keep your young man waiting."

"It's not—" I began, but she shooed me out the door with a smile.

"Have fun," she called as I made my way to the elevator.

I waited until I heard the snap of her deadbolt before I punched the Down button.

CHAPTER TWELVE

$\mathcal{J}$'D BEEN IN THE OLD CHART HOUSE RESTAURANT ONLY
once since it had become Eugene's. Situated at the back of Palmetto Bay Marina, it provided a spectacular view across the tidal marsh to Bishop's Reach, the wide expanse of water that emptied into Calibogue Sound. Because most of its windows faced west, diners on clear evenings could expect a ringside seat to Hilton Head's spectacular sunsets.

I checked in at the maître d's stand about ten to eight to find Ben Wyler hadn't yet arrived. I strolled back onto the deck and seated myself on one of the long benches set among pots of trailing bougainvillea and lush hibiscus. Sleek sailboats and smaller craft plied the Reach, most heading in as the light faded into the pearly gray that signaled the onset of evening.

I turned at the sound of an engine. A massive old Jaguar pulled up to the curb, and an elderly woman stepped out of the passenger side. Across its gleaming black top, I caught the flash of sunlight reflected off the glass windows of a building rising among the trees on the other side of the parking lot. Several boats on trailers were pulled up around its perimeter. I wondered if this could be the yard where Karen Zwilling's rapist had brought his boat for repair. I had just about decided to take a walk over to check it out when someone called my name. I glanced back to find Ben Wyler moving toward me across the deck.

He raised a hand, and I waved back in acknowledgment. He wore a yellow Ralph Lauren polo shirt tucked into crisply pressed tan slacks. In the waning light of the soft evening, he looked almost handsome.

"Sorry," he called. "Traffic."

Our window table along the side of the room overlooking the water made it seem as if we were floating. I smiled as a young woman pulled out my chair and set menus in front of us.

"Nice job, Wyler. Who'd you have to bribe to get such a good seat?"

A waiter appeared at his shoulder before he had a chance to reply. "What'll you have to drink?" Ben asked me.

"Just water for now," I said, and he frowned.

"Dos Equis," he said, and the waiter moved off. He cast a quizzical look across the table. "You don't drink?"

"Every day," I said, stung a little by the brusqueness of his question. "I believe you die if you don't."

He snorted. "You know what I mean. Alcohol. A wee nip now and again?"

"I've never seen the point of it. Besides, most of it smells like gasoline."

"You mean you've never tried it? Not anything? Where'd you go to college, Temperance State?"

I had to laugh. "I've had the occasional glass of wine. Even tried beer once," I added as the waiter set our glasses in front of us. "Nasty."

Wyler poured his in a slow trickle down the side of the frosted pilsner glass while the young man in flowered shirt and white shorts rattled off the evening's specials. We decided on grouper. I sipped at my water and watched the fingers of twilight spread themselves across the sky. It surprised me how quickly we'd dropped into this easy companionship.

"So what did you want to discuss?" I asked. "Did you get anything more out of the sheriff's office on our mystery corpse?"

"Geez, Tanner, I thought maybe we could at least get through the first course before we start discussing dead bodies."

"Sorry. I thought that was the point of getting together." I reached into my bag and pulled out the copies of the articles Erik had down-loaded from the Atlanta papers. "Take a look at these."

Wyler skimmed the stories, pausing to give the grainy photo-graphs more attention. "Hmmm," he said, tapping his index finger against his chin.

"What?"

The waiter slid our salads in front of us. When he'd moved away, Wyler pointed at the figure of Randolph Wade. "How tall do you think this guy is?"

"I don't know. How can you tell without knowing how tall every-one else is? And what difference does it make?"

Wyler set the papers down beside his plate and attacked his Caesar salad. He wiped dressing from his mouth with his napkin. "I had a peek at the file today. Strictly against regulations, but not everyone at the sheriff's office thinks of me as a pariah."

I studied him across the table. I had a feeling the pariah reference had been directed at my brother-in-law.

"And?"

"And the dead man was six-one, one-ninety or thereabouts. The guy in this picture looks bigger than that."

I reached for the copies and studied the photos under the light of the candle in its glass globe. Outside, the setting sun had burnished the tops of the trees to a hazy gold, and streaks of burnt orange lit the water as if a fire glowed beneath its smooth surface.

"I don't know. It's hard to judge."

The grouper arrived, and I set the papers aside. Not until we had relaxed back into our chairs with tea and coffee did we return to the os-tensible reason for our meeting.

"So you're doubting it's really Wade, is that it?" I asked.

"I don't know. Just a couple of things nagging at me."

"Like why whoever killed him left his driver's license in his wallet? If the whole purpose of disfiguring his face was to conceal his identity, that was pretty stupid, wasn't it? Even tossing his ID into the water doesn't make sense. Why not just take it with him and burn it or something?"

I hadn't often seen Ben Wyler smile, except in that sardonic way he had that made you feel as if you'd just said something incredibly stupid. This one softened his eyes, and I found myself marveling at the transformation.

"I always said you were more than just a pretty face. That's exactly what I've been thinking. And then there's the watch."

"Right! If it's worth so much money, why did the killer leave it behind? And—" I stopped, suddenly realizing I had been showing off, like a well-prepared pupil basking in the glow of approval from her teacher. I snapped my mouth shut and sat back in my chair.

"Hey, don't stop," Wyler said, leaning forward, elbows on the table. "You're on a roll."

"I'm sure you've already thought of all this," I said quietly.

"Yeah, you're right. But I didn't have the ability to chase down these newspaper articles. Me and the computer aren't normally on the most cordial of terms."

That brought a smile. "Me either. Erik's the one with the keys to the mysteries of the Internet. I can barely retrieve my e-mail." It was a small exaggeration. Under my partner's tutelage I had become pretty adept at navigating my way around search engines.

"Anyway," he went on, "we're definitely on the same page on this thing. Trouble is, we've got squat to take to the coroner. I don't think they're gonna spring for any kind of DNA tests or fingerprint checks unless this Zwilling woman comes forward with her rape accusation. From what I heard today, it sounds as if they're pretty well satisfied the dead guy is Wade. They've got no cause to pursue it any further without some solid reason."

"I don't know. Karen's resisted the idea of involving the police right from the get-go. And you know as well as I do we can't violate her confidence without her permission."

Ben Wyler grunted. "So talk her into it. We need to give them a reason to dig a little deeper and make sure they're burying the right guy."

I thought about it while the waiter set the check beside Wyler's plate.

"Why should she?" I said finally. "What's in it for her?"

"Knowing the guy who raped her is dead."

"She knows that already. Or she will as soon as I tell her they've found his ID. She was already half convinced just by the vague description in the paper. I told you before, she's not eager to call attention to herself with the cops."

"You mean considering her profession?" Wyler laughed. "Gimme a break. As long as she doesn't roll anybody or start passing around nasty diseases, they won't hassle her. They got better things to do with their time and manpower."

I couldn't challenge his assertion, but it didn't sound right to me. I shrugged. "It doesn't matter what we think. All I can do is ask and see what she says. But I wouldn't hold out a lot of hope."

"Damn it!" He snatched the newspaper photos and jabbed his finger at the hazy face of Randolph Remington Wade. "I'm telling you this guy is not our corpse!"

Our poor server picked that moment to approach the table. He jerked his hand back at Wyler's words as if he'd been slapped on the wrist with a ruler.

I waited, but Wyler made no move. Finally I leaned over and pulled my American Express card out of my wallet. "Don't mind him," I said with as wide a smile as I could manage. "He has a very vivid imagination."

Ben Wyler tried to talk me into a nightcap at the bar, but I declined.

"Hey, you can have a ginger ale or a Coke," he said, but I pleaded fatigue.

We stepped together out into the soft June night, a light breeze off the Reach stirring the leaves of the ancient oaks towering over the restaurant. Lights sparkled in the windows of the condominium complex next door as well as on the rigging of the sailboats moored in the compact marina. Across the way rose the massive mansions of Bram's Point.

Wyler stopped next to my car, his hands thrust deep into the pockets of his slacks. This should have been the moment when I said something about having had a good time and thanked him for the evening. That is, it would have been if this had been an actual date. And if he had actually paid for dinner. Instead I slid behind the wheel and busied myself with keys and seat belt. Wyler watched as I started the engine and eased down the side windows.

"Well," I said, "I'll let you know what Karen says. I'll be in the office on Monday if you want to check back with me."

"You better do it tomorrow," he said, his face unreadable in the dim glow of the overhead lights. "There's no telling when the coroner will release the body."

"Release it to whom? If there's no next of kin, what'll they do?"

He shrugged. "I guess the county will pay to bury him. I'm not sure how you handle these things down here." He jiggled the coins in his pocket. "I do know they'll try their damnedest to find a relative first."

"A relative of Randolph Wade?" The sudden thought made me shiver in the humid night air. "If it's not really him, that would be unbelievably cruel."

"So call the girl. As soon as possible."

Ben Wyler raised his hand in a brief wave and sauntered away toward the back of the parking lot.

"You're welcome," I muttered.

I had no idea what kind of car he drove, so I sat for a few minutes watching several vehicles wind their way around the marina and back onto the road toward the highway before I shut off the engine and slid out from behind the wheel. The gravel crunched beneath my high-heeled sandals as I picked my way toward the building I'd spotted earlier in the evening. As I got closer I could see a spotlight illuminating the name on one of the stucco walls: Palmetto Marine Services.

The area around it was sparsely lit, but I passed several boats either resting on trailers or up on some sort of stands. I had difficulty reading most of the names, although the couple I could make out were exceedingly clever. I guessed the captain of the *Mary No* had a wife who hadn't been thrilled with the idea of watercraft ownership. I peered at another, a massive yacht whose gleaming white superstructure rose to what looked to me like a couple of stories above the ground. The black hull, almost invisible in the darkness, seemed to be pitted. The smell of the ocean, dank and musty, drifted to me from what I suddenly realized must be barnacles and seaweed still clinging to its sides. What I know about boats would fill a thimble.

So this one had recently been in use. I stared again at the huge craft towering above me. How did they get something so big out of the water? I walked around to the back—the stern, I corrected myself—and peered up to the spot where I expected to see the name. A tarp or piece of canvas had been draped across it. I squinted into the dim light, looking for a ladder or some way of getting onto the thing, but I saw nothing. Not that I intended to try to scramble aboard, especially not in the middle of the night and especially not in a dress and heels.

A car door slammed, close at hand, making me jump back and stumble on the loose gravel. The boat repair place probably had security, patrols of some kind. Or dogs. I edged back into Eugene's parking lot. I had almost reached the Thunderbird when a flurry of activity caught my eye. Voices and lights wafted to me from the direction of the marina, and I headed toward them.

I approached the docks and stopped at the end of a short, manmade channel. Straddling it was a massive blue crane, its wheels sunk into tracks on either side, and a sling of some sort connecting the tall pillars. I could make out a tangle of heavy steel cable and hydraulic lines.

So this is how they get yachts that size out of the water, I thought.

People streamed by me, chattering and laughing as they shed jackets and sweaters. I looked up to see an excursion boat, the kind meant to carry tourists on dolphin-watching or sunset cruises. I meandered down the other side of the dock and gazed out at the variety of watercraft moored in close or riding at anchor farther out in the sheltering arms of the marina. I caught the flare of a cigarette lighter and the clink of glasses, a short burst of laughter suddenly cut off. I wondered if people actually lived on board some of the larger boats and if Randolph Wade's had been tied up here when he'd raped Karen Zwilling and her friend. I shuddered in the warm glow of the dock lights and moved toward the car.

Forty-five minutes later I pulled on my favorite oversized T-shirt and climbed into bed, pillows piled against the headboard, an old Dashiell Hammett hardcover next to me. Since I'd officially become a private investigator, I'd found myself drawn to rereading the classic noir novels of the thirties and forties. I loved the "mean streets" of prewar Los Angeles and San Francisco and the hard-boiled detectives who prowled them. I had a date with Sam Spade and *The Maltese Falcon*.

I pulled my bag onto the bed and searched its depths for my reading glasses. As I retrieved the case, I realized something was missing. I pawed through the contents, but it was obvious the papers were gone. I closed my eyes, conjuring up the last time I'd seen them: next to my companion's plate on the snowy white tablecloth in the restaurant. I was positive they hadn't been there when we'd risen from our chairs.

So Ben Wyler had walked out of Eugene's with the photos of Randolph Wade tucked into one of his pockets, and I was damned if I could figure out exactly why.

CHAPTER THIRTEEN

I TRIED TO REACH KAREN ZWILLING ALL DAY SATURDAY with no results except a growing frustration. In between trips to the grocery store and the dry cleaner's and an extended run along the beach, I dialed her number, each time reaching her voice mail. After the fourth or fifth try, I stopped leaving messages.

In the evening, I filled a glass with iced tea, tucked the Hammett novel under my arm, and flopped down on the chaise in the screened-in area of my deck. I'd called Erik after he'd gotten home from work and brought him up to date on my meeting with Wyler. I set the portable house phone as well as my cell on the low table beside me in case our wandering client decided to get in touch.

But the inevitable interruption came in the form of a vigorous pounding on my front door. I crossed the great room into the foyer and keyed the intercom.

"Yes?"

"Bay, it's me. Open the door."

Red Tanner did not sound like a happy camper. I sighed and flipped the lock.

"Hey! Come on in."

In dark green shorts and a faded gray T-shirt sporting the Marine

Corps logo, my brother-in-law looked fresh out of the shower. He pushed past me without further greeting.

"I'm out on the deck. Want a tea or something?"

"I don't mind if you don't want to go places with me," he said, his face set in grim lines. "Well, hell, that's not true. Of course I mind. But you're a free agent. You've made that perfectly clear in more ways than I care to remember. What I won't stand for—"

"Whoa! Hold the phone there, pal." I folded my arms across my chest, and we faced each other across the expanse of hardwood floor like two boxers sizing each other up from opposing sides of the ring. "I don't think you want to have a conversation with me that begins with, 'I won't stand for.'"

Red ran his hand through his thick, light brown hair in one of those familiar Tanner gestures that made me want to smile and cry at the same time. "Okay, okay. Point taken. What I want to know is why you blew me off on the ballgame so you could go schmoozing around with that . . . with Wyler."

I really hadn't given a thought to how it might look to Red when I'd accepted Ben's invitation. I'd considered it a business meeting and directly connected with our client's case. I didn't wonder how he'd found out. Devoid of its tens of thousands of summer visitors, Hilton Head is a small town. I should have anticipated some mutual acquaintance rushing to carry the tale back to my brother-in-law.

I watched the expression on Red's face morph from anger into hurt. I brushed past him and into the kitchen, pulled a beer from the depths of the refrigerator, and carried it back to him.

"Come on outside and let's talk."

I didn't wait to see if he followed. I dropped back onto the chaise and tucked my hands behind my head. A few seconds later he took a seat in the cushioned chair opposite me.

"I'm just sayin', if you don't want to go somewhere with me, all you have to do is tell me. You don't have to make up . . . excuses."

I could tell by the hesitation he'd been about to say "lies." I shook my head. "Red, you really piss me off sometimes, you know? It was business. Not that I owe you an explanation."

He took a swallow of beer and leaned forward, his elbows resting on his knees. "Of course you owe me an explanation, and you damn well know it." He sighed and lowered his voice. "Look, how long since that day my brother first introduced us? What is it? Fifteen, sixteen years ago?"

I cast my mind back to our first meeting, his brother Rob and I bathed in the glow of our newfound passion. It had been at some sort of Tanner family gathering, maybe Thanksgiving. What I did remember with crystal clarity was that nothing and no one else but Rob had even registered on my radar.

"About fifteen," I said. "Which means you should know me well enough by now not to accuse me of blowing you off. On the rare occasions when I have, it's been necessary. I wouldn't waste a good lie on something as stupid as a baseball game."

That brought the beginnings of a smile.

"The truth is, I didn't talk to Wyler until Friday morning. It was business, Red . . . Wait, I can prove it."

I levered myself off the chaise and strode toward the bedroom office. From one of the wire baskets on the desk I plucked the credit card receipt from the dinner at Eugene's and carried it back to the porch.

"See?" I thrust the slip of paper at him. "I bought dinner. Company American Express card. Is this enough proof for you, Sergeant Tanner?"

Red took the receipt from me and tossed it on the side table without looking at it. "Okay. I guess I owe you an apology."

"Damned straight." I smiled to take any sting from the words. "Well?"

"Well what?"

"I'm waiting for the apology. And it better be good. I want to see lots of heartfelt contrition. A tear or two wouldn't be out of order."

Red grinned. "I humbly beg your pardon, Mrs. Tanner. If you can find it in your heart to forgive me, I promise to make it up to you over a plate of shrimp at Bubba's." He paused. "And I guarantee I won't stick you with the check."

"Deal," I said, relaxing back against the cushions. The silence stretched out as we sipped our drinks. Outside in the palmettos, a barn owl screeched, startling us both.

"So what did you and the New York City reject find to talk about?" my brother-in-law finally asked.

"You're cattier than an old woman," I replied, shaking my head. "And what we discussed is confidential. I think I've explained it to you about a million times."

"I thought he wasn't going to get involved in the day-to-day running of things."

"Well, he's obviously changed his mind." I paused and formulated my next question carefully. "What's happening with the murder victim you guys found on the beach? Has he been identified?"

Red studied my face. "What's it to you?"

I could feel his antennae quivering, and I shrugged. "Nothing. Just trying to make conversation."

"Why do I have the feeling it's more than that? Are you messing around in an official investigation? You want to get your license yanked?"

"Quit preaching. If you don't want to talk about it, then don't." I sipped diluted tea and set the glass back on the table. "So what do you think of the Braves' prospects this year?"

Red laughed. "Okay, okay. I guess it can't hurt. I'm not directly involved in the case, you know, but Morgan says no one's come forward to identify the body. All indications are it's this Wade guy, the one whose wallet washed up, but the coroner's not ready to make that call just yet. They have feelers out to the Atlanta PD since that's the address on his driver's license, but nothing's been confirmed." Red tipped the bottle back and drained the last of his beer. "I heard they asked the paper up there to run a brief story, see if anyone responded to it."

"I hope they didn't use his name," I said, appalled at the thought some relative of Randolph Wade's might find out about his supposed death from a newspaper article. "What does the coroner make of the injuries?" I asked, and immediately Red's face closed up.

"What do you know about the injuries? Has Wyler been shooting his mouth off? The guy has no damned business sneaking around the office. He's officially a civilian. I'm going to have a few choice words for the duty people—"

"God, Red, give it a rest, will you? Does it matter how I know what I know? Answer this: If the murderer went to the trouble of beating the guy's face in, why would he be so careless about the wallet? And why didn't he remove the license along with the credit cards and cash?"

Red's cell phone chirped, and he pulled it from the case strapped to his belt. "Tanner."

"Saved by the bell," I muttered as he rose and moved away into the great room.

Maybe one of the reasons our relationship hadn't blossomed into anything other than wary friendship was that we were both too enamored of our secrets.

Whatever the situation which had prompted the call to Red, it had apparently not been anything urgent. A few minutes later I heard the refrigerator door close, and my brother-in-law wandered back onto the deck with a fresh beer. Since he deftly parried every attempt I made to steer the conversation back to the corpse from the beach, we spent a pleasant hour reminiscing about old times and old friends.

Around ten o'clock, Red checked his watch and said he had to be on duty at seven the next morning. We parted with mutual pecks on the cheek and promises to get together soon for shrimp and oysters at Bubba Mitchell's hole-in-the-wall restaurant on Skull Creek. I watched from the kitchen window as Red maneuvered his restored Ford Bronco around and out of my driveway.

I went through my nightly ritual of buttoning down the house, checking windows and arming the security system, then tossed my clothes in the hamper. I climbed into bed and opened the detective novel to page forty-seven. I never used a bookmark because my father had believed it would stimulate my mental development to make me memorize the page numbers instead of marking my place. I didn't know how much it ever did for my IQ, but the practice had long since become habit.

And so had Red's and my bickering every time we were in the same room for longer than five minutes. In my head I replayed the evening's conversation as the print blurred before my eyes. I couldn't put my finger on the reason Red and I seemed to be so at odds with each other all the time. After Rob's murder, I accepted his brother's concern as a natural protectiveness born of our shared grief and my own physical injuries. But lately it had become almost cloying, smothering, as if Red couldn't stand to see me make it on my own.

Don't be ridiculous, I said to myself. Both the Tanner boys were brought up to be fine men by a stay-at-home mother and a school-teacher father who had been the quintessential Southern gentleman. The truth was, I didn't want to examine the real reason for our prickliness with each other. I forced my attention back to Sam Spade and Brigid O'Shaughnessy.

By Monday morning I still hadn't heard from Karen Zwilling.

As I unlocked the door of the agency, I heard Erik's footsteps behind me. I held the door open for him and called "Good morning" over my shoulder, then carried my briefcase into my office.

"Morning, boss," Erik said, following me in and dropping into the client chair. "How was your weekend?"

"Frustrating," I said. "Do we have any messages on the machine?"

He rose and stepped back out into the reception area. "I'll check the service," he said, punching buttons.

I worked my neck around on my shoulders before settling behind my desk. I'd spent Sunday working the phones, trying to track down both our unresponsive client and Win Hammond's elusive old cronies.

I'd begun to wonder if the entire county was avoiding me. I'd struck out all the way around, and the aggravation of it had left me tossing most of the night.

"Have you been trying to reach Karen Zwilling?" Erik called as I pried the lid off the Chai tea I'd picked up at Starbucks on my way in.

"Only for the past forty-eight hours straight," I said.

"She called Saturday afternoon, said she's going to be out of town for a few days."

"Damn it! Did she leave a number?"

"Nope."

"Figures. Anything else?"

Erik carried the pink slip in and handed it to me. "This one's interesting. Someone who wants an appointment for first thing this morning. I think you'll recognize the name."

I took the paper from his extended hand and had about five seconds to register the words STAR RYAN KENNEDY before the outer door opened and the woman herself stepped into reception.

CHAPTER
FOURTEEN

I PRACTICALLY PUSHED ERIK OUT OF MY OFFICE, INDI-
cating with wild hand-waving he should pull the door closed
behind him. I could hear his muffled query about helping our unannounced visitor but not her soft reply. I straightened my already pristine
desk, stuck the Starbucks cup in a file drawer, and grabbed a random
folder. When the intercom buzzed, I had the stage pretty well set.

"There's a Mrs. Kennedy to see you," Erik said in a formal voice
with a hint of amusement riding just below the surface. "I'm afraid she
doesn't have an appointment." He paused dramatically. "It concerns a
Mr. Randolph Wade."

"I know. Tell me you can rearrange a couple of things as if I've asked
you to."

I heard him riffle the pages of the nearly pristine appointment
book. "I can push your ten o'clock back to ten thirty if you'd like."

"Ask her to wait, then get yourself in here."

I was in the process of smoothing my hair when Erik stepped in and
eased the door closed. A wide grin split his face. "What's this all
about?"

I took a deep breath. How could I explain my visceral reaction to
Star Ryan Kennedy's sudden appearance in my office?

"I know her. I mean, I thought she looked familiar when I saw her pictures in those newspaper articles you downloaded, but they were so blurred it didn't register until I saw her in the flesh. She used to live around here, back when I was in high school. An old mansion over on The Point in Beaufort. She and my mother cochaired some charity functions, maybe for the Historical Society. I don't remember exactly, except her name wasn't Kennedy then." I studied the ceiling for a moment. "Something French, like Beaumont or Belmonde. She was quite a bit younger than my mother and absolutely gorgeous."

"I'm surprised you'd forget someone called Star."

"That's what threw me. She was Étoile back then. Come to think of it, I'm pretty sure that's French for star."

"So why are you acting as if the Pope just dropped by?"

"I don't know exactly." I shook my head. "It's silly, but she was one of the few of my mother's society groupies who could really intimidate me."

"Well, you're not a kid anymore. And she could be the solution to our problem of identifying Wade's body. Play nice."

I smiled and exhaled deeply. "You're right. I'm being ridiculous. Send her in."

I folded my hands on the desktop like a schoolgirl waiting for the teacher, then quickly dropped them into my lap and ordered myself to quit acting like a ninny as Star Kennedy preceded Erik into my office. I waited for the older woman to offer her hand before extending my own, just as my mother had taught me. I indicated the chair as Erik slipped back out the door, and the elegant woman in the creamy St. John knit suit lowered herself in one fluid motion onto the edge of the seat.

"I'm sure you don't remember me," she began, settling her Isabella Fiore bag onto her lap and crossing her long, slender legs at the ankle.

I couldn't get a good look at the shoes, but I knew they'd be designer, too. "Of course I do," I said. "You were a great friend of my late mother."

A little *moue* of sadness briefly puckered her full lips. Not enough to generate any wrinkles on her perfect face, but sufficient to indicate her reaction. "So sad. And so sudden. I considered Emmaline my mentor, my counselor, if you will. I was quite devastated to learn of her death."

Apparently not devastated enough to send a formal condolence, but I let it slide. Before I could ask what had brought her to my office first thing on a Monday morning, she continued.

"I remember you quite well, Lydia. I must say you've grown up to be a lovely young woman. Emmaline would have been proud."

Nothing is more guaranteed to raise my hackles than this social pandering, but I bit back the retort hovering on my lips and said, "Thank you. I prefer to be called Bay, if you don't mind."

For the first time she looked a little flustered. "I understand. My given name was not one I would have chosen for myself. No one could ever quite figure out how to pronounce it."

The gracious smile changed her whole demeanor, and I felt myself relax.

"I always thought it was beautiful," I said.

"Why, thank you, dear." Her right hand, sporting a magnificent emerald-cut diamond, smoothed an already perfectly arranged, faux blond pageboy. "My second husband simply couldn't get it right. Changing it to Star seemed so much easier than trying to teach that great, hulking redneck how to speak French."

She said it with a laugh, softening the harshness of her words.

"How can I help you, Mrs. Kennedy?" I said. "My associate tells me it has to do with a Mr. Wade."

"Star. Please, you must call me Star. Otherwise, I'll feel like a frumpy old dowager."

Fat chance, I thought. *That face has had a whole lot of overhauling to make certain you look anything but.* "Of course. If you're interested in engaging our services, I'd like to tape our conversation."

Her eyes narrowed, and I watched the calculating look of the intelligent woman replace the bland façade of the society matron. "I'm not certain that's necessary. Let me give you the particulars, and then we can decide, all right?"

I inclined my head slightly in capitulation. I pulled a legal pad from the desk along with a pen. "I'll just take notes for the time being." I didn't pose it as a question because it wasn't open to debate.

"As you wish." Star Kennedy lowered her bag to the floor and leaned slightly forward in her chair. "I've spoken with your associate, Mr. Wyler. That's why I'm here."

I didn't have to fake my surprise. "You talked to Ben Wyler? Why?"

She squared her shoulders and looked directly at me. "He indicated you might not approve, but he felt I had a right to know." Her chin rose a fraction, and she appeared to be struggling for control. "About Remmy."

It threw me for a moment until I dredged up the supposed victim's complete name: Randolph Remington Wade. Apparently the newspaper photos showing an adoring older woman gazing up at her handsome escort had been right on. "Remmy" sounded like the kind of intimate nickname one might give a particularly close friend. Or a lover.

"You're acquainted with Mr. Wade?" I asked.

"Yes. He was . . . is a friend as well as a . . . business advisor."

"So you've known him a long time."

She hesitated. "I wouldn't say . . . Sometimes it isn't a matter of years that allows one to develop a . . . relationship of trust with another person. It's simply a question of being . . . in *tune,* as it were. I'm sure you understand."

All too well, I thought. "When did you actually meet?"

"Last November," she said reluctantly, her face again tightening in an expression that dared me to comment. "At the Daughters of the Confederacy ball. A mutual friend introduced us."

"I see. And the name of this friend?" I waited, my pen poised over the legal pad.

Star Kennedy hesitated long enough to make me realize she really didn't want to part with the information. "Lucy Whitcombe. Her husband and mine were partners in some . . . ventures."

"Would that be your second husband, Mr. Kennedy?"

The mask slipped back onto her beautiful face. "I fail to see how any of this is pertinent to the present situation."

I gave up the pretense that we were just two former acquaintances settling in for a chat about the old neighborhood. "I'm assuming your purpose here is to determine if your friend Mr. Wade is in fact the murder victim found on the beach last Wednesday night. Am I in error?"

My bluntness brought fire to her fine hazel eyes. "There's no need to be coarse, Lydia."

"I'm sorry if I offended you. But Ben Wyler called you because of some photos we located in the Atlanta paper's Internet files. Photos of you and Wade. There's some question as to the identity of the corpse, and my guess is he's hoping you can clear that up. I'm assuming that's the reason you agreed to come. You want to know for certain, too."

Her eyes blazed, but she controlled her voice. "You're right. Mr. Wyler gave me the particulars, and it does sound like Remmy. It must be."

"But yet you have some doubts?" I asked softly. Whether or not the late Mr. Wade had been the answer to the prayers of an aging belle or an opportunistic gigolo, there had obviously been something between them. "Can you tell me why?"

Star Kennedy cleared her throat and resettled herself in the chair. The slim skirt of her designer suit rode up over her knees. I couldn't help noticing she had beautiful legs for a woman who had to be pushing sixty, as well as a body kept taut by regular trips to the gym.

"Your Mr. Wyler told me the . . . person had been staying at some motel or other. Some tourist place." Her perfect nose wrinkled in distaste. "Remmy comes from a fine old Virginia family. He never traveled unless he could get a suite at the best hotel."

"How nice for him," I muttered, but she caught my tone.

"We're not snobs, Lydia. We have money. Perhaps I didn't work for mine, but I enjoy it." She paused and shot me that enigmatic smile. "Although some would say being married to Francis Aloysius Kennedy for fifteen years may have earned me sainthood along with his fortune."

Again she hesitated. I could see the calculation flicker in her eyes as she decided whether or not to put me all the way in my place. "I believe Emmaline saw to it that *you* were quite well taken care of yourself."

I had sat through enough of my mother's interminable teas and socials to know how this game was played. I could have leaped into the battle with colors flying, my own verbal guns blazing. Instead I drew a deep breath and took the high road.

"So your only reason for supposing the victim might not be Randolph Wade is that the man was staying in an inferior hotel?"

That made her angry. "Of course not! But it's not something Remmy would do. Or, if he was traveling in his yacht, he would have slept there."

"Do you know the name of his boat?" I asked.

That brought a brief smile. "He named her *Wade in the Water.* Like the jazz song. I always thought it rather clever."

I made a note on my pad. "And you know for a fact this boat is here on Hilton Head?"

"No, not for certain. But he did talk about bringing her up from the islands to have some sort of overhaul performed. I assume there are places here where that can be done."

It tallied with Karen Zwilling's story, but of course I couldn't tell Star Kennedy that. "When's the last time you saw Mr. Wade?"

Her chin came up. "About two weeks ago. We had dinner, and he told me he was going to be out of town for a little while. I assumed it was about the boat. We were planning a trip to the Virgin Islands, and he wanted to make sure everything was in order."

She *assumed.* Which meant Wade hadn't told her exactly where he was going.

"And when were you scheduled to leave?" I asked.

I noted her hesitation and the rapid blinking of her eyes.

"We hadn't set a specific date."

Not exactly urgent, then, to have the boat repaired. I leaned back in my chair and regarded Star Ryan Kennedy. I could pick out the little telltale signs of nervousness and anxiety, although she appeared outwardly composed. I knew she hadn't told me everything, but I could also sense she probably wasn't going to. And something about her posture and the tone of her voice made me uneasy. Her words were those of a woman trying hard for composure in the face of almost certain bad news, but somehow it rang false. Or maybe I was just getting cynical.

"What would you like us to do for you, Star?" I asked. "If you want to view the body, you're going to need to see the coroner." I saw her shoulders stiffen. "I'd be glad to come with you, if that would make it any easier."

"I have no intention of . . ." She stuttered to a halt.

I couldn't blame her. The prospect of trying to identify someone whose head had been pounded to a pulp wouldn't rank high on my list, either.

"Then I don't quite understand why you're here."

Her greenish blue eyes fixed themselves on mine. "There was a watch. Your Mr. Wyler mentioned it when we spoke."

I wished she would quit referring to Ben as *my* Mr. Wyler. "And you think you can identify it?"

She leaned down and retrieved her bag from the floor. Head bent, she studied the contents before removing a slip of paper and handing it across the desk to me. When she didn't speak, I glanced at the precise printing laid out on what looked to be a scrap torn from some very expensive stationery.

" 'To Remmy,' " I read aloud, " 'from his own shining Star.' The inscription on the watch, I take it?"

I looked up to find Star Kennedy's eyes locked on my face as if daring me to comment. "Yes. A Cartier. A gift last Christmas."

I matched her unblinking stare while my mind whirled. She'd just told me she'd met Wade in November. That meant this woman had given a ten-thousand-dollar watch to a man she'd known less than a month. She had to be either incredibly gullible or in love.

"You can go to the sheriff, you know. Ask him to find out if this inscription is on the watch they took from the victim. In fact, you could have done it with a phone call. You don't need us for that."

"I don't want my name involved in this . . . this awful thing. I just want to know for certain it's him." She had a red leather organizer in her hand. "Just tell me how much you need to take care of it for me." A hint of a smile worked its way across her lips. "Be generous with yourself. I can afford it."

I shook my head. "I can't take your money for something as simple as making a phone call."

She nodded, as if I'd passed some test. "At least let me pay you for your time this morning."

The accountant in me couldn't disagree. I glanced at my watch. "Our standard rate is a hundred dollars an hour."

Star Kennedy scribbled with her gold pen for a moment and ripped off the check with a flourish. "I'm at the Westin," she said, "the Governor's Suite. You'll let me know?"

"Of course." I slipped the check into my center desk drawer and rose with her.

She extended her hand. "It was lovely to see you again, Bay. Please give my best regards to your father."

Her fingers brushed mine, and she let herself out of my office. I heard her murmur good-bye to Erik as he opened the outer door for her.

I flopped down in my chair and expelled a long breath.

"Well?" Erik asked, materializing in front of me. "Does she think the dead guy is her boyfriend?"

I chuckled. "You do get right to the heart of a thing, don't you?" I picked up my pen from the desk and idly twirled it in my fingers. "There's something more going on here," I said and tossed the paper with the inscription across to him.

"Maybe she just wants the watch back," he said with a grin.

"No, I'm sure that's not it. But . . . I don't know how to explain it."

"You think she was really in love with the guy?"

"I don't know. Maybe. But it's more than that." I looked up to find Erik studying me intently. I shook my head and finally put into words the vague feeling I'd been trying to grab onto.

"It's almost as if she's more afraid it's *not* him."

CHAPTER FIFTEEN

EITHER WYLER WAS AVOIDING ME, OR HE HAD SOMEHOW managed to screw up both his home and cell phones and their accompanying voice mails.

Erik and I had discussed the situation at some length and come to the conclusion we couldn't directly approach the sheriff's office or the coroner without entangling both Karen Zwilling and Star Kennedy in a murder investigation. Even Red couldn't be relied on to check out the watch's inscription without having to answer to someone higher up. That left Ben Wyler. And he'd suddenly dropped off the radar screen. We decided to think about it some more over lunch.

We locked up and rode in Erik's black Expedition to the little Italian place in Port Royal Plaza. Both of us ordered pizza and salad. Over Diet Cokes, Erik cast a quick glance around and lowered his voice. "I meant to tell you something this morning before we got sidetracked by our Atlanta visitor."

"About what?"

"Chuck Matheson and Cliff Morningside."

It took me a moment to recall the case we'd just been bounced from. *How soon they forget,* I said to myself, although a lot had happened in the intervening few days. I smiled at the waitress who delivered our salads and waited while Erik moved his plate next to mine so I could unload the black olives, green pepper, cucumber, and tomatoes.

"Why don't you just order lettuce?" he asked, passing me the salt and pepper.

"A question posed over the years by just about everyone who knows me," I said. "I guess it's because I don't want to be any trouble. A lot of places have the salads already made up ahead of time."

"So this is a magnanimous gesture on your part," he said, grinning.

"Certainly. And you reap the benefits in the form of double vegetables. Now what about the CM² guys? Is Cliff going to be okay?"

"Chuck got to him before he had a chance to hurt himself." Erik swallowed and wiped his mouth on the paper napkin. "I heard he had a gun. Planned to blow his brains out in the motel room. I guess he didn't want to make a mess at home or at the office."

"Let me guess. Turns out he was the one doing the embezzling."

Erik pointed his index finger in my direction. "Bingo! You were absolutely right on the money with figuring out how he'd been doing it. We just had the wrong partner. Seems Cliff had the scam going with a couple of guys who worked the big hotels. He'd dump them stuff on the side, and they'd take it to Savannah or Charleston and sell it under the table. Then they'd all split the cash."

An unsettling thought wormed its way into my mind. "Do you think our investigation of Matheson had anything to do with Cliff's . . . attempt?"

Erik shrugged. "I don't know. Could be. Maybe Grace let something slip to her husband. He obviously knew he wasn't the one cooking the books. Maybe he confronted his partner."

Erik's words made me push the half-eaten salad away. The thought of starting some sort of investigative agency had initially been a lark, a harebrained scheme born from my successful solving of a couple of crimes involving family and friends. Retired from my accounting profession and financially secure enough not to work unless I wanted to, I'd considered it something to keep me from spending the rest of my life in the kind of pampered, useless pursuits I'd always despised my mother for. I hadn't really weighed the possibility that my little foray into detective work might drive someone to suicide.

Erik smiled at me from across the table. "Not your fault."

"I know. I guess."

Neddie Halloran, my old college roommate, always told me I had a God complex, a belief I could somehow control everything and everyone if I just put my mind to it.

"Where'd you get the scuttlebutt?" I asked, dragging the salad back in front of me and spearing a hunk of carrot.

"Around. I hit a couple of bars over the weekend. It's the talk of the food and beverage crowd since most of them know both Cliff and Chuck. And I happened to overhear a couple of off-duty deputies discussing it over beers at Moneypenny's."

Erik moved his salad plate aside as the waitress set huge slices of pizza in front of us. "I wonder how Mrs. Matheson plans on explaining hiring us to her husband."

I snorted. "I wouldn't worry about little Gracie. If ever I saw a woman likely to land on her feet . . . She'll probably tell him she suspected poor Cliff all along."

"I wonder if she still plans to divorce Chuck."

"My guess is it depends on how he ends up financially."

We finished our lunch and stepped out into the sun, the shopping center's usual noontime bustle swollen by the addition of a couple of hundred tourists. I pulled my cell phone from my canvas tote bag and tried Wyler again.

"Where the hell did he disappear to?" I asked rhetorically as I stabbed the disconnect button. "It's just like him. Stir up this hornet's nest with Star Kennedy and then take a powder."

"Got anything for me the rest of the afternoon?" Erik slid behind the wheel of the Expedition.

"Not that I know of. Unless you want to head over to Beaufort and try to track down Win Hammond."

I'd almost forgotten about that mission in all the excitement of having Star Ryan Kennedy appear unannounced in my office.

"I can do that. Give me the addresses of those two guys you've been trying to get in touch with, and I'll see what I can scare up."

A few minutes later we pulled into the office parking lot a couple of spaces from a sleek, deep green Jaguar XJ6. I jumped down from the high seat of Erik's huge SUV to find Ben Wyler, puffing on a long black cigar, leaning casually against the front fender of the Jag.

"Took your sweet time over lunch," he said, uncrossing his ankles. His khaki shorts revealed the nicely formed legs I remembered from our previous encounter at Jump & Phil's. His faded maroon T-shirt looked as if he'd taken a shower in it. A battered Yankees cap rode low over reflective, wraparound shades. "Hotter 'n Hades out here." He blew smoke into the humid midday air. "I should have a key."

"Right this second, or can we go inside first?" I dug my own ring out of my purse and fumbled for the one to the outer door.

The air conditioning hit us like a slap. I marched ahead into my office, dropped my bag on the side table, and pulled the Hammond file from the top cabinet. Ignoring Wyler, I handed Erik the paper with the addresses and phone numbers of Bobby Delacroix and Ray Don Rydel.

Over Erik's shoulder I could see Wyler inspecting the magazines on the low table next to the armchair. A faint, but unmistakable odor drifted in on the frigid air.

"Take that cigar outside!" I yelled, then exhaled slowly and lowered my voice. "You need directions?" I asked Erik.

"I'm sure I can find my way around okay," he said and hustled after Wyler, who had surprisingly taken my orders without a murmur of protest. "I'll keep in touch."

It looked as if they were fighting for the opportunity to be the first one out the door.

By the time Wyler returned, cigar-less, I had seated myself behind the desk and gotten my temper under control.

"Where the hell have you been?" I asked as he flopped himself unceremoniously into the client chair. "I've been trying to reach you all morning."

"So she showed up, huh?" Both his demeanor and his tone seemed orchestrated to tick me off.

"If by 'she' you're referring to Star Kennedy, yes, she did."

I flipped open the folder I'd made up after our new client had taken herself off to her luxurious suite at the Westin. I pushed aside the check, made out to Simpson & Tanner in the amount of one thousand dollars. The figure was, of course, ridiculous for one hour's time and maybe a couple of phone calls. I didn't intend to deposit it. I extracted the scrap of paper with the inscription written on it and handed it to Wyler.

"On the back of the watch, so she says. Think you can get some of your pals to check it out without dragging her name into it?"

He tossed the note back onto my desk. "What's the matter? Did your brother-in-law crap out on you? I thought he was your pipeline into the sheriff's office."

I leaned back in my chair and drew a long, calming breath. "Look, either you can or you can't. Just tell me. I'd think they'd be thrilled to get a positive ID on this guy without having to go to the trouble and expense of checking all those fingerprint and DNA banks."

Wyler's lips twitched in the half-smile that made me feel like a bad-tempered child. "Any other assignments?"

He probably wasn't the most annoying man on the planet, but he sure as hell had to be running a close second to whoever was.

"You were the one who insisted the dead guy isn't Wade. And you also said it wouldn't do much good for anyone to try identifying the corpse. This seems like the best chance of saying one way or the other if it's Randolph Remington Wade tucked into that morgue drawer or not. Am I missing something here?"

His face lost its smug, know-it-all look. "It could help. I'm not sure that would cinch it, though. If it was my case, I'd want something more to back up the watch. Jewelry of that caliber can be stolen."

"Sure it can. But if you couple it with the driver's license?"

"Again, if it was my case, I'd be happier if the wallet had been found in his pocket. It may be a reasonable assumption the two of them go together, but I never like to assume."

"At last! Something we agree on." When he didn't respond, I said, "So can you do it? Find out if the watch has an inscription?"

The smile he turned on me could only be described as wolfish. He rose up a little on the chair and stuffed his hand into his back pocket. He tossed two crumpled color photographs onto the desk. "It doesn't," he said.

I looked from him to the pictures. The first showed the magnificent gold watch, its face studded with diamonds, strapped to a hairy wrist. I shuddered at the blue-tinged skin, wet sand pressed into the folds of the fingers. There was nothing on the reverse side.

"You knew already? About the inscription?"

He shrugged. "I had a feeling."

The phone in the outer office rang. I punched a button and picked up, more to give myself space to think than because I was expecting anything important. "Simpson and Tanner."

"Bay, it's me." Erik's voice sounded tinny and far away.

"What's up?"

"Is Ben still there?"

I eyed Wyler, picking at a hangnail on his left thumb and pretending not to eavesdrop. "Yes," I said.

"Good. I checked in with Miss Hammond on my way out of town. To see if she'd heard anything from her brother in the last couple of days."

Something I should have thought of myself. "Good call." I swiveled myself around until I had my back to Wyler. "Is there a problem?"

"I'm not sure. She said she hasn't talked to Win since the night he took off, but that guy's been back. The Jamaican. The one you tossed out of her place?"

I sat upright in the chair. "He came to her apartment again?"

"Yeah," Erik said. "Just a little while ago. She didn't let him in. Didn't even answer the door. But she says she looked through the peephole, and it was definitely the same man."

I didn't like the sound of that at all. "I'll get over there and talk to her. Thanks, Erik. Good work."

"You should take Ben with you. In case this guy's still hanging around."

I gritted my teeth and said calmly, "I can handle it."

"I know, but if—"

"I said I can handle it."

"You're the boss. I'll let you know how I make out over here. Seems there might be more urgency than we thought about locating Mr. Hammond."

I sighed. "I'm afraid you're right. If you run into any problems in Beaufort, call the Judge. He can smooth out any wrinkles you might encounter."

"Gotcha. I'll be in touch."

I glanced back to find Wyler studying my face as I hung up the phone. "Trouble?" he asked.

"Could be. I have to leave now." I filed Star's folder in the pending drawer and pointed at the photos of the watch still resting in the center of my desk. "Can I have those? I'll need to show them to Mrs. Kennedy."

"I'll get copies made for you. I think I should hang on to these for a while." He stuffed the pictures back into his pocket.

I shrugged and picked up my bag. "Suit yourself." I waited for him to get up out of the chair, but he simply sat and stared at me. "I'm leaving now. I need to run something down. For a client," I added as an afterthought.

"I'll come with you," he said, uncrossing his legs and rising. "Since it's business."

I bit my tongue and headed for the door. "Suit yourself," I repeated, "but you'll have to drive your own car."

I locked up, and we headed for the parking lot.

"Sure you don't want to try out my little beauty?" he asked, stopping at the front fender of the Jaguar.

"Another time. I really need to get to Miss Addie's. She lives at The Cedars."

"I know," Wyler replied.

I pondered on that as I slid behind the wheel of the Thunderbird and whipped the air over to max. How did Ben Wyler know where Miss Addie lived? And why was it of any interest to him? As I glanced in my rearview mirror to watch the beautiful classic Jag ease behind me into the traffic, I also pondered the discussion Erik's call had interrupted. We'd never gotten around to the real mysteries of the dead man on the beach: Why had he been impersonating Randolph Remington Wade, and who the hell was he?

CHAPTER
SIXTEEN

THOUGH MOST OF THE THREE O'CLOCK TRAFFIC WAS headed off the island, it was still slow going. I took advantage of a red light at the entrance to Palmetto Dunes to call Miss Addie and tell her she had company on the way. I also needed passes to get through security.

Wyler stayed right on my tail around the Sea Pines circle and out Palmetto Bay Road. When I turned left a couple of miles later, the Jaguar got stuck at the light. I slowed to a crawl until Wyler caught back up, and he followed me into The Cedars. I pulled up to Miss Addie's building and stepped out into a dizzying wave of heat and humidity. I waited for him to park the Jaguar at the far end of the lot. I assumed he didn't want any careless old folks leaving dents in his vintage car. I couldn't say I blamed him.

"I need to fill you in," I said as we approached the door to the lobby.

I gave him a quick rundown of the Hammond family history and Win's disappearances, both the one twenty years ago and that of the week before. I described the man I'd encountered that night and his seeming knowledge of Hammond's background, including the false name he'd been using in the islands.

"Hang on a sec," Wyler said, waving an index finger at me as he moved back outside.

I waited until he'd walked up and down the entire row of vehicles parked next to the building and stepped back into the lobby.

"What are you looking for?" I asked. "I already did a quick check of the parked cars. There's nobody lurking inside any of them."

"I know," he said, gesturing toward the elevator. "We goin' up?"

"Then what was that all about?" I punched the Up arrow and tapped my foot in frustration at both his clipped answer and the slowness of the elevator.

"Looking for rental tags," he said as the doors slid open. "If the guy you're talking about came here from the Caribbean, he sure as hell didn't drive his own car."

Score one for the professionals. "I didn't think of that," I admitted.

Ben Wyler shrugged. "Takes practice. You'll get better."

I hoped to hell he was right.

Miss Addie did me proud, demanding in a loud voice to know who was there when I rang the bell. The pause between my reply and the opening of the door made me certain she'd taken the time to check us out through the peephole as well. I introduced Wyler as an associate of the firm, and she seemed to accept it without question, ushering us both in and immediately offering iced tea.

I smiled watching my companion study the incredible jumble of priceless antiques, paintings, and bric-a-brac, as my father called it, while Miss Addie scurried around in the kitchen. He seemed especially interested in several crude figures I'd always assumed were pre-Columbian artifacts, although I didn't know enough about them to be certain.

It also did my heart good to watch his veneer of New York cynicism melt under Adelaide Boyce Hammond's considerable Southern charm. The fluttering little bird had the big bad wolf eating out of her hand in a matter of minutes.

Wyler even went so far as to remove his baseball cap in her presence. *Lord have mercy!*

After a few minutes of general chitchat, Wyler took over the conversation.

"Does your brother have a key to your apartment?" he asked while Miss Addie refilled his glass from an icy pitcher on the butler's tray.

"Why, of course he does. I gave him my spare the first night."

"Any others floating around?"

She took her time considering the question. "The cleaning people. And the office in the administration building. They keep a copy in case any of the residents misplaces theirs or needs assistance, and so they can let the pest control folks in once a month."

"So three besides your own. Are all these people trustworthy? Ever had any trouble with theft or vandalism?" Wyler leaned over and rested his elbows on his knees.

Miss Addie glanced at me before replying. "A long time ago," she said, "but that's been resolved. No one here now has ever given me the slightest cause for concern."

"I'd like the names of the other key holders, if you have them."

Again Adelaide Hammond flicked her gaze at me. "Oh, dear, well, I suppose . . . I don't quite understand what you're getting at, Mr. Wyler. Sally and her sister have been taking care of me for years. And I really don't know about the bug company. They're hired by the condominium association, although I've never heard the first hint of any problems."

I knew Wyler had to be thinking about someone being bribed for a key. Miss Addie wasn't stupid, and I could tell by the stricken look on her face she'd figured that out, too. I tried to get his attention so I could send him a silent signal to quit scaring the old lady to death, but he ignored me.

"I don't think it's a huge problem," he said with the engaging smile that transformed his face. "Still, it doesn't hurt to explore all the possibilities. Once we eliminate the unlikely, we can concentrate on what we need to do to keep you safe."

Miss Addie seemed flustered under his continued stare. "I have the information on Sally and Janet in my papers. Because of taxes, you understand." She half rose from her chair before sinking back down with a sigh. "Lydia, you know where I keep my records. Would you mind . . . ?"

"Of course not." As I passed Wyler, who still refused to look at me, I jabbed his arm in an attempt to get him to shut up about stolen keys and danger. He didn't even flinch. "Why don't you give Ben a little history of some of your things?" I said on my way down the hall to the bedrooms. That should keep him from getting another word in, at least until I got back.

I stepped into Miss Addie's room and crossed to her beautiful rosewood desk tucked into the corner near the windows. The expansive view across the marsh drew my eye, and I paused to watch a flock of ibis probing with their long, curved bills in the pluff mud glistening in the afternoon sunlight. The tall, green marsh grass undulated in the breeze off Bishop's Reach where a lone sailboat glided toward the Intracoastal Waterway.

I pulled my gaze away and opened the right-hand drawer.

The folder I needed still bore the heading for Lawton Merriweather's firm, along with his office address and phone numbers. But he was gone, dead just a few months after my father's close call the previous summer. The grief struck me like a slap, and I sank onto the worn needlepoint seat of the delicately carved chair.

Law had gone to the office, as he always did, despite the fact that his clients had dwindled to a few old friends like Miss Addie. And me. When he didn't come home for lunch, his wife had called the Judge, who'd alerted the two remaining members of the Thursday night poker club. Boyd Allison and Charlie Seldon found their friend slumped over his desk.

A massive coronary had been the ruling, quick and final.

The funeral at St. Helena Episcopal Church in Beaufort had necessitated shutting down streets for blocks around the eighteenth-century landmark. No one could remember another service which overflowed that huge old sanctuary and spilled out onto the porches and lawns. My father had delivered a stirring eulogy for his oldest and dearest friend, his first truly public appearance since the onset of his strokes almost a decade before.

Within a few weeks, Miss Amelia, Law's wife of more than fifty years, had grieved her way into the plot next to his in Riverdale Cemetery.

I crossed to the nightstand and pulled a tissue from the box, blew my nose, and ordered myself to snap out of it. Lawton Merriweather had been more than just my attorney and my friend. All my life he had been a calm, soothing counterpoint to my father's fiery temper and frequently disappointed expectations of me, and I had loved him. He and the Judge and Miss Addie were all nearly the same age. I refused to examine the cold lump of fear that thought laid on my heart.

Since Law's death, I'd taken over the financial part of Miss Addie's personal business. I sniffled back the last of the tears, copied out Sally Ann and Janet Effie Jones's address and phone number onto a slip of paper, and headed back to the living room.

"My late father absolutely despised Constable," I heard Miss Addie saying as I resumed my seat. She stood before the fireplace gazing fondly at the dark landscape in its heavy gilt frame. "Papa always called him 'that overpriced dabbler,' but Mama wouldn't be swayed." She smiled at me. "Lydia knows, don't you, my dear? Mama may have been a lady, but she almost always got her way."

I thrust the paper at Wyler. "I think this is a waste of time, but here's the information on Sally and Janet. They've been helping out Miss Addie for years."

He rose and picked up his baseball cap from the side table next to the sofa. "I'm sure you're right, Lydia," he said with a wicked grin, "but better safe than sorry, no?" Before I could formulate a suitably stinging rebuke for his use of my hated first name, he spoke to Miss Addie. "Thanks for your hospitality and for the chance to see all your wonderful antiques. When I get ready to furnish my own little house, perhaps I could call on you for advice?"

Miss Addie tittered and batted her eyelashes. "Why, I'd be honored, sir."

Wyler took her tiny hand in both of his. "You keep that door locked, okay? I don't want you letting in anyone you haven't known since the Hoover administration. Except for me, of course."

I stared openmouthed at this blast of unexpected charm from the generally taciturn former New York detective. Miss Addie chirped her birdlike laugh as I led the way to the door. "You'll call me if you hear from Win?"

"Of course, dear. But I'm really not all that worried anymore, especially since one of your father's friends saw him in Beaufort over the weekend. I'm sure he's just off renewing old acquaintances and reminiscing with his friends." She patted my arm. "Don't you put yourself out trying to track him down. He's just like Papa. When he's ready to come home, he will."

Again I paused in the hallway until I heard the locks click into place.

"I don't like leaving her here alone," Ben Wyler said, stabbing the elevator button with more force than was necessary. "Why don't you take her to your place?"

"First of all because she wouldn't come. Miss Addie may appear to be a dithering old darling, but she's got her head screwed on right. Most of the time, anyway. She sees it as her mission to safeguard the Hammond family treasures." I stepped ahead of him into the narrow car and punched the button for the first floor. "Besides, I think maybe between the two of us we've impressed on her the need to take this whole mystery man thing seriously. She'll be okay."

"I hope you're right."

We crossed the lobby and moved out into the heat. "Now what?" I asked, stopping under the shading limbs of a tall sycamore.

"Hey, you're the one with her name on the stationery," Wyler said with a twist of his lips before adding, "Lydia."

"I'm glad you find yourself so amusing," I said, with only a little rancor. I hated to admit it, but the guy was growing on me. I dug my keys out of the tote bag. "Are you going to check out Sally and Janet? They live over in Hardeeville."

"I don't think it's urgent," he said, sobering, "although I don't like the idea of all these people having keys to her place."

"You're not in the big, bad city anymore, Detective," I said. "Granted we have our share of crime down here, but there are still lots of folks who don't think a thing about leaving their doors unlocked. In the older communities like Beaufort and St. Helena, it's almost a way of life."

"A stupid one, if you ask me." He raised a hand before I could reply. "I'll save the cleaning ladies as a last resort." He jingled his own keys at me. "I think I'll take a run at the rental car companies over at the airport, see if I can find out what kind of car our Jamaican friend is driving. It could help us track down where he's staying."

"So you are taking that part of Miss Addie's troubles seriously."

"I take it all seriously. Haven't you worked out yet what's probably going down here?"

I bristled at the implied criticism in his voice. "No, I guess I haven't. Why don't you enlighten me?"

Wyler shrugged. "Well, it's just a crazy-ass theory at this point, but haven't you wondered about the connection between this Hammond and the dead guy on the beach?"

I stared at him as if he'd lost his mind. "What connection?"

"Boats," he said without missing a beat. "Hammond drove one. Wade owns one."

"Along with a few million other people," I said. "Besides, we've just pretty much proved the murder victim isn't Wade." I gestured toward his back pocket and the photos he'd stuck there. "No inscription on the watch."

"Assumption," he replied. "We haven't *proved* a damn thing. But say you're right. Then who is the dead guy? Why was he impersonating Wade?" He paused, apparently waiting for me to comment on the brilliance of his deductions. When I remained silent, he added, "And most important of all, where is the real Randolph Remington Wade?"

"You still haven't connected all this to Win Hammond."

"Did the Kennedy broad tell you about the little voyage she and her boyfriend had planned?"

It took a moment for the pieces to click into place. "The Virgin Islands," I said, and Wyler smiled.

"Old Edwin's home turf. Still think I'm nuts?"

"Yes," I said with a grin, "but you're sure as hell not stupid."

"Neither are you. I can tell by your face you'd already worked most of this out for yourself."

"Everything but the connection to Win." I watched an elderly couple roll sedately into the parking lot and pull their huge Cadillac in next to Wyler's Jaguar. "I still think that's pretty tenuous."

He noticed the Caddy and edged away from me toward his car. "You told me a long time ago you don't believe in coincidences." His eyes darted back and forth between me and the Jag.

"I don't. But sometimes things that look as if they're connected really do turn out to be happenstance."

Wyler backed up a couple of steps.

"Serendipity," I added.

"I'll be in touch," Wyler called over his shoulder as he jogged toward his car.

I watched him reach the Cadillac seconds before the sprightly woman in the bright yellow warm-up suit could swing her door open more than a few inches. Wyler caught it and eased it the rest of the way, his body protecting the gleaming finish of his restored Jaguar. They were too far away for me to hear the conversation, but I could pretty much guess the dialogue from the old lady's bubbling laugh.

First Miss Addie, and now this. I wondered if a woman had to be over seventy to touch Ben Wyler's heart. *Not that I really give a damn,* I told myself.

I drove back to Port Royal Plantation and eased into my garage just before five o'clock. The usual late-afternoon thunderheads marched silently across the horizon and seemed to merge into the flat gray of the ocean. My cell phone chimed the first few notes of Beethoven as I dropped my bag on the console table in the foyer.

I checked the caller ID. "Hey, Erik, what's up?"

"I think I know where Win is hanging out," he said, "but I haven't actually seen him."

"Where?" I mounted the steps into the kitchen and pulled open the refrigerator door.

"At Delacroix's place. I talked to one of the neighbors, and she said there'd been a lot of traffic in and out for the last couple of days."

"And she volunteered this information because . . . ?" I'd had to reprimand Erik a couple of times before for implying he was a police officer, even if he didn't come right out and say so. The ploy generally worked, but it could also get our license pulled. Not to mention put Erik's butt in the slammer for a few months.

"Strictly legit," he said, reading my mind. "I told her I was an old pal of Bobby's, and he'd invited me to stay with him anytime I happened to be in town. She doesn't know him, just moved in herself a couple of months ago, but she remarked he'd have to buy more groceries since he seemed to be running a B&B over there. I'm assuming that means Win Hammond, but I don't know for certain." He paused. "I'd like to stick around and stake the place out."

"Okay, but remember you're on your own time now. We aren't billing Miss Addie."

"Understood. I don't have to be at work tomorrow until noon, so I'll just sit here and see what shakes out."

"Be careful," I said before hanging up.

Nothing in the freezer looked appealing, and besides I wasn't really hungry, so I poured a glass of tea. I set it on the counter while I changed clothes, retrieved a pad and pen from the office, and carried it all out to the screened deck. Time for one of my famous lists. Maybe it was the accounting, but laying out a problem in neat rows and columns always helped me get a better grip on things.

I sipped tea and jotted notes as the sky darkened over the ocean and lightning flashes lit the bottoms of the clouds. I paused to watch a sheet of rain move across the water parallel to the beach and just offshore. The wind, salt-laden and almost chilly, felt wonderful. I dropped my eyes back to the legal pad.

What do we think, what do we know, what can we prove? It had been my late husband's formula for examining a case when he had been the head of a special task force attached to the state attorney general's office, his mission to track down the money end of the drug trade. I had been trying to apply it to the circumstances surrounding the body on the beach.

Under the second category, I listed the facts. A man claiming to be Randolph Wade had taken a room at the Holiday Inn Express, engaged the services of at least two women from local escort services, and subsequently raped them on a boat he claimed to own. In one instance he had used a not very clever variation on that name as an alias. Shortly after the attack on Karen Zwilling, a man answering his description had been bludgeoned to death and left on the beach. The body had been stripped of identification except for a distinctive watch. Later, a wallet containing a driver's license issued to Wade had been found in the vicinity of the attack. Newspaper photos linked Wade to Star Ryan Kennedy, who claimed she had given him an expensive watch with an inscription on the back. The watch found on the body carried no such inscription.

Ergo, I said to myself, *the murder victim is not Randolph Wade.*

I studied the list and could find no holes in the logic. My stomach growled, but I ignored it and pressed ahead.

Win Hammond had been a boat captain on Virgin Gorda. He insisted unnamed creditors had followed him back to the Lowcountry to settle old scores. I moved that second item over to the What Do We Think? column, since I had no independent verification of it, although the appearance of the Jamaican at Miss Addie's door—twice—gave a certain credence to his claim. Less than twenty-four hours after arriving back in the States, Win had disappeared from his sister's condo, apparently with nothing more than the clothes on his back and a supposedly empty suitcase. He might have been spotted in Beaufort, but that couldn't be proved. He could be holing up with one of his old friends, but again that had to remain an assumption.

I leaned my head against the back of the chaise and studied the lists. Nothing there hinted at any connection between Win Hammond and Wade. Or whoever the murder victim turned out to be. Unlike Wyler, I discounted Star Kennedy's claim she and her lover had been planning a cruise to Win's old stomping grounds in Virgin Gorda. Lots of locals with oceangoing yachts sailed to the Caribbean. Besides, the American and British Virgins were made up of dozens of little islands. No matter what Wyler said, sometimes things really were just coincidence.

I set the pad aside and let my mind drift as the sun fought its way out of the storm clouds now moving south toward Savannah. Long trails of Spanish moss dripping from the twisted limbs of the ancient live oaks surrounding the deck swayed rhythmically in the breeze . . .

I couldn't have been dozing for more than a few minutes when the shrill of the phone inside the house jerked me awake. I stumbled across the great room and up the steps into the kitchen but didn't make it before the answering machine kicked on. I shook my head to clear the cobwebs just as the canned message ended and a familiar voice blasted from the speaker.

"Bay? If you're there, pick up the phone. I mean it. Pick up."

I smiled as Doctor Nedra Halloran, child psychologist extraordinaire, took a breath and gathered herself for another attack.

"Damn it, Tanner, don't you screen me!"

"Okay, okay," I said to the disembodied voice. The outburst was so typically Neddie. But as I reached for the phone, I heard a catch in her voice, and her next words came out almost as a wail.

"Bay, please! For God's sake, pick up the phone! I need your help. Now!"

I snatched up the receiver.

CHAPTER SEVENTEEN

$\mathscr{I}$T TOOK ME A GOOD TEN MINUTES TO CALM MY OLD college roommate down. I carried the portable phone back out to the deck and dropped once again on the chaise, the legal pad I'd been using to work out the mystery of Randolph Remington Wade flipped to a clean page.

Professionally, Neddie Halloran had always been the quintessential shrink: calm, logical, soft-spoken. Once she'd stepped out of her designer suits and sensible pumps, however, she could be as erratic and flamboyant as one would expect from a woman whose wild red curls tumbled down her back and whose flashing Irish eyes seemed to dart from place to place looking for mischief. In the brief time we'd spent together at Northwestern, Neddie had led me into more trouble than I'd managed to stir up in the previous twenty years of my life put together.

"So let me get this straight," I said, pulling up my knees and resting the notepad on them. "You have a patient who's gone missing, and you want me to find her. Does that about sum it up?"

"In a nutshell. So what do you think?"

"If you're that concerned, I think you should call the police, which is what I told you from the start."

"And I told you I can't do that. At least not yet."

There seemed to be some sort of epidemic of women in distress who refused to do the logical thing. Karen Zwilling I could sort of understand. And Star Kennedy. But Neddie's reluctance was harder to fathom.

"I realize you feel responsible because this teenager disappeared from your office, but that's no reason for you to take on the responsibility of tracking her down. The cops have resources I can't even approach. They put out a missing-persons alert, and you've got thousands of pairs of eyes looking for her. What the hell can I do that's better than that?"

"Are you going to make me go through it all again? What do you need, Tanner, words of one syllable?"

"I need you to quit being a smart-ass and start making some sense. This girl had an appointment in your office. You got an emergency call and asked her to step into the reception area while you took it. When you went to bring her back in, she was gone. How does any of that make this your problem?" I lowered my voice to a more reasonable tone. "In fact, I still don't understand why you're so worried about her. What aren't you telling me?"

I waited while she decided how much information she could share without violating the girl's doctor-patient confidentiality.

"You know I take some pro bono cases, usually juvenile court referrals, and most of the time those kids aren't exactly the cream of Savannah society. This one is . . . really messed up." She sighed. "Let's just say Yancey may have a little problem with putting things up her nose God never intended to go there."

"Doesn't she have parents? Other relatives?"

"I've called every contact number I have, including her social worker and her public defender. I even went to her house. No one's heard a word from her in three days."

This time the silence lasted for a full minute before I broke it.

"Neddie, look. You said Carolann told you the girl took a call on her cell phone, then simply walked out the door under her own power. It's not exactly a kidnapping. And I certainly don't believe anyone can hold you civilly liable when a fifteen-year-old girl voluntarily leaves your office. Don't you think you might be overreacting again?"

I heard her sharp intake of breath a second before the crash of the phone slamming into the cradle.

I waited a moment, then clicked the Off button and walked back into the kitchen. I refilled my glass with sweet tea and pulled a box of graham crackers out of the cupboard. Back on the deck I watched the sun spread fingers of orange and plum across the bottoms of the dissipating storm clouds. When the phone rang, I checked my watch. A little over five minutes. *Not bad,* I thought to myself. Neddie's snits generally lasted a good fifteen.

I picked up the handset and waited.

"I'm sorry, okay? I know you're right, but it doesn't matter. Legal or not, I *feel* responsible."

Again she hesitated, and the silence stretched out. I crunched a few crackers and washed them down while I waited.

"I know you understand that I'm severely limited in what I can reveal. But let's say—hypothetically—that a young girl runs with a rough crowd, and she has a boyfriend who has a hard time distinguishing her from a punching bag. Let's further assume that her mother disappeared when she was barely ten, and her father is . . . well, not a particularly good influence. And let's say she may know some things that . . . certain people might prefer she didn't divulge. Would any of that change your mind?"

"Not really. Hold on!" I snapped before she could work up a good head of steam. "Hear me out. It's tragic, it stinks, I hate it. I don't know how you can put yourself in the way of these kinds of kids day after day after day. It would absolutely break me. But if you have reason to believe that this child has been taken against her will or is in serious danger, I don't see one single way you can avoid involving the authorities."

"But I can't! That's why I called you." Neddie took a deep breath. "There's more to this than I can tell you, Bay." Again the pause. "I promised to keep her safe."

"You had no business making a promise like that, Neddie. And it's really unfair of you to ask me to keep it for you."

The anger rushed out of her in a long, muted sigh. "You're right. I just don't know what else to do."

I lowered my own rhetoric a few notches. "I'm telling you what to do. If you honestly believe she could be in jeopardy, get her description into the hands of the police. Let them handle it. There's really no other viable solution, and you know it."

"I'll think about it," she said. "I'm sorry I hung up on you."

"Not a problem. I'm kind of getting used to it after all these years."

"I can be a giant pain in the ass, can't I?"

"Mammoth," I agreed.

I waited through another charged silence. "Listen, Bay, can I call you again? If she doesn't turn up?"

"Of course you can. Don't be a dolt. But think long and hard about calling the police. Deal?"

"Deal," she said. "See ya."

"Bye," I said to the dial tone buzzing in my ear.

I ate peanut butter out of the jar, dropped the spoon into the empty dishwasher, and called it close enough for dinner. I tried to settle again to the three-columned assessment of the Randolph Wade scenario but gave up when I found my mind wandering to Neddie's problem. How did two nice girls like us, from good families, with superior educations, manage to get ourselves into such messes? And Neddie's function lately had been to get me *out* of disasters, not create new ones.

More black clouds were massing on the horizon as I gave up the effort and carried all my paraphernalia back indoors. In the office, I pulled out the local phone book and jotted down the number of the Westin Hotel. Star Kennedy's suite didn't answer, so I left a voice mail with the automated system. On impulse, I slipped on a pair of slacks and cotton sweater, grabbed my bag, and headed for the garage. Perhaps the former Beaufort socialite was having dinner, and I could catch her in one of the dining rooms. I suddenly felt the need to deliver the news in person. It seemed cruel to make her wait any longer to find out the body on the sand was not her Remmy.

It took less than five minutes to make my way to the grand resort hotel sprawling across the beach just a few dozen yards from the roiling ocean, which had turned a deep gray-green. The outer edge of the next approaching storm sent whitecaps slapping onto the wide stretch of sand. Most of the hotel's visitors had been chased inside by the earlier rain squall, but a few hardy souls wandered along the edge of the surf, their clothes flapping in the freshening wind. Early twilight had set in, and most of the resort's lights had clicked on in the gloom.

I let the young man at the valet stand park the Thunderbird and wandered inside to the massive lobby. Straight ahead through tall windows I could see a few diehard tourists still stretched out on chaises next to the pool. I moved along a hallway to the swankiest of the Westin's three restaurants. I figured anyone who could afford the Governor's Suite wouldn't eat anywhere except the Barony Grill with its understated elegance and unique wine-tasting room.

Star Kennedy sat in solitary splendor at a damask-covered table just inside the door. She'd exchanged her suit for a clingy crepe dress in a fabulous blue that highlighted her deep tan and champagne blond hair. In the muted overhead light and a single, flickering candle, she looked younger than I did. At least from a distance.

She glanced up over the rim of her glass of ruby red wine as I stepped through into the low hum of conversation in the sparsely populated restaurant, and I saw the jolt of alarm go through her. I bypassed the hovering maître d' and walked quickly to her table.

"It's not him," I said without preamble, and her trembling hand returned the sloshing glass of wine to the white cloth.

"Ma'am?" A waiter had materialized beside me.

"Thanks," I said, and he pulled out the chair, a menu appearing in front of me before I had a chance to drop my bag onto the floor.

"No, thank you," I said, "not right now," and he disappeared as quietly as he'd come.

"Tell me," my mother's former protégée said as I pushed the gold-rimmed charger away and folded my hands on the table.

"The watch didn't have any inscription."

"You're positive?"

"I saw photos of it myself. It looks like what you described, but the back is blank."

I don't know exactly what I had expected her reaction to be, but Star Kennedy continued to frown at me across the gleaming stemware and cutlery.

"I thought you'd be relieved," I said.

"Of course I am. Thank you. It's just . . ." She dabbed absently at the corners of her mouth with her heavy napkin and returned it to her lap. She gathered herself and forced the semblance of a smile. "I'd steeled myself for bad news. It seemed so likely. And now—"

"You're not quite sure how to react," I finished for her.

"I appreciate your coming in person. It was kind of you."

"Not a problem. By the way, I'll be returning your check. I assume I can send it to the address that's printed on the face of it."

Light crackled in eyes which a few moments before had seemed opaque and lifeless. "You'll do no such thing!"

"Look, Star, I didn't earn a penny of it. The information fell into my lap without my even having to make a phone call."

"Nonetheless, I insist you keep it. Now we'll say no more about it. I've quite made up my mind." She paused only long enough to wave a hand heavy with diamonds in the direction of someone behind me. "You'll join me for dinner," she said, and the taciturn waiter appeared at my elbow. "A menu, please, for my guest."

"I've already eaten," I said, but the massive, tasseled bill of fare snapped open in front of my face, and I had no choice but to take it.

"A salad then, perhaps," Star said. "They do a wonderful Caesar with lobster and crab."

Water and ice tinkled from a crystal pitcher into one of the glasses in front of me. The waiter stepped back and eyed me expectantly.

"Fine," I said. Sometimes you just have to take the path of least resistance.

"Excellent choice," the young man crooned before gliding away.

Star beamed her approval. "Well, this is lovely. I've so wanted to catch up on things in Beaufort." She eased back in her chair, a lot of her former anxiety seeming to ebb away as she raised the glass to her lips.

I really didn't want to get into a history lesson on the past twenty years in the Lowcountry, so I decided to get my own questions into play before we got lost in the potholes of memory lane. "What will you do now?" I asked.

"What do you mean?"

"I'm assuming you haven't heard from Mr. Wade and haven't been able to contact him, otherwise there'd be no reason for you to expect him to have been the . . . victim. Do you have any idea at all where he could be?"

The haughty mask I remembered from my girlhood snapped into place over the well-tended face of Star Kennedy. "I really don't think that need concern you," she said in the same imperious voice my late mother had often employed to put upstarts in their place.

"Sooner or later you're going to have to talk to someone about it," I said, leaning back as the waiter set a basket of rolls on the table between us.

"I don't understand."

"It's fairly obvious this man, whoever he is, has been impersonating your . . ." I paused and saw her eyes darken in alarm. "Your friend. The police are going to want to know who he is, why he had Wade's driver's license on him, and where the real Randolph Wade is." I didn't want to be unnecessarily cruel, but the question had to be asked. "Aren't you afraid this imposter may have harmed the real Wade in some way? How else would he have gotten his identification and wallet?"

I watched the superior smile die on her lips. "You think this other man may have killed him?" she croaked.

"Don't you?" I countered. "Unless you've got another explanation."

Suddenly the hand bearing the impossibly huge diamond shot

across the table and gripped my wrist. "You have to find him," Star Kennedy said. "I have to know if he's dead or alive."

I twisted my arm away from her clawlike grasp and dropped my hands into my lap. Unconsciously I rubbed the scratch where the ring had bitten into my skin.

"That's not the way to go about soliciting my help," I said as evenly as I could manage.

"Oh, my dear, I'm sorry! Truly! You must forgive me. It's just . . . Well, you have no idea the strain I've been under these past weeks."

Weeks? I thought. The body had been found only a few days before. There was another agenda boiling just below the surface of Star Kennedy's stricken expression, and I intended to find out exactly what it was.

CHAPTER EIGHTEEN

I FOUND BEN WYLER'S MESSAGE WHEN I TRUDGED INTO the house shortly after ten o'clock. I debated whether or not to call him back while I stripped off my clothes and pulled on the old T-shirt that had become my nightwear of choice since I'd stopped sharing my bed with anyone except Sam Spade and his fictional brethren.

In the end I decided just to get it over with. The drop in the barometer accompanying the rumbling storms which seemed destined to pound the island for the rest of eternity had set my face throbbing and a pain like a sharp knife spiking through my right eye. I tossed back two sinus tablets and put the kettle on for tea before punching in the number.

"Yeah? This is Wyler." His voice sounded raspy, the few words slightly slurred, and I wondered if he'd been drinking or if I'd gotten him out of bed.

"It's Bay. Your message said you had some news?"

"Right." He paused as if gathering his thoughts. "I took a little spin over to Savannah when I struck out at the local airport. Henry Littlejohn."

I frowned, which only made my head feel worse. "What the hell are you talking about?"

"Wake up, woman. The Jamaican. The guy who's been bugging Miss Hammond?"

"Well, why didn't you just say so? Look, Wyler, I'm not in the mood for any of your games right now. I've got a sinus headache. I just want to drink some tea and crawl into bed."

His low chuckle could have been interpreted in any number of ways I didn't like, but I couldn't muster the energy to call him on it.

"Anything else?" I asked.

"He's driving a blue Ford Taurus with Georgia plates. You want me to give the old lady a heads-up?"

"Don't call Miss Addie 'the old lady.' And no. I'll take care of it."

"We *are* cranky tonight, aren't we? Maybe I'd better save the rest of it for another day."

"What rest of it?"

"I had a little informal chat with Morgan, the death investigator for the sheriff's office. Without mentioning any names, I let him know he needs to ramp up his investigation of the dead guy. Fingerprints, DNA, the whole shot. I pretty much guaranteed him it's not this Randolph Wade."

The kettle whistled, and I tucked the handset between my cheek and shoulder and set about making tea. "How'd he take it?" I asked, pouring the steaming water over the chamomile in the old, chipped Wedgewood teapot. I dunked the bags up and down a few times and set it aside to steep.

Ben Wyler snorted. "Not too great, actually, but I think he knows me well enough—at least by reputation—that he took it seriously. You talk to the Kennedy woman yet?"

"I just got back from the Westin." I pulled a mug from the cupboard and filled it, then inhaled the fragrant steam. I could almost feel the tightness in my face easing a little. "There's something weird going on there, too."

"Weird like how?"

I sipped and exhaled gratefully, maneuvered my way down the steps, and curled up on the white sofa in the great room. Outside, thunder rumbled, reverberating off the open water and enveloping the house in waves of sound, and lightning crackled along the beach. It felt as if the storm were raging inside my head.

"I can't do this right now," I said. "Can we pick it up tomorrow?"

There was a long silence before Wyler answered. "Sure, no problem. Take care of yourself, okay? Put a slug of whiskey in that tea and get yourself to bed."

"Okay, Mom," I said, and he laughed.

"I'll check in on you in the morning. Good night."

I pondered on the sudden softness in his voice as I left the half-drunk tea on the side table and stumbled off to my room.

I dreamed Rob and I were building a house—*this* house, it seemed, although it wasn't on the beach. It must have been somewhere up north because I could feel myself shivering, a cold wind blowing across my bare arms and legs. I was pounding on a nail, one specific nail, and in the way of dreams, no matter how hard or how often I struck it, the head never moved any farther into the wood. Again and again I slammed the hammer into it while the piercing wind whistled around me and . . .

"*Señora?*"

I jumped into wakefulness as Dolores gently shook my shoulder. The remnants of the previous night's headache still lingered behind my eyes, and I kept the lids firmly shut against the slivers of light trying to force their way through.

"What?" I mumbled.

"*Señora, discúlpeme. Miles perdones.* But Mr. Red, he says he must see you. *Ahora.* Now."

Even with my eyes closed I could sense her tiny hands fluttering in distress. I squinted up at her through narrow slits. "Tell him to go away."

"But *Señora* . . ."

I groaned and gathered myself to roll over when I realized I was sprawled on my stomach, crossways on the bed, with half the length of my legs hanging over the edge. I clutched at the sheet and found it bunched up beneath me.

"Please, Dolores! For God's sake, make him go away."

"I'm not going anywhere, Bay, so make up your mind to it. You've got some explaining—"

The cannon of his voice was cut off by Dolores's screech of outrage.

I opened my eyes to see my tiny Guatemalan housekeeper pushing ineffectively at my brother-in-law's chest as he stood open-mouthed in the doorway to my bedroom, and at the same moment I realized I was absolutely naked.

I made him wait while I showered and dressed, taking my time in the hope I'd be able to gather the few remaining shreds of my dignity about me before I had to face Red Tanner. Half an hour later, covered nearly from head to toe in slacks and a long-sleeved shirt, I raised my chin a fraction higher than normal and strode into the kitchen.

Dolores had covered her own embarrassment, as she did most problems, with food and silence. My brother-in-law sat at the round table in the bay window sipping coffee, an empty, egg yolk–smeared plate in front of him. Toast crumbs littered the placemat. I held up my hand as my housekeeper turned toward me, her spatula raised expectantly.

"I don't want anything, Dolores. Really. I just need some tea."

For once, she simply nodded and lifted the simmering kettle from the stovetop.

Red set down his coffee cup and blushed. "Bay, I'm really sorry. I—"

"Just shut up, Tanner, okay?

He slumped in his chair.

"Were you banging on the door earlier?" I asked him as Dolores set the mug of Earl Grey in front of me.

"*Es culpa mía, Señora*. I was in laundry. Not hear the bell."

"Don't worry about it. It's just that . . . I was dreaming about pounding nails." I sipped tea and regarded Red over the rim of my cup. "So what's so damned important you have to come invading my house in the middle of the night?"

"First of all," he said, suppressing the beginnings of a smile, "it's after nine o'clock in the morning. And I'm sorry about barging in on you like that. I should have waited for Dolores to wake you up."

"Damn straight. You're lucky I wasn't sleeping with the Seecamp under my pillow."

The smile erupted into a genuine grin. "Would have served me right."

The restorative power of the caffeine had worked its way into my bloodstream, and I felt myself relax. Red had looked so shocked standing there in my doorway with the diminutive Dolores beating on his chest. I could almost begin to see the humor in the situation. After all, it wasn't as if other men hadn't seen me naked. Not a lot of them, but I was far from a blushing virgin.

Still, in the shower earlier, with warm water cascading across my skin, I'd faced the real reason for my embarrassment. Red was now one of only a handful of people who had looked fully upon my disfigurement, the ugly raised scars crisscrossing my left shoulder, the puckered skin at the edge of the grafts. I was certain it would be this, more than my bare rear end hanging out in the breeze, that would be the image my brother-in-law carried around in his head for a long time.

"Bay . . . ," he began softly, somehow reading my face, and I looked across to see pity welling up in his eyes.

"Not a word. Not now. Not ever. Case closed. Are we clear?"

He held my gaze and nodded.

"Good. So what's so all-fired important?"

Red straightened his shoulders and put on his cop face. "Scuttlebutt around the office this morning is that you and Wyler have cracked the Wade case wide open."

"Really? It's news to me." I dropped my eyes so he couldn't read the evasiveness I knew would be reflected there.

"Come on, Bay, don't bullshit me. Wyler told Morgan you had a client who could prove the dead man wasn't Wade. He wouldn't say any more than that, except for a few hints here and there, but it was enough to send Morgan running for the FBI databases."

"So why are you busting my chops about it?" I asked. "Why aren't you muscling your way into Wyler's house and catching him naked in bed?"

The image must have struck us at the same moment, for suddenly we both broke into laughter. Dolores, carrying a pile of folded sheets and towels from the laundry room, paused on her way down the hall to cast a quizzical glance at us. When we'd gotten ourselves under control, Red wiped his eyes and shook his head.

"Have I ever mentioned that you are the most exasperating woman I've ever met in my life?"

"Once or twice," I said. "Seriously, Red, you know I can't divulge the confidences of my clients unless I know there's a direct link to a crime under investigation. If someone waltzed into my office and confessed to bashing this guy with a two-by-four, I'd be on your doorstep in a heartbeat."

"I know that. But we've wasted a lot of time when we could have had the identification process already in the pipeline."

I shrugged. "That's the breaks, although it's not as if the body's going anywhere. Try to look on the bright side. If Wyler hadn't spoken up, you'd still be spinning your wheels thinking it was Wade. At least this way you're headed in the right direction."

The phone rang before Red had a chance to reply. I crossed to the built-in desk, checked the caller ID, and picked up. "Hey, Erik!"

"Good morning. I've got news."

What with Wyler and Star Kennedy and now Red Tanner, not to mention the storm-induced headache of the night before, I'd completely forgotten about Erik's stakeout of Bobby Delacroix's house in Beaufort.

"Did Win turn up?" I asked.

"A few hours ago."

"Don't tell me you've been there all night?" I glanced over at Red, who had leaned forward in his chair and was eavesdropping with unabashed interest. I carried the phone down into the great room and curled up on the sofa. "Did you sleep in the Expedition?"

"Sure," Erik answered with more enthusiasm than he had any right to feel. "I've done it before, on long trips and when I couldn't afford a motel room."

"I think you need a raise," I said.

"I won't turn it down. But listen. Mr. Hammond showed up about six o'clock this morning. A taxi let him off in front of Delacroix's, and either the door was unlocked or he had a key, because he didn't knock or anything. Just went right in."

"Well, at least we know where he is. And that he's okay. I'll let Miss Addie know as soon as we hang up. You'd better get yourself some sleep. Call in sick at the computer store. I'll make up whatever you lose in pay."

"Wait, Bay. I haven't gotten to the good part yet. He had the suit-case with him."

"The one you saw him with at the airport?"

"Right. That old beat-up thing. And it wasn't empty."

I sat up straighter on the sofa. "How do you know?"

"Because he had to use both hands to drag it along the sidewalk. I thought he might not make it up the front steps. Whatever's in there has to be pretty heavy."

A dozen scenarios flitted through my mind, none of which made any sense. "Anything else?"

"Yeah. I wrote down the license plate number of the cab. I thought maybe we could figure out how to track down where he was coming from. And get this—I think someone followed him home."

My hand shot out to where the cigarette box used to sit on the coffee table in front of me. I wondered how long it would be before my body stopped reaching for nicotine of its own accord. "Why do you say that?"

"A car cruised by right after the cab pulled away. Going real slow."

"It could have been somebody on the way to work. Or maybe a tourist who got lost."

"At six o'clock in the morning?"

"We'll have to think about it. At any rate, great work. Can you stay awake long enough to write it up?"

"Already did. I'm at the office. I'll leave a copy on your desk."

"Thanks. Now go get some sleep. We'll talk later."

"I'm fine," Erik Whiteside said with the resilience of youth. "I'm gonna go get cleaned up and head in to the store."

"Up to you."

"I hope all this turns out to help Miss Hammond."

"I'm sure it will," I lied, wondering how long it would take to get rid of Red so I could grab Wyler and get to Bobby Delacroix's house before Win decided to take another midnight jaunt. Maybe one of our cases had a prayer of a good outcome, I thought as I rose and put on my poker face for Sergeant Red Tanner.

CHAPTER NINETEEN

*T*HE DELACROIX HOUSE SAT TUCKED BACK BEHIND A chipped wrought-iron fence just outside the historic district and a million miles from the magnificence of its neighbors only a couple of blocks away. At one time it must have been a tiny jewel of a place, perhaps a dower house, I thought, or maybe a home built for an unmarried sister of the planter who owned the property. Regardless, it had been allowed to fall into shabbiness, its wide front porch sagging, a once neat row of azalea bushes running rampant over the cracked front walk.

Ben Wyler pulled the Jaguar to a stop on the dusty shoulder of the narrow street and cut the engine. "Looks like Hammond's buddy's come down in the world," he said, lowering his side window.

Immediately the car filled with humid air carrying the faint scent of honeysuckle and the oppressive weight of the noonday heat.

"I don't know anything about the family," I said as I lifted the damp, heavy hair off the back of my neck. "I guess they didn't move in my mother's exalted circles."

Wyler smiled. "Their loss. Ready?"

We'd discussed our game plan during the long drive from Hilton Head, and I still wasn't entirely comfortable with the retired cop's insistence we should simply walk up and knock on the door. I'd taken the precaution of slipping my little pistol into my tote bag, but even that couldn't dispel the anxiety coiling in the pit of my stomach.

"What's wrong with trying to get some information out of the cab company before we go barging into a situation we know nothing about?" I'd made the argument more than once as we slogged along in the weekday traffic, but Wyler had been insistent. He was afraid Win Hammond would skip out if we gave him too much time.

"The easiest way to find out where he was last night is to ask him," he said, pushing open the car door and hauling himself out into the blazing sun. "I thought we decided that already."

"*You* decided that," I said, sighing in resignation as I struggled out of the low bucket seat and joined him on the street. "I don't remember there being a vote."

He studied the house through the heat waves shimmering across the gleaming hood of the car. "I got a feeling."

Tough to argue with that, I thought. Wyler pushed on the gate, which swung silently open, and I followed him up the heaving sidewalk, careful to avoid the knobs of tree roots poking up through the concrete slabs. The second step creaked, announcing our presence in the somnolent quiet before we ever reached the porch. Through the closed front door, its paint worn completely off in patches, I thought I heard the muted voices of a television program.

Ben Wyler punched the rusted doorbell, his head cocked to one side as he listened for its notes inside the house. A moment later he banged on the door. I hitched my bag up a little higher on my shoulder, resisting the urge to slip my hand inside and wrap my fingers around the comfort of the Seecamp. The TV voices droned on, but not another sound disturbed the silence. Wyler and I exchanged a look, and he rapped again, more loudly.

I surveyed the houses on either side, both closer to the street, their side windows almost level with Bobby Delacroix's front porch. Not a curtain twitched, and both places seemed deserted. I wondered if Erik's nosy informant had a day job.

"Hammond! Open up!"

Wyler's voice boomed and echoed across the confines of the narrow porch, his fist punctuating each word with a vicious attack on the door frame. A Volvo station wagon, its occupants gazing out from air-conditioned comfort, rolled by on the blacktop, the passenger's hands wrapped around an SLR camera pointed in our direction.

"Let's check around back," Wyler said, startling me out of my pre-occupation with the tourists.

"Wait!" I grabbed at the sleeve of his T-shirt as he moved toward the steps. "We can't do that! We're trespassing. If he shot us from one of the upstairs windows, he'd get off without a fine."

"You read way too many detective novels," Wyler said, trotting down the steps and disappearing around the side of the house.

I jogged after him.

As had been the case in the front, all the windows on the side were closed, wooden shutters half-sagging across some, faded drapes conceal-ing the interior on others. Out back we found a rusted swing set slowly sinking into the yard. A tumbledown building, which might once have been a storage shed, hunkered nearby. The dirt driveway had been com-pletely overgrown. Wyler squatted down to inspect the dim impression of tires where the weeds had been flattened by some sort of vehicle.

"Not recent," he said, rising and dusting off his hands.

I wanted to ask how he could tell but decided that particular lesson in detecting could wait for another day. As he studied the small back porch and its railings tilting precariously outward, I moved toward the outbuilding. The roof looked to be in good shape, although the sides were cracked and warped. I leaned over to peer into a narrow gap be-tween two boards, wishing I'd thought to bring a flashlight. I rested one hand on the lower piece of siding and nearly toppled over when a chunk of the board all but disintegrated at my touch. With a squeal of alarm I jumped back.

"Jesus, Tanner, why don't you send up a flare?" Wyler moved quickly to my side as I rubbed my grimy hand on the seat of my shorts, then inspected my palm for splinters.

The implied reprimand stung. "I didn't make any more noise than you did! If all that pounding didn't get their attention, they must either be out to lunch or dead."

Ben Wyler raised one shaggy eyebrow. "You think they're dead in there?"

"No, of course not! It's a figure of speech, for God's sake!"

He moved closer to the gaping hole I'd inadvertently made in the side of the old shed and peered inside.

"See anything?" I asked, craning my neck to peer over his shoulder.

"Cobwebs, rusty garden tools." He twisted his body around to a different angle. "A dead rat."

"Let me see," I said, and he moved aside.

I cupped my hands around my eyes to cut off the glare and scanned the dim interior. As I shifted my head, a gleam of metal caught my eye.

"There's something shiny in the far corner," I said, straightening so Ben could take my place. "On the back left wall."

"Looks like a couple of gasoline cans," he said. "Fairly new."

"Well, there's nothing sinister in that. Lots of people keep gas for their lawn mowers."

He rose and dusted off his hands. "You see any evidence this place has seen a lawn mower in the past decade?" He flung his hand around the dismal backyard. "Hell, there's hardly any grass left to worry about."

I followed him around to the front of the sloping building. An old-fashioned doorknob turned under his hand, but the narrow door remained firmly shut.

"Locked," he said unnecessarily. "I wonder why."

A loud screech of unoiled hinges split the noonday silence, and we spun simultaneously toward the back of the house. A tall man dressed only in rumpled shorts stepped out onto the rickety porch. I had a quick glimpse of a well-muscled chest covered in curly gray hair and the bulky legs of a weight lifter before Wyler moved in front of me.

"Afternoon. Would you be Mr. Delacroix?"

The man let the screen door bang shut behind him. "Who's wantin' to know?" Despite his appearance, his voice held the soft drawl of our Southern aristocracy.

I peeked around Wyler. Bobby Delacroix had to be around six-foot-two or three, and his mane of black, wavy hair curled toward his shoulders. He had the body of a gym rat. His face, partly hidden in the shadows of the porch, sported at least a week's worth of stubble working its way into the start of a decent beard. His large hands clutched an old wooden baseball bat, its handle bound with smudged white tape. He looked ready to take a swing at anything that might be standing in his path.

"I'm Ben Wyler, and this is my associate, Mrs. Tanner. We're looking for Edwin Hammond." Ben's voice matched Bobby's in its soft, non-confrontational timbre.

"Why?" He tapped the barrel of the bat into his hand to punctuate the question.

Obscured by Wyler, I slipped my pistol from my bag into the pocket of my shorts. "I'm a friend of his sister Adelaide," I said, stepping out into the open. "She's worried about him."

I thought I saw a flash of anger in my companion's eyes as I moved to stand shoulder to shoulder with him in the relentless noonday sun.

"No one here by that name," the big man said, lowering the bat and leaning his weight against it as if it were a cane. "Sorry."

"But he is staying with you." Wyler didn't make it a question.

The towering figure stopped and fixed us with a hard stare. "Keep off my property," he said before disappearing into the gloom.

I hadn't realized how tightly I'd been holding myself until the door squealed shut behind him. I felt my shoulders sag and breath rush out of my lungs. "Jesus, Mary, and Joseph!" My knees wobbled as I followed Wyler back to the car. He turned the key and adjusted the air conditioning controls.

"You recognize him?" he asked as we pulled away from the run-down house.

I thought about it for a moment. "No. I couldn't see much of his face through all the hair, although it's not a body you're likely to forget. But I never knew him to begin with, so . . ."

"So it's not necessarily Delacroix."

"Who else would it be?"

Wyler shrugged and turned left onto Carteret Street. "He never did identify himself. And he wasn't the only one in the house."

We crested the hump of the bridge to Lady's Island and rolled down the other side. "How do you know that?" I asked.

Wyler answered my question with one of his own. "You see a remote control in the guy's hand?"

"No."

"The TV went off."

I wondered how long it would be before my powers of observation got that fine-tuned. Probably never. It suddenly occurred to me we were headed away from Hilton Head. "Where are we going?"

"To see your father. Maybe you'd better get on the horn and let him know we're coming."

As I reached toward the cell phone in the bottom of my tote bag, my hand paused in midair. "You know, I'm beginning to feel a little like Effie Perine here, and I can't say I'm liking it much."

"Who?"

"Sam Spade's secretary in *The Maltese Falcon.* The one he calls 'doll' all the time. Did somebody die and elect you king of the hill when I wasn't looking?"

"Am I stepping on your toes, Miss Lydia?"

Suddenly he swung the car violently to the right and skidded to a halt in a cloud of dust just across from the little airfield that serviced Lady's Island.

"What the hell are you doing?" I demanded, fumbling for the contents of my bag, which had been flung across the floor at my feet. "I can't ask a question without you going nuts on me?"

But Wyler wasn't looking at me, and I realized his reaction had nothing to do with my complaining. His gaze was locked on the cluster of buildings and small planes gathered along the short runway of what was affectionately known among the locals as Frogmore International Airport.

"That could be the ticket," Wyler mumbled to himself as he checked the side mirror and whipped back onto the highway.

"What are you babbling about?" I asked, craning my neck around to see what about our little airstrip had caught Wyler's attention.

"What's security like?"

"At the airport?"

"Seems to be a lot of ways to get in and out of this place without attracting too much attention," he said, more to himself than to me.

He slowed to let oncoming traffic pass, then darted left onto the road to Presqu'isle.

"Answer me," I said.

"About what?"

I scrambled to get all my thoughts in some semblance of order. "One, why do you think the guy in the cutoffs wasn't Bobby Delacroix? Two, what has you so interested about the airport?"

The shock of the Jaguar's low-slung chassis negotiating the first of the potholes which line the avenue of oaks leading up to Presqu'isle jolted my teeth.

"Hang on a couple of minutes. I hate to have to go over everything twice." He made no effort to keep the smug superiority out of his tone and off his angular face.

I worked my tongue around inside my mouth to make sure I hadn't cracked a molar. I straightened my shoulders and planted my gaze firmly on his profile before replying. "We need to talk, Wyler, and soon, about just who's running this show."

"Agreed."

That stopped me for a moment. "And I want an answer before we go bursting in on my father. If the guy on the porch wasn't Bobby Delacroix, just who do you think it was?"

Wyler's grin made me want to slap it off his face. "Figure it out," he said in the mocking tone that made my jaw ache. "Who's missing besides Hammond?"

It didn't take five seconds for the light to click on. "Randolph Remington Wade."

"Bingo!" Wyler said as he whipped the Jaguar into the drive in front of Presqu'isle, spraying gravel into my mother's prize rosebushes and leaving me absolutely speechless.

CHAPTER TWENTY

A S I EXPECTED, LAVINIA INSISTED ON FEEDING US, AL-
though I tried to talk her out of it. Ten minutes after stepping
into the dim interior of Presqu'isle we found ourselves seated at the old
oak kitchen table with cold chicken sandwiches and redskin potato
salad in front of us. The ever-present iced tea pitcher sweated on the
counter just behind me.

My father hadn't blinked at this disruption of his usual after-lunch
siesta. In fact, he leaned forward from his wheelchair, the elbow of his
good arm resting on the placemat, his gray eyes sparkling.

"So you think the man you saw on the back porch of the Delacroix
place wasn't Bobby? That maybe it was this Wade fella?" the Judge
asked.

Wyler nodded, his mouth full of sliced chicken breast and warm
sourdough bread.

"What about you?" My father cocked his head in my direction.

I swallowed and gulped down some tea. "I don't know. I couldn't
pick either one of them out of a crowd. I don't remember Bobby at all.
If he's a friend and contemporary of Win Hammond, he'd be twenty or
so years older than I am." I speared a piece of potato. "As for Wade, all
I've seen is a grainy photo in a newspaper."

"Vinnie, would you please bring me the phone?"

I was pleased to hear him treating Lavinia with the proper deference for a change, and I could tell by her quick smile as she placed the handset in front of him that she appreciated it as well. The Judge laid the portable on the table and punched buttons with his good hand.

"Who are you calling?" I asked, although I pretty much knew it would be one of his Bay Street Irregulars, the old men who were the remnants of his now defunct Thursday night poker games. The thought brought a tinge of sadness. Law Merriweather was dead, and two others had dropped out due to frail health. Only Boyd Allison and Charlie Seldon were still ambulatory.

My father shook his head at me and spoke into the phone. "Boyd? Tally . . . Fine, you? . . . Listen, you remember the Delacroix clan?"

I tried to disguise my blatant eavesdropping by speaking to Wyler, but I still had one ear tuned to the Judge's conversation. "If the guy on the porch was in fact Wade, are you thinking the stiff in the morgue is Bobby?" I whispered.

Ben Wyler's head snapped up from his plate, and I smiled at the dab of mayonnaise on the end of his slightly crooked nose. He saw me staring and swiped it off with the back of his hand. "Good job, Lydia! I have to admit that hadn't occurred to me."

I wasn't so sure, but I let it ride. The counterpoint seemed logical. I sat back in my chair as the Judge handed the phone to me, and I clicked the Off button.

"Well?"

"Bobby Delacroix is five-ten and about one-eighty soakin' wet," the Judge replied. "Somewhere in his fifties according to Boyd." His grin told me he had more, even though his description had blown my theory out of the water.

"And?" I prompted.

"And he spent a couple of years in prison."

"What for?" Ben wiped his mouth and set his napkin on the table.

"Boyd wasn't certain, but he'll find out. Charlie may remember, since he probably prosecuted the case. He thinks it might have been something like forgery or receiving stolen property. Nothing violent, at any rate."

"Interesting," Wyler muttered.

"So what does all this prove?" I asked as I rose and carried our two plates and silverware to the sink. Lavinia had left one side full of soapy water, and I slid our dirty dishes into it.

"Sit down, Bay, honey. I'll get those."

"You sit down," I said, waving her back into her chair. "Relax."

"I still think there's some connection between Hammond and Wade," Wyler said.

He sat hunched over, his arms crossed in front of him on the table, and I noticed for the first time the scar running from the inside of his elbow and disappearing into the sleeve of his T-shirt. It looked old and faded, but I could still make out its pale, ragged outline against his deepening tan.

Knife, I thought, rinsing the plate and transferring it to the drainer.

"And I think you're reaching," I interjected before my father could work up a head of steam. "We have no proof at all Randolph Wade is the man we saw this afternoon or that he and Win Hammond even know each other. The guy could have been a friend of Bobby's or his cousin or someone entirely unconnected to this whole thing. Maybe Delacroix doesn't even live there anymore."

I pulled a towel from the rack next to the sink and began drying the dishes.

Wyler shrugged. "All good points. Any way to find out if the house has been sold or rented out?"

"I'll have the whole rundown before long," my father said with smug confidence. "I told Boyd to get me everything he can about Delacroix. I have a few other sources I can tap if he comes up empty."

Lavinia rose as I sat and carried a glass pie pan and a stack of dessert plates back to the table. "Apple pie, Detective Wyler?" she asked. "Fresh this mornin'."

"Yes, ma'am," he replied with enthusiasm, and she laughed.

"What had you so interested about the airstrip that you nearly ran us off the road back there?" I asked as the fragrance of warm cinnamon drifted across the table.

"Gas cans." He smiled at my raised eyebrows. "I was thinking how easy it is in a place like this for folks to come and go. You people who've lived here all your lives probably think you can't make a move without the whole town knowing what you're up to. But it's really just as easy to disappear from these islands as it would be, say, in Manhattan."

"I don't follow. I'd think a person could get pretty lost in a city of several million people without too much trouble."

"You're right in one sense. If you just want to become invisible, there's plenty of holes you can crawl into in New York. But I'm thinking more of coming and going undetected. All the boats in and out, small deserted landings and little uninhabited islands. And I can't believe that airport has the tightest security. If you were, say, someone who grew up around here and knew everybody and his brother, you could pretty much wander in and out without raising any suspicion whatsoever."

I scraped the last apple off my plate. "You could be right, but what does all this have to do with the body on the beach or Randolph Wade, Win Hammond, and Bobby Delacroix?"

"The detective is simply ruminatin' on the possibilities, Bay," my father said with a trace of annoyance.

Wyler smiled at him. "Right you are, Judge. I'm just thinking about people disappearing overnight and sneaking in at the crack of dawn. About empty suitcases that suddenly get filled up. Two men with an interest in boats who both hang out on the same out-of-the-way island and who both show up here at about the same time. People impersonating other people and ending up dead." He stopped and grinned at me. "You have to admit it's an intriguing puzzle."

"And that's why you've decided to butt into the agency after all this time?"

I knew the question sounded snide and whiny the second it was out of my mouth, and it took my father less than that to call me on it.

"If Ben wants to interest himself in one of our cases, he's more than earned the right. You should be glad of his expertise and experience instead of actin' like some spoiled little kid who has to share her toys."

It wasn't fair, but I didn't have a rebuttal. I pushed my chair back from the table and leaned down to hug Lavinia. "Thanks for lunch. It was fabulous as usual."

"You're welcome, I'm sure." She patted my hand where it rested on her shoulder. "Let me fix you a plate to take along."

"No, thanks," I said, unhooking my bag from the back of the chair and hefting it onto my shoulder. "We need to be getting back."

I stared at Wyler who returned my gaze with a look I couldn't quite decipher.

"Right. I've got some things I want to check out back on Hilton Head. You'll let me . . . *us* know what you find out about Delacroix?" he asked the Judge, ducking his head away from my stare.

"Call me on the cell," I said to my father, striding toward the hallway without my usual affectionate pat on the arm or peck on the cheek.

I left the front door standing open and stormed across the verandah and down the steps. I wrenched open the door of the Jaguar and flung myself inside.

Fine, I told myself, *just damn fine.* If the two of them wanted to play boys against the girls, it was okay by me. I had a couple of aces up my sleeve neither one of them knew about, and I intended to play them.

The ride back to Hilton Head passed in an uneasy truce once it finally got through Wyler's thick skull I didn't want to talk. After I'd responded to his conversational gambits with noncommittal grunts a few times, he got the message and tuned the radio to an oldies station. I concentrated on the familiar scenery whizzing by the side window while the detective sang along to Motown memories of the sixties. He had a scratchy baritone voice, but he sang with gusto and seemed to know all the words. I covered my mouth a couple of times to hide the twitchings of a smile and wondered exactly just how old he was.

I got us through the security gate into Port Royal Plantation, and we pulled up in my driveway a little past four o'clock. Dolores's battered blue Hyundai sat just off the concrete pad under one of the two towering oaks shading my house. Wyler cut the engine but made no move to get out of the car.

"See you," I said, reaching for the door handle.

His hand on my arm stopped me. "You gonna tell me what's bugging you?"

"You're the hotshot detective. Figure it out." I winced as his grip tightened.

"You are a spoiled little Southern belle, aren't you? Your father's got you pegged pretty good."

I wrenched my arm out of his grasp. "Go to hell."

My exit from the low-slung Jaguar wasn't as dramatic as I'd have liked due to the considerable time and effort it took to uncoil my five-foot-ten-inch frame from the bucket seat. I had to bend over nearly double to fire my parting shot through the open window.

"My family and I are none of your concern, Wyler. Your name's on the PI license, so you've got the right to stick your nose into this case. I can't stop you. The Judge is right about that, at least. But until you come up with the cash to buy me out, it's still my business, and I don't need your help to run it. So go play whatever games you want. Just stay the hell out of my way."

As I straightened, I heard two slow, dull claps as he brought his hands together in mock applause.

"Hey, c'mon! I'm kidding!" he called as I turned on my heel and marched toward the side of the house.

As I passed the front of the garage, I glanced up to see Dolores framed in the bay window of the kitchen. I had only a brief glimpse of her face, mottled in the reflection of oak branches and Spanish moss quivering in the eddies of wind off the ocean, but the stiffness of her shoulders and her hands clenched in front of her told me something was wrong.

I tuned out Ben Wyler's shouted commands for me to stop and sprinted up the steps to the front door.

"Dolores?" I called as I fumbled my key into the lock. "Dolores!"

She met me in the entryway, her short, stubby fingers bunching the hem of her smock into fistfuls of wrinkles. "*Aiyee, Señora! Gracias a Dios!* You must come."

She turned and scurried down the hallway.

"Wait!" I caught up with her just outside the guest room. I halted her with a soft hand on her shoulder and spun her around to face me. "What's wrong? What's happened?"

"The *doctora,* she say tell no one. She say no call."

Now that I could see her up close, Dolores looked more agitated than afraid, and I let myself relax a little. *Doctora.*

I stepped around my housekeeper and pushed open the door to the guest room. Neddie sat in the overstuffed armchair near the window, her bare feet propped up on the ottoman. As I entered, she looked up from the book in her lap and brought her index finger to her lips in the universal signal for quiet. My gaze flew to the bed where a lump of sheets and blankets was topped by a cascade of dirty blond hair. I whipped my head back around to Neddie just as she padded across the carpet toward me.

"Sorry, Bay, but I didn't know where else to go," she whispered, taking my arm and guiding me back into the hallway.

I waited while she pulled the door shut behind her. Neddie Halloran folded her arms across her chest and planted her feet defiantly in front of the room like some ancient, red-haired eunuch guarding the entrance to the harem.

"So you found Yancey," I said, and Neddie smiled.

CHAPTER
TWENTY-ONE

"WHERE'S YOUR MERCEDES?"

We sat at the kitchen table with glasses of sweet tea in front of us. I glanced out the bay window to watch Dolores maneuver her beat-up old car onto the driveway and roll toward the street.

"It's at the Westin," Neddie said, picking a grape off the stem and popping it into her mouth.

I toyed with a cube of cheddar cheese, stabbing at it with a cocktail pick. "You walked down the beach?"

"Yup. Just in case."

"Just in case what?"

"You know."

"You thought someone might be following you?" I made a conscious effort to keep the annoyance out of my voice, but I must not have succeeded.

"Don't say it as if I'm some lunatic! It was a definite possibility."

"Oxymoron," I said and ducked as she pitched a grape across the table at me. "Hey, it's a grammatical term, not an insult."

"I know that, Tanner. I'm actually a college graduate myself, if you recall." She sighed, and the teasing light went out of her face. She looked over her shoulder toward the bedroom. "The poor kid is scared to death."

"Of what?"

"Pretty much everything and everybody."

"That's helpful."

"Look, her boyfriend has beaten her badly enough to put her in the hospital. Her father drives a truck, so he's gone for days, sometimes a week or more. She's on her own more often than not."

I crossed to the refrigerator and pulled out the tea pitcher. I topped off our glasses and sat back down. "You said her mother disappeared? What's the story there?"

"I'm not sure. She isn't ready to talk about it yet." Neddie sighed. "We were just beginning to get into that at the last session. The one she took off from."

"Are you going to be able to give me any details, or are we still hung up on this doctor-patient privilege thing?"

"No, Yancey gave me permission to discuss everything with you." Neddie smiled. "I told her you'd be picking at me until I finally caved anyway."

"So let's have it. Is this related to her drug habit?"

"In a way. I don't really have the whole picture. There are some things, like her mother's disappearance, she won't open up about. But the bottom line is that she witnessed some sort of . . . I don't know what to call it. Something that scared the hell out of her, at any rate. That phone call she got in my office sent her on the run. She's been moving around Savannah for the past few days, panhandling for food and avoiding her usual hangouts."

"How'd you find her?" I asked.

"I didn't. She showed up on my doorstep at home this morning, dirty and hungry and convinced someone was following her." Neddie swiped a hand through her tangle of red hair. "She absolutely refused to let me call the police. She almost has me convinced I'm in as much danger as she is."

"Why?"

"Because, in her convoluted logic, whoever is after her will think she spilled her guts to me."

"Did she? I mean, if a patient reveals a crime to you, aren't you bound to tell the cops?"

"It's a lot more complicated than that." Neddie tipped back her glass and drained the last of her tea. "The truth is, she hasn't given me anything specific."

I nibbled around the edges of a piece of cheese. "So why bring her here? She's what, fifteen? Have you considered that your little freckled butt could end up in jail for transporting her across state lines?"

Neddie dismissed my concern with a flip of her hand. "I didn't kidnap her, for God's sake. And my intentions are certainly not immoral. You read way too many detective stories."

I let that familiar crack slide for the moment, and we sat quietly across from each other. The psychologist seemed to be grappling with some decision.

"Who do you know who could give us some advice?" she asked. "About where we stand with the cops. Your brother-in-law, maybe? I don't want to drag you into anything illegal."

Wyler's name popped immediately into my head, but we hadn't parted on the best of terms, and I'd be damned if I'd go crawling to him for help. Still, he was retired, which made him a better candidate than Red, who'd be bound to report the kid if she really was mixed up with some crime.

"I'll have to think about it," I said.

The telephone sounded loud in the quiet warmth of the kitchen. I stared at it across the room and waited.

"You *do* screen," Neddie said, the accusatory tone of her voice only slightly tinged with humor as I made no move to answer.

"Deal with it," I said and waved her to silence when the last of my tinny answering machine words faded.

"Listen, Bay, it's Ben." Pause. "Wyler." He sounded serious. "We need to talk. About the case. Call me." There was another moment of silence during which I thought he'd finished before I heard him add quietly, "Please?"

"Who's that?" Neddie pounced like a kitten with a new catnip toy.

"Down, girl," I said. "It's business."

I could tell she was waiting for me to elaborate, but I'd given her all the information she was going to get about Ben Wyler.

"So what's the plan?" I asked, folding my arms on the table in front of me and leaning toward her. "You know I love you like a sister, but you've put all of us in jeopardy, Neddie, and you damn well know it. If she's really on the run because she witnessed some sort of crime—"

"You callin' me a liar?" Both of us jumped at the sharp voice.

The girl stood at the foot of the steps leading up from the great room to the kitchen. Neither of us had heard her barefooted approach. She glared up at us from a more than pretty face framed by fine, blondish hair falling well past her shoulders. She wore the standard teenage-issue skimpy shorts that hugged her long, slender legs and an even skimpier cropped T-shirt that revealed a pale white stomach, a little leftover baby fat still pouched around her pierced navel.

Neddie leaped up and crossed the room to reach down and clasp the girl's hand in her own. "Come on, Yancey, settle down. I want you to meet a friend of mine."

The sullen expression softened a little, and the girl allowed Neddie to lead her to the table. "Hello, Yancey, I'm Bay Tanner." I held out my hand, and the teenager took it reluctantly.

"Hey." Her eyes avoided mine, ranging around the gleaming kitchen and coming to rest on the food in the middle of the table.

"Are you hungry?" I pointed at the plate of fruit, cheese, and crackers Dolores had set out for us before she left. "Help yourself."

Somewhere along the line someone had taught the girl at least a few rudimentary table manners. She spread a napkin across her lap before diving in.

I took a glass from the cupboard and poured her a tea. Neddie and I exchanged a look as we watched the teenager clean the serving plate down to the last crumb.

"How about if I fix us some dinner?" I said. Parading through some restaurant crowded with tourists didn't sound like the best idea.

"I don't eat meat," Yancey said with an imperiousness that set my teeth on edge.

"How about fish? Or shellfish?" I forced my voice to remain neutral.

"That's cool."

Bet your ass it's cool, sweetheart. I caught Neddie watching me, her eyes scrunched up in anticipation of one of my legendary outbursts, and I shrugged. *Cut the kid some slack,* I ordered myself.

Apparently the shrimp and rice passed muster, and an hour later Neddie and I sat over empty plates discussing how best to extricate ourselves from this mess she'd gotten us into. Yancey Sullivan had stuffed herself, thanked me grudgingly, and taken herself off to the shower. Neddie had thrown a few of her own things in a bag before taking it on the lam, but the girl had literally nothing but the clothes on her back. I left the kitchen long enough to hunt up a few things of mine I thought she might be able to wear without looking like a kid playing dress-up and left them draped across the bed in the guest room. I picked up her discarded shorts, T-shirt, and underwear from the floor and dropped them into the washer on my way by.

I headed back to the kitchen and made it as far as the entryway when the doorbell pulled me up short. I glanced at Neddie, hovering halfway down the steps, a look of fear trembling on her face.

"Who is it?" she hissed.

I shrugged and moved toward the door.

"Get rid of them!" Her urgent whisper sent a shiver along my arms.

I pushed the intercom button.

"Yes?"

"Bay, it's me. Erik. Open up."

He sounded excited, out of breath. I unlatched the door, and he pulled open the screen. "Thanks."

He didn't step inside, instead glancing over his shoulder into the dark tunnel formed by the shrubs that lined the front walk. I craned my neck, but could see nothing—or no one—behind him.

"What's the matter?" I asked, his furtiveness communicating itself to me on some instinctive level. "Is something wrong?"

Erik Whiteside reached behind him and motioned with his hand. A woman stepped out of the bushes and bolted up the steps to hover beside him, and I recognized the pale face immediately.

"What's she—?"

"Can we come in? It's important," Erik said.

I shrugged and stepped back.

He pulled the woman in behind him and quickly shut the door.

Karen Zwilling turned her face up to me, and I could see the quivering of her bottom lip. "You have to help me," she said. Her fingers gripped the strap of her shoulder bag as if it were a lifeline.

"What happened?" Behind me, I heard Neddie move down the remaining steps from the kitchen.

"I saw him!"

"Who?"

"The guy! The one who raped me!" Karen Zwilling swallowed hard. "And I think he saw me!"

CHAPTER
TWENTY-TWO

ANCEY SULLIVAN, FRESH FROM THE SHOWER, HAD AT-
tached herself to Erik like a limpet. My old clothes hung on
her, the shorts riding so low on her hips I felt certain they'd be around
her ankles at any moment. She'd tied the tails of the sleeveless blouse
tight underneath her small breasts so that her navel ring gleamed in
the lamplight. She'd immediately staked out her territory and huddled
on the sofa as close to Erik as she could get without actually sitting in
his lap.

I'd done the hostess thing, making introductions, then offering
drinks as if this were some sort of cocktail party. After everyone had declined, we sat in silence for a moment, staring awkwardly at each other.
Except for the teenager, whose adoring gaze seemed permanently attached to the side of Erik's face.

"Look," I finally said when it became apparent the kid wasn't going
to take my subtle hints, "I have business to conduct here, Yancey. And
it's confidential. You understand what that means?"

The scorn on her face as she tore her eyes away from my partner's
profile made me want to reach out and slap her. "What do you think,
I'm some kind of moron?"

"Come on," Neddie said, "we need to leave Bay and Erik and Karen alone." She rose and extended her hand. "Let's go watch TV in the other room."

Again Yancey favored me with the withering look that comes as standard equipment on every person under the age of twenty regardless of race, creed, or national origin. "I like it here." She fixed Erik with an adoring smile that made him inch a little closer to the edge of the sofa.

"Yancey, please," Neddie coaxed.

I'd had enough of diplomacy. "You're not welcome in this conversation, Yancey. You're a guest in my home and not even an invited one at that. So go with Dr. Halloran. Now. Run along like a good little girl."

I knew my tone would tick her off. She shot me a glare and leaped off the couch, flouncing down the hall with Neddie close on her heels.

They're so easily manipulated, I thought with a smile.

"I'll take that drink now," Karen Zwilling said into the sudden quiet.

I found the remains of the bottle of Scotch that Win Hammond had been working on, poured out a measure, and added ice and water. I carried it back into the great room and handed it to our client.

I retrieved my spare voice recorder from my handbag and switched it on. "So tell me what happened."

Karen took a good hit on the Scotch and glanced at Erik.

"It's okay," he said with a reassuring smile. "No one's here to judge."

"You had a date?" I asked.

Her voice held evidence of the fear bubbling just beneath the surface. "Yes. A date. Guy here from Cleveland on a golf trip."

"Where'd you hook up with him?" I flinched at my inadvertent word choice, but it skipped right by Karen.

"The Crowne. We met in the bar, had a couple of drinks, and he'd already decided on a place called Eugene's for dinner." She shook her head, and a crooked smile twitched at the corner of her mouth. "He actually just wanted to go to dinner."

"Who drove?"

She looked momentarily disconcerted by the question. "He did. A Navigator. A rental, I think."

"Go on."

"So, he seemed like a nice enough guy. I had an aunt who used to live in Cleveland, so we talked a lot about how things had changed since I used to visit her in the summers. You know, just talk."

"Where did you see Wade?"

She took another slug of Scotch. "Just as we were leaving the restaurant. You know how dark it is around here, which is something I just can't get used to. I mean, why can't they put up streetlights like everybody else?"

"He was in the parking lot?" I asked. I couldn't figure out why she kept going on these little conversational side trips.

"Yeah. Those Midwestern guys are brought up right, I don't care what anybody says. He had me wait while he went to get the car. I was just standing out in front of the restaurant, looking around at the boats and stuff, and suddenly it dawned on me. This was the place Wade took me." She swallowed hard. "Where he . . ."

"Take it easy," I said softly. "You're sure it was the same marina?"

"Pretty sure. And then I spotted these two men. Toward the back, under some trees. At first I didn't pay much attention, I mean, why should I? Then when my guy brought the car around, the headlights sort of struck them for a minute, and they looked up." Karen Zwilling knocked back the last of her drink. "Jesus, I almost fainted."

"You're sure it was Randolph Wade? The man who raped you?"

She hesitated, and Erik reached across to pat her gently on the arm. She smiled at him. "Sure as I can be in just that brief glance. He didn't look *exactly* the same. His hair was different."

"Okay, take it easy. You said earlier he saw you, too. How did that happen?"

She shivered. "As we swung around, he looked right at me, through the window of the car. I couldn't have been five feet away from him."

"Did he act as if he recognized you?" I asked, and she shrugged.

"I don't know. But he had to see me. I mean, the windows weren't tinted or anything."

I shifted in my chair next to the fireplace and tucked one leg up under me. "What about the other man? The one Wade was talking to. Did you get a good look at him?"

Karen Zwilling shook her head, and her newly bleached hair swirled around her face, gleaming in the lamplight. "Not really. He turned his back as we drove past."

I leaned in and tried to fix her with my stare. "Think. This is important. Can you tell me anything about the other man? Clothes? Age? Height? Anything at all."

Erik shot me a questioning look, and I realized he had no idea about Wyler's and my adventures of earlier in the day, about the man with the baseball bat on Bobby Delacroix's back porch. I shook my head at him just as Karen spoke.

"I think he might have been old—I mean, older than us."

"What gave you that impression? Was he stoop-shouldered? Gray hair?"

"Yeah, that's it. He had this sort of salt-and-pepper hair. Long. Hanging over his collar. And he was a lot shorter than Wade." The animation on her face faded almost as quickly as it had arisen. "What do you think I should do?"

"Karen, there are only two possible scenarios here. One, this is a case of mistaken identity. The man you saw just looks like Wade, and the real rapist is tucked away in a drawer at the morgue."

"Or it's really him." Her voice rose, and I could see the panic on her face.

"Yes, or it's really Randolph Wade you saw, and the body on the beach is someone else."

"But . . ."

"But even if you really did see Wade at the marina, why would he be any kind of threat to you? Think about it. As far as he's concerned, he bought your silence with his five hundred dollars. There's no way he could have any idea you hired us to find him. And you told me you never took him to your condo, so he has no way of knowing where you live. Or your real name."

I said the words with an assurance I was far from feeling. That afternoon's encounter in Beaufort suddenly loomed much larger in importance.

Erik spoke for the first time since Karen Zwilling had begun her story. "I agree with Bay. I'm sure it gave you a shock to see someone who looked like this guy when all along we'd all assumed he was dead. But either way, I can't see that you're in any danger."

"You don't think so?" Apparently my opinion carried far less weight than that of my handsome partner. "Really?"

"If you're that concerned, why don't you take a few days off? Go visit friends or family."

"I can't. I . . . I just can't," she said, her eyes downcast.

"Whatever you say." I caught Erik's eye and shrugged.

"Why don't I take you back to the office, and we can pick up your car. I'll follow you home and make sure everything's okay."

His smile seemed to reassure her.

"I'm sorry I barged in on you like this," Karen Zwilling said, rising. "I'm just lucky Erik answered his cell and agreed to meet me at the office. I didn't know what else to do."

"You did the right thing," I said, following them toward the entryway. "Try not to worry."

Karen paused, one hand on the front doorknob, and looked back. "Are you going to, you know, investigate this? I talked to Layla, and we're willing to pay whatever it takes to find out whether this bastard is alive or dead."

"We'll keep on it," I said, again catching the quizzical look on Erik's face, "until we know for certain one way or the other."

"Thanks."

I tugged at Erik's sleeve as he prepared to follow our client out onto the porch. "Get back here as soon as you can," I whispered.

I closed the door behind them and rested my head on the cool wood. *Where does all this fit into the equation?* I asked myself. *Could the older man with the guy Karen thought was her rapist have been Win Hammond?*

Neddie's voice at my shoulder made me jump about six inches off the carpet. "Bay? Are you all right?"

I tuned back in to see her face wrinkled in worry. "I'm fine. Sorry about all that." I linked my arm with hers and guided us both up into the kitchen. "I need a nice cup of tea. How about you?"

Neddie dropped into one of the chairs around the breakfast table. "What I could use is a good stiff shot."

"Trouble with the girl child?" I asked, carrying the nearly empty bottle of Scotch and a glass to her. "Ice? Water?"

She shook her head and poured herself a stiff measure. "Since when did you take to keeping the hard stuff in the house?" she asked after drawing a long, slow sip.

"Since alcohol-needy people started dropping in on me at all hours of the day and night," I said lightly.

"If you want us out of here, just say the word," she snapped, a clear note ringing out as she set her drink none too gently back onto the glass-topped table.

"Hey, lighten up." The microwave dinged, and I pulled out the steaming mug of water. I dunked a teabag into it and seated myself in the chair across from Neddie. "You asked the question."

Her shoulders sagged, and she shook her head. "You're right. Sorry. I'm more pissed at myself than anyone else. What the hell was I thinking?"

"You talking about the little prima donna in there?"

That got a smile. "Yeah. When she showed up on my doorstep and told me her story, I just reacted. It seemed so clear to me at the time. You know, that I should get her out of Savannah, away from whoever was threatening her." Neddie Halloran ran a hand distractedly through her thick, bright hair. "Now . . ."

"Well, you can't go back tonight, so let's follow the advice of your favorite literary belle and worry about it tomorrow."

"I'm afraid she's going to take off again," she said, the smile fading into a worried frown. "It's the main reason I came to you instead of taking her to a hotel."

"Once I set the alarm system, she won't get out of here without waking the entire island. You can rest easy on that score."

"I know." The face my friend turned up to me carried a fear I'd never seen before. "And no one can get in. I'm counting on that, too."

By the time Erik trudged back up the steps a little before midnight, both my guests had retired to the spare room. Yancey hadn't been too happy about sharing the bed with Neddie, but I'd convinced her it was that or the floor. I tried to dismiss the girl's total disregard for others as simply the defense mechanism of a scared kid, but she made it tough to be sympathetic.

Which is why Neddie's the shrink and you're the bean counter, I'd been telling myself when the phone jangled again in the kitchen. I let it ring, and Ben Wyler's voice, more irritated this time, ordered me to call him back immediately. He'd apparently gotten over whatever twinge of conscience had softened his tone on his earlier message.

"You can be pissed at me all you want," he grumbled, "but this is business."

"Whatever," I said to the empty kitchen. I nuked another cup of tea and sank down onto the sofa. My partner's soft knock interrupted my contemplation of the empty fireplace.

"Everything okay?" I asked, following him into the kitchen.

"No problem." Erik swung open the refrigerator door and pulled out a beer. "I'll tell you what, though," he added as he twisted the cap off the chilled bottle. "We're definitely in the wrong business. You should see her place."

"Oh, yeah? Swanky?"

We perched on either end of the sofa. "Classy. Third floor, ocean-front, complete wall of windows facing the beach. Everything inside looks brand-new."

"Maybe she comes from money," I said. "Wouldn't be the first time a poor little rich girl decided to try life in the fast lane."

He shook his head. "I don't think it's that. There's something . . . I don't know, almost *sad* about Karen."

I didn't want to get into a discussion of our client's psyche in the middle of the night. "I need to tell you about what happened today. Wyler and I went to Beaufort to follow up on your lead about Win Hammond staying with Bobby Delacroix."

"Did you find him?"

I related the tale of our encounter with the scruffy, bat-wielding man on the back porch, told him about Ben's theory that the guy might be the real Randolph Remington Wade.

"How does he figure that?" Erik asked, setting his empty beer bottle on the carpet beside the couch.

"I don't know exactly. He has this idea Win and Wade must know each other because they're both involved with boats and both have ties to the Virgin Islands."

"So that's why you questioned Karen about the other guy she saw." He paused, then shrugged. "I suppose it's possible, but it sounds pretty thin to me."

"That's what I said. Anyway, the Judge is checking on Delacroix, but first reports are that Bobby's not built like the back end of a Mack truck like the guy we saw today. Maybe Wyler's on to something."

It occurred to me then that maybe I should have taken Ben's calls. Both times he'd said it had something to do with the case. Or maybe that was just an excuse. He'd sounded pretty contrite the first time, as if he felt bad about his performance in the driveway. I glanced at my watch. I had no idea if he was a night owl or if . . .

"Bay?"

"Hmm? Oh, sorry. You were saying?"

"Look, it's late. And you've got company. Why don't we try to sort all this out in the morning?"

"You haven't asked anything about my visitors."

"None of my business," he said without a trace of rancor.

"Well, it's going to become our business whether we like it or not. Want another beer?"

"No thanks. I'm half asleep as it is."

I remembered then that Erik had spent the previous night curled up in his SUV in front of the Delacroix house waiting for Win Hammond to show up, then driven back to the island, cleaned up, and gone to work.

"Oh, God, Erik, I'm sorry! You haven't really slept in almost forty-eight hours. Go home. We'll talk about it tomorrow."

"I'm fine. What do I need to know?"

"Nothing more tonight. Sleep in. I've got some things to take care of myself, so let's meet at the office around noon."

He uncoiled his long frame from the soft cushions. "Whatever you say. But I'll probably go in at the regular time."

I followed him to the door for the second time that night.

"It's your body," I said, and he grinned.

"Anything you want me to get started on?" he asked.

I thought about it for a moment, my eyes drawn to the hallway and the closed door of the guest room. "Yes. Check out the name Yancey Sullivan. See if she's got a record or any kind of paper trail."

"Will do," he said. "Good night."

I watched him jog down the steps before closing the door and setting the alarm system. I stepped up into the kitchen, suddenly bone tired. I piled dirty glasses into the dishwasher, looking up as the sweep of Erik's lights flashed across the ceiling. I moved to the window as he backed his big SUV around and headed out of the driveway. I have no idea why I stood there, gazing out into the dark after the hulking silhouette of the Expedition had been swallowed up by the night.

I had just begun to turn away when I saw a pair of headlamps click on out by the street, and a vehicle pulled slowly after my partner's retreating taillights.

CHAPTER
TWENTY-THREE

J AWOKE TO WONDERFUL SMELLS DRIFTING UNDER MY closed bedroom door. I rushed through my shower, threw on shorts and a T-shirt, and hurried out to the kitchen.

Neddie stood at the stove, the spatula in her right hand poised over a sizzling frying pan. "Good morning," she called.

"Hey! What are you doing?"

"I believe they call it cooking. Yancey, have you finished setting the table?"

The young woman barely glanced up from the newspaper spread out before her.

I crossed the hardwood floor and snatched the *Island Packet* out from under her fingers. Her icy stare fixed itself on my face. "Plates and glasses to the right of the sink, silverware in the drawer beneath. Hop to it, kiddo."

I heard Neddie's low chuckle as the teenager made a production number out of banging utensils onto the blue flowered placemats while I sat and scanned the headlines. Randolph Remington Wade's case had already been relegated to a small paragraph on page three which reiterated the scanty details and again asked for help from the public in identifying the victim. I wasn't certain how long I could keep Karen Zwilling's involvement—not to mention Star Ryan Kennedy's—out of the hands of the sheriff. What we needed was a positive ID on the guy. I wondered if Ben Wyler's hints to the death investigator had been enough to push him toward seeking assistance from the FBI. Our own State Law Enforcement Division could certainly help if the decedent had been from South Carolina.

"How long?" I asked Neddie as I passed behind her to the built-in desk on the other side of the kitchen.

"Couple of minutes."

Quickly I dialed Wyler's number, waiting through nearly a dozen rings before the machine picked up. "This is Bay. I got tied up last night. Call me."

I punched in the office number as I walked down the steps and out onto the deck.

I'd debated a long time the night before about whether or not to call Erik on his cell and alert him to the possible tail. I wasn't certain exactly what had held me back. Maybe the fear of making a fool of myself if it turned out to be something completely innocent. I didn't like the idea that I'd begun to question my own judgment, but the events of the past few days seemed to have eroded my confidence in some insidious way I didn't want to examine too closely.

Erik answered almost immediately.

"Hi, it's me." I took a deep breath and plunged in. "Anything unusual happen last night after you left here?"

"Like what?" Erik asked, his voice surprisingly chipper for the small amount of sleep he must have gotten over the past two days.

"I think someone followed you." Above me, in the branches of the moss-laden oak that shaded the deck, I watched a pileated woodpecker attack a thick, twisted limb.

"What do you mean?"

"I watched out the window after you pulled out. A pair of headlights came on all of a sudden, from the side of the road, as if the car had been waiting back a ways from my drive. He went in your direction."

"Coincidence. Could have been visiting one of your neighbors. Maybe someone had a party."

"Could be, but I don't like it. Did you go straight home?"

"We could classify that as technically none of your business," he said, the grin coming through in his voice, "but I'll let it slide."

"Erik, I don't think this is anything to laugh about."

"Yes, I went home," he said, his tone sobering, "but I think you're worrying over nothing." He paused a moment. "Did you get a good look at the car? Make or model? Color?"

"No, nothing," I said. "The light's bad out there. All I saw were the headlamps snap on, then the vehicle move after you."

I jumped as fingers tapped against the glass of the French door and saw Yancey motion for me to come to the kitchen.

"Then don't worry," Erik said. "Listen, I was just about to call you. I'm not having much luck with the girl. Juvenile records are sealed, and their firewall is pretty sophisticated. It could take a lot of effort to crack into it. I'll be glad to have a go at it, but—"

"That's okay. We'll reserve that for later if Neddie and I can't get her to open up. I plan on taking a run at her right after breakfast. How about other stuff? Like a birth certificate?"

"Piece of cake. You want the details now?"

I thought about that for a moment. "Just print out whatever you've got and open a file. And check out the mother. See if you can find anything about her disappearance around five years ago. Maybe it was under suspicious circumstances, and it made the papers."

"I'm on it."

"Great. Listen, we need to have a sit-down. There's been too much going on, and I'm losing control. Give Ben a call and see if he can meet us at the office, say, around three. I'll try to be in before then, and we can go over whatever you've found out about the girl."

I glanced through the French door to see Neddie and Yancey already seated at the table, both their faces turned in my direction.

"Will do. Anything else?"

"Yes. Check in with the Judge. He may have more information on Bobby Delacroix. And call the Westin and see if Star Kennedy is still registered. I may need to talk to her again."

"Got it."

"Thanks," I said, slipping through the door. "See you later."

I hung up and slid into my chair before a plate heaping with bacon and scrambled eggs. A platter of toast and English muffins sat in the center of the table. "Ladies," I said, the fork poised halfway to my mouth, "eat up. Then we need to talk."

I made it to the office a little after two thirty to find Erik's Expedition missing from the parking lot and the front door locked. I let myself in and found three message slips neatly stacked next to my telephone alongside a note telling me my partner would be back in ten minutes. I tossed my bag on the client chair, seated myself behind the desk, and picked up the pink forms.

Star Ryan Kennedy was still registered at the Westin but hadn't answered her calls or picked up her messages as of one thirty. Ben might be late but would make it as close to three as he could. The third slip left me massaging my forehead as I stared at the name and tried to dredge up its significance. I'd heard it before, and recently.

I slid open a bottom drawer, slipped off my shoes, and propped up my bare feet. I leaned back and closed my eyes, willing myself to remember. *Henry Littlejohn, Henry Littlejohn . . .*

"If you're that tired, you ought to go home."

I jerked forward, my feet sliding off the edge of the drawer to land with a thump on the carpet. Ben Wyler stood grinning from my doorway.

"Jesus, Mary, and Joseph, Wyler! You scared the hell out of me!"

"Let that be a lesson," he said, picking up my bag by its handles and dropping it on the corner of the desk before seating himself in the single chair. "Falling asleep with the place wide open could get you hurt. I coulda popped you from the outside door there, and you never would've known what hit you."

"I wasn't sleeping." I pushed myself up straight in the chair. "I was thinking."

Wyler snorted. "Yeah, right."

I was saved from killing him by Erik's arrival. "Sorry," he called as he shut the outer door behind him. "I thought we might need some sustenance."

Breakfast seemed light years in the past. "Bring it in here, please," I hollered as I slid my feet back into my shoes.

Erik set a six-pack of Diet Coke and a bag of corn chips on my desk, then pulled the receptionist's chair in from the outer office. "How did it go with—"

I shook my head and gestured toward Wyler who grinned and didn't even pretend not to have noticed.

I ignored him. "Interesting," I said to Erik. "I'll fill you in later."

The former police officer pulled one bare ankle across a knee and leaned back. "Business?" he asked.

"Yes, but not yours." I popped the top on a cold soda and ripped open the bag of chips. "You have something to share, Mr. Wyler?"

He looked blankly back at me.

"About the case? You left me a couple of messages last night."

"Oh, yeah. That. Well, I wanted to let you know I found the Jamaican."

Henry Littlejohn. The lights clicked on in my head. I picked up the message slip. "He called."

"Here? When?" Wyler's voice boomed in the small office.

"About an hour ago," Erik said. "Is he the guy who's been bothering Miss Hammond?"

"The same," Wyler said. "What'd he want?"

"You first," I interrupted.

He shot me a look I couldn't quite read, then shrugged. "He's at the Motel 6. Down on 278 next to Tony Roma's."

"Did you speak with him?" I asked.

"Nope. Just located the car. License plate checks out with what I wormed outta the rental car company at the airport."

"What time was this?"

"Right before I called you. I was sitting in the motel parking lot and thought you'd want to know." When I didn't reply, he said, "I waited around for a couple of hours, but he never left, so I went home. Got his room number, though."

I did the math. So it had to have been sometime in the middle of the evening, say maybe eight or eight thirty, when Wyler gave up his surveillance. Plenty of time for Mr. Littlejohn to have been parked outside my driveway waiting to follow Erik. I wondered how long he'd been there. Had he trailed Erik and Karen Zwilling back to her place? The concern must have registered on my face.

"What is it, Bay?" Erik asked. "Trouble?"

"He could be the guy who followed you last night. Could he have tailed you and Karen?"

"I don't know. I wasn't really looking—"

"Wait a minute! Hold it!" Wyler dropped both feet to the floor and sat up straighter. "What the hell are you talking about? Someone's tailing the kid?"

Wyler was oblivious to the red flush of anger rising up Erik's neck and into his face. "Excuse me?" my partner said in a too-quiet voice.

Wyler ignored him. "Why would the Jamaican be interested in the kid and the hooker? And what the hell were they doing at your place anyway?"

"We'll get back to that." I waved away his protest and spoke to Erik. "There's only a name and number on the message. What did the guy actually say?"

Erik shot Wyler a venomous look and shook his head. "Nothing. Just asked for you and left his contact info when I told him you weren't here. Looks like an out-of-area cell number to me."

"This is weird."

"That makes three, in case anybody's counting," Wyler said.

"Three what?"

"Three guys from the same neck of the woods who all seem to have converged on Beaufort County in the last week. Don't you think that's getting a little past coincidence?"

He had a point. "But what's the connection? All we have are about a million loose threads with nothing to hang a theory on." I paused. "Unless you'd care to give us the benefit of your years of experience?"

Ben Wyler grinned. "You don't like my theories, remember? Besides, I'm trying to win my way back into your good graces. I'm just here to take orders like the rest of the grunts."

The image made me laugh, and I saw that Erik had also relaxed back into his seat with a smile.

"Maybe this Littlejohn guy can shed some light," I said and picked up the phone.

I watched Wyler pop the tab on a can of Diet Coke while I listened to the ringing. I had about decided to give up when the voice I remembered from outside Miss Addie's door said, "Yes? Who's calling?"

"Mr. Littlejohn?"

"Who is this, please?"

"It's Bay Tanner. We met a few nights ago at The Cedars. I'm returning your call."

The pause stretched out, and I glanced up to find both Wyler and Erik studying my face.

"Mr. Littlejohn?"

"Yes. Sorry. I believe we have a mutual acquaintance."

"Win Hammond," I said, and he laughed.

"I know him as James Holland, but I'm certain we're talking about the same man."

I leaned back in the chair and propped my feet back on the open desk drawer. "What's your interest in him?"

"I was about to ask you the same thing, Mrs. Tanner." The soft cadence of his Jamaican accent took any hint of the sinister from his words, although his tone held more than a little challenge.

"Look, Mr. Littlejohn, I don't feel the need to explain myself to you. Whatever the man may have done in the islands, it has nothing to do with us. My primary concern is with his sister, the woman you've been harassing. If you've got business with Win, tend to it. Just leave Miss Hammond out of it. Do I make myself clear?"

"That sounds remarkably like a threat," the Jamaican said softly.

Wyler leaned forward, snatched a pen from the holder, and scribbled across my desk pad. I had to twist around to make out the words "arrange a meet" scrawled in red ink. I nodded.

"Maybe it wouldn't be a bad idea for us to get together. You could be here . . ."

Wyler made frantic slashing motions across his throat while mouthing, "Don't let on you know where he's staying!"

". . . in just a short time, no matter what part of the island you're on. My office is about halfway from either end."

"I don't think so, Mrs. Tanner," the smooth voice replied.

I shook my head at Ben and Erik.

"Why not? Perhaps we could help each other."

His laugh was rich and throaty. "I doubt it." Then all the amusement seeped out of his voice. "Unless you know where this Hammond can be found. If so, it would be in your best interests to tell me. Now."

I pulled myself upright in the chair. "*That* sounds remarkably like a threat, too, Mr. Littlejohn."

"Believe me, I mean you no harm. I have no quarrel with you or with the sister. But it is imperative I locate Mr. Hammond without delay."

"Are you a police officer?" I asked, remembering Erik's suggestion of a few days before.

"Good-bye, Mrs. Tanner. Think about what I've said."

I was listening to dead air. I lowered the phone to its cradle.

"Well?" Wyler folded his arms on the desk and leaned over them. "What did he say?"

I relayed the conversation.

"He's a cop," the detective said, settling back into his chair.

"Why do you say that?" Erik asked.

"Just a feeling. If he was a hit man or an enforcer, he wouldn't have bothered talking, either to you or to Miss Hammond. And he wouldn't be running around in a crappy car and staying at some low-end motel."

"I don't know," I said. "There's something about this whole thing that doesn't ring true. If Littlejohn is a cop, he has no jurisdiction here on his own. Wouldn't he have gone to the locals and asked for their help? It doesn't do him any good to find Win if he can't serve a warrant or whatever he's got."

The low hum in Wyler's throat reminded me of the Judge when he was mentally chewing on a problem. "Good points," he finally said. "But you're assuming he's on the up and up. There are places in the world where they aren't as concerned with the legal niceties as we are."

Erik cleared his throat and glanced sideways at Wyler. "I don't understand what it is Mr. Hammond's supposed to have done that would make him a target for either the police or some goon."

"Another good point," Ben conceded. "Maybe we've been going at this the wrong way." He glanced at Erik. "Can you get hold of the local papers down there where Hammond's been living?

"Sure, online. But what am I looking for?"

"I don't know. This Win guy showed up here a week ago today, right? Do we know when he booked his flight?"

Both Erik and I shook our heads, then my partner said, "Didn't Miss Hammond say she'd bought the ticket for him?"

"Right." I closed my eyes and conjured up the scant belongings I'd rifled through in Miss Addie's spare room. "You know, now that I think about it, I don't remember seeing anything like a return ticket in the stuff he left at her condo."

"Could be he wasn't planning on going back." Wyler paused. "Or, maybe he has a return, and he had it with him when he took off."

I mulled over the implications of that, none of which I liked.

"Why don't we ask the old . . . Miss Hammond what kind of ticket she bought him and when he first called her about being in trouble?" he asked.

"Why?"

"Give us a time frame," Wyler said. "Something happened right around then to spook him into running. I'm not buying that bullshit story about angry creditors. Unless it's a huge amount of money, and he owes it to the mob, no one would go to all the trouble of sending Little-john after him, especially not the cops."

I shook my head. "I don't want her upset any more than she already is. If we start suggesting her brother is involved in some sort of crime or that he may be planning on running out on her again . . ." I let the thought trail off, unwilling to put my fears into words.

"No problem," Erik said, rising from his chair. "I'll just start checking the papers for a robbery or some other big crime, say, a week or two before he left. I can get started on it now." He pushed the chair ahead of him into the reception area, and almost immediately I heard his fingers on the keys of his laptop.

I leaned back in my chair and sipped at the warm Diet Coke. Something niggled at the back of my mind, and I bent my concentration on it. Something about . . .

"So tell me what happened last night."

Wyler's voice sent the tenuous thought scurrying back into its hole. I sighed and let it go.

"Karen Zwilling showed up at the office, and Erik brought her over to my place." I gave him a thumbnail sketch of her encounter with the man she thought might be Randolph Wade. And his companion. "She was pretty spooked," I finished, "so I had Erik follow her home. Then he came back, we kicked it around for a while, and he left. That's when I saw the car pull out behind him."

"Hmmm. So you're thinking this other man the hooker saw might have been Hammond?"

I slammed the nearly empty soda can down on the desktop, and the clang made Wyler jump. "Quit calling Karen 'the hooker,' damn it! She has a name."

"Hey, take it easy, okay? I'm sorry. Force of habit. Anyway, did you buy her story?"

I closed my eyes and let out a long, slow breath. "I don't know. I haven't had time to turn around today let alone sit and think anything through." I eased the bottom drawer closed and slid my bare feet back into my sandals. "I'm going home."

Wyler reached into the open bag on the desk and pulled out a few corn chips, popping them into his mouth.

"You can sit here and stare at the walls if you like," I said, slinging my bag over my shoulder. "Make sure you lock up."

I moved out into the reception area. "Yancey?" I mouthed, and Erik slipped a file folder out of the center drawer. I shoved it into my bag and told him to call me if he found anything about Win. I was halfway to the outside door when Wyler spoke.

"You wanna grab a bite to eat later? You know you get cranky when you're hungry."

"Not in this lifetime," I said sweetly and slammed the door behind me.

CHAPTER
TWENTY-FOUR

J FOUND THE HOUSE EMPTY AND THE BED IN THE
guest room neatly made up. Propped against the mirror on
my dresser, a note announced that Neddie had taken Yancey to buy
some clothes. I peeled off my dress, kicked my sandals into the closet,
and flopped myself across the bed, the file Erik had slipped me spread
open on the duvet.

His research confirmed much of what I already knew about the girl.
Yancey Sullivan had been in and out of trouble since she was ten years
old. Her school records showed multiple suspensions for truancy, fighting, petty theft, and generally being an all-around pain in the ass to her
teachers and principals. Neddie had told me her most recent brush with
the authorities involved shoplifting. Her boyfriend, one Delbert
Watkins, was nineteen and had multiple arrests for a wide range of minor offenses, most pled out to time served in the city jail. Neddie said
there were allegations of drug possession, but nothing stuck.

More interesting were the birth certificate and two brief articles
from the *Savannah Morning News* Erik had copied for the file. Deirdre
Sullivan had been reported missing in October five years before by her
grandmother, with whom she and Yancey had been living. No mention
of the father. Deirdre had said she was meeting friends for drinks after

work but never showed up. Police requested information from the public, but with no signs of foul play, the story died after only a week.

I closed the thin file and tucked it back in my bag. Yancey had refused to discuss her mother when I'd tackled her that morning, insisting the disappearance had nothing to do with her current troubles. She was probably telling the truth, at least about that part of it, but you had to wonder how much that abandonment—whether intentional or not—had contributed to screwing up the poor kid.

I rolled onto my back and let the soft, rhythmic rotation of the ceiling fan cool the sheen of sweat on my face and neck. A light wind in the giant oak outside my window sent sunlight flickering in kaleidoscopic patterns against the backs of the drapes, and I felt myself sinking into a foggy haze of light and shadow . . . light and shadow . . .

I am drifting on the water, the gentle undulation of the waves like the tender rocking of a cradle. I lie on my back, my arms flung out from my sides. I float effortlessly, my eyes shielded somehow from the blistering sun as I stare directly into the cloudless dome of the sky. Something brushes my fingertips, and I turn my head. Rob's hand closes over mine, and I smile into his face.

"How are you, sweetheart?" he seems to whisper, although I hear no sound save the low murmuring of the ocean . . .

"I miss you," I answer, "every day . . ."

"Bay? Bay, honey, wake up."

I struggled to hold on to the vision, but it slipped away on the receding waves. "Oh, no, don't . . ."

I felt a hand on my bare shoulder, and I tried to slap it aside.

"Honey, I'm sorry." I opened my eyes to see Neddie's concerned face just inches from my own. "You were talking in your sleep."

I forced myself awake as Neddie seated herself on the edge of the mattress.

"I was dreaming," I said. "About Rob."

"I know. It must have been a good one." She reached out a tentative hand and pushed a lock of hair away from my forehead.

I looked up into her soft smile. "Yeah, pretty good."

Across her shoulder I spotted movement. Yancey Sullivan shifted

from one foot to the other as she stood poised in the doorway to my bedroom. I tugged a corner of the duvet across me, embarrassed to have
been found asleep in the middle of the day in my underwear. I wondered
how long she'd been standing there eavesdropping on my dreams.

"Want to talk about it?" Neddie asked.

I shook my head. "No, I don't think so."

"Whatever you say." She studied me for a moment, then forced a
smile. "Hey, we had quite a shopping spree this afternoon. You should
have come with us."

I swallowed against the dryness in my mouth. "Get out of here and
let me get dressed." I glanced at the girl. "We have to talk."

"Sure. I'll pour us some tea and meet you in the kitchen." Neddie
rose and patted my shoulder before turning toward the empty doorway.

Yancey Sullivan had slipped silently away.

A dash of cold water against my face and the comfort of old shorts and a
T-shirt made me feel almost human again as I wandered into the
kitchen. Yancey sat hunched over the table, studying her nails. Across
from her, Neddie twisted her glass around in circles. The silence seemed
to vibrate with tension. I pulled up a chair and downed half my iced tea
in one long, icy swallow.

"Okay, then," I said, "have you two had a chance to talk over what
we discussed earlier?"

They exchanged a look I couldn't interpret, but neither of them
spoke.

I'd spent the better part of the morning trying to pry the details of
Yancey's troubles out of the sullen teenager. She'd swung from stubborn
silence to anger and back again, but all the time I'd been aware of the
current of fear running just below the surface. Neddie wheedled and
coaxed; I yelled and demanded. In the end, I felt we'd gotten about as
much out of her as she was prepared to give. For the moment.

Yancey squinted against the glare of the late-afternoon sun through
the kitchen window. "I don't know what else you want me to say."

"I told you this morning. I want you to tell Dr. Halloran and me the truth."

The long blond hair glinted as she flipped it over her thin shoulder. "I did! What do you want from me? You want me to make something up?"

Neddie opened her mouth, but I got there before her. "I'm sure you're a very accomplished liar, Yancey. And you've spent enough time in the system to know just how to work it." I leaned forward on my elbows and held her gaze. "But I'm not a social worker. Or a shrink. I'm the person whose bed you're sleeping in and whose food you're eating, and I'm not buying your story."

"And I'm supposed to give a damn?"

"Yes, you are. You came to Dr. Halloran. She came to me. Do you want our help? If not, we can drop you off in Savannah, and you can get back to your life. Just say the word."

"Bay—"

I cut Neddie off with a wave of my hand. "Let her answer. You want to talk, or shall I get the car keys?"

I watched Yancey try hard to hold on to the bravado, the teenage defiance that twisted her pretty features into an ugly scowl. But she couldn't quite disguise the trembling lower lip. Reluctantly, she shook her head.

"Okay. So let's have the story. All of it."

"Delbert's going to kill me."

"Do you mean that literally? Has he threatened you?"

Yancey's eyes refused to meet mine. "I saw . . . I saw him and this other guy, Randy. They beat up some old dude, some drunk. They beat him bad. And they took his wallet." She swallowed hard. "There was a lot of blood. I was supposed to stay in the car, but . . . I think they killed him."

Neddie's hand reached across the table and patted the girl's arm. "Why didn't you just say so in the first place?"

"Because." She hesitated. "You know that call I got? In your office?"

"Yes."

"That was Delbert. He knew where I was. He said if I told you anything, he'd . . . he'd kill both of us. I didn't want to get you in the middle of this, honest, but I just didn't know where else to go!" She ended on a wail.

Neddie continued to stroke her arm and let her cry. When the bout of tears subsided, I handed Yancey a handful of tissues from the box on the counter, and she blew her nose loudly.

"If you'd told me all this back in Savannah, we could have gone right to the police."

"Don't you get it? That's why I didn't say anything. Del said if I went to the cops he'd say I was part of it. Randy, too. They'd both say I helped them. But I didn't do it. Honest. I don't want to go back to jail."

"You're not going to jail," I said with more conviction than I had any right to feel. "Let me check on something." I crossed to the phone and dialed the office. "When did all this happen, Yancey?"

"Last Saturday."

"Erik. Good, you're still there. Can you check something out for me?"

"Sure," my partner answered.

"See if you can find anything in the Savannah papers about a robbery last weekend. Someone beaten to death in the course of getting mugged."

"Do you have a name or anything else?"

"Nope, that's it."

"You want me to call you back?"

"Can you do it now?"

"Sure. Hold on."

I smiled reassuringly at Yancey while I listened to the tapping of Erik's fingers on the keyboard. Neddie brought the iced tea pitcher to the table and topped off everyone's glasses. In a moment, Erik was back.

"Nothing. There was a mugging all right, in an alley off Congress, but the victim was treated for a head wound and released. He claims the thieves got about a hundred bucks and his credit cards."

"Nothing else?"

"Nope. That's it."

"Okay, thanks."

"You got it, boss. I'm still checking on any crimes down in the Virgin Islands, but so far I'm coming up dry. I'll keep you posted."

"Thanks."

I looked up to encounter two anxious faces. "Did this happen around Congress Street?" I asked, and Yancey nodded.

"Somewhere in that area."

"Then Delbert is a worse liar than you are. The man walked away. Minor injuries."

"Really?"

"Really. If you like, I'll have a friend of mine in the sheriff's office double-check. I can ask him without having to give up any names. Okay?"

Relief radiated from the teenager, and the beginnings of a smile crimped the corners of her mouth.

"So let's get you back to Savannah. We've imposed on Bay's hospitality long enough." Neddie rose and worked the tension kinks out of her neck. "Your father should be back by then, right? We're all going to the police about Delbert and his pal Randy. When they're locked up, you can forget this whole ugly episode and concentrate on getting yourself straightened out. Deal?"

Yancey didn't reply, but I had no doubt Neddie would bring her around.

"Tell you what," I said, forcing cheerfulness into my voice, "let's do something fun tonight. You guys can take off for home tomorrow. How about dinner out and a cruise?"

"Great idea. What do you think, Yancey?"

"That'd be okay, I guess."

I tried not to be overwhelmed by her unbridled enthusiasm, but at that point I'd drag her along if necessary. I had a few plans of my own that had nothing to do with scumbag boyfriends or muggings, and I needed some cover.

"Good. Let's get changed. Nothing fancy," I said, "but we'll need sweaters for out on the water. There's a great little Greek place down in

Coligny Plaza. Market Street. They have plenty of vegetarian things on the menu. We can eat outdoors, then head down to the marina and catch the excursion boat. There's one going out around eight."

Yancey followed Neddie into the guest room while I loaded up my tote bag with what I thought I'd need for the second part of the night's mission: a black sweatshirt, a navy blue baseball cap, a small but powerful flashlight. And the Seecamp.

We sat beneath a green umbrella at a round table and watched the world go by. Tourists of all sizes and shapes and ages, most of them a shiny pink from their first days in the relentless South Carolina sun, streamed past. Yancey Sullivan, in a white tank top and a tiny piece of denim that barely qualified as a skirt, garnered more than her share of appreciative glances from the males of the teenage species who swaggered their way past us. Their sharp digs in each other's ribs and their squeaky, self-conscious laughter carried me back a few decades. While Yancey preened, Neddie and I exchanged do-you-remember grins behind her back.

I devoured my cheese steak sub—minus the green peppers, of course—and my companions, too, made short work of their dinners. We topped them off with luscious, warm bread pudding drowned in whipped cream. It would have been nice to linger a while in the fading heat of a summer's evening with the soft breeze off the ocean ruffling the tops of the trees, but duty called. We piled back into the car, three of us crammed into the T-Bird's two bucket seats. Yancey had insisted on having the top down, even though the thermometer still hovered in the high eighties. With both the air conditioning and the radio blasting, we wheeled into Palmetto Bay Marina in high spirits. I picked up the tickets I'd reserved at the little office on the pier, and we joined the throng of visitors waiting to board the double-decker boat.

I wandered along the dock, my gaze lingering on every large vessel moored or anchored, but I saw nothing that looked the size of the craft Karen Zwilling had described. Star Kennedy had referred to it as a yacht, and even with my limited knowledge I figured that meant something at least the size of the one I'd seen the previous Friday when Wyler and I had had dinner next door. Maybe it was still up on blocks being worked on. I drew in a deep breath and headed back to where Neddie and Yancey leaned against the rail of the dock.

I felt a stirring in the group around me as I came up to Neddie.

"Looks like they're getting ready to let us on," she said.

One of the cruise company's employees had begun to maneuver a set of wooden steps into position alongside the boat.

I scrunched up my face and made a show of running my hand across my temple. "Hey, I'm really sorry," I said, keeping my voice low and strained, "but I've got a headache coming on."

Neddie immediately opened her bag and began rooting around inside. "I've got some aspirin in here somewhere," she said.

"No, I think it's sinus. It's sort of making me sick to my stomach, too." Through my half-closed eyes I saw Yancey's face sag in disappointment. "I think you guys should go ahead. I'll just sit it out here, maybe go wait for you in the restaurant."

"Bay, if you're that sick, we should just go on home. Yancey won't mind. We'll do it another day."

"No, really. I don't want to spoil it. You two get on the boat and enjoy yourselves. I'll be fine." I swallowed hard for emphasis. "I just need to sit quietly. I'll be here when you get back."

"You're sure?" Neddie asked, and I felt a pang of guilt at the genuine concern on her face.

"Positive. Count how many dolphins you see."

"I'm sorry you're not coming with us," the teenager said in what I thought might have been the first show of real, unselfish emotion I'd seen from her.

I thanked her and watched as they joined the queue. The young man at the boat's railing took considerable time helping the coltish teenager on board, and I could hear her clear laugh at some comment he made as he moved on to assist Neddie onto the deck. I waited until the excursion boat had maneuvered its way out into Bishop's Reach and motored toward Calibogue Sound. I waved until I felt certain they could no longer discern me in the falling twilight. I meandered back along the dock, pulling the dark sweatshirt and baseball cap from my tote bag and tucking both the pistol and the flashlight into the pocket of my slacks. Weaving my way among the tightly packed cars and vans, I made a beeline for the boat repair shop at the far edge of the parking lot.

The big, oceangoing yacht loomed over me as I stepped around the side of the building. A lot of the barnacles and stains had been scraped and scrubbed from its hull, and I noticed some shiny metal rods in the vicinity of a propeller. The overpowering smell of dead vegetation and old fish had gone as well.

I set my bag down and pulled on the sweatshirt. It took a few moments to wind my hair into a ponytail and push it up under the cap. I slipped around to the far side of the huge boat and pulled out the flashlight.

When Ben Wyler had begun trying to take over the case, I'd decided to keep my feelings about the significance of the yacht to myself. I firmly believed it held the key to everything, and I was determined to find the answers on my own.

I'd purposely worn sneakers, but the loose gravel still crunched beneath my feet. In the stillness of the humid night, the slight noise sounded as if it would wake the dead. I paused every few steps to listen for any hint of activity inside, but I could detect neither light nor sound. It seemed as deserted as the silent thicket of scrub palmetto crowding in on me from the edge of the lot. I made a complete circuit before returning to the stern and gazing upward. The tarp which had hung down on my previous visit had been shifted enough for me to make out the gold letters, outlined in black: *Wade in the Water.*

No doubt now this was Randolph Remington Wade's floating love nest.

I moved again to the side screened from view of the marina and ran my light quickly over the wide expanse of fiberglass. Another gleam of metal caught the light, and I fixed the beam on it. About ten feet above my outstretched fingers the bottom rung of a boarding ladder hugged the side of the boat. I flexed my knees and jumped, but my momentum carried me nowhere near it.

An engine roared to life in the parking lot just a few yards away, and I started, nearly dropping the flashlight.

"Damn it!" I cursed under my breath and risked a peek beneath the curve of the bow to make certain no one was paying me any attention. The parking lot lay in shadows except for the lights of a minivan backing around and heading for the exit.

Surely there had to be some way for the men working on the boat to gain access to the upper parts of it. A quick glance around the exterior of the repair shop proved fruitless. I saw nothing, not even an old barrel or concrete blocks I might stack up. Whatever sort of ladder or platform they used must be hidden away somewhere.

I crouched down and studied the underside of the yacht. I thought perhaps there might be a trapdoor, some way of gaining access to the engine and whatever mechanism ran from it to the propellers. A drive shaft of some kind, I supposed. But nothing marred the smooth surface. Lost in concentration, I almost missed the sound of a car door being eased quietly closed.

Almost.

I watched a pair of denim-clad legs ending in crepe-soled deck shoes begin moving in my direction.

I rose slowly and darted a glance over my shoulder. In that spot the thicket had encroached to within a few feet of where I stood, and I edged my way toward it, moving backward one deliberate step at a time while my eyes stayed riveted on the approaching figure. Because he made no noise, I had to be extremely careful not to disturb so much as a pebble. I wasn't moving fast enough. He would be on me before I had covered even half the distance to concealment.

I'd just about determined to make a run for it when a huge *boom* split the night. Seconds later a flash of bright orange burst over the condos lining the harbor as fireworks exploded in the black sky. Another rocket whistled, and another concussion rocked us. The feet paused, then turned in the direction of the marina. I sprinted to my left, ducking down in front of a huge motor home while above me the weekly fireworks show down the way at Shelter Cove drew oohs and ahs from the crowd now gathering on the dock.

In a crouch I crept to the next line of parked vehicles, not daring to stick my head up until I had worked my way close to the restaurant. I waited for a group of tourists to move out into the parking lot before straightening up and easing my way into their midst. Together we headed in the direction of the dock, and I made certain to stay well within their protective cover.

By the time I felt safe enough to risk a look back toward the towering yacht, my stalker had disappeared.

CHAPTER
TWENTY-FIVE

*T*HIS TIME I DIDN'T HAVE TO FEIGN THE HEADACHE THAT had Neddie clucking over me like a mother hen. Oblivious as usual, Yancey chattered away about the dolphins and the sunset and the fireworks as we made our way home.

In my room, I stripped off my fear- and sweat-soaked clothes and climbed into the shower.

Who was it? I asked myself over and over as the steaming water eased away the tightness in my shoulders and head. Possibilities came readily to mind—security, or maybe one of the owners or employees of the repair shop. Win Hammond. Bobby Delacroix. Randolph Wade.

Had he seen me? I wondered, stepping out onto the bathmat and toweling my hair. Did he know someone lurked just a few feet away, watching his stealthy approach?

I slipped into my favorite cotton pajamas and decided I needed advice. As I moved down the hallway, I could hear a soft murmur of voices coming from behind the closed door of the guest room. I smiled, remembering many such times in the shared apartment of our college days when Neddie and I had sat up late into the night, wrapped in blankets against the bitter Lake Michigan winds rattling the windows, and planned our future. I hoped Neddie had a prayer of setting Yancey on the right path.

I nuked water for tea and longed for the calming ritual of a cigarette as I punched in Ben Wyler's number. He answered on the first ring.

"It's Bay," I said after his gruff, monosyllabic greeting.

"Where've you been?" he demanded, and I felt my hackles rise.

"Out. And now I'm back." I dropped a teabag into the steaming cup and banged it on the kitchen table. *Damn him!* The man knew the location of every single one of my buttons and exactly how hard to push them.

"Do you ever think about picking up messages? Just on the off-chance that—oh, I don't know—say, maybe someone might be trying to get in touch with you?"

I glanced guiltily at the blinking red light on my answering machine. I'd shut down my cell phone on my way to reconnoiter the boat.

"Sorry. Circumstances prevented. What did you want?"

I could almost feel him reining in his temper like a rider trying to control an unruly horse. "We need to talk," he said in a much softer tone.

"What do you call this?" I knew the wisecrack was a mistake a moment before the dead silence descended on Ben Wyler's end of the line. I waited a beat before backtracking. "Sorry. I'm tired, and it's been a long day." I sipped tea. "Ben? Are you there?"

My thumb was moving toward the Off button when I heard his voice, the barely suppressed anger evident in every syllable. "I'm coming over. Call me in a pass for the gate."

"That's not a good idea, Ben. It's late. And I've got company."

This time the silence lasted much longer. It never occurred to me how my last pronouncement must have sounded until he said, "Then tell your boyfriend to get his pants on and stay the hell out of my way. I'll see you in twenty."

I listened to the dial tone for a few seconds before bursting into laughter.

I thought about getting dressed again but instead settled for a white cotton robe buttoned chastely from knees to neckline over my pajamas.

I'd been watching at the bay window in the kitchen for the sweep of his headlights so I could intercept him before he rang the bell. The lights were out in the guest room.

By the time Ben Wyler emerged from the old Jaguar and mounted the steps to the front porch, I had the door standing open. I leaned against the inside wall, one hand on my hip.

"You look just like my mother used to when I came home at three in the morning," he said, edging around me into the hallway. "Actually, you're kinda dressed like her, too."

"Excuse me?"

Wyler moved into the great room, his head swiveling from side to side as if he'd entered a crime scene and had to be certain no more danger lurked in the far corners. "You know, the pj's thing," he said. "I didn't think women wore those anymore." He twitched aside one of the drapes drawn over the French doors out to the deck.

It suddenly occurred to me that Ben Wyler had not been in my home since the day he'd executed the bogus search warrant nearly a year before. I decided not to think about the implications of that. "You want something to drink?"

"Got a beer? Or doesn't a good little teetotaler like you keep anything alcoholic on hand?"

I ignored the sarcasm, and he followed me up the steps.

"Nice," he said, his gaze roving around the kitchen.

I retrieved a beer from the fridge and handed it over. "Glass?"

"Nope, this is good." Wyler twisted off the top and again studied the room. "Are these granite countertops? The color goes great with the floor."

"Look, Wyler, can we get down to business? Or did you come barging in here at midnight to give me a real estate appraisal?"

The laugh escaped in a short grunt as if he'd been trying to hold it back. He shook his head. "You know, I really like you, Miss Lydia."

I watched the amusement in his eyes slip into something softer, and I turned quickly back to the refrigerator. I popped the top on a can of Diet Coke and, avoiding his gaze, led the way back into the great room.

I perched on the edge of one of the wing chairs by the fireplace. Wyler took the near end of the sofa.

"I didn't see the sergeant's car," he said, the flip words belied by the intensity in the gray-green eyes locked on my face.

I shook my head. "I hope you were a better cop than you are a private eye. My company is my old college roommate and her . . . niece." Yancey's problems were none of Wyler's business unless and until I decided they were. "They're both asleep, which is where I'd like to be as soon as you get whatever it is off your chest."

"Your roommate," he said, smiling. "Well okay." He relaxed into the cushions.

"Ben . . . ," I began, and he waved his hand.

"Okay. Right." He took a long swallow of beer and set the bottle on the end table. He rested his elbows on his knees and leaned over, nodding. "I got a call this afternoon, late. From Morgan down at the sheriff's office."

I sat up a little straighter. "Something happening with the Wade case?"

"Yup, you could sure as hell say that."

I waited, but he seemed determined to drag it out. "So tell me."

"Got a couple of reports back in. Fingerprints and the official coroner's ruling."

I sucked in a lungful of air and let it out slowly. "And?"

"Made me feel like a complete idiot. Care to take a guess at who it is laid out on that slab?"

"How should I know? I thought running prints was the whole point of the exercise. To find out who the guy really is."

"You already know who it is," Wyler said, his eyes again studying my face intently.

I ran a hand through my tangled hair. "For God's sake, Ben! I don't feel up to your games. Just tell me." I watched the smile play around his thin lips for a moment before closing my eyes in concentration. They popped open a second later. "Wade! The dead guy really is Randolph Remington Wade."

"Bingo," Wyler said, and I slumped back in my chair.

"I don't believe it! But what about the watch? And the disfigurement? What was the point—"

"Slow down there a second," he interrupted me. "I told you before we were making a lot of assumptions."

"Occam's razor," I said.

"What?"

" 'One should not increase, beyond what is necessary, the number of entities required to explain anything.' "

"You mean like the KISS principle?" He read the confusion on my face. "Keep It Simple, Stupid."

"Exactly." I sipped on the Coke to give myself a chance to focus. "So the guy in the pictures with Star Kennedy and the body on the beach are the same person." I rubbed my temples. "But what about the height discrepancy? That's one of the things that originally had you convinced they weren't."

"It's still a problem, as far as I'm concerned," Wyler said. "I'd swear the man in those photos is at least two inches taller than the vic."

"But that would mean . . ." I scrunched up my eyes. ". . . the murder victim is the real Randolph Wade and the guy with Star is the imposter."

Wyler smiled. "Exactly where I'd gotten to. It's the only thing that makes sense."

"None of it makes sense. So who's the rapist?"

"I'd say the dead guy. He fits the . . . our *client's* description better."

"Agreed. But is he the one who was staying at the Holiday Inn Express or was it . . . ? God, this is so confusing!"

"It gets better." Wyler set the empty beer bottle on the floor. "Or worse, depending on how you look at it."

I tucked one leg up under me and waited for the detective to gather his thoughts.

"I haven't told you about the coroner's report yet."

"I thought that was pretty cut-and-dried. He died from multiple blows to the head."

"That was the preliminary ruling. On further examination, they determined the original wound to the back of the head was made a considerable time before the body was found."

"How considerable?"

"Hard to say exactly. At least a few hours, maybe as much as a couple of days."

I stared at him. "Are you telling me the guy was dead before somebody beat him up?"

Wyler shrugged. "That's what the coroner's saying. The blow to the back of his head, which is what ultimately killed him, was delivered before the whacks to his face."

We sat in silence, the only sound the whirring of the ice maker as it dropped precisely measured cubes into the waiting tray in the freezer. Ben Wyler sat back against the soft cushions of the sofa, one bare arm draped along the top as he studied me across the room.

"I can't make any sense of it," I said at last, shaking my head. "I need sleep and time to sort this all out."

"Never let it be said I can't take a hint." He pushed himself up and looked down at me. "But I do think we need to sit down with the kid and his computer and do some serious brainstorming. There's something at work here I don't like, and it worries me." He paused as I glanced up into his concerned face. "There's a chance you could be in danger."

"Me? Why?" I rose and pulled the crumpled robe back down over my knees. I expected Wyler to step back, but he stood his ground, and our eyes met and held just a few inches apart. For the first time I noticed how tired he looked, the lines around his mouth and nose more pronounced, his eyelids drooping with fatigue.

"You have a certain reputation for . . . let's say, leaping before you look. For sticking your nose in where it doesn't belong. Sound familiar?"

"Don't be silly," I said. I moved a step to my right, taking me out from under his intense gaze. "I'm not in any kind of danger." I stopped short, remembering the powerful pair of legs approaching the yacht as I'd hunkered, trembling, in the darkness of the parking lot. I glanced down at Wyler's feet.

"What? What are you thinking?" Wyler's hand clasped my upper arm and spun me back to face him. "Are you holding out on me?"

Again our eyes locked for what seemed like hours before I jerked my arm out of his grasp. "Give it a rest, Wyler. I'm fine." I pushed past him and out into the entryway. "Now get out of here so I can go to bed."

I flung open the door and waited as he took his own sweet time crossing the wide expanse of white carpet.

"Set that alarm system," he said without looking at me. Our arms brushed as he moved onto the porch. "I'll call you tomorrow."

I closed the door and punched in the codes, then leaned my head against the cool wood. In the distance, I heard the muted roar of the Jaguar's powerful engine as Ben Wyler sped out into the street.

CHAPTER
TWENTY-SIX

I EXPECTED TO SPEND THE NIGHT WITH THE CONUN-
drum of Wade's death running endlessly around in my head,
and I wasn't disappointed. I woke feeling as if I had slept a total of fifteen minutes. I crawled out of bed, brushed my teeth, and ran a comb
carelessly through my hair, then followed the sound of light, feminine
voices toward the kitchen.

Dolores presided over the stove, her practiced hand flipping pan-
cakes on the griddle as if she'd been a short-order cook all her life. Beside her a giggling Yancey, also armed with a spatula, tried to emulate
her precise movements. Splatters of pancake batter around the edges of
the counter and down the front of the cabinets made it plain her tech-
nique still needed work.

"Good morning!" Neddie called from her place at the table, and the
other two looked up.

"Good morning," I echoed, smiling at the contrast between the
tall, leggy teenager and my dark, diminutive housekeeper. *Light and
shadow,* I thought, brushing away the remembered dream.

"Mrs. Santiago is teaching me to flip," Yancey said with another
bubble of laughter. "I haven't quite got it yet."

"Ah, *Señora,* this one, she is *un tesoro.*" Dolores beamed at the young
woman.

"A treasure. To be sure." I joined Neddie at the table and lowered my voice. "You taking off today?" I asked.

"We'll head straight for the police station," she said, her voice low. "The sooner her crazy boyfriend gets locked up, the safer I'll feel."

"You're welcome to come back here," I said.

"What are you guys whispering about?" Yancey appeared at Neddie's shoulder.

"Nothing—" I began, but my friend shook her head.

"No more secrets, Bay. Everyone tells the truth up front. I was saying that we're going directly to the authorities when we get back to town, Yancey. We'll wait until Delbert and Randy are rounded up and charged, then we'll get you back to your father's."

"Will I have to testify?" the girl asked.

"I'm sure you will," I said, "but don't worry about that now. Dr. Halloran will take good care of you, and you can both come back here if you like until it all dies down."

Dolores distributed plates of hotcakes, some of them crimped and slightly out of round. We ate in silence except for occasional requests to pass the syrup or butter, and the lack of distracting conversation allowed the questions surrounding Randolph Wade to rise front and center in my head again. While Dolores saw to the washing up and the other two wandered off to pack up Yancey's new wardrobe, I carried a fresh cup of tea into the office.

Erik would be at work at his other job by this time, I figured, so I left a message on his cell phone voice mail asking him to call me at his earliest opportunity. I pulled out the legal pad with the Wade list I'd been working on when Neddie first called me about Yancey, but it was based on what I now knew to be an entirely false set of assumptions. I tried to rearrange the items in the columns into some semblance of logic, but nothing fit.

I'd just about convinced myself it was time to take up smoking again when a tap on the closed door was followed by Neddie's soft voice.

"Bay? We're leaving now."

I stepped out into the hallway. "Good luck," I said, hugging my old friend. The girl surprised me by stepping awkwardly into my offered embrace. "Tell the truth," I whispered against her soft cheek.

I watched from the kitchen as they slipped into Neddie's Mercedes and disappeared onto the street.

"*Señora?*" Dolores said at my elbow. "They will be fine," she added, her head nodding to emphasize her words. "You no worry."

I smiled. "I hope you're right."

"I do the shopping now," she said more briskly, and I realized she had her purse draped over her arm and the ever-present list in her hand.

"Fine. See you later."

Back in the office I tried to concentrate on the tangled mess of the Wade case, but my mind kept wandering back to the boatyard and the stealthy visitor I had nearly interrupted. When Erik hadn't returned my call by eleven o'clock, I decided to put it all out of my head and take a swim.

Visitors and their children packed the beach for as far as I could see. I wove my way among the coolers and blankets, dropped my T-shirt on the sand just beyond the tide line, and plunged into the warm Atlantic. I paddled out into the small rollers, dodging inflated rafts and boogie boards, finally reaching a point where I could stretch myself into a steady crawl. I let the soothing salt water and the rhythmic cadence of my strokes ease the tension from both my body and my mind.

When I had pushed myself nearly to the point of exhaustion, I dragged myself back to the house, took a long, hot shower, and collapsed onto the bed.

I hadn't intended to fall asleep, but I must have dozed. I vaguely remembered a soft tap on the door and Dolores's voice. Bright sunlight through the partially open drapes and a low rumbling in my stomach told me I had slept into the middle of the afternoon. In the bathroom, I splashed cold water over my face and ran a brush through my matted hair. I listened for a moment, but the house lay in blessed stillness.

I found Ben Wyler sitting in one of the wing chairs, a book open on his lap. He glanced up as I stopped in the entrance to the great room, my heart nearly dropping to my feet at the shock of seeing him there.

"Well, look who's finally up." He closed the pages against his index finger, marking his place. "Good thing you've got some decent reading material."

He held the book up for my inspection.

"You're a noir fan?" I asked, eyeing the lurid cover of a reprint of Raymond Chandler's *The Big Sleep* he'd pulled from my bookshelves next to the fireplace.

"Those guys could really write," he said with a smile. "Hammett. Chandler. Ross-MacDonald."

I padded barefoot across the carpet and curled myself into a corner of the sofa.

"What are you doing here?"

He set the book aside. "I want to know what's going on."

"I don't know what you mean." I looked over his shoulder toward the kitchen. "Where's Dolores?"

"Don't blame her. I pretty much bullied my way in here."

"Why?"

"Why what?"

"I want to know why I wake up from a well-deserved nap and find a man making himself at home in my living room. I want to know why you 'bullied' your way in. And I want to know where Dolores is. Are the questions too tough for you, Detective?"

"One, because I want to talk to you. Two, because your housekeeper is a little terrier when it comes to protecting you. And three, I told her to take the rest of the day off."

"You told—?" I stopped at his upraised hand.

"Don't get all excited, Bay. Apparently one of her kids needed a ride home from school, and she couldn't get her husband on his cell phone, so she had to make the pickup. She said to tell you she'll be back tomorrow to finish up."

I bit back my anger as I untangled my legs and headed for the kitchen. I dropped two halves of an English muffin into the toaster and pulled the peanut butter jar out of the cupboard.

"Why don't you let me buy you dinner?" Wyler's voice next to my ear made me jump.

Once again he forced me to step away from the intensity of his eyes. I leaned back and steadied myself against the counter. This habit he'd developed of crowding me, of hovering as if waiting for an opportunity to pounce, grated on my nerves. Time to clear the air. I drew a deep breath.

"Look, Ben, let's get something straight. I'm not interested—"

"You're a liar, Bay Tanner." He propped his hands on the counter on either side of my waist, effectively blocking me in. "Look me in the eye and tell me you haven't felt this . . . pull, this attraction, whatever you want to call it. The first time I walked in this house with that search warrant I could feel it. You hated my guts that day, but it was still there, somewhere underneath all that outrage. Go ahead. Deny it."

He stood so close I could feel his breath on my lips. My body trembled, whether from anger or fear, I couldn't tell, but I knew for certain it wasn't desire. I forced myself to speak calmly.

"You're wrong, Ben." I stared steadily into his eyes, and something he read there convinced him

He stepped away, but his gaze never left my face. He raised his hands in a gesture of surrender.

"Hey, no problem." The sardonic grin I'd come to expect settled across his craggy face. "So how about tossing a couple more of those in the toaster? I'm starving."

"Sure," I said, and my hand shook only a little as I drew a knife from the drawer.

Over our impromptu lunch, Ben carried on as if the earlier episode had never happened, and I did my best to shrug off the feeling of unease his words had created.

We kicked around the Wade case for a while, though neither of us had anything further to add to the already tangled mess. What we did agree on was that the man Star Kennedy had been wining and dining and introducing to her Atlanta socialite friends had to be an imposter. Where he'd come from or how he'd acquired enough information—and identification—to impersonate the real Randolph Remington Wade remained open questions, along with what his motive might have been.

"Have you heard anything from your father about the Delacroix guy?" Ben asked as he gathered scattered crumbs from the table into a neat pile next to his plate.

"No, now that you mention it. I haven't talked to him since we had lunch with him at Presqu'isle." Almost two days with no word from my father. I felt the familiar niggling fear worm its way into my stomach. "I'll call."

I glanced at the clock over the sink as I punched in the numbers. At a little after three in the afternoon he might still be napping. I had worked myself into a state by the time I finally heard Lavinia's breathless "Hello?"

"Is everything okay? Where's Daddy?" I blurted.

"Land's sake, child, calm down. We're fine," she said in that annoyed voice I remembered so well from my childhood. "I was out on the back porch clippin' herbs for a gumbo. I'm not exactly up to sprintin' for the phone anymore."

I swallowed and waited a moment for my heart to resume its normal rhythm. "Sorry. Is he still napping?"

"Now how on God's green earth would I know that? Didn't I just tell you I've been outside?"

"Yes, ma'am, you sure did." I glanced at Wyler, his grin indicating he was enjoying my end of the conversation. "Will you see if he's up? I need to speak with him."

The clatter of the receiver on the kitchen counter was all the answer I got, but I could picture Lavinia stomping through the old house to my father's room. She was probably muttering under her breath as well. The mental image brought a smile.

"He's still asleep," I heard her whisper a few moments later. She must have picked up the extension on his nightstand. "You want me to wake him?"

"No! That's okay. Just have him call me as soon as he's up."

"I'll do that. Good-bye."

The click in my ear seemed much louder than usual, and I paused to wonder what had Lavinia in such a bad temper. Nothing I could do about it, whatever it was, I decided and returned to my seat at the table.

"He'll call," I said, and Ben nodded.

When he didn't add anything, I reached for the plates and empty iced tea tumblers and carried them to the sink. He stayed silent for a long time, his fingers drumming lightly on the glass of the table in time to some rhythm only he could hear as I stacked things in the dishwasher. At one point I thought I heard him murmur, "I wonder . . . ."

"Well." The word dropped into the stillness, and I jumped. Ben pushed himself up from the chair and stretched inelegantly. "God, I'm tired. Let's give it a rest and get back on this thing tomorrow."

The switch seemed so entirely out of character. His shoulders slumped, and his head appeared too heavy for his neck to hold up. I studied his face, mostly his eyes, and they told an entirely different story. For some reason, Wyler wanted to get out on his own, and he didn't want to tell me where he was going or why. I gave a thought to challenging him but decided against it. If he wanted to escape, who was I to stop him? God knew I'd felt that way plenty of times myself.

I followed him through the front entryway. "See you tomorrow," he said without turning around. "I'll call," he tossed over his shoulder, almost as an afterthought, as he trudged down the steps.

I wandered into the living room and picked up the book he'd left lying on the side table. I flipped through the first few pages of *The Big Sleep*. I dropped onto the sofa, my attention caught by a line of dialogue: " 'My God, you big dark handsome brute! I ought to throw a Buick at you,' " I read aloud, then laughed. I didn't remember who the speaker was, but I knew who she was talking about—Phillip Marlowe.

I scrunched down into the cushions and flipped back to the beginning. Maybe I'd have to throw Sam Spade over in favor of this "big dark handsome brute." Besides, I didn't like the way old Sammy talked to poor Effie Perine. I was pondering on his resemblance to a certain former New York homicide detective when the phone interrupted.

"Hello?" I said in the middle of the third ring.

"Mrs. Tanner?"

I recognized the singsong cadence immediately. "Yes, Mr. Littlejohn. What can I do for you?"

"I believe I may have been somewhat hasty during our last conversation." He paused. "I think a meeting may be to our mutual advantage."

His words took me completely by surprise. I scrambled around for an appropriate response. Ben Wyler may have thought me naïve, but I wasn't stupid.

"Fine. Someplace public. And in the daylight."

I heard his soft chuckle. "Of course. How about right now? Or in, say, thirty minutes. You name the place."

Again I fumbled around in my head, testing and discarding options. "Okay. Do you think you can find the Palmetto Bay Marina? It's off Palmetto Bay Road at the foot of the Cross Island Parkway." A plan was forming somewhere in the back of my head.

"I'm certain of it." Another pause. "Shall we say four fifteen?"

"Perfect. There's a little restaurant near the entrance. The Sun Rise Café."

"I'll be there." The line went dead.

I depressed the Off button, my hand hovering over the keypad while Wyler's phone numbers floated through my head. I slapped the handset back in its cradle and headed for the bedroom to change.

Two can play this game, I thought as I peeled off my shorts and T-shirt and pulled a pair of khakis from the closet. Even before slipping on my Birkenstock sandals I tucked the Seecamp pistol into my pocket.

CHAPTER
TWENTY-SEVEN

I FOUND HENRY LITTLEJOHN SEATED AT A ROUND PLAStic table on the narrow verandah of the small café. The smell of strong coffee drifted to me as I made my way slowly up the steps.

He lifted his eyes to meet mine. "Mrs. Tanner. Right on time. Thank you for agreeing to see me."

Up close and in full daylight, he looked much less sinister than he had in the dim hallway outside Miss Addie's door. "No problem." I pulled out a chair and sat down, settling onto my left hip so that the pocket holding the pistol would be in easy reach.

"May I offer you something? Coffee?" He signaled for the waitress who had been hovering just inside the door to the restaurant.

"Sweet tea," I said. "Thank you."

When she'd moved away, I leaned back and folded my arms across my chest. Neither of us spoke until my drink had been delivered, and we were once more alone.

"So?" I asked, and waited. Littlejohn had called this meeting, and I wanted him to make the first move.

"We seem to have reached something of an impasse," the big man said. Both his expression and his posture as he slouched casually in his chair were intended to put me at ease.

"Indeed. What do you have in mind?"

He smiled. "Americans are always so direct."

"I find it saves time." When he didn't respond, I added, "Let's start with who you are and why you're chasing Win Hammond. Or James Holland, as you call him."

He studied me for a moment, and I watched his eyes narrow in calculation. I could almost hear the monologue running through his head while he decided whether or not he should tell me the truth. I tensed when he suddenly rose and reached into the back pocket of his wrinkled pants, but his hand came away with a fat, tattered wallet. He flipped it open and slid it toward me as he reclaimed his seat.

The picture was fuzzy but recognizable. Some sort of official seal adorned the well-worn card which identified Henry Aaron Littlejohn as a licensed employee of Security 1 International.

"You're a private investigator?" Of all the scenarios Erik and Wyler and I had kicked around, that one had never surfaced.

"A fellow traveler, as it were."

"So you're not a cop."

"Former," Henry Littlejohn said.

I waited, but he simply stared back at me. In this game of conversational tennis, the ball was apparently back in my court.

"What's your interest then?" I swirled the ice around in my glass and sipped tea as if I didn't give a damn about his answer.

He smiled to let me know I wasn't fooling him for a minute. "I'm afraid that's confidential. Client privilege. I'm sure you understand."

"Then I see no point in continuing this conversation." I pulled my bag onto my lap and fished inside for my wallet.

I was surprised when the simple ploy seemed to work.

"Please, Mrs. Tanner. A little patience." I set the tote back on the concrete floor of the verandah. "I believe we can be of mutual assistance to each other. Within certain parameters."

Henry Littlejohn didn't talk like a private eye, or like a former cop either, for that matter.

"I'm listening," I said as he used the paper napkin underneath his unused silverware to wipe away the sweat beading on his coffee-colored forehead.

"I'm not interested in your Mr. Hammond or Holland or whatever he chooses to call himself."

He paused, inviting comment, but I merely tilted my head and waited for him to continue.

"I . . . *we're* attempting to locate a missing person. I'm convinced Mr. Hammond either knows where this man can be found or will eventually lead me to him."

"Why?" I asked. He looked puzzled, his narrow eyebrows scrunched together in a frown. "Why do you believe Win can help you? And if that's the case, why don't you just ask him? Why all this skulking around, harassing his sister and"—I decided to toss it out and see what kind of reaction I got—"and following my partner all over the island?"

The smile told me everything I needed to know, although he made no acknowledgment. Littlejohn *had* been tailing Erik the night I saw the car headlights at the end of my driveway. I was certain of it. And I also suddenly had a pretty good idea of who the missing person might be.

I stared into the detective's steady brown eyes and waited for him to answer.

"Let me tell you a story," he said, leaning back in his chair.

The waitress picked that moment to pop out the door, refilling Littlejohn's coffee cup. I waved away her offer of more tea. In the silence that followed I heard the guttural roar of a boat engine rumbling to life somewhere in the marina behind us.

The Jamaican cleared his throat. "Hypothetical, of course." His smile this time seemed genuine, and I relaxed a little.

"Of course."

He steepled his fingers beneath his chin. "A family spends more than a couple of centuries amassing a considerable fortune, prestige, a well-respected name. The embodiment of the American dream, if you will. Each generation manages to produce at least one member who demonstrates the ability to take the legacy and carry it forward." He paused, as if inviting comment.

I shrugged. It sounded like the tale of every wealthy, aristocratic family in the Lowcountry. "Go on," I said.

"This family is admired, powerful. They have their fingers in a lot of pies, from industry to agriculture to politics. Then, suddenly, a child comes along who doesn't fit the mold, doesn't want to toe the company line. A black sheep." He paused again. "Too much inbreeding, or at least that's *my* theory," he said with a rueful shake of the head.

A brief memory of Geoffrey Anderson flashed across my mind, but I forced it away. Instead I pictured Win Hammond as he must have been in his youth—wild, handsome, preferring bedrooms to boardrooms—skulking off to self-imposed exile in the sunny Caribbean. Perhaps that was the reason Littlejohn thought Win and his quarry might be connected. Birds of a feather.

"At any rate," the detective continued, "if such a person were the next in line, so to speak, and if he preferred to throw away his legacy in the pursuit of pleasure rather than preparing himself for his responsibilities . . ." He let the thought trail away. "Everything the family had worked for all those decades could be destroyed."

"So your company keeps him under surveillance?" When he didn't answer, I added, "And he's slipped your net."

Henry Littlejohn paused and looked directly into my face. "It's particularly bad timing." I watched him come to some conclusion in his head. "Look, Mrs. Tanner, the patriarch of this family—the man's uncle—is in frail health. He could go at any time." The detective sighed. "Unfortunately, my . . . assignment is the principal heir."

I should tell him, I thought, but I was convinced he held the key to the mystery I found myself embroiled in. A little more . . .

"And you're afraid he may have gotten into some kind of trouble?"

Littlejohn looked decidedly uncomfortable. "He's been known to . . . drink a little more than is good for him. And he's attached himself to some unsavory companions."

"Criminals?" I asked.

The cop mask slid down over his face. "I've been very forthcoming, Mrs. Tanner. Time for the quid pro quo. Do you know where this Hammond, or Holland, can be found?"

I shook my head and decided it was time to toss all the cards on the table. "No, I don't. But if the man you're really looking for is Randolph Remington Wade, I'm afraid I've got some bad news for you."

The sun had glided to the other side of the building, blocked now by the tall condominiums flanking the little harbor. Though not a breath of breeze stirred the bougainvillea twining up the roof supports, the temperature had dropped considerably.

Henry Littlejohn stared at me a long time before speaking. "You're certain?"

"My sources in the sheriff's office say the fingerprints came back with his name on them." I paused. "Although no one has actually made a positive ID of the body. Face to face, that is." Again I hesitated. "Do you know Wade by sight? Could you say for certain it's him?"

His head was shaking before I finished. "I've never met the man personally. I only picked up the assignment when my predecessor . . . allowed Mr. Wade to elude him. But I do have photos. Would you like to see them?"

"I'm not sure what good it would do. His face had been . . . battered. Our coroner says it may have been done postmortem."

I saw no reason to withhold the information. Henry Littlejohn's quarry was dead. His case was closed. I wondered what the remnants of this hypothetical family or their attorneys would do now. I assumed there'd be a secondary heir. Maybe the Wades wouldn't mourn too long or hard over their lost sheep.

Littlejohn interrupted my pointless speculations. "Postmortem? They're certain?"

"They say the fatal blow occurred anywhere from four to forty-eight hours before his face was disfigured. We always assumed it was done to obscure his identity, confuse the police." I shook my head. "We—my partners and I—were operating on the theory that the dead guy had been impersonating Wade."

The detective jerked himself upright in his chair. "Why did you think the dead man was an imposter?"

I gave him the rundown on the photos from the Atlanta paper, the height discrepancy, the watch with no inscription on the back. I kept Star Ryan Kennedy's name to myself. Then the thought of why we had gotten involved in this mess in the first place popped into my head.

"Let me ask you something," I began. "Was there any indication Wade had ever been suspected of rape down in the islands?"

"No," Littlejohn said, shaking his head for emphasis, "not that I'm aware of." He paused, a flush of embarrassment creeping up from the open collar of his white polo shirt. "Mr. Wade's quite generous allowance made it unnecessary. He could well afford to purchase whatever, um . . . *pleasures* he required."

So he preferred hookers, I said to myself. A pattern?

"However, his file does indicate he may have had one or two run-ins on that score as a much younger man. I believe his family had some success in getting it hushed up," Littlejohn added.

But not before Wade's prints had found their way into the system. It was a question both Wyler and I should have asked the minute we heard about the positive ID: Where and when—and *why*—had Randolph Remington Wade been printed in the first place.

I sipped at the warm, diluted tea in my glass and thought about Karen Zwilling and her friend Layla. If Littlejohn was right about Wade's preference for professionals—and if, as seemed pretty undeniable, Wade was the dead man—then the women could be pretty certain their attacker wouldn't be bothering them again. Although I still wasn't convinced the imposter was completely out of the picture. I shook my head, the possibilities and contradictions swirling around in my brain like a kaleidoscope, the patterns settling and reforming at an alarming pace. We needed a positive identification.

"If you wouldn't mind sharing one of those photographs, I have a couple of people I'd like to have take a look at it," I said.

"No problem. The file is in my car."

He rose, and I realized for the first time how powerfully built he was. Though he stood an inch or so under my own five-foot-ten, his broad shoulders strained against his polo shirt, and his brown forearms looked like hunks of polished oak. I was admiring the graceful way he moved down the steps when my cell phone chimed.

The screen revealed an unidentified number.

"Bay Tanner."

Erik's voice sounded as if he had laryngitis. "Hey, it's me. I'm at work. Can't talk long."

"What's up?"

"Well, it's been slow here, so I've been prowling around the Internet."

"On company time?"

I could envision his shrug. "Better than standing outside smoking, which is what the other guys are doing."

"Did you find something?"

"Maybe. Yesterday I looked all through the local papers down there, at least the bigger ones online, and pretty much came up empty as far as any kind of robbery or drug bust or anything like that. I even went back a month rather than two weeks. Anyway, today I brought them up again and started reading some of the smaller articles, the ones I skimmed over before."

I heard the muffled sounds of an in-store loudspeaker message in the background, and Erik's next words were lost in the confusion.

"Say again. I missed the last part."

"I said, I found this small item about a case of financial fraud involving a wealthy woman on St. Thomas. Seems some guy bilked her out of a lot of money and most of her jewelry, then split. They indicted him in absentia because they're pretty sure he fled the islands."

I watched Henry Littlejohn make his way back up the steps, a large brown envelope clutched in his hand. "They give a name?"

"Yeah, but they're pretty sure it's an alias. Robert Dubois."

I sat up straight as Littlejohn dropped back into his seat. I held up a finger and turned in my chair, away from his inquisitive eyes.

Robert Dubois. The idea seemed absolutely preposterous, and yet . . .

"Anything else?" I asked, lowering my voice.

"Yes. The part that really made me sit up and take notice." He paused in typical, dramatic Erik fashion, before adding, "He posed as a boat captain. The lady who got taken hired him to pilot her yacht."

CHAPTER
TWENTY-EIGHT

IT TOOK ME A FEW MINUTES TO MAKE MY ESCAPE.
I thanked Henry Littlejohn for the tea and the photo and
wished him a safe trip home. He tried to prolong the conversation, reluctant to let me go. I didn't quite understand why he seemed so intent
on pumping me for details since his search was over, but I finally managed to extricate myself by promising to keep him informed of how the
case turned out. We exchanged cards and a handshake, and I left him in
the shade of the restaurant's verandah staring after me as I scurried away.

I broke one of my own cardinal rules as I pulled out onto Helms-
man Way. I punched Wyler's number into my cell phone and drove with
one hand while I listened to the endless ringing. His voice mail finally
kicked in, and I fumbled to compose a message that would convey the
urgency of my need to talk without sending him charging to the rescue.
I hung up, cranked the volume on the ringer to full power, and shoved
the phone back in my bag.

At the light at Palmetto Bay Road, I turned left. Maybe I should
stop at the office-supply store and spring Erik, I thought. And I needed
to get hold of my father. He'd be the best source of information about—

And then my own stupidity slapped me in the face. I whipped the
T-Bird into the entrance to the Audubon Nature Preserve, earning myself an angry horn blast and a raised finger as the pickup truck behind

me blew by. I executed an illegal U-turn and veered back across the four lanes, my heart racing as I retraced my steps. I only hoped Henry Littlejohn had headed back to his motel.

The interior of the marine repair office was spartan but pleasant. I approached the young woman behind the short counter.

"Hi! Can I help you?" Gleaming white teeth contrasted nicely with the burnished tan of her pretty face. A long, black braid hung over one shoulder.

"I'd like to inquire about the boat you have under repair outside. The big one. *Wade in the Water?*"

"She's a beauty, isn't she? The inside is like a palace."

"You've been on board?"

The girl ducked her head. "My dad let me take a peek while they were working on her. He said Mr. Wade wouldn't mind."

"You've met Mr. Wade?" I asked, wondering if, after everything we'd been through, it would turn out to be this easy. I should have known better.

"Oh, no. My dad deals with all the owners. I just, you know, take care of the office and the phone and stuff. During the summer."

"Home from college?" I asked.

"Yes, ma'am. Furman. I'm an early childhood development major."

"Good for you." I groped for a way to extract the information I wanted without spooking her.

The girl stuck out a slender hand. "I'm Lizzie, by the way. Lizzie Barrett."

"Nice to meet you." I decided to keep my own identity to myself for the time being. "I may be interested in buying something like *Wade in the Water*. You wouldn't by any chance know if it's for sale, would you?"

She shook her head, and the braid bounced up and down on her chest. "No, ma'am, I sure wouldn't. I kind of don't think so, because Dad said Mr. Wade was going to be heading back out by the weekend."

"Really?" For a moment, the jumbled events of the past few days made my head spin. I concentrated hard and decided on Thursday. Yes, it was definitely Thursday. And Wade was supposedly leaving the island in about forty-eight hours. Pretty tricky move for a dead guy.

"Maybe I should approach him directly. Do you happen to have his local phone number?"

Lizzie Barrett's face lost some of its childish eagerness to please. "I don't think I should do that. I mean, my parents don't actually own this place. They just manage it. And I'm, like, not supposed to give out information about the customers. Company policy."

Dead end. Maybe. I plastered on a smile. "I understand. It's just that if he's leaving soon, and he might be interested in selling, it seems a shame for us not to get a chance to discuss it."

I left the implied question hanging. Most people, especially well-brought-up young Southern women like Lizzie, usually tried hard to be accommodating. I kept the hundred-watt smile cranked up. I could feel her discomfort at disappointing me warring with her respect for the rules.

"Well, maybe I could call him and see if he wants to talk to you. Would that help?"

"That would be great! But I don't want to get you in trouble."

"Oh, don't worry about that!" she said with a bouncy confidence I vaguely remembered from my own days of twenty-something invincibility.

I watched her thumb through a sheaf of work orders attached to a clip hooked on the pegboard covering the wall behind her.

"Here it is."

She pulled out the paperwork and slipped it onto the top of the stack, then picked up the phone. Her slender body blocked my line of sight, but I counted the beeps. Seven. Local number. That could mean anything from Daufuskie Island to Beaufort.

We smiled politely at each other while she listened to the rings, and a wave of panic washed over me. What in the hell was I going to do if someone actually answered? I swallowed hard, my mind whirling, but I needn't have worried. Lizzie shook her head and pushed the Off button.

"Sorry. No one home, I guess."

The back door eased open, and a tall, muscular black man stepped inside. Backlit by the late-afternoon sun, his face seemed to shimmer with the sweat he wiped away with a greasy rag.

"Hey, Wilson. Need something?" the young woman called over her shoulder.

"Hey, Lizzie," he replied, his voice deep and mellow. "Just a bigger wrench. Afternoon," he added, nodding in my direction.

"Good afternoon."

The interruption seemed to break my tenuous hold on the girl's willingness to be helpful. "Well, sorry," she said and slipped the clipboard back on its hook. "I'll tell my dad to ask Mr. Wade when he talks to him next time. You want to leave your number or something?"

Did I want whoever was impersonating Randolph Wade to have my name and phone number? Not a tough decision.

"No, thanks, that's okay. It was probably a long shot anyway. I wonder if I could take a closer look at her, though. Just out of curiosity."

"Oh, no, I can't do that," the girl said. "That's, like, *really* against the rules."

The mechanic emerged from a side room, a shiny chrome wrench in his huge hand. "Oh, what the hell, Lizzie. Let the lady take a look around. Ain't gonna hurt nothin'. I'm right out there workin'." He winked at both of us. "I won't let her run off with the boat."

The girl returned his wide grin and shrugged. "Sure. I guess it'll be okay."

"Thanks for all your help," I said, easing around the counter.

"No problem."

I looked past her narrow shoulder to the work orders hanging on the wall. I could make out the name "Wade" handwritten on the top line and the start of a phone number: A five, maybe a two . . . *Damn!* New glasses for certain. But at least I now knew it was probably a Beaufort exchange. Nothing to shoot down the theory I'd been forming since my recent chat with Henry Littlejohn.

"Ma'am?"

I turned reluctantly toward where Wilson the mechanic held the back door open for me. "Thanks," I said again and followed him out.

Wade in the Water still rested on its supports, although all the tarps had been removed. The hull gleamed with what looked like a fresh coat of paint or a thorough cleaning. I shaded my eyes with my hand and gazed up at the towering superstructure.

"She's a honey, all right," Wilson said, his hand once again mopping his brow with the stained rag.

"Ever met Mr. Wade, the owner?" I asked without looking at him.

"No, ma'am, I sure haven't. Like to, though."

"Why's that?"

"Kinda like to ask him how he come to mess up the propeller so bad. Scraped the sh— I mean, the daylights outta the bottom, too. Musta run 'er aground pretty good on somethin'. Shame, pretty thing like this."

Wilson shook his head and moved off toward a much smaller craft on a trailer. He stepped up onto a series of cubes of ascending height, and I realized how they got up into the taller boats. I looked around and saw several more of the wooden platforms stacked along the side of the building. I'd missed them during my aborted reconnaissance of the night before, or else they were locked inside after closing. I glanced at the mechanic, his head bent over the engine compartment of the smaller boat, and tried to formulate a plausible reason to ask him about it. I came up empty.

The outside of *Wade in the Water* had nothing to interest me. I needed to get on board. There had to be personal items—clothes, papers, *something* I could use to try and figure out just what the hell was going on.

I took another turn around the huge yacht, my eyes recording the layout, committing to memory just where everything was located. When I came back I wouldn't have the brilliant sunlight to guide me.

"Thanks again," I called as I picked my way across the rough gravel of the work area.

"Most welcome," the black man called. The hand he raised still held the wrench.

As I moved back toward the Thunderbird I wondered how a man like Wilson must feel, spending every day tinkering with these toys of the wealthy. I had no doubt the money Randolph Wade—or his family—had spent on the yacht could keep the mechanic and his kids in comfort for the better part of a lifetime.

I pulled into the parking lot of the sprawling office-supply center just before five thirty. I parked as close as possible to the front door and cut the engine. I didn't know what time Erik got off work, but his black Expedition still sat under a tree in the employee area. I extracted my cell phone and leaned back in the bucket seat.

Neddie answered on the third ring.

"Hey," I said, "how's it going? How's Yancey?"

"Surprisingly good. I think she's relieved to have it all out in the open."

"Did you talk to the cops?"

"Briefly. Enough to get them tracking down the boyfriend and his pal. She'll have to go in and make a formal statement, probably tomorrow."

"That's good. Is she still with you?"

"For now. The cops don't think we need to take Delbert's threats too seriously. Still, we're locked down for the rest of the evening. I picked up a few groceries and some DVDs on the way home from the police station. Girls' night in. Wish you could join us."

"Sounds like fun." I kicked the air conditioning up a notch and kept my gaze focused on the main door. "Did Yancey's father get home?"

"Not yet. He's due in from Sante Fe in another day or so. But she talked to him on his cell phone. Sounded to me as if he's going to try to get shorter hauls so he can be around more. Yancey needs the structure."

"You were eavesdropping?"

"Of course! That's one of the first things they teach you in shrink school."

I laughed and glanced up to see Erik striding out the front door. He called something to a short, stocky young man with a wispy goatee and headed toward his car.

"Gotta run," I said. "Keep me posted on what happens. And remember you can always use the spare room if you need to get outta Dodge."

"Thanks. Later."

I pushed open the car door and intercepted my partner as he pulled his keys from his pants pocket.

"Bay! What are you doing here?"

"I need to talk to you. Got dinner plans?"

He shook his head. "Nope. Just me and a frozen pizza. What's up?"

I thought a moment. "Let's run over to Jump & Phil's. I have a lot to tell you."

"Sure. I'm right behind you."

Thursday was turkey night, so we both ordered the special. I'd picked a table in the near corner where the noise and chatter of the after-work bar patrons would prevent us from being overheard. With drinks in front of us, I filled Erik in on the bizarre happenings of what had become a marathon day, from Yancey's situation to my meeting with Henry Littlejohn and my daring daylight reconnaissance of the boatyard. The bizarre confrontation with Wyler I kept to myself.

"Thanks, Debbie," I said as our usual waitress set the heaping plates in front of us. "So what do you think?" I asked Erik between bites of dressing and gravy.

"You sure do pack a lot into a few hours," he said with a grin. "Of course, the stuff with Dr. Halloran and the girl is none of my business, but I'm glad it seems to be working out." He paused to bring a forkful of mashed potatoes to his mouth. "But I really don't know what to make of this guy Littlejohn. You think he's on the level?"

"He seemed to be. He gave me a picture of Wade." I leaned over and extracted it from my bag. "Here, take a look. It's definitely not the man in the newspaper with Star Kennedy."

He studied it for a moment before handing it back. "You're right, although the guy in the paper seemed to be turning his head every time someone snapped a photo. Did you notice that?"

"Yes. I didn't think much of it at the time, but for a good-looking man he certainly was camera-shy."

"You're right."

"You know what I don't get? How did he expect to get away with it when the real Randolph Wade was alive and kicking? So many wealthy people vacation in the Caribbean, you'd think he'd be afraid someone would tumble to his little charade. All it would take is for one of Star's friends to come back from a trip to the Virgin Islands and announce they'd run into the genuine article, and the game would be up."

Erik sipped his beer and nodded. We ate in silence except for the occasional burst of laughter or greeting as the crowd lining the bar ebbed and flowed. I decided I couldn't stuff another bite in my mouth and sat back, craving a cigarette. Erik laid his silverware across his plate before speaking.

"So the imposter had to kill the real Wade to keep from getting exposed."

The idea didn't shock me. "Of course that makes the most sense," I said, nodding, "but where is he then? Skipped back to the islands? On the run? Star said she hadn't seen him in a couple of weeks."

"What about Ben's theory that the guy you saw at this Delacroix's place could be the imposter?"

I shrugged. "Beats the hell out of me. Insufficient data, as you're so fond of saying." I looked up as Debbie dropped the check on the table. I fumbled in my bag for my wallet. "Here's what I think our game plan should be. First, we show this picture to both Karen Zwilling and Star Kennedy. See if either of them recognizes it." I paused. "And then we need to get on that boat. I think that's where we'll find the answers."

I signed the credit card slip and gathered my things as we headed back out to the parking lot.

"This is going to be strictly illegal," I said, stopping next to my car. "I'm pretty sure it's breaking and entering even if the thing isn't locked up." I paused for emphasis. "And if it is, I'm going in anyway. If you don't want to be involved, I'll completely understand."

"Have you thought about getting hold of Red? Giving him all this information and letting him take it from there?"

A logical and sensible course of action, to be sure. But what did I really have? Intuition and a few scattered clues that added up to precisely nothing in the way of provable evidence. Red would scowl and tell me to stay out of it. The Judge would no doubt do the same.

I shook my head. "The girl at the boatyard told me 'Mr. Wade' is planning on leaving this weekend. Since we know he's dead, that must mean the imposter is planning on claiming the boat and skipping. We're running out of time."

"Okay, count me in."

"You sure?"

"Absolutely." A wide grin lit his face. "Besides, what'll I do if you end up in the slammer all by yourself? I sure don't want to spend the rest of my life selling computers."

I returned his smile. "Great. Here's the plan."

We stopped at Erik's store, and I made photocopies of the picture while he waited in his car. I gave him one and sent him off to track down Karen Zwilling. Back home, I dialed the Westin. Star Kennedy was still registered, although again her room failed to answer. At dinner, I told myself as I headed for the bedroom.

There'd been a message from Ben, returning my earlier call, but I'd decided not to involve him in the evening's entertainment. It seemed to me even former police officers still belonged to some sort of secret society from which the rest of us were eternally excluded. They might, like

238 ⌒ K A T H R Y N R . W A L L

Wyler and Henry Littlejohn, retire or move on to a civilian profession, but the loyalty, the fierce commitment to the law, remained an integral part of who they were. I couldn't see either of them aiding and abetting me in the invasion of Randolph Remington Wade's private property, even if he was dead.

Besides, I needed to put some distance between Wyler and me, at least for a while.

Erik and I had agreed to meet at the marina around eleven. I figured there would still be some people milling around the docks and restaurants, plenty of cars in the parking lot. Enough activity to make us inconspicuous, but not enough to interfere with what we had to do. I pulled on a pale green jersey shift that ended well above my knees and slid my feet into flat leather sandals. I could hardly go hunting for Star Kennedy through the swanky restaurants of the Westin in the clothes I'd already laid out for the evening's later rendezvous.

I hummed to myself as I pinned up my hair. *Rendezvous. Reconnaissance. Reconnoiter.* The detecting business certainly had its own vernacular, a delightfully sinister and secretive vocabulary. I smiled at myself in the mirror. Sometimes I felt more like fourteen than forty, despite the tiny lines beginning to radiate from the corners of my eyes. The phone rang as I fastened plain gold hoops in my ears.

"Do you ever stay at home?" my father demanded in his booming courtroom voice before I'd even managed to say hello.

"I have a cell phone. You have the number. I'm available damned near twenty-four/seven. Did you want something in particular?"

"Of course I wanted something in particular. Have you ever known me to call you up just for idle chitchat?"

I sat down on the closed toilet seat in my bathroom and drummed my fingers on the marble vanity top. I gave myself ten long seconds before I answered. "I'm sorry. I should have realized."

Admitting guilt always worked wonders with the Judge. "Well, don't ask inane questions. I brought you up to be precise with language."

"Yes, sir, you did."

His decibel level dropped to normal. "I have some news you might find interesting. About Bobby Delacroix."

"Tell me." Couldn't get much more concise than that.

"His stint in jail took place several years ago. In Georgia, which is why it took so long to track down the information. He pled guilty to fraud by deceit for bilking a woman out of her life savings in a phony investment scam." He paused for a moment, and I could almost see his leonine head shaking in disbelief. "From everything I've heard, I wouldn't have thought the boy had that much sense. Something of a dim bulb, or so everyone says. At any rate, he still owns the house in Beaufort, although he rents it out from time to time. Neighbors aren't too happy with the caliber of his clientele, but there hasn't been any trouble with the law."

"Where is he now?"

"Unknown, but rumor has it he's spent time in the islands." He paused as if he somehow knew his next piece of information would be the clincher. "I hear he hires himself out as a boat captain."

CHAPTER
TWENTY-NINE

I FOUND STAR KENNEDY IN THE BAR.

As I stepped into the dim, elegant room, I spotted her champagne blond hair glimmering under the soft light of a discreetly placed wall sconce. At first I thought she was alone at the small table tucked into the far corner diagonally across from the entrance. I made my way past the row of elevated booths, remembering the times I'd spent huddled there with the Herrington men and their sister Jordan.

When I stopped at the table, I thought my client might have a coronary on the spot. She looked more than surprised. The word that sprang immediately to mind was *stricken.*

"Lydia! I mean, Bay! What . . . that is, why . . . ?" She bit hard on her lower lip. "Is there some problem, dear?"

I had no idea what was making her so jumpy, unless it was the man seated with his back to me. Obviously *not* Southern, I thought, as he made no attempt to rise or even to turn around in his chair.

"No problem," I said evenly. "Just some news I thought you should hear. Mind if I join you for a moment?" Without waiting for permission, I pulled over a chair from a nearby table.

An unforgivable breach of manners, but my curiosity had been aroused, both by the man himself and by Star Kennedy's uncharacteristic dithering. I waited for my mother's protégée to rise to the occasion, but she simply sat, staring at me in dismay.

I looked straight at the man, younger than I'd first supposed. "I'm Bay Tanner," I said, extending my hand across the table. "I'm a friend of Star's from the old neighborhood."

His smile was guarded, but he had nice eyes. Sort of a bluey green, almost like sea glass. I guessed him to be about twenty-five, maybe thirty. Good tan against a crisp white shirt, its long sleeves rolled back at the cuffs. Hard to judge the height of a sitting person, but I thought he'd stretch out to around average.

"Hello." A soft voice with a deliberately sensuous undertone. That was it. No name offered, but his handshake was firm and dry. He seemed reluctant to let go of my fingers. Or it could just have been my imagination.

I switched my attention back to Star Kennedy. She looked ready to explode, though whether from embarrassment or anger I couldn't tell. She folded her elegant hands on the table in front of her and made a conscious effort to regain control of the situation.

"I do wish you'd called first, dear," she said in that voice which reminded me so much of my mother's—painstakingly polite with a heavy undercurrent of condescension.

"I tried. No answer." I paused a beat, then added a tilt of my head that said, *Over to you.*

Her pointed glare might have been intimidating when I was a gawky teenager, but those days were gone, along with my youthful naïveté. If I had any doubts about exactly what the relationship was between these two, Star's escort dispelled them with his next words.

"Want me to take a hike, babe? I could use a trip to the can anyway."

I nearly choked on the laugh bubbling up in my throat as Star's skin color deepened to a shade reminiscent of ripe tomatoes. The young man rose and smoothed his hands over narrow hips encased in a pair of designer jeans so tight they left absolutely nothing to be imagined about his primary attraction. I leaned down to retrieve my bag from the floor and used the time to recover my composure.

"I want you to look at something," I said, handing her a copy of the photo Henry Littlejohn had given me.

Without meeting my eyes, the older woman glanced down at it, briefly, before shaking her head. "I've never seen this man before. Although he does bear some resemblance . . ."

"It's Randolph Wade," I said.

"It most assuredly is not."

"Yes, Star, it is. I got this from a man hired to track him down. He disappeared from Virgin Gorda about two weeks ago, along with his yacht." I waited a moment for her to digest what had to be an alarming revelation. I laid my hand gently against her arm. "I'm afraid he's the man they found murdered on the beach last week."

"There must be some mistake."

My head was shaking before she finished the sentence. "I'm sorry, but there's not. The fingerprints are a match."

"I don't understand." She looked as bewildered as an abandoned child.

"The man you've been seeing in Atlanta is an imposter. He may even be responsible for the real Wade's death." I watched her lift a trembling hand to her lips. "You need to tell me everything you know about him."

"May I get you something from the bar?"

I looked up into the face of the hovering waitress. "No, thank you. Nothing for me. Star?"

The older woman's face had sunk into folds and creases she'd spent a fortune trying to keep at bay. A twinge of guilt flitted across my conscience, but there was nothing I could do about it. The truth was the truth.

"Bring my friend another of whatever's she's been drinking," I said.

"And the gentleman?" the waitress asked.

Again I looked to Star. This time she shook her head. "He won't be staying," she mumbled and collapsed against the back of her chair.

———

A folded hundred-dollar bill, exchanged discreetly during a perfunctory handshake, left Star Kennedy and me alone a few moments after her "escort" returned from the men's room.

"Would you rather talk about this in your suite?" I asked, watching her down her fresh drink in one long, desperate swallow.

"Why? Are you trying to save me embarrassment? Humiliation? Ruination?"

Her voice rose on each word, and a couple of people at a nearby table glanced in our direction. I thought she might be more than a little drunk.

"Come on," I said, attempting to rise when her hand clamped down on my forearm.

"What difference does it make?" she asked more quietly, shaking her head. "They'll all know soon enough."

"Know what?"

"What a complete and utter fool I've been. What a stupid, gullible . . ." The rest of the sentence trailed off into silence.

I tried to think of something comforting to say, some words that would ease the pain. "Will you tell me? Maybe you can help us catch him."

A little of the old sparkle snapped in her eyes. "Catch him? I mean to kill the bastard!"

I smiled, and she joined me. For more than a hundred and fifty years, people had been deceived by the outward gentility of Southern women, sadly underestimating their grit and determination. Like my own, Star Kennedy's female ancestors had fought to keep the vast agricultural holdings of the Confederacy intact through four dreadful years of loneliness, privation, and war. They had borne and reared children, overseen plantings and harvests, and held the shreds of their tattered lives together while their husbands fought and died hundreds of miles from home. While most people idolize the Scarlett O'Hara of the first half of *Gone with the Wind*—the pampered belle with an indulgent mammy and scores of wealthy young gentlemen swooning at her feet— I'd always identified more with the postwar Scarlett: angry, determined, ruthless when it came to defending herself and her family.

We came from good stock.

While Star Kennedy summoned the waitress for a pot of coffee, I slipped my spare tape recorder out of my bag and set it on the table between us.

"Mind?" I asked, and she shook her head. "Okay, so let's start at the beginning. You told me earlier that a friend of yours introduced you to Wade." I'd decided we might as well call him that, as neither of us had a clue about his real name. "Lucy somebody, if I remember correctly."

"Whitcombe. Lucy Whitcombe."

"Do you think she knew he was a phony?"

"No." The shake of her head was emphatic. "Absolutely not. Lucy and I have known each other for dog's years. She met him when her husband entertained some business associates. He was wealthy, charming, unattached. She figured we'd be perfect for each other. Remmy . . ." She stumbled over the nickname, then cleared her throat. "The man claimed to have been acquainted with my late husband. Frank and Thorne Whitcombe had done some business together." She held up a hand as I opened my mouth. "And don't ask me what kind. Frank was involved in lots of things: real estate development, property management, other kinds of investments. He owned several restaurants and some office buildings. I believe he and Thorne bought a race track together, but they sold it a long time ago."

"Anything offshore?" I asked.

"I suppose." Star sipped at her coffee, and a little of her natural composure began to reassert itself. "I'm pretty sure they had an interest in a casino at one time. In the Caymans, I think. Or maybe it was the Bahamas."

I'd have to look it up, but I was pretty certain there was no legalized gambling in the Virgins, either American or British. But then, none of the islands down there were so far apart they couldn't be reached easily by short plane hops. Or large, oceangoing yachts. The connection was possible.

"Go on," I said. "Lucy introduced you. Then what?"

Star Kennedy shrugged and looked directly into my eyes. "What do you think happened? Don't be coy with me, Lydia. We became lovers. Almost immediately." The corners of her lips turned up into a sardonic smile. "I don't have a lot of time to waste on foreplay. He was a good-looking, cultured, eligible man. Or so I thought."

I waited a moment before saying, "When did he start stealing from you?"

I had expected flustered denials, but Star surprised me. "Almost immediately," she repeated. "Of course, I didn't know it at the time. It seemed so . . ." She groped for the appropriate word, ". . . so *plausible*. He seemed to know a lot about Frank's businesses, tossed out the names of mutual acquaintances. Of course I have a firm to handle all my finances, but . . . but Remmy convinced me they weren't doing enough. I could make more, risk-free. He had friends, connections." She sighed. "It really wasn't until he disappeared that I began to suspect anything at all."

"You told me he was getting his yacht repaired. Did you believe him at the time?"

"Of course. He'd been gone about a week when my financial advisor called to ask why I'd converted such a large chunk of my bonds to cash."

I didn't have any trouble predicting the next part. "You'd given Wade power of attorney?"

Star Kennedy shook her head. "Stupid. Just plain stupid. I spent days pacing around the house trying to decide what to do."

"And then you heard about the body washed up here and the possibility it might be Wade."

"Yes. And I had to know. One way or the other."

"Of course." Her spur-of-the-moment trip to Hilton Head on the slim chance presented to her by Ben Wyler now made a lot more sense.

Star poured herself more coffee and added cream. Around us, the buzz of conversation provided a muted backdrop.

"I'm not broke, you know," she said, nodding for emphasis. "It was a blow, I won't deny that, but Frank believed in diversity. I still have cash, the properties, other investments. I'll be all right."

"That's good." I waited for her to elaborate. When she didn't, I said, "I got the feeling, almost from the beginning, that you'd prefer it if the body turned out to be *your* Randolph Wade. I guess I can understand. It would make things easier." I paused. "No explanations." Again she remained silent. "So what's your primary concern now? Getting your money back or keeping anyone from finding out how easily you were duped?"

"Very perceptive of you, Lydia," she replied. "I can live without the money. Reputation and standing are much harder to hold on to."

I understood that all too well.

CHAPTER THIRTY

ERIK PULLED IN ALMOST RIGHT BEHIND ME, THE LIGHTS of his SUV blinding in my rearview mirror. I led us to a pair of parking places close to Eugene's restaurant, but at the far end of the lot. I gathered up my tools and stuffed them in my fanny pack before stepping out into the soft, humid night.

I left the doors unlocked in case I had to make a fast getaway. The idea made me smile.

"What's so funny?" my partner asked. He had raised the rear hatch of his Expedition and was checking the contents of the carpeted storage area. I spotted a folding ladder and a couple of oversized flashlights.

"Nothing," I mumbled and bent to help him.

We piled all the gear on the ground and pushed it beneath the vehicle for easy access later. Everything except the pistol. I'd exchanged my cell phone for it at the last moment.

"I just want to take a short stroll around," I said, "and check for security."

Erik tilted his head toward the darkened boatyard on our right. "Is that it? The big one?"

"Yes. Pretty spectacular, isn't it?"

"How much does something like that cost?"

"I have no idea," I answered with a shrug. "I'd guess at least a few million."

At the dock, we passed the towering mobile boat hoist with its lines and pulleys before stepping out onto the wooden planks. Ahead of us, a dozen small sailboats bobbed gently in the nearly placid water. Farther out, several of the larger craft riding at anchor showed lights in their salons and cabins, and snatches of conversation and brief bursts of laughter floated on the humid night air.

I rested my forearms on the railing and stared out across the water. "I've never liked boats," I said.

Erik leaned next to me, his voice low. "How come? You've lived by the ocean almost your whole life."

"I don't know. The Judge and I went out fishing a few times, mostly with his legal cronies. Maybe because everyone was usually drunk before the day was over. I can remember trying to calculate how far we were from shore in case I had to swim for it."

"Your father would never have put you in any danger."

"I suppose not. Didn't stop me worrying, though."

His laugh brought an answering smile. "Does anything?"

"Point taken." I tapped the slight bulge in my right pocket. "But I always believe in being prepared."

"You would've made a good Marine," he quipped, following me back toward the parking lot.

We ambled around, gawking like tourists, but in reality both of us were checking for anything resembling a security patrol or night watchman. I particularly didn't want to encounter dogs, although I couldn't figure how they could leave any running loose with this many people still moving back and forth from the restaurant to the marina, not to mention the folks who lived in the condominiums flanking the harbor.

By the time we found ourselves back at the Expedition, we'd covered almost every foot of the perimeter completely unchallenged.

"Next stop, the yacht itself," I said softly. "You take the lead. Wander around as if you're just curious. If anyone stops you, apologize, claim you didn't know it was private property, and get the hell out of there."

"Fine. What are you going to do?"

"I'll check out the building, look for cameras, any other kind of security. I sort of know my way around there now. I also want to see if I can locate those platforms they use for access. I'm not sure that little ladder you brought is going to do us much good."

"What, you don't want to stand on my shoulders?" His smile flashed in the dark.

"Tempting, but I'd rather be a little less obtrusive. Meet you back here in about fifteen minutes."

"Aye, aye, Captain," he said, moving off.

In moments his black shirt had been swallowed up by the night.

It was close to midnight by the time we rendezvoused at the rear of the Expedition.

"Find anything?" Erik asked.

"They keep those risers out behind the building, underneath a tarp. If I hadn't seen the mechanic using them this afternoon, I never would have known what I was looking for."

"Cameras?"

"Not that I could see. I'm guessing the sheriff sends a patrol through here a couple of times a night. Their main concern has to be vandalism. There's no way anyone could steal a boat."

"Don't be too sure," Erik replied.

"How about you?"

"I think the ladder will work. All I have to do is be able to reach the bottom rung of the one attached to the side of the boat. I can pull you up behind me."

I'm not exactly a petite woman, and I thought he might have been a tad optimistic, but I agreed. We could use the risers for backup.

The parking lot had thinned as we'd made our reconnaissance and stood whispering at the back of the SUV. Most of the noise had died in the marina, and only a couple of windows still glowed in the condos across the way. The restaurant was dark. The only real activity came from Captain Woody's, the bar just behind the little café where I had met with Henry Littlejohn. A snatch of music drifted to us as someone opened the door, stepped outside, and lit a cigarette.

Thoughts of the Jamaican detective brought me up short. "Hey, I forgot to ask. Did you locate Karen Zwilling?"

Erik shook his head. "No. She wasn't home or answering either of her numbers." He studied his feet, and I could feel his discomfort.

"What?"

"Well, I thought it was important. For her to identify the picture, I mean, so I made a little detour on my way here." He stopped speaking again and toed the gravel with his dark Nike running shoe.

"Hey, what? We need to get moving here." I punched him lightly on the arm to punctuate my point.

He swallowed. "I stopped at The Club. I thought she might be . . . you know . . ."

"Hustling?" The upscale nightspot had a reputation for scantily clad showgirls and lots of people of both sexes looking for a good time.

I could tell he didn't like my choice of words. "Whatever. But she wasn't there. I did meet her friend Layla, though. Wow! What an incredibly beautiful woman. Long black hair, these incredible dark brown eyes. Exotic. Maybe from India or the Middle East. And her voice was deep and just . . ."

"Incredible," I said, and he laughed.

"Yeah."

"Did she recognize the photo?"

"Yes. She said that's definitely the man who raped her."

I swore under my breath. One of my theories had just been shot to hell, but I wasn't quite sure how it affected the overall picture. We didn't have time to worry about it. The solitary smoker moved back inside the bar, and I touched Erik on the shoulder.

"We'll sort it all out later. Let's get moving."

We retrieved our gear and skirted the edges of the gravel area, keeping close to the overhanging limbs and undergrowth on the perimeter. Luckily for our first foray into breaking and entering, the access ladder hung from the far side of the boat. Without consultation, we both dropped into a low crouch as we approached the towering vessel. Erik quickly unfolded the compact extension ladder and laid it against the hull. He cast a look at me over his shoulder. I nodded, and he scrambled up.

The beam of the security light on the corner of the building fell just short of the stern of *Wade in the Water,* but even its dull reflection off the stones in the work area seemed like a blinding glare as I watched Erik make his way up the side of the boat. I braced the bottom of the ladder and scanned continually left and right. My bravado of earlier in the evening was fast dissolving. A tight knot of fear made my breath come in short, labored gulps. So absorbed was I in trying to quell my urge to bolt, I almost missed Erik's urgent whisper.

"Bay! Come on!"

I stood and searched the blackness, but I couldn't see a thing.

"Come on! I think you can reach it yourself."

I swallowed hard, hitched the fanny pack around to the back of my waist, and began climbing.

I wouldn't have made it without someone above me.

Erik's strong hand gripping my wrist provided the impetus to propel me across the gap between my outstretched fingers and the bottom rung of the boarding ladder. A few moments later I lay panting on the teak deck of the huge yacht, my grinning partner beside me. He flexed his hand and worked his wrist around in circles.

"Are you hurt?" I whispered, my words carried away on the breeze. It had kicked up, rattling the palmettos and sending trailing wisps of Spanish moss swaying in its wake.

"I may have overestimated my strength just a bit," he said with a smile.

"Or underestimated my weight."

"Let's not go there," he said wisely.

I scrambled to my feet and surveyed the open deck. Dark humps which could have been stacked chairs or equipment of some kind lined the sides. The glow from the edges of the security light glinted against glass.

"That must be the door," I said, moving forward.

I tripped over what might have been a coil of rope and would have fallen flat on my face without Erik's restraining grip on my upper arm.

"Careful."

I inched my way more cautiously, sliding my feet in front of me like an inexperienced ice skater. I looked back over my shoulder as I approached the door, buoyed by Erik's nod of encouragement. I grasped the metal handle and twisted.

And nearly fell into the main cabin.

"You okay?"

"Fine." I pulled myself upright and groped in the dark for a handhold. "Watch out. There's a sill of some kind there."

I'd done a little research on the Internet after leaving Star Kennedy in the bar of the Westin and before heading out to meet Erik. I had no idea what company had manufactured *Wade in the Water,* or even how long she was. Still, a number of yacht brokers had provided layouts of the interiors of their offerings, enough so that I had a rough idea of how they were usually configured.

Behind me, I felt Erik move inside and ease the door shut. "First thing we have to do is close the curtains," I said. "Give me a flashlight."

He unclipped one from his belt and handed it over. I risked a couple of brief bursts to orient myself, then moved around, drawing the thick material across the surprisingly wide windows.

"I think if we keep the light aimed at the floor, it won't be noticeable from outside."

"Right," he whispered.

"You take the left side, and I'll get the right. We'll alternate turning on the flashes. We're looking for papers—a desk or maybe a brief-case. We'll do this room, then move on to the bedrooms."

"Got it. You go first with the light."

After a few minutes, we developed a rhythm as we worked our way around the main salon of the huge yacht. The sofas and chairs were the same size and material to be found in any upscale house or apartment. I had expected it all to be cut down, miniaturized I suppose, because of the limited space available on a boat. By the time we'd met at the door-way leading into the dining and galley area, I'd come to realize the en-tire contents of my great room could have fit comfortably in the space.

"Now what?" Erik asked as we paused in the dark.

"Sleeping quarters. I'll stay on the right. Tap on the wall with the flashlight if you find anything."

"Bulkhead," Erik corrected me. "They're called bulkheads."

"Whatever."

I hit pay dirt on the first try. The spacious room with its full-sized bed was strewn with dirty clothes, discarded shoes littering the floor. I spotted a dresser with two drawers hanging open, and next to it, a built-in desk with papers tossed carelessly across its inset leather top. At first I thought the place might have been searched—and by someone in a damn big hurry—but on further inspection I decided the occupant was simply a slob. I scooped the papers onto the floor and knelt down beside them.

A lot of them appeared to be correspondence, and I recognized a few names immediately: Francis A. Kennedy, Thorne Whitcombe—and Randolph Remington Wade. The heading on all of them read WHITE STAR CASINO, FREEPORT, GRAND BAHAMA ISLAND. I glanced up as Erik materialized in the doorway.

"Find something?"

"You bet. I don't know what it means, but it's a definite tie between whoever's been on this boat and Star Kennedy."

"No kidding!"

"I'm taking them with me." I set the flashlight on the floor and straightened the edges of the papers before folding them in half and stuffing them in the waist of my black pants.

"You think that's a good idea?"

I scrambled to my feet and ignored the question. I picked up the light. "Let's check the rest of this room. You take the closet."

I began pulling open the desk drawers, which were mostly empty except for the one on the top right. My groping fingers encountered smooth leather and raised lettering on the nearly square little booklet. I knew what it was even before I eased it out. I tucked the flashlight under my arm and opened the well-worn passport.

"Gotcha!" I whispered. The face looked younger, the photo probably taken a good five or six years before. Clean-shaven, but still recognizable. The shape of the jaw and the wide-set eyes were the same, minus a few creases.

I opened my mouth to call to Erik when I realized the quality of the darkness had changed. I turned to find the doorway filled with a tall, bulky shadow. I gasped and fumbled with the flashlight while my right hand dived into my pocket. I had just wrapped my hand around the grip of the pistol when a familiar voice said, "What in the hell do you think you're doing?" and Ben Wyler stepped into the room.

CHAPTER
THIRTY-ONE

MY BREATH WHOOSHED OUT OF MY LUNGS, AND MY knees threatened to buckle, but I managed to stay upright.

"Jesus, Mary, and Joseph!" I hissed, my own heartbeat nearly drowning out my words. "Where did you come from?"

Wyler slouched in the doorway, and I could feel his eyes scanning the room. "Find anything of interest?" he asked, ignoring my own question.

Erik moved out of the deep shadows, and Wyler whipped around in his direction, the gun appearing as if by magic in his hand. "Freeze!"

"It's Erik!" I nearly shouted.

"Don't sneak up on me like that, kid," Wyler said, lowering his arm to his side.

"Don't call me kid again if you don't want that thing shoved up your—"

"Hey, let's all calm down here, okay?" I moved between the two glowering men.

I heard Wyler exhale slowly as he holstered his weapon. "You make this mess?" he asked.

"No. I think our Mr. Wade or whoever's been staying here is just a pig by nature."

He gestured toward the little booklet I still clutched in my hand. "That his passport?"

"It's somebody's," I said.

Wyler took it and flipped it open. Erik and I moved closer as Ben shined his own penlight over the two-by-two-inch photo. "Well, well, well," he muttered, "what have we here?"

The handsome face, much more in focus than any of the newspaper photos had been, smiled back at us. The name—Randolph Remington Wade—and a birthplace in Virginia were printed neatly alongside.

"That's certainly Star Kennedy's Wade, but it isn't the real one," I said, and Wyler's head snapped in my direction.

"How do you know?"

"Because I've seen a picture of the real guy, and this isn't him." I took the passport and handed it to Erik. "You agree?"

"Absolutely. They have some similarities, but it's definitely not the man in the pictures."

"Hold up," Wyler said, his eyes darting between us. "What pictures?"

It took me a moment to realize Ben had been out of the loop about my meeting with Henry Littlejohn. He hadn't taken my call that afternoon, and I'd never returned his.

"Long story," I said. I bent my head again to the passport photo. "But you know who . . . ? With longer hair and maybe a beard . . ."

"What the hell are you talking about?" Wyler asked, jerking the folder out of my hand. "You've got some explaining—"

We all heard the noises at the same time: two car doors slamming and voices raised in some sort of argument. Wyler flicked off the light, and instinctively I dropped into a crouch below the level of the window over the bed. None of us spoke. I strained to make out who it might be or what they might be yelling about, but everything sounded muffled. High above the parking lot, behind thick glass meant to withstand the pounding of storm-driven ocean waves, we were cocooned in the luxurious yacht.

"Stay here," Wyler whispered out of the dark.

Before I could protest, he'd slipped through the doorway and disappeared.

I scooted next to Erik and put my lips close to his ear. "What do you think?"

He shrugged and shook his head.

Outside I could still hear voices. Hard to tell how many for sure, I thought, shifting around a little to ease my cramped legs. Before I could work up the courage to stand and risk a peek out the window, Wyler was back.

"Two drunks," he said in a fairly normal tone of voice. "They're arguing about who's sober enough to drive home. Nothing to do with us."

I let my breath out slowly as I rose, flexing my knees one after the other. "We need to finish up and get out of here," I said, turning back to the desk.

"Hold on," Wyler said, one hand on my shoulder.

I shrugged it off and pulled open another drawer. "You can go. Just make sure to leave the ladder so we can reach it."

I heard his snort of exasperation. "Tanner, do you know you've broken about fifteen different laws with this stunt of yours?"

I flipped open the checkbook I'd found tucked in among some unopened mail. "Erik, get me something to stash this stuff in, will you? There's too much here to put in my pockets."

Wyler didn't move, so Erik stepped around him and stripped the nearest pillow. I retrieved the papers I'd stuck into the waistband of my slacks along with the checkbook and the mail and dropped them into the musty-smelling pillowcase. Having to touch even the edges of it made me wish I'd thought to bring gloves.

As if reading my mind, Wyler said, "Your fingerprints are going to be all over the place."

I gave him a pitying look. "Gosh, Mr. Big City Detective, I never thought of that. Come on, what's he going to do, call the cops?" I scooped the remaining paperwork from the desk and added it to my bundle. "Erik, you find anything worth a second look?"

My partner spoke from the depths of the closet. "Only that all the clothes in here look new. Some of them still have tags." He stooped and studied the jumble of shoes on the floor. "These, too."

I doused my light and listened to Wyler's feet whisper across the carpet to the other side of the stateroom.

"Any indication of where they came from?" he asked.

"Here," Erik replied. Only someone who knows him as well as I do would have been able to detect the suppressed anger in that single word.

So someone had bought a complete new wardrobe. Recently. And cleaned out the real Wade's clothes. I wondered if that could have been what was in the suitcase Win Hammond had lugged up the sidewalk the night Erik had been watching him.

No time to worry about it now, I said to myself. Aloud, I added, "Okay. Let's go."

"I'll leave first," Wyler said, materializing out of the darkness at my side. "You two wait just inside the door out to the deck." He paused as if anticipating I'd make some objection, but I held my silence, waiting. "Okay. My car is parked in the far corner of the lot. Close by yours. I'll check things out. When I'm sure it's clear, I'll flash the penlight once. Then you get the hell out of here as fast as you can go. Got it?"

I knew he couldn't see my smile or my nod, so I said, "Got it."

He moved out into the hallway, and Erik and I trailed behind him. I was surprised how much my eyes had adjusted to the dark. We made it to the far side of the living area without so much as a stumble. Wyler didn't stop, simply eased the door open, and stepped over the raised sill. I positioned myself to one side of the glass and managed to pick out his hunched form a moment before he slipped over the rail and disappeared.

I didn't want to risk a betraying strobe of light, so I had no idea what time it was or how long Ben had been gone. I'd counted seconds for a while, losing track somewhere after three minutes because my mind kept wandering to the documents we'd found strewn around the bedroom. I itched to spread them out on my desk back home and begin to

piece together the mystery of Randolph Remington Wade. I felt certain
I knew who the imposter was and probably how Win Hammond had
gotten mixed up in this whole sordid mess, too.

Poor Miss Addie, I thought, glancing across to where Erik stood
sentinel on the other side of the door. His eyes were focused on the spot
where we'd left our cars, but no beam of light flickered in the darkness.
His voice startled me.

"What do you think's taking him so long?"

"I don't know," I whispered back. "You know Ben. He's nothing if
not thorough."

"So why do you think he just happened to show up here?"

I'd already had a chance to work that one out. "Because I think he's
the mystery man who interrupted me last night. I may have been wrong
in believing I was the only one who'd figured out the importance of getting on board." I shrugged. "We probably scared each other off."

"Right. Well, I'm giving him another minute, and then we're out
of here."

"Okay." I could feel the coiled tension in him from across the few
feet separating us.

I forced my brain to concentrate on counting down the seconds. I
was at fifty-two when Erik said, "Nothing. I'll go first, make sure everything's okay. Step outside with me, and I'll snap my fingers if it's clear.
You join me at the rail, and I'll help you down."

He didn't give me a chance to protest. I scrambled out behind him
into the humid night and watched as he hunched his shoulders and trotted silently across the deck. I lost sight of him for a moment among the
bulky shapes lining the sides. I held my breath and strained for the sound
of his fingers, but nothing came. I could feel my stomach muscles knotting. I had just made up my mind to spring after him, signals be damned,
when I saw him running full-tilt back toward me. He grabbed my arm
without a word. I opened my mouth to protest when he spun me around
and, in one fluid motion, jerked open the door and flung me inside.

"What the hell are you doing?" I hissed, trying to jerk my arm out of his grasp, but he held on and pushed me farther into the salon. "Erik! What . . . ?"

"The ladder's gone," he said.

I grunted as I banged my shin against the edge of a table, then stumbled onto one of the soft leather couches spread around the room. I heard Erik drop down beside me.

"I'm sorry. You okay?"

I rubbed my leg and visualized the purpling bruise I'd have to deal with when I got home. *If* I got home.

"Something must have happened to Ben," I said, the pain giving way to panic.

"Or else he bailed out on us."

There had been a time last year when I would have agreed with Erik's implications, a time when I had been certain Ben Wyler could be my most dangerous enemy. But not now. Not since . . . I shook my head. "Don't be ridiculous! He must be hurt. Or he ran into trouble. Which could mean someone knows we're here."

"Not necessarily," Erik said, his voice surprisingly calm. "If someone saw him coming off the boat, they might think he was alone."

"If they've got the brains God gave a chicken, they're sure as hell gonna check to make sure." I drew a deep breath and exhaled slowly. "Okay. How else can we get off this tub? We have to find Ben."

"We can't jump. This thing is high as a two-story building. We need to find some rope."

"There was lots of it out on the deck."

"I know, but we can't exactly go roaming around out there, now can we? If whoever . . ." He stopped, and I knew what kind of gruesome thoughts had to be rattling around in his head because they were rattling around in mine, as well.

"If whoever took the ladder," I finished for him, "is still out there, we'd be sitting ducks." I paused. "Why don't we go out on deck and start yelling like maniacs? If we can attract anyone from the bar . . . or maybe those guys from before are sleeping it off in their car."

"No good." I looked in the direction he'd tilted his head to see glowing numerals on a clock I'd missed during our initial search: 2:41. "The bar closed at two. I doubt there's anyone around at all. At least not anyone who'd be on our side."

"Cell phone," I said, scrabbling in my pocket until I remembered I'd exchanged it at the last moment for the comfort of the Seecamp pistol. "You bring yours?"

I could just make out the shake of his head. "Didn't see any reason to. I didn't want it falling out of my pocket or banging up against something in the dark." He sounded almost amused. "I guess you don't have yours, either."

"Nope. The fanny pack's filled with my burglar tools."

"Where on earth did you get burglar tools?" Again it seemed as if he were on the verge of bursting into laughter.

"On the Internet," I said with as much dignity as I could muster. "And I'm pretty good with them, too. I've been practicing. If this thing had been locked, I could have had us inside in less than two minutes."

He did laugh then, a soft snort that made me smile into the darkness, even though he couldn't see me. "Aren't we just a pair of idiots? Okay," he said, sobering, "so let's go see if we can find anything in here to use for a rope." He held out his hand and pulled me to my feet.

I paused for a moment, eyes closed, trying to remember details of the rooms we'd searched one brief burst of light at a time. I bit the inside of my mouth to quell the anxiety surging through me, but it was as if my mind had shut down. I felt my way around the salon, afraid to risk even the smallest telltale light, but nothing I touched seemed the least bit useful. Across the carpet I could hear Erik doing the same. In unspoken agreement, we moved on to the other cabins, ending back where we'd stood not long before in whispered consultation with Ben Wyler.

"How about knotting sheets?" Erik asked, flicking dirty clothes from Wade's bed onto the floor.

"That only works in bad movies and worse novels," I said. "Do you really think you can tie something that thick and heavy into a knot that will hold?"

"No," he said glumly.

"Look, why don't we just go down the boat ladder and drop from there to the ground? How bad could it be?"

Erik paused. "I thought about that. But one, it's a really long drop, and two, that's the way Ben went down. I wanted to use the other side."

"I understand, but it looks as if we're out of options. Come on, we have to get out of here."

Reluctantly he followed me back into the main salon. We hesitated at the door out to the deck. "Let me go first," Erik said. "That way I can try to catch you, or at least cushion the fall a little bit for you."

If you don't break your own leg on the way down, I thought. "Okay. Let's do it."

"Give me two minutes, then come ahead. Stay as low as you can when you're out in the open."

Before I could answer, he was out the door and gone.

I watched the red numerals on the clock face across the room flip to 2:56 and then 2:57 before I eased out the door and dropped into a crouch. I moved crablike across the teak deck, now damp with dew, and made it to the rail in a matter of seconds. I half rose and peered over the side, searching for Erik's face against the dark backdrop of the thick bushes.

I drew a long breath and slung one leg over the polished rail, clutching the pillowcase full of papers in my sweaty hand. My foot found the first rung of the boarding ladder, and I'd just begun to swing the rest of my body over when I heard a grunt followed by a soft rustling in the wild tangle of underbrush at the edge of the boatyard.

I looked down to find the ground below me empty.

CHAPTER
THIRTY-TWO

I DON'T KNOW HOW LONG I HUNG THERE, FROZEN IN disbelief, before the fight-or-flight part of my brain kicked in, and I scrambled back over the rail to land with a thud on my bad shoulder. A jolt of pain sent colored lights dancing in front of my eyes, and for a moment I thought I might pass out. I waited for my vision to clear, then began crawling back across the deck toward the doorway.

It was slow going. I paused every few feet to allow my breathing to quiet, straining through the blood drumming in my ears for the sounds of someone making his stealthy way up the side of the boat. At one point I encountered the coil of rope I'd stumbled over on my first trip toward the cabin door, and I hooked it through the crook of my arm and dragged it along with me. Interminable seconds later, I bumped into the raised sill.

I transferred the pillowcase and rope to my left hand and reached tentatively for the handle with my right. I took a deep breath and counted to five. In one fluid motion, I pushed the door open, tossed the rope and papers inside, and rolled in after them. I kicked the door closed and lay there on my back, panting with relief.

It took a few moments for the adrenaline rush to ease and the pain to take center stage.

My shoulder felt as if it were on fire. I sat up and tried to rotate it, but only succeeded in making things worse. The fingers of my left hand tingled, a pins-and-needles sensation that wouldn't go away. I eased myself into a sitting position, my back against one of the sofas, and took stock.

I had no cell phone, and Erik and I hadn't come across anything resembling one in our search. There had to be a ship-to-shore radio in the—my fuzzy brain couldn't wrap itself around the right word—wheelhouse? bridge? Wherever they steered the damn thing from, but I had no idea how to work one even if I could find it. I had a rope, but no clue how I'd go about using it with only one good arm.

I forced myself to relax, focusing on my breathing as if I were preparing for meditation. I concentrated on feeling each inhalation, holding the air in my lungs a long time before releasing it in a slow, steady stream. In minutes, I had cleared my head and assigned the throbbing pain in my damaged shoulder to a mental box I shoved into a far corner of my brain.

My first decision was to secure myself in the cabin. Ben Wyler and Erik Whiteside had somehow been taken out of the game by the bogus Wade and his partners. Captured or injured or both, I had no idea. Win Hammond's weathered face flashed in front of me, and I pushed the pain of his treachery into another compartment in my mind. *I'll just think about that tomorrow,* I told myself.

It soon became apparent that anything small enough for me to maneuver to block the door into the cabin was already bolted to the floor. It made sense. In rough seas, furniture sliding from side to side could pose a serious danger of injury, not to mention cause tremendous damage. I explored the door latch with my good hand but could find no means of locking it from the inside. It appeared to work like a deadbolt. I could probably use one of my picks to set the lock, but that wouldn't keep out anyone with a key. The panic threatened again, and I clenched my jaw to quell the trembling I could feel working its way into my body. I pushed myself up onto the sofa and tried to think.

My eyes strayed to the tiny red numbers on the clock sitting atop the side table. Eleven minutes after three. At least several hours until sunrise, until the faint rose of dawn over the ocean would give me even the slimmest hope of spotting my adversaries. That long, too, until the first early risers would be out walking their dogs or strolling the docks, steaming mugs of coffee in hand, sharing the quiet moments before the island stretched itself awake.

Somehow I had to stay safe until then.

I hefted the rope and the pillowcase and maneuvered my way through the maze of furniture to the hallway leading to the bedrooms. I bypassed the one in which we'd found all the clothes and papers and stepped into the doorway across from it. I couldn't see much, that side of the boat being the farthest from the soft glow of the security light, but I could make out a bed, neatly made up, and a small dresser in one corner. I dropped my burdens onto the floor and headed back down the hall.

In the compact galley, I flung open cupboard doors. A full complement of dinnerware lay inside the first one, and I removed the largest plates and stacked them on the narrow counter. Crystal wine goblets filled another section, and I added those to my pile. I felt my way back into the main cabin, finding I had become quite proficient in negotiating around the tables. I remembered a bookcase just to the right of the largest sofa, and I removed all the hardbacks I could locate. I paused occasionally to listen, my ear pressed against the heavy door, but no sound penetrated from the outside. I risked a quick glance through the glass, but again found nothing to cause alarm.

I worked steadily, arranging the books against the doorsill until I had created a shelf that reached above its lip. I made several trips from the galley, able to carry only a few pieces at a time. My left hand remained numb and unresponsive. The red clock numbers had flipped over to 3:42 when I placed the last wineglass on my carefully constructed pyramid and stepped back. It wouldn't make a lot of noise against the carpet covering the cabin floor, but at least I'd have some warning.

I moved back down the hall and retrieved the rope. If I couldn't use the bolted-down furniture as a barricade, at least it could provide another early-warning device. I knotted one end of the strand around the legs of a table and stretched it across the path anyone entering the cabin would have to take. Estimating I had it about a foot off the floor, I secured it to the bottom of the entertainment center on the opposite side. By using my legs for leverage, I managed to pull it taut.

I felt desperately thirsty as I made my way back toward the bedroom I'd chosen for my sanctuary. I stopped in the galley and took a large tumbler out of the cupboard. The taps in the sink yielded nothing. Two cans of beer rested on the middle shelf of the refrigerator. I pulled open the door to the freezer and found a single plastic ice cube tray, its contents shriveled to nothing. I retrieved one of the beers and carried it with me into the unused cabin.

I pulled the bedspread off and rolled it up against the headboard so I could sit upright in some degree of comfort. I gripped the can between my knees and popped the top with my good hand. It tasted like gasoline, and I couldn't suppress the shudder that traveled down my back, but at least it was wet. I rested the two pillows across my lap, then eased the Seecamp out of my pocket and wrapped my hand around the pistol's grip. I lifted my left arm onto the cushion of the pillows and immediately felt some of the pain let up.

My ambush laid, I drew a deep breath and focused my eyes and the gun on the open bedroom door.

I don't know how much later I fell asleep.

When my head snapped up of its own volition, I felt a surge of panic, the kind you get when you wake suddenly in a strange place and your brain can't register exactly where you are or how you got there. The throbbing pain in my shoulder brought it all into focus in a frightening rush.

The gun had slipped from my hand, and my fingers scrabbled frantically over the crumpled sheets until I felt the reassuring touch of cold metal. I pushed myself up straighter on the mattress and swung my legs over the side. On my feet, the pistol gripped tightly, I felt some of the tremors of fear subside. I edged my way toward the doorway, my ears straining for any repeat of whatever sound had awakened me, but all was silence.

I darted a quick look into the darkness, but no one crept stealthily along the narrow hallway. I stepped back into the bedroom, unsure of whether I should make my stand there as I'd originally planned or try to sneak up on my adversaries under cover of darkness. The more I thought about it, the less I liked the idea of being trapped with no possible escape route. Earlier, afraid and disoriented by pain, I had hunkered down, my first instinct to find a safe hole to crawl into. With the benefit of a little sleep and a clearer head, the obvious flaws in my plan were becoming more evident by the minute.

I groped behind me for the beer can I'd set on the bedside table, my throat achingly dry and scratchy. I debated a quick foray into the salon to check out the digital clock versus risking a flick of the flashlight I'd earlier dropped into the pillowcase along with the stolen papers. Without consciously making the decision, I eased my way out the door and planted my back against the wall.

Bulkhead, I heard Erik whisper inside my head, and I shuddered with the jolt of fear that stabbed my chest. *Where was he? What could have happened to him down there?* He had disappeared in the matter of seconds it had taken me to sling my leg over the railing. *And Ben . . .*

I inched my way along, pausing every couple of steps to listen intently for any sound disturbing the eerie quiet inside the huge yacht. I moved past the galley, leading with the pistol but holding my arm close to my body so someone couldn't swat the gun out of my hand. Just like Red had taught me. I paused at the entrance to the main cabin, drew a calming breath, and jumped into the doorway, my body bent in a running crouch as I sprinted to my right and dropped down behind one of the long sofas.

Blood pounded in my ears, but no shot rang out, no angry voice demanded to know what the hell I was doing there. I counted to fifty, then eased my head up slowly. The red numerals on the clock on the side table glowed brightly against the deep black of the night. 5:28. I ducked back down behind the comforting solidity of the leather sofa.

Again I made myself wait before popping up again to survey the booby trap I'd laid in front of the only entrance into the main cabin. My carefully constructed pyramid of glass and dinnerware sat undisturbed on its base of well-worn novels and travel guides. I could discern nothing which might have jerked me out of my short nap in the bedroom.

Without consciously making the decision, I prepared to effect my escape. If someone was coming to check out the boat, they had probably decided to wait for sunrise, unsure of who or how many of us might be waiting for them on board. Getting out before they discovered their sole adversary was a single woman with a miniature handgun and only one working arm seemed like a helluva good plan to me.

I pushed the Seecamp back into my pocket and set to work on the knotted rope.

Within seven minutes by the little clock I kept glancing at, I had the rope undone and draped over my right arm. I'd tossed the piled glasses and plates of my booby trap onto one of the couches and kicked the books away from the door. I'd also pulled a long shoelace from a sneaker in the bedroom and used it to tie shut the pillowcase of evidence and secure it to one of my belt loops. I'd threaded another of the laces through the trigger guard on the pistol, fastening it around my neck so the gun hung down near my waist. I figured in a pinch I could get my hand around it in time to . . . well, to do whatever I needed to do. I made a conscious decision not to think about that.

With a few surreptitious peeks through the closed curtains, I'd chosen my spot: a cleat just outside the cabin door on the marina side of the yacht. Fastened to the top of the deck below the rail, its chrome prongs gleamed in the waning moonlight. I was pretty sure I could loop the rope around it several times so I didn't have to worry about knots, toss the rest over the side, and slide down after it. How I'd manage it with only one useable hand, I hadn't figured out yet.

I moved about the room, again sneaking little darting glances around the edges of the closed curtains until I felt reasonably sure no one lurked in the immediate area. At least not that I could see. I had just stepped to the door and wrapped my fingers around the handle when the roar of an engine split the predawn air. Startled, I stumbled back, my foot connecting with the discarded books strewn across the floor. My arms flailed, windmilling as I tried to keep my balance. I felt myself tilting backward, the insistent, pounding howl growing louder and nearer.

Suddenly, my feet flew out from under me. I twisted in midair, my one thought to protect my damaged shoulder. As if in slow motion, I watched the corner of the table rise to meet my forehead . . .

CHAPTER
THIRTY-THREE

"*B*AY? BAY, HONEY, COME ON NOW. WAKE UP."
The hoarse whisper, delivered in a deep masculine drawl,
made me frown in concentration. What was Law Merriweather doing
in my bedroom?

"Bay! You've gotta wake up. We have to get you out of here."

I felt my eyelids flutter, but they didn't seem to want to cooperate. I
knew, however, that my lips had curled up into a smile. Law always called
me "honey" or "darlin'" as if the endearments were middle names. But really, he shouldn't be in my room. What would his wife think? Or Lavinia?

"Damn it, girl, what are you grinning about?" The muffled voice
seemed to come from far away.

And I remembered then. Law Merriweather was dead.

I forced my eyes open to find Win Hammond's creased and weathered face only inches from my own. In the same instant it all came
flooding back: the boat, the noise, Erik. My right hand touched the tender spot on my forehead, and I winced.

"You okay? Got a nasty bump there."

"What are you doing here?" I tried to raise my head, but a wave of
nausea washed over me, and I collapsed back onto the pillow. "I think
I'm going to be sick."

"No you're not," the urgent whisper came back. "We don't have time for you to be throwin' up."

I felt a cool hand tenderly brush my hair back.

"Take a few deep breaths and swallow hard."

I did as I was told, and the dizziness subsided a little. I ordered my brain to get its act together.

"What are you doing here?" I repeated. "What happened to—"

"Later," Win Hammond said tersely.

"No!" I said through gritted teeth. "Where's Erik? And Ben?"

He sighed. "They're okay. Tied up, gagged, and tucked away out in the scrub behind the boatyard." He almost smiled. "They're gonna have a couple of bad headaches and maybe a few chigger bites, but nothing worse."

I didn't know whether to believe him or not, but there was nothing I could do about it either way. Not yet.

"Can you stand up?"

He moved around to slip a supporting arm under my shoulders while I eased my legs over the side of the bed. In a distant part of my mind I registered that I was in the same cabin where I'd fallen asleep. It seemed like an hour and a half before the hammers in my head settled into a dull, manageable thudding. With Win's help, I finally stood on wobbly legs, my good hand bracing myself against the closet door.

Upright, I also noticed for the first time that the boat was moving.

"Where are we? Did . . . ? How . . . ?"

"Never mind all that. They're puttin' her in the water right now. You have to be ready as soon as we're underway."

I couldn't decide if the confusion paralyzing my thought processes came from the blow to my head or if Miss Addie's brother had completely lost his mind. I felt myself propelled toward the doorway, my stumbling, weaving gait counterbalanced by Win's supporting arm.

"Hold it!" I whispered, my jerking attempt to pull myself out of his grasp sending the jackhammers back to work behind my eyes. "What's going on, Win? What the bloody hell is going on?"

"Do you want to sit here and satisfy your damned curiosity, or would you prefer to get the hell off this boat?"

I stared at him for a moment, unable to understand why he sounded so angry. His face looked deadly serious in the gray predawn light.

The motion I'd finally realized had to be the hoist carrying the huge yacht down to the dock area suddenly ceased, and I grabbed for Win to steady myself.

"Almost there," he mumbled. "We gotta move."

"Wait! I don't understand."

"For once in your life will you just shut up and do as you're told?" He gripped my arms in hands made strong by twenty years on the ocean, and his voice dropped to a normal pitch. "Listen to me. Charlie and Bobby are getting everything ready to head out to sea. They went straight to the dock as soon as the boatyard guys came with the hoist. I'm supposed to make sure everything is battened down tight in here before we sail."

"But why—?"

"No whys! They don't know you're in here, don't you get it? I found you moaning on the floor and dragged you out of sight. If there hadn't been so many guys around, I would have . . . Well, never mind that. The point is, you're going to have a chance to get away, but not until we're on the water." He ran a spotted hand through his thick, graying hair. "I'm pretty sure Charlie wouldn't . . . But he's been acting sort of weird lately. We can't take the chance."

"Who's Charlie?"

"Charlie Forester. I met him through Bobby. They knew each other back in Georgia. Two of them used to be . . ."

"Cellmates?" I guessed and saw him wince.

He sighed and looked at me in what I thought might be supplication, as if he were seeking absolution. "God, nobody was supposed to get hurt! They promised me! I didn't want anything to do with their damn schemes, but it seemed like the only way to get myself out from under." Win Hammond shook his head. "The first part worked great, just like they planned it. But then Bobby got caught and . . . Charlie's not a bad guy, really, but—"

"Not a bad guy? He bilked Star Kennedy out of half her fortune and killed the real Randolph Wade. What exactly is *your* definition of a bad guy?"

"No! No, that's not how it happened! Sure, Charlie got mad when he came back to Gorda and found Bobby and Wade gone, but he didn't mean to kill anybody. By the time Charlie tracked them down here, Wade was stoned out of his mind and babbling something about roughing up a couple of prostitutes he got mixed up with. If he'd gotten himself arrested, it would have blown the whole thing. They ended up in a fight, and things just sorta got out of hand."

Outside I could hear the groaning and creaking of the chains and lines as the boat was maneuvered closer to the water. A disconnected part of my brain wondered how anyone in the condominiums around the harbor could possibly sleep through such a racket.

"Is that what Charlie told you?" I asked, forcing myself to concentrate. "Randolph Wade was killed by a blow to the *back* of his head delivered at least four hours before he rolled up on the beach. And someone deliberately pounded his face into mush to keep him from being recognized." I watched Win Hammond's eyes, surprised by his lack of reaction. "But you knew that, didn't you? Were you the one who dropped the wallet where the cops were sure to find it? Did you *want* Wade identified?"

Miss Addie's beloved younger brother turned his face away, and I could see him trying to gather himself to deny it.

"You wanted someone to stop them. That's why you came racing up here. You didn't have any creditors on your tail. You knew what was likely to happen, and you thought you could prevent it. You just showed up a day late."

A sudden lurch sent me crashing against the closet door. The hoist had begun lowering the yacht into the water. Win Hammond stumbled, then righted himself.

"You don't know what you're talking about, Bay," he finally said, but his voice lacked conviction. He sounded like a tired, defeated old man.

I made myself speak slowly and calmly. "Look, Win, why don't we just end this? There are people around now. All I have to do is get out on deck and begin screaming my head off."

Again Win Hammond gripped my arms, but this time all pretence of gentleness was gone. "I don't want you to get hurt, Bay, but I'm too damn old to go to jail! They're going to set this thing in the water, and I'll help you get overboard before we get too far from shore. Once we hit the open sea and cross the twelve-mile limit, there's nothing anyone can do." He paused, his head cocked to catch the shouts being exchanged between the dock and the men operating the hoist. "Come on, we don't have much time."

Win Hammond had removed my sneakers before laying me across the rumpled bed, and he bent now and helped me slip them back on, his knobby fingers struggling with the laces. He'd untied the makeshift gunnysack I'd stuffed full of papers and dropped it just inside the door. Not surprisingly, he'd also taken my gun.

I scanned the dark room for it to no avail. The only good news was that a little feeling had returned to my left arm, and I no longer felt like throwing up. Trains continued to collide inside my head, but I thought I could deal with that.

Win and I sat side by side on the bed as the boat continued to sink toward the water. I calculated how much coordination it would take for me to push past him, sprint through the cabin, and fling myself out onto the deck. Would he pursue me? Could I make myself heard above the din of the motorized hoist? Was it possible to convince whoever operated the huge machine that I needed help?

I glanced again at my companion. As if reading my mind, he produced the Seecamp from his pocket, and the little gun now dangled from his hand. I didn't think he'd use it, but I couldn't be certain. He lifted his lined face to mine, and suddenly he looked very old and very tired. Maybe words would be more effective.

"We can work this out, Win," I said softly. "I'm sure you had no idea anyone would end up dead. I know damn well you didn't have a hand in that."

He stared at me, his eyes unreadable in the dim light. "How can you be so sure?"

I shrugged. "Because I know who you *were,* where you came from. Because your sister couldn't love you as much as she does if you were capable of anything like that."

His voice sounded husky, as if he were fighting tears. "You don't know me at all, Miss Lydia. And neither does Sissy. Not anymore." His deep sigh rippled out across the room. "I've done things you wouldn't . . ." The words trailed off into silence.

"Then make me understand." Very carefully I laid my hand on his forearm. "Talk to me, Win."

Again that almost pitiful sigh. "There's no time, darlin', no time. Story of my life."

The boat didn't drop into the water, probably because the hoist operator knew his business. She settled onto it, gently, the slight rocking motion the only real indication she was back in her element.

Win's head snapped up. "Listen to me now, Bay. Listen closely. Stay in this room. It's going to take Bobby and me a little time to run through all the checklists. They're gonna want to see my face up on the bridge, to hear everything's secure down here, so I have to leave you alone. I'm going to lock you in, but I need to trust you not to try anything." He paused, as if waiting for some pledge of honor from me, but I remained silent. "And you need to trust *me* to get you out of here in one piece. It's the only way. Deal?" He crossed to the door, slipping my little pistol into his pocket as he went. He paused there, one hand on the knob. "Deal?" he asked again.

I didn't see I had much choice, so I nodded. Besides, promises made to liars and cheats didn't count. Everyone knew that.

The door slid closed, and I heard the snick of the lock.

———

I figured it didn't matter anymore, so I groped for the light switch and flicked it on. A small lamp on the bedside table didn't do too much to dispel the gloom, but I felt better for it anyway. Through the small window I could see the other boats in the marina rocking at anchor. By kneeling on the bed and craning my neck, I could just make out the rooftops of the mansions on Bram's Point across the Reach. And something else.

A dark line of thunderheads obscured the horizon off toward the mainland. Cocooned in the big yacht, I couldn't hear the thunder, but intermittent flashes of lightning split the sky. That explained why the cabin had grown darker while Win Hammond and I had sat huddled together on the bed. I tried to think. Did this make things better or worse? If Win's plan was to slip me over the side as the boat made its ponderous way down the channel, how would the chop kicked up by the storm hamper my ability to swim for it? For that matter, how much would my injured arm hold me back? I flexed the fingers of my left hand and tried rotating my shoulder. The pain had dulled, but my range of mobility was still seriously impaired. I was a strong swimmer, but how well would I do with only one arm?

I felt the engines rumble to life and knew I didn't have much time. Fight or flight? I couldn't believe Win Hammond would actually shoot me if I made a run for it now. But would I get the chance? I leaned back against the headboard and felt the bulk of my fanny pack dig into my side. The burglary tools! I pulled the leather pouch around in front of me and fumbled with the zipper. In seconds I was kneeling by the door, one of the slender picks inserted in the flimsy lock.

It took less than a minute for me to pop it open.

I unhooked the pouch and tossed it on the bed. I couldn't tell if we were moving yet or not, but I slipped off my shoes anyway. If I had to dive from the rail, I didn't need anything extra to weigh me down. In the middle of June the temperature of the water would be like a soothing bath. I undid the button on my pants and let them drop to the floor as well. I peeled off my T-shirt and added it to the pile.

Half naked, I ran through a couple of stretches, concentrating on loosening my cramped muscles and psyching myself up for the next few moments. I drew three deliberately calming breaths and visualized the course I would have to take through the salon, out onto the deck, and over the side. Fifteen seconds. Twenty, max. I imagined myself knifing into the water, rising to the surface and striking out for shore. I forced myself into calm determination and yanked open the door.

And nearly collided with the tall, bearded man from Bobby Delacroix's back porch.

"What the—?" I heard him growl a second before I planted my arms squarely against his chest and pushed with everything I had.

Charlie Forester stumbled against the raised sill and went down like a giant oak, his head bouncing off the door frame of the cabin across the way. I didn't wait to see him land. I vaulted over his tangled legs and sprinted for the salon.

One one thousand, two one thousand . . . I began the countdown in my head as I threaded my way around the sofas and tables. By ten I was out the main door. By fifteen I had oriented myself and clambered up onto the rail.

We were out into Bishop's Reach, the yacht gliding slowly along in the No Wake zone like a practiced dancer across a polished floor. Thunder rumbled over the water, and the rising wind kicked up a slight chop that slapped playfully against the hull of the big boat. I took it all in a second before I inhaled deeply, flexed my knees, whipped my arms up over my head, and dived.

CHAPTER
THIRTY-FOUR

THE SHOCK OF THE ENTRY NEARLY TORE MY ARMS FROM their sockets.

Immediately I arched my back and kicked, clawing for the surface. My head finally broke through the murky haze, and I gasped as a cold, driving rain pounded into my face. I treaded water, turning myself in circles, but I could see no farther than a few feet in any direction. All my landmarks had been swallowed up by the fury of the storm.

I bit down the panic and ordered myself to stay calm. I was in a creek, not adrift on the vastness of the ocean. The yacht had been almost in the center of the channel, so I couldn't be any more than a few hundred yards from either shore. I could hang there and wait for the storm to pass, get my bearings, and then strike out. Besides, my left arm could use the rest. It seemed to be functioning, but I'd need it able to withstand the strain of a long swim. I pushed the weight of my hair away from my face and let myself float onto my back. The rain stung, but I could breathe more easily.

I closed my eyes and listened to the rumble of the thunder, the usually placid creek undulating beneath me. I figured the tide had been nearly high, the primary reason Charlie Forester had rousted out the dockworkers at that ungodly hour of the morning. Too much delay and he would have been stuck in the marina for another twelve hours. I wondered how much it had cost him—or rather how much it had cost Randolph Wade—to lure them from their beds.

The skin on my face had begun to go numb, so I allowed my legs to drop back down. My mind wandered as I paddled and slowly circled. Maybe Win Hammond was right. Maybe Wade's death had been an unfortunate accident resulting from a fistfight with Forester. No, that wouldn't work, I reasoned. The coroner had said the man had sustained a blow to the back of the head *before* all the damage had been done to his face. Then I remembered the words of the boatyard mechanic as I'd prowled around the yacht. He'd been lamenting the damage to *Wade in the Water,* wondering how her skipper had been careless enough to allow it to happen. Maybe Wade had hit his head when the boat ran aground. Maybe his death really had been accidental, a delayed reaction to head trauma.

There's someplace you don't want to go, I thought, my hand finding the lump hardening on my forehead.

The wind had dropped a little, but driving rain still obscured the land in both directions. I tried to stay alert for any sound of a motor. I didn't think anyone would be stupid enough to take a small boat out in this weather, but I knew I'd be impossible to spot until they were right on top of me. I also had no way to calculate how far I might be drifting. The thought sent a wave of fear down my spine.

What if I was floating downstream, away from the marina? If the tide had turned, the ebbing water could carry me on its natural course toward the ocean. I knew it was a long way around the tip of Hilton Head, past mysterious, privately owned Buck Island, secluded Daufuskie, and the famous Harbour Town Lighthouse in Sea Pines. How long would it take for a body bobbing along on the current to be whisked out into the ocean?

I could feel myself flailing in the water, the mental images of my drifting forever sending subconscious messages to my arms and legs. I bit the inside of my mouth and gave myself a stern admonition to keep it together. Long before that happened, the storm would be gone, blown out to sea by the same westerly wind which had carried it from the mainland.

Westerly wind! I eased myself slowly around, turning until I felt the full force of the wind against my upraised face. I'd been good at geography. I moved a hundred and eighty degrees to my right, kicked myself up onto my stomach, and began a slow, steady crawl back toward the marina.

I'd begun to count my strokes as a way of keeping my mind focused on the task. I thought the sky might be lightening just a little, although the rain continued to fall in steady sheets. My left arm felt pretty good, but I knew it had its limitations, so I stopped every time the tally reached fifty to rest it and try to get my bearings. Which is probably the only reason I heard the slap of the oars ahead and a little to my left. A sharp cry escaped before I even realized I'd made the sound, but I was certain no one could have heard it above the whine of the wind.

Decision time. I had no reason to suspect Charlie Forester had stopped the yacht, lowered a skiff, and come looking for me. It would be a stupid move when in a couple of hours, even in the storm, he could be beyond the reach of U.S. law enforcement, free to lose himself in any of a thousand islands where no questions would be asked and money could buy anything, including anonymity. If the man had any sense, he'd write off his scheme and get the hell out of here.

But I wasn't stupid, either. With a smooth sidestroke, I eased myself quietly to the right and stopped. The creak of the oarlocks pinpointed the boat's location, and I kept myself moving, a foot or so at a time. If I worked it right, I could submerge as they neared, then resurface behind them. I'd know in a glance if these were rescuers or pursuers.

The forward movement of the boat slowed, and I stopped, quietly treading water. Had they seen me? Heard me? I fought the urge to dive and swim like hell away from them.

Suddenly the rain stopped, gone in an instant as if someone had flipped a switch, and the shiny black sides of the rubber dinghy materialized out of the mist, almost on top of me. I gulped a lungful of air and dived a second before I registered the spit from the suppressed handgun, and a bullet went whizzing by my left ear.

Swimming underwater is disorienting enough, but worse when you can't see a damned thing. The storm had churned up the bottom, making visibility nonexistent. I pulled for what seemed like hours, my lungs on fire and my bad arm vibrating with pain, before forcing myself to rise slowly, ordering my needy body not to gasp for air the moment I broke the surface.

Long, slender shafts of sunlight poked through the remaining storm clouds and danced across the water of the Reach. I breathed slowly, re-oxygenating my body, then filled my lungs and slid under until only my eyes and the top of my head remained visible.

He was still there, farther away, but not far enough. I checked around me to find I'd figured things out exactly right. Although slightly downstream, I was very close to the marina, close enough to shout if anyone was awake and prowling the dock. But the storm had chased all the sensible, law-abiding folk indoors. Charlie Forester and I seemed to be the only two people left in the world.

I sank lower, completely submerging myself, and began working my way again toward the rear of the dinghy. I had no plan other than staying alive long enough for this crazy man to realize he should cut his losses and get the hell out of there. I eased up again, took a reading, and slipped back under. In a couple of minutes I had gained my objective.

My adversary knelt in the bow. With an oar in one hand, he paddled the small craft, slowly turning it as he scanned the water. A burst of sunlight glinted off the muzzle of the gun, which he held ready but close to his side, making it practically invisible to a casual observer.

"I know you're out there."

His voice, floating disembodied on the heavy, humid air, made me gasp, and I sank, afraid he might have heard me. He had. The bullet ripped the water in almost the exact spot I'd occupied a second before. I kicked away from the dinghy, pulling with every ounce of strength I could muster, again staying under until my lungs nearly exploded. Despite the danger, my body had its own agenda. I shot up out of the water like a geyser, coughing and choking. He whipped around, his gun hand rising.

I gulped air again and dived.

I knew there could be only one winner in this game if the rules didn't change and fast. I also knew I had maybe one more of these underwater escapes left in me. I could feel my head throbbing from a lack of oxygen, and I could no longer tell if my left arm was working. My legs had lead weights attached to them, and I'd lost all sense of direction. I was nearly spent.

I surfaced after what seemed like hours and found myself staring directly into the side of the dinghy. Another foot and I would have come up directly under it.

Under it!

Through the pounding in my ears, I could hear him muttering, although I couldn't make out the words. He stood now in the little craft, back to me, his legs splayed out to keep his balance. I watched his head swivel from side to side. Only a matter of time before he spotted me. I breathed shallowly through my nose, trying to load up on oxygen. This would be my last shot.

I slipped under the water, keeping my eyes open and my face tilted up so I didn't drift away. When I had positioned myself directly under the dinghy, I let myself sink a little farther by expelling a slow stream of the precious air from my lungs. I gathered myself and shot straight up, striking the bottom of the rubber boat with my shoulder and pushing hard with my one good arm.

He hit the water with a satisfying smack as the boat flipped over.

I saw the gun drift past me toward the bottom.

Charlie Forester had on shoes and a full set of clothes, and I'd taken him by surprise. I had only a few moments to take advantage of the situation.

Quickly I checked my position and set off toward the marina. At first all I could manage was an erratic sidestroke, but once I found my rhythm I put my mind on autopilot and concentrated on bringing the long dock a little closer with each kick. I tried waving, desperate to attract someone's attention on shore, but my left arm refused to respond.

Surely someone would be out soon. It had to be after seven o'clock in the morning. The storm had passed. Where were all the damn dog walkers? I could feel myself flagging, my breathing no longer smooth and regular. I choked and spit water as the effort to keep my head up became almost impossible.

Close now, I told myself, *just one more. Come on. One more.* I could make out the names on the anchored boats now, a few more yards and I could stop. *One more.*

I heard a grunt, and a hand grasped my ankle, pulling me under for the last time.

CHAPTER
THIRTY-FIVE

*T*HE LIPS DIDN'T FEEL FAMILIAR, BUT THE SENSATION wasn't entirely unpleasant.

"Come on, Bay, come on. Breathe, damn it!"

When I coughed and started spewing up creek water, he jumped back.

"God, woman! At least give a man some warning!"

I couldn't see Ben Wyler in the glare of the sun overhead, but I'd know that New York accent anywhere. The face hovering over me, however, wasn't his. Then strong hands eased me onto my side, and I found myself staring into the cold, gray features of Charlie Forester. A puddle of pink water pooled around his head.

A muted voice said, "This one's gone," and a blanket dropped down, mercifully obscuring the staring, lifeless eyes.

I felt myself being lifted, then things went fuzzy for a while. I remember the pain stabbing through my shoulder as the gurney bumped over the planks of the dock, but I couldn't muster enough energy to complain to the paramedics. I think I threw up again, but I'm not sure. The only certain memory I have of the next few fractured hours is of Ben Wyler's steady, reassuring gaze every time I opened my eyes.

It would be a long time before either of us spoke of it.

"You're right about one thing. The old guy probably did save your hide."

"Why can't you ever call anybody by their right names?" I shifted myself around on the cushion, reaching for the glass of tea on the side table, but Erik was there before me. "Thanks," I said as I took it from him, "but I'm not an invalid." He shrugged, and I turned back to Wyler. "Win Hammond. Win Hammond. Memorize it, for God's sake."

"Okay, okay, whatever. He put the other dinghy over the side once he realized the dead—"

I pulled the sunglasses down to the end of my nose and glared at him.

"Okay. Once he realized *Forester* had gone after you."

"Mr. Hammond must have whacked him pretty good," Erik added, shaking his head. "I didn't think one of those aluminum paddles could do that much damage."

We sat on my deck, the ocean rolling peacefully by across the dune, an unhappy blue jay scolding at something over our heads. I lounged on a chaise, the painful, receding knot on my forehead the only visible reminder of my ordeal in the water.

"How's Win doing?" I asked. "Anybody talked to him?"

"He's okay." Erik's smile faded. "Miss Hammond posted bail, and he's staying with her while the indictments get sorted out."

"A lot of jurisdictions want a piece of him," Ben added. "I'm afraid the old guy's in for a bad time."

"But you said yourself he saved my life. That has to count in his favor."

"Maybe a sentence consideration, but there's no doubt he's going down for something."

We sat in silence for a few moments. Wyler leaned over in his chair and dug at his right ankle.

"Leave that alone. You're only making it worse." I pointed to one of the red splotches scattered across his bare legs.

Chigger bites. Erik had them, too, and judging by the way he occa-

sionally squirmed in his chair, in a few places he couldn't scratch in polite company. I'd yet to hear the story of how they'd managed to get
themselves loose, but I felt certain one of them would share it with me
sooner or later.

Wyler glared back at me and continued to dig.

"How close do you think we were to figuring out the actual scam?"
Erik looked across at me, but it was Wyler who answered.

"Pretty close, although we probably threw enough monkey
wrenches into the works so he'd never have been able to make a play for
Wade's inheritance, even if he'd survived."

I worked my left arm around, amazed at how quickly it had
bounced back from its pounding. "I think Henry Littlejohn might have
had something to say about it, too." I fidgeted, wishing I still smoked.
Somehow a conversation about crime and death always made me long
for a cigarette. No doubt something Freudian there. I'd have to ask
Neddie. "Does anybody know if Henry's still in town?"

"Why?" Wyler shot the question at me.

"Just curious," I said. "He might be able to fill in some holes about
the real Wade's life down in the islands."

"Why, you gonna write his biography or something?"

I stared back into his glowering face. "What the hell's your problem?"

"Nothing. I just don't like the guy."

"You never met him."

"I know his kind."

"Sort of reminds you of yourself, does he?" I asked sweetly.

"I don't understand how Forester expected to get away with it,"
Erik said into the charged silence. "Surely they'd make him prove his
identity. Or would the phony passport and papers we found on the boat
have been enough?"

I set the glass of iced tea back on the table. "I think Forester had
been positioning himself to make a play for the whole enchilada by impersonating Wade in different places like the White Star Casino in
Freeport to see if he could pull it off. And then in Atlanta after he'd in-

gratiated himself with Thorne Whitcomb. Judging by the photos, Forester and Wade looked a lot alike. If you saw them together, you'd be able to tell them apart, but dressed in the same kind of clothes, with his hair cut the same, Forester could probably fool a lot of people who only knew Wade casually. And, according to Henry Littlejohn, no one in the States had seen Wade in years."

I paused, waiting for Wyler to interrupt, but he just stared and waited for me to continue.

"But there's where the whole thing falls apart, because Forester couldn't have known the family had been keeping Wade under surveillance for quite some time. The minute Charlie made his move, Littlejohn or one of his partners would have blown the whole thing out of the water." I shook my head. "Forester basically killed Wade for nothing."

"Stupid," Wyler said, "just like I always told you. I mean, Forester and Delacroix met in jail, for God's sake! You'd think that would've told them they weren't as good at this scam business as they thought they were. And I'm guessing Hammond had done his share of charming the heiresses out of a few bucks by way of his charter business, and look where it got him. Broke and up to his ass in debt and willing to throw in with these other two losers. None of them was ever gonna win an IQ contest."

Erik ignored Wyler and directed his question to me. "But if Mr. Hammond was one of them, why did he try to mess things up?"

"I don't think Win had any idea how far Forester was prepared to go," I said. "Once Charlie had cleaned out Star Kennedy, he probably planned to lie low on Virgin Gorda, wait for Wade's uncle to kick off, then make his move. But Bobby Delacroix got caught with his hand in some rich widow's cookie jar and needed to get out of town fast. Imagine how pissed off Charlie must have been when he got back and found out Delacroix had convinced Wade to use his boat to smuggle him off the island."

"So Forester tracked them to Hilton Head, found Wade, and killed him." Wyler made it sound like a natural progression.

"It could have happened the way Win said it did. A fight that just got out of hand."

Wyler snorted and shook his head as if I'd just said something incredibly stupid or naïve.

"Look, I agree with you that Win was probably in on the scam, but I don't believe he thought Wade would end up dead." I shrugged. "I think he spun that story about the creditors so Miss Addie would send him enough money for a plane ticket. Until I see some evidence to the contrary, I refuse to buy the idea that he had anything to do with Wade's death."

Something in me needed to believe Miss Addie's brother hadn't been involved in cold-blooded murder. Maybe it was because he'd saved my life. Or maybe I just didn't want the poor old woman to have to deal with any more heartache.

"More likely he was just worried about getting cut out of the payoff," Wyler said.

"And you still think Mr. Hammond is the one who threw Wade's wallet on the beach?" Erik asked. "So they'd be sure to identify the body?"

I nodded. "Once Win realized Wade had been killed, I believe he thought it was the only way to keep Forester from getting away with it and still keep himself out of jail."

Ben cleared his throat and shook his head. "That's wishful thinking. If Hammond had really been on the up-and-up, he would have gone straight to the cops. And he wouldn't have gotten on that boat or let you risk your life in the water."

"But he ended up saving me. And the fact that both of you are still alive is pretty good evidence in his favor, too. Like it or not, I think Win may end up being the hero of this whole sorry business."

"Think we'll ever find out the whole truth?" Erik asked.

"Probably not," Wyler said with a shrug of his own. "But, hey, that's how life goes, kid. Especially when you're dealing with scum like these guys. They may drag some more out of Hammond and Delacroix when they come to trial, but they're both gonna be looking to cover their own butts. Mark my words, they'll dump the whole thing on Forester. Dead guys can't do a real good job of defending themselves."

"If Forester had just kept on going once they got the boat launched, they'd all be sipping piña coladas on a beach somewhere." I shook my head. "Win says Forester was convinced I'd set the Coast Guard on them before they could get out of U.S. waters."

"I'm telling you, these guys operate on a different wavelength than the rest of us," Wyler said.

"I hear you. I guess it's just the accountant in me. And the computer guy in Erik." I smiled at my partner. "We like to see all the ends tied up nice and tight."

"Then you better find another profession," Ben answered with a sardonic grin. "You're almost never gonna know all the answers when you're dealing with con men and murderers."

I threw them out a few minutes later. Time for another dose of pain medication, and the damn things made me drowsy. I reminded myself of my tendency toward addiction and made a solemn vow not to get too dependent on the delicious sense of calm and well-being the little white pills provided. I curled up on the duvet and fell immediately and deeply asleep.

It was dark outside when the faint ringing of the telephone finally registered. I hitched myself up and picked up the bedside extension.

"Bay, I'm sorry. I know you probably still feel like hell, but . . . damn it, I just don't know what to do."

"Whoa, Neddie. Slow down. What's the matter?"

Without thought, I'd swung my legs over the side of the bed, and for a moment the room swam in front of my eyes. I shook my head to clear the wave of dizziness.

"She's gone!"

The usually unflappable Dr. Nedra Halloran sounded distraught, and I could almost picture her tugging at her hair.

"Calm down a minute. Are you talking about Yancey? What do you mean, gone?"

"Split. Hit the bricks. AWOL."

I scrunched up my eyes and tried to clear the fog from my head. "When did this happen?"

"I don't know. I just got home. I had a patient in crisis, and I was gone most of the day. Then I stopped at the grocery store." She swallowed hard around the catch in her voice. "She was gone when I got here."

"Maybe she just went . . ." I fumbled for words through the fuzziness of the pain pill.

"Right. You can't think of anything plausible, either." I heard Neddie draw a steadying breath. "I can't believe Yancey would just walk out without leaving me any word."

I transferred the phone to my right shoulder and sipped from the glass of water on the nightstand. "There's no sign of . . ." I paused, wanting to phrase the question so it would raise the least amount of alarm. "No sign of a struggle? What about her clothes? The ones you bought on your shopping trip the other day."

"Gone," Neddie said quietly. "And no, I didn't see anything out of place."

"So there's your answer," I said in a soft voice, "don't you think?"

"I can't believe she would just take off like that without any explanation. Not after . . ."

"After everything you've done for her?" I sighed. "Neddie, you're the expert on kids, not me. But judging by her performances over the past few days, I'm not entirely surprised. Are you? I mean, if you think about it rationally, doesn't it seem pretty much in character?"

She waited a long time before answering. "Maybe," she said grudgingly. "I guess you could be right. But what if it wasn't voluntary? What if her pig of a boyfriend forced her or something?"

"You've been hanging around me too much. Seeing bad guys and conspiracies everywhere is my bag, not yours. You're the calm, rational one, remember?"

That brought a short laugh. "Okay, I get the point." Then she sobered. "But I want you to check it out."

"Check what out? You can't hold the kid prisoner. And you haven't got a legal leg to stand on. If she decided to go home or back on the street, there's not a damn thing either one of us can do about it. Have you contacted the father?"

"I tried. He's not back in town yet, and I don't have his cell number. Do you think maybe Erik . . . ?"

"I don't know. I'm not sure how it works tracking down records of cell phones. Do you have Yancey's number?" I pulled a pen from the bedside table and scratched the digits on a notepad. "I'll ask him, but I wouldn't hold out a lot of hope."

"So what am I supposed to do?" It had been a long time since I'd heard that level of desperation in her voice.

I kept my tone even. "Forget about it and take care of the patients who really want your help. Notify the police that she's no longer in your care and let them worry about it. I don't see what other choice you have."

"I hate it when you're right."

"I know. Get over it."

A little of her usual optimism seeped back into her voice. "She could have gotten bored. Maybe she'll just turn up again."

"Maybe," I said, although I had serious doubts. Totally self-absorbed kids like Yancey Sullivan wouldn't give a damn how much worry and trouble they caused. If Neddie had served her purpose, the teenager would likely not feel a second's compunction about bailing out on her without a word.

"Well, thanks. I feel a little better. You'll let me know if Erik comes up with anything?"

"Of course. Now go have a glass of wine and try to forget about it."

"Okay. See you— I'll see you soon. Bye."

I hung up wondering what that hesitation had been all about, curled back up on the bed, and dropped off in seconds.

I dreamed of blood and water.

CHAPTER
THIRTY-SIX

J LAY BACK AGAINST THE SOFT LEATHER SEATS OF THE
      Expedition, my eyes closed against the late-afternoon glare.
The car had slowed to a crawl as Erik did his best to avoid the potholes
peppering the narrow lane up to Presqu'isle.

"I don't know why the hell I had to drag myself off my deathbed for
some stupid birthday dinner," I muttered, grimacing as one of the tires
caught the edge of a rut.

"Your father wanted to celebrate your birthday with you." Erik
spoke softly, ignoring the hyperbole. "You're his only child. Give him a
break. Who knows how many more he'll be around for."

"Oh, great. More guilt. Are you by any chance in touch with the
spirit of my mother?"

I lapsed into silence over the last few yards. Erik parked in the
semicircular drive, then came around to help me down.

"You look nice," he said.

"Thanks," I mumbled ungraciously.

Dolores had insisted I needed to dress properly, one's fortieth birthday being an occasion of some importance, or so she informed me. I'd
refused her suggestion of a dress and heels, compromising on tan gabar-
dine slacks and a pale green silk sweater which complemented the
darker green of my eyes. *All this fuss for a damned birthday I'd just as soon*

skip anyway, I thought as Erik followed me up the sixteen steps and through the front door.

"Mrs. Smalls?" he called loudly over my shoulder, and I turned to stare at him. "We're here."

I headed automatically toward the kitchen, but with a firm hand in the middle of my back, Erik ushered me toward the front parlor. I stopped dead, digging my heels into the heart pine floor. I knew what was coming, and someone was going to pay dearly.

"Oh, no!" I cried. "No! I'm going to kill—"

The shrieks of "Surprise!" echoed through the ancient hallways, rattling the dishes on the sideboard.

"You're a dead man," I muttered over my shoulder as I plastered a smile on my face and went to greet my father.

I couldn't believe how many people had been privy to the secret and how well they'd all kept it. Bitsy and Big Cal Elliott had dragged their kids along. I could tell the teenagers would rather have been cleaning their rooms than stuck in this crowd of old people, but they all hugged me and wished me well. Chris Brandon, the attorney with whom I'd worked on a couple of cases, was there, minus his new wife. I really couldn't blame her, considering the part I'd played in her family's recent troubles. Her absence seemed to make Chris uncomfortable, and I tried to smooth it over as best I could.

Red and his ex-wife Sarah hovered together in a corner, their heads bent toward each other. I wondered what the subject of their earnest conversation could be. Probably my niece and nephew, Elinor and Scotty, who had insisted on giving their Aunt Bay big, sloppy birthday kisses. The last survivors of the Thursday night poker games, Charlie Seldon and Boyd Allison, hovered in deep conversation with Miss Addie, who held court from one of the blue silk wing chairs near the window.

A subdued Neddie chatted with Ben Wyler, whose eyes seemed to be on me every time I glanced in their direction.

The Judge accepted congratulations at his coup in pulling off the surprise, and Lavinia bustled around, overseeing the two waiters she'd engaged for the evening, checking on the hors d'oeuvre trays and making certain the champagne flowed freely. The heavy silver Tattnall family punch bowl, one of my late mother's treasures rarely unpacked except for the most festive occasions, held center stage on the long mahogany table in the dining room, whose connecting pocket doors had been thrown open to accommodate the mob.

Early on Lavinia had hugged me, whispering, "I know you don't like this sort of thing, but he wanted to do it for you. Pretend to be happy about it. For him. And me." She kissed my cheek. "Happy birthday, honey."

I managed to find a quiet spot by the window, gazing out toward the Sound at the herons and curlews picking in the mud along the narrow strip of marsh. The noise and conversation drifted around me, and I had to admit it was a wonderful party. So many people I'd known my whole life had taken time out to share the occasion with me. And my father had come up with a wonderful idea. Instead of gifts, the guests had been asked to make a donation to a charity in my name, and the table was strewn with the acknowledgments from places like Literacy Volunteers, the local public television endowment fund, and the Deep Well food project.

Lost in thought, I didn't hear the whir of the wheelchair until I felt my father's hand on my arm. "Having fun, sweetheart? Forgiven me yet?"

I sat down on the low bench beneath the window so we could look at each other eye-to-eye. "Of course. It's a lovely party. I can't believe so many people could have kept it to themselves."

"You had me worried yesterday. I wasn't sure you'd be in any condition to be here."

I watched him swallow against his emotion, and I lowered my head to avoid the fear I saw rising in his eyes. "I'm fine, Daddy."

"We've had some close calls lately, daughter," he said softly.

"Yes, we have." I raised my gaze and smiled. "But we're still here."

The Judge's good hand fumbled in the pocket of the dark gray suit coat he'd dusted off for the occasion and came out with a long, parchment envelope. "This is for you," he said. "You don't have to open it now."

I didn't have to feign my confusion. The heavy envelope seemed to be stuffed full of papers. "What is it?"

He lowered his voice and maneuvered his chair a little closer. "It's the deed to Presqu'isle. I've signed it over to you."

"But Daddy, I don't want—"

"Hush! Let's keep it just between us for now. I asked Law to take care of things before . . . well, it's all legal—notarized and recorded down at the courthouse."

"But what are you and—"

"Don't worry, Vinnie and I aren't goin' anywhere. This is just so you know you'll always have a place. No matter what happens to me."

I fought against the treacherous tears, and I could see the emotion reflected on my father's face.

"Now, no gettin' all sloppy on me, hear? The house would have come to you anyway. This saves all that probate mumbo jumbo down the road." The familiar twinkle lit his eyes. "Just don't think you can start charging me rent."

I stared at him, unable to process all the feelings whirling around in my chest.

One of the waiters drifted past then, and the Judge hailed him. He placed a crystal champagne glass in my hand, then took one for himself. "I think we need a toast."

"No big fuss, Daddy, please." I tilted the flute in his direction. "Just a quiet one. Between the two of us."

"Happy birthday, Princess. I'm very, very proud of you. Your mother would have been, too."

We clinked glasses and sipped.

The arrival of a huge cake with forty blazing candles broke the spell, and the low murmur of conversation rose in anticipation. As my

friends and family began to move toward me, I caught the glint of another glass raised in my direction. Across the room, Ben Wyler held my
eyes for a long moment. He said something I couldn't make out, and a
slow smile creased his face.

Maybe it was the champagne, but I found myself smiling back.